*"I conceive of nothing in philosophy, that is mor[e]
to wear, for a while"*
*— Charles Hoy Fort,
"Wild Talents"*

THE FALL OF THE SEA PEOPLE
VOLUME 1

VENUS AND THE SEA PEOPLE

BY

HENRY HALLAN

To Amber

Henry Hallan

LEABHAR CNOC MHUILINN

ISBN 978-0-0571585-0-4

http://www.henryhallan.me

Edited by Órfhlaith ní Chonaill

Cover art by Linda R. James.

For Rachael

"Θεοσ δε θεοσ […] εν νομοισ βασιλευων, ατε δυναμενοσ καθοραν τα τοιαντα, εννοησασ γενοσ επιεικεσ αθλιωσ διατιθεμενον, δικην αυτοισ επιθειναι βουληθεισ, ινα γενοιντο εμμελεστεροι σωφρονισθεντεσ, συνηγειρεν θεουσ παντασ εισ την τιμιωτατην αυτων οικησιν, η δη κατα μεσον παντοσ του κοσμου βεβηκυια καθοα παντα οσα γενεσεωσ μετειληφεν, και συναγειρασ ειπεν:-"
"Κριτιασ", Πλατον

"...The god of gods, who rules according to law, and is able to see into such things, perceiving that an honourable race was in a woeful plight, and wanting to inflict punishment on them, that they might be chastened and improve, collected all the gods into their most holy habitation, which, being placed in the centre of the world, beholds all created things. And when he had called them together, he spake as follows:-"
translated by Benjamin Jowett

Prologue

Long long ago, after the ice had receded but before the myths that foreshadowed our history were established, a mother was arguing with her daughter. They lived in a small village in the northeastern corner of their land; it was just a few one-room huts of stones and thatch gathered around the stream that became the Teorainn river. The daughter had hair the colour of straw and blue eyes, like her parents. She was considered handsome rather than pretty, with a shy face made serious by a strong nose, but a mouth that would betray it with a smile of mischief. The daughter was a singer and piper, talented beyond her years, and word of her skills had reached the far-off City. The rulers of the City had sent for her, to entertain them and their guests on this day, the Day of Autumn.

Éirime's mother owned a big pottery bowl, large enough to stand in and almost too large to lift. Éirime was standing in it, naked in front of the fire, and her mother was pouring water on her from a small pot. As she helped her daughter to wash, she spoke about what would happen that day. Mother was excited.

"They're coming to take you to the Festival of Selection, in the City of the Sea People. You will be performing for the Mentor and the City. Nobody from our world has ever done that before. To think: someone from our village going to the big City to entertain on the Day of Autumn."

Éirime didn't want to go. She felt cold and self-conscious, her mother was making far too much fuss, and the journey to the big City filled her with vague fears. She had complained so much that, for one of the very few times in her life, she had fought with her father. Normally she could rely on his calm, but since the news had come that she was to sing, he had fretted nearly as much as her mother. It was too much. She felt too old for this kind of attention, and the soap was getting in her eyes.

But soon the soap was gone, and her mother took honeysuckle, the last of the summer blooms, and rubbed it on her arms and legs to scent her. The sensation was ticklish and unpleasant, but she felt grown-up that her

7

mother would waste the flowers to make her smell good.

Her mother helped her to step out without tipping the bowl, wrapped her in a woollen blanket to dry, and opened the chest by the door. She rummaged around a bit while Éirime shivered, then lifted out a linen dress. Éirime was horrified.

"I can't wear that, Mammy."

"Why not? It's the best dress we own, and it's the only thing we have that could be good enough."

"But Mammy, that's your wedding dress. That will be my wedding dress."

"Well, maybe you'll meet a husband in the big City."

"Mammy, that's stupid!" Éirime objected. "If I wear it when I meet him, what will I wear on my wedding day? And anyway," she added "I don't want a husband from the big City. I want to marry a shepherd and take care of his sheep on the hill."

"If you wear your old woollen thing, you won't be marrying anybody from the big City."

"I don't want anybody from the City," she repeated.

"Éirime," warned her father, and she remembered how they had fought and she blushed.

Her mother brought the dress over.

"Come on, put it on," her mother said.

Éirime put her arms out, and lifted it over her head. The fine cloth felt strange, harder and less scratchy than the wool she was used to. Her mother had other things too: a pebble of turquoise from the river, pierced and with a leather thong; fine sandals with small beads of polished bone; and a garland of flowers that her cousin, Óire, had woven from the bushes and pasture: autumn chrysanthemums in brilliant yellow. Each one was put on her. Her hair combed and towelled, was pale next to the yellow gold of the blooms. Her mother opened the doorway, letting in light and air, and led her over into the sunshine.

"There," said her mother when she was dressed in everything. "You look beautiful now, fit to meet people from the big City. Don't you feel beautiful?"

Éirime stood in the unfamiliar clothes, the beads on the sandals pressing on her feet, the weight of the flowers in her hair, the strange feeling of the linen around her waist and knees, the cold turquoise on her chest and the scent of honeysuckle in her nostrils. It surprised her, but dressed up, she did feel more confident, more happy.

"I feel better, Mammy," she said reluctantly.

"There you are, then."

"But I don't want to marry a man from the big City."

Before her mother could speak, her father said, "You don't have to marry anyone you don't want to. But dressed like that, you can marry anyone you like."

Whatever her mother was going to add was lost. Éirime had been looking out of the door, hoping that nobody would see her and also hoping that someone would. She saw Óire looking across the river to the south. Then she turned around. She saw Éirime come out of their house, and Éirime could see in her cousin's green eyes that she was shocked by how pretty Éirime was. Then Óire saw something else, and pointed into the sky, to the south.

"They're coming," Óire shouted.

Faces appeared at every doorway in the village. Éirime saw the shepherds running back to their houses, her brother among them. She grabbed her goatskin jacket.

"You can't wear that smelly old thing to the big City," her mother objected.

"Maybe not," her father replied, "but if she doesn't wear it on the Flyer, she'll die of cold before she gets there."

But Éirime didn't hear the conclusion of the argument: jacket in hand, she ran out to see the Flyers for herself.

As the Flyers descended towards the village, the villagers did not know what to stare at most. They had rarely seen Flyers, and even more rarely seen one with the turquoise blue of the Sea People's cloaks in it. But then there was Éirime. People knew she was the prettiest girl in the village, as well as being the best singer. People also knew that she might be the best singer in the province, or maybe even in the world: the visits of the Flyers, bringing strangers to hear her voice and her performance for the entertainment of others were proof enough of that. But seeing her ready for the City, she seemed like she must be the most beautiful peasant girl in the world too: not a farmer like them but as attractive as the Sea People themselves.

The Flyers landed. As well as the Sea People, there were servants or guards: tall people whose grey clothing was completely unrecognisable to the villagers. "People from the City," they whispered, "not like us."

Éirime was led quickly to the Flyers, and sat among the tall strangers. Among them and the Sea People she seemed tiny, a little speck of white and gold among the blue and the grey. Then the command was given, the Flyers lifted, and they were swallowed up by the sky.

Éirime's brother caught up, breathless, and stood with his parents at the doorway of their little hut. His father looked up into the sky, shading his eyes from the bright morning sun, but his mother wouldn't look.

"I can still see them," his father said, "They look so high, like a bird."

"I will watch when they bring her home to me," his mother replied.

"It might be dark," his father pointed out. "The Festival of Selection at the City might last all day."

"I will watch them when they bring her home," his mother repeated. "Not before."

— 1 —

The Shepherdess

Two men were in the Forest. They were both tall and they both wore turquoise blue cloaks but, other than that, they could not have been more different.

"What I still don't understand is why it's important, my love," the rider said.

He was tall like his companion, but his soft, deep brown skin was stretched over a sparse frame, over elegant high cheekbones. His voice was high and musical.

"I know that you want any news you hear of her," he continued, "but why not simply track her and ask?"

"I don't want to find her, Miotal," his companion growled, "I want to find out *about* her."

As tall as Miotal, Aclaí was pale-skinned, with a heavy frame, short fair hair and a stubble that could almost be a beard. He picked his way through the Forest, leading his companion and the other horse through the overhanging branches of a willow, following the alarm-call of a bird.

Aclaí asked, "How long have you known her?"

"Long enough," replied Miotal.

"Then you know why I am curious. Have you ever known her go into the Forest by choice?"

"I don't remember her doing so. But why is that important?"

"People don't do things without a reason, Miotal."

"I understand that," he replied. He was about to ask again why Aclaí didn't simply ask her, but then he remembered why. Instead he asked "What do you think that reason is?"

"She is Retired. She is going somewhere to make a new life."

"How far do you think she has gone?" Miotal remembered something Éirime had said, something she had always said. "Do you think she is looking for Iolar? She always thought he survived, didn't she?"

"She is not looking for Iolar," Aclaí replied, with surprising vehemence.

11

"He went into the Forest only a month after she was Selected. The Forest was much more dangerous then. You would have to go a lot deeper today to encounter the sort of monsters we met every day. Nobody does that."

"Except for those that March on Chaos," replied Miotal, regretting it almost as he said it.

"People don't Retire in order to March on Chaos, Miotal. Marching on Chaos doesn't need any permission. The Mentor knows that people die in the Forest – that is why it is an honourable death, even if it is a futile one."

"Futile? Those who March on Chaos destroy monsters that would otherwise be a threat to us. Someone of Immortal Rank would kill many of them before they died."

"And antagonise a lot more. When Novices choose to keep going deeper into the Forest and never turn back, they won't get far before something eats them. But when Immortals do, they will go deeper than we do normally. It happens every few generations, and there are monsters that never see a human being for generations. What would we do if a type of monster we'd never seen before came into our world, killing all before it?"

"We would track it back and make sure it never happened again."

"And what do you think they do? We see surges of monsters sometimes, and who is to say that they don't follow a March on Chaos back to the City?"

"If you really think the March on Chaos is a Tradition that causes the City so much destruction, why encourage it?"

"Who says I encourage it?"

Miotal seemed about to answer, then he thought.

"You don't speak out against it, my love," he answered, weakly.

"I don't. Sometimes it is the only escape for someone. I don't speak out against everything that is wrong with the City. Do you?"

"Aclaí, I have learned not to speak out against anything in the City."

"That is healthy," observed Aclaí.

"Especially for the rest of us, love. We're not all favourites."

"Favourites are more likely to be overheard," Aclaí commented. They rode on. Then he added, "She has not Marched on Chaos, Miotal."

"How do you know?"

They rode on more, Aclaí following the trail, and the mysterious paths that stitched the woodland together to make the Forest.

Eventually Aclaí answered, "I don't know. If she is Marching on Chaos, if she has found that much courage, then I will try and change her mind."

"And if you can't? What then, Aclaí my love?"

"Then I will March by her side," he answered, simply, "and –"

He stopped, lifted his head to see. He had heard something.

Then Miotal heard it himself. It was the metal ringing of a sword: a sword of the Sea People. Aclaí climbed on to his horse, nudged it into a run with a kick of the heels, and leaned forward, to guide the horse with his breathing. Miotal kicked too, and his horse sped to follow. They drew their swords as they rode.

Ahead they could hear screams, and shouting, and the strange cries of the wild monsters of the Forest. Aclaí and Miotal both had armour on their Silver Cords, and as soon as they thought of the Silver Cord, they were wearing the armour. As they were both Immortal Rank, within the armour their bodies became insubstantial, and so immune to simple physical injury. It was not something they felt, but they both knew it was true.

Then they were among the monsters. These were some sort of *fo-mórach*: primitive lesser giant types, with humanlike bodies, long legs with hooves, and goat-like heads. Aclaí was the first there, and he was met with spear-points, surrounding him, all tipped with roughly-made heads of Metal. As he breathed calmness to the horse, he swept his sword about one-handed, the razor edge chopping easily through the shafts of spears, or through the limbs of any of the giants that were foolish enough to get close. Behind him he heard Miotal shout Words of Power, calling for a Manifestation of Fire, and he felt rather than heard the pressure wave as the surrounding woodland exploded into flame. Aclaí thought that he would not have chosen fire, not in the woods in the Month of Darkness, but their problems were more immediate than that.

The giants fell back, and Aclaí urged his horse on, towards the source of the human sounds. The giants were too well organised for their intelligence, though, and Aclaí and Miotal knew there must be another creature leading them. As they rode into the clearing, Aclaí saw a figure with a hooded robe, and two vast spiders. The hooded shape was twice the size of a man, and from the front of the robe, tentacles were reaching over twice a man's length. Clutched in them was a girl from the City, armoured but with her helm missing, struggling to get her sword to the tentacles that enfolded her. She was small, and brown, with eyes from the Great Ocean, and she looked terrified. Another girl was fighting off the spiders, and by her feet was the body of a boy. The one in the tentacles had a broad nose, and her hair was already streaked with grey, but the girl fighting the spiders was young, with delicate dark features and thick black hair. She looked around as they rode in, and one of the spiders leaped on her.

Aclaí sighted along the edge of his sword, and breathed Power: green light flashed from the tip, and the spider was gone. Then he swung the blade right around his head, and cut down and through the robed creature, the whole weight of the horse's charge bearing through the sweep. The creature was cut right through, and the parts collapsed. Miotal, riding just behind him, enveloped the fallen body in fire, before it could re-form and attack them again.

That just left the other spider, and now Aclaí called Words of Power, this time to summon a Manifestation of Ice. The spider didn't seem affected, it just stood still, although hoarfrost was now forming on it. But the girl who was fighting it was shaking, and suddenly she fell to the ground, convulsing.

Aclaí looked at the two that had fallen. The venom of the spider would swiftly overcome the girl, and the fallen boy had the chest part of his armour open, and Aclaí could see internal organs. The girl who had been in the tentacles rushed to him.

"My lord Aclaí," she begged, "he's still alive."

Aclaí could see that both of them would need the Words of Restoration, and that Miotal would be of no help there.

He called out, "Miotal, circle around and make sure they don't have reinforcements. I'll get these back on their feet."

He had only a few moments, and he knew he must work without Miotal watching if he was to save them both. As Miotal rode away into the woods, Aclaí leaped down. The boy was nearest. A closer look told him that he was right: the boy's entrails were not only exposed, but a significant portion was missing. He was still awake, somehow, and he spoke, fighting for breath.

"Lord Aclaí," he gasped, "help Blátha. Please, my lord."

Something about the words reminded Aclaí of why they were in the Forest, and he went over to the girl instead, the Words of Restoration already forming in his mind. The Words of Restoration are a powerful Formula of Words, and Aclaí had to concentrate on his breathing, to feel the Power so he could utter them and make them work. The girl had puncture marks from the bite on the side of her head, one deep into the neck, the other behind the ear, under her long hair, into the skull, planting the venom straight into the brain. Still exhilarated from the fight, and then again by such powerful Words, he watched as the wounds closed up, and the colour returned. He didn't even wait to see her rise: he had to get back to the boy before Miotal returned.

The other girl was cradling the boy.

"You can't die," she wept, shaking him. "You might not be able to live without her, but how am I supposed to live without you?"

Aclaí spoke to her as he hurried up to them.

"He might not be dead. Let me see."

But as he bent down, he heard Miotal ride back.

"He's dead, Aclaí," Miotal said. "There's nothing we can do."

And, listening to Miotal's voice, Aclaí knew he was right. To raise the dead was a forbidden Art, and had been longer than Aclaí had been at the City.

Aclaí held out his hand to the girl, still trying to remember her name. He couldn't. He could see that she was of the seventh Novice Rank from her sword. The other girl, Blátha, he recognised. She had been among the Favourites for a while, a few years back, and she was five Ranks above the other two. She came over, and the girls embraced.

"I'm sorry, Féileacána," Blátha whispered. "I know you loved him."

Aclaí saw it, and felt angry, angry at Miotal for returning too quickly, angry at all the things that the City forbade.

"I am sorry," he told Féileacána.

"You did everything you could, Lord Aclaí," she replied. "We all know the rules of the City."

He wondered then if she knew what he had wanted to do. But the rules were about more than not getting caught. They were deeper than that, burned into him. Every time he broke the rules of the City, it tore at his heart. He was enchained by Words of Power, and he believed that he would never break free.

It was raining, and it was getting dark, but she was not cold. Her blue cloak was not just a symbol of her order, but it also kept her warm and dry, no matter how cold or wet it was. Beneath her the horse was warm, too, and she was not urging it on: they were walking along the old road to the village. Riding faster than walking pace needed concentration, even with her Rank and training, and she felt no need to hurry. If she had wanted speed, she would have used a Flyer. She was through the Forest now, the part of the journey that had made her afraid when she was planning. Now that was behind her, and she had surprised herself with how little there had been for her to fear. She wanted the journey to finish as it had been: the horse to do the walking while she sang, while she daydreamed, while she remembered. She had waited long enough to come home. A few more hours would not hurt.

Peering through the falling rain, the fading light, she could see that the buildings were not as she remembered them from when she was a girl. Things had changed since the representatives from the City had arrived, in the years since they had taken her away to Selection, since she had been chosen to live in the Land of the Forever Young. The buildings were still made of stone and thatch, but they were bigger, more spacious, better at keeping out the weather. Modern conveniences came from the City: lights; warmth; healing for injuries and illness; and the Visions for their education, to teach them about the Sea People. Every building she had known as a girl had been rebuilt, extended, enlarged.

She rode past the unfamiliar houses, past an unfamiliar inn, to the new bridge where the ford had been, and over to where her parents house had stood. She imagined she could see a lump in the ground where the stones had been, but the building she could see was new: another inn, in an orchard by the river, next to a wharf with merchants' boats tied up. The sign showed a girl in a sheepskin, sitting on a rock, a wooden flute in her hands, the mouthpiece hovering by her lips, and a shepherd's looped staff by her feet. Beside her a bird was perched, singing. The girl looked very like she had when she was younger: straight straw-blonde hair that covered her neck, framing a serious face with a strong nose, and a slight, boyish figure. The sign showed the name of the inn, without writing: the Songbird and the Shepherdess. She guided her horse over, stepped down, tied the halter of her horse to the rail, and went in.

The innkeeper had heard the horse walking along the road, and so had many of the guests. A horse on the road north of the river was unusual, as most visitors arrived by boat: they were looking around as the door opened. As she stood in the haze and the firelight, the first thing they noticed about the visitor was her cloak. Only the Sea People were permitted to wear the blue and her cloak marked her as one of them. She pulled the hood back and her hair and face were dry, for all that she must have ridden for hours in the rain. Her face was young, but in her eyes there was a look suggesting she had seen too many things. Well, they had all heard tales of what happened in the Forest.

She came over to the innkeeper, the locals getting quickly out of her way and bowing their heads. As she walked through them, he could see that she was shorter than him by at least a head height. For those who thought the Sea People were all seven feet tall, their eyes flashing fire, the little sad-eyed girl did not match the glory of her cloak.

Beneath her cloak she was wearing boots, tall and practical for riding, and a loose white dress on her slim frame. The dress was a simple design, but the linen of it was more finely woven than anything a village girl would wear to travel. He guessed she was young, with less than twenty summers, not long at the City. She would not have reached the Eighth Rank, so she was here on her Forest service. At her hip there was no sword, which would have given her Rank at a glance. Instead he saw a flute and a harp on her belt, such as might be played by anyone in the village, but made of fine materials: beautiful things. He could also see that she was beautiful, as the Sea People always were.

"Good evening, sir. Do you have space for me, and for my horse?" she asked.

Her accent was local, which surprised him, but his caution won over

his curiosity and he didn't ask. Her voice was soft, hardly more than
a whisper. Her tones were gentle, honestly asking it seemed, not giving
orders, a courtesy that she had no reason to extend.

"Of course, my lady," he replied.

He was an older man, with only a small amount of silver-grey hair
around his ears, and a badly-trimmed beard.

"My stable-boy will take care of the horse," he continued. "Let me show
you our best room. It is not much, but this is a country place."

She smiled at him, reassuring.

"I was born in a one-room hut, such as your ancestors lived in. I have
slept on silk enough. Whatever you have will be fine with me."

He led her out of the commons, to where the private rooms were, and
showed her the room under the eaves, with the hearthstone under the
smoke-hole, and the small bed. The sheets may not have been silk, but at
least they were linen.

"This is all we have, my lady."

"What can I give you for letting me stay?" she asked.

"I cannot take anything from someone like you, my lady. It is our duty
to the City..."

Instead of arguing, she found a thong at her neck, untied it, and removed
a little gold statuette of a rabbit.

"I will pay you this gold piece for your room and for the horse," she
told him. He recognised beneath the softness of her voice the tone of an
order given. She continued, "Have ye been expecting one of us here?"

"We had asked for a Steward, my lady. We had hoped so, anyway. We
are a long way from Port Teorainn."

"The Mentor has given me permission and I would like to try and be
yere Steward, at least for a while." She was looking at him with something
in her eyes he could not identify, not in a blue-robe like her. "That is," she
added, "if ye will have me."

"Of course we will have you," he replied, hoping to get the tone right.
"We hoped to be so honoured, my lady."

"I am afraid I have never been a Steward before, not even for a small
village. I might not be any good at it. I might not do it for long. But we
can try."

"We've never had a Steward, my lady." He looked at how she was, and
began to suspect that she really was as unassuming as she seemed. It was
most strange. "I am sure everyone will try to make you feel at home, my
lady," he added, knowing it was probably too familiar.

"I am home."

"You were born in Anleacán, my lady?" he asked, wondering.

"I was," she replied. "I was born and raised here, not sixty paces from this spot."

"I never heard of it, my lady," he replied.

"Well," she mused, "it was a long time ago. I left when I was no more than a girl, and I never came back. Nobody will remember."

He did remember: there had been a blue-robe born and raised in the village, a long time ago. But she was a legend, not a quiet, serious-faced young woman. He felt the hollow weakness in his belly as he suspected who she was.

"Who are you, my lady?" But he knew. "Are you really her?"

"I am," she answered, a little disappointed. "I thought ye would have forgotten."

"We hadn't forgotten you, my lady," he stammered. "This house is named for you." He tried to steady his breath. "I am sorry if my words have caused offense," he blurted. "I thought you were much younger than you are, my lady. I did not realise that a village like ours would get such a Steward. I did not realise that an Immortal, one of your Rank, a Favourite, would ever be a Steward. Not of a little place like Áthaiteorann."

"Don't be afraid," she replied. "I liked being unknown. I told you, I chose to come here, I asked the Mentor to be permitted to leave the City, to come and be yere Steward. I wanted to come home. I hoped people would have forgotten, after so long, but I should have guessed when I saw your sign."

"Nobody has forgotten, my lady, people remember you. Especially in this house. You are one of the proudest stories our village knows. We always imagine that you remember us fondly and that you protect us and speak in our favour. That is why we asked, my lady."

"If ye only knew, the story might not seem so proud," she mused. But then she added, "I do remember ye. I want ye to continue to think that. But perhaps it would be better if my name was not used. Would you call me 'Caora' and vaguely remember my going to the City? You can remember my name as 'Caora' with the name of your inn? I would like to be yere Steward, but I couldn't bear to be myself. Would you tell people that I am my own Favourite?"

"Are you sure, my lady?"

"I don't want to be her. Does the rest of the village care?"

"We all care, my lady. My family especially. We are your brother's family, my lady. You are the oldest of our family, my lady. Our ancestor, and ancestor to most of the village."

"I am not, landlord. I am nobody's ancestor: I have no children. The Sea People do not marry."

"But you are our many-times-great-aunt, my lady, and that counts you an ancestor to us. The blood of your parents flows in us too, and the spark of talent that goes with it. It is Anleacán's Gift. And we remember you."

"Then I will have to be 'Caora'."

Liús worked the brush over the pony's neck, and down to the flanks.

"They do get you in a mess in the Forest," he whispered. The skin on the horse twitched and flicked beneath the hair as he picked out the mud and blood. "You don't want to go out there any more than I do."

He was a blond man, with fair eyes, from the land east of the Archipelago. He put the brush and comb down, and went out. Outside the stable he saw that Lord Aclaí and Lord Miotal had arrived.

"My lords," Liús said.

He took the halters to control the horses' heads, held them while the lords dismounted, then shooed the horses into the stable, remembering to use his breath on their heads the way his father had taught, not the way they taught in the City. The way they taught in the City was so hard.

The larger of the Immortals followed him into the stables. Liús looked around.

"My lord Aclaí?" Liús asked.

"You were Selected only this year, weren't you, Liús?"

"I was, my lord," Liús replied, astonished that the Oldest should even remember him.

"Where is your lover?"

Liús felt a moment of fear.

"My lover, my lord?" he replied.

"You know what I am talking about. Ye must keep it secret from the Mentor, you know," Aclaí advised him. "Keep it secret even after she is Initiated. If he finds out that there is a real love between two of the Sea People, he might choose to break it. The broken pieces remain, but the love can never be mended. The Sea People do not marry, Liús: remember that, and love in secret, if ye have to love at all."

Liús was about to deny it, but Aclaí had already turned to leave.

"My lord?" Liús asked.

Aclaí turned back.

"Was there something else?" Aclaí asked.

"Lord Aclaí, would you be able to get Éise to the Mentor, get her Initiated soon?"

"Is that what you want?"

"It is what needs to happen, my lord. It is for the best."

"It is. I will see what I can do."

"Thank you, my lord," Liús replied. He stared after the departing Lord Aclaí and he remembered whose departure it was that Aclaí and Miotal had been tracking. For half a second he thought the obvious, but then his mind shied away from the possibility. Lord Aclaí was too cold and powerful a man to love anyone, least of all someone so gentle, so dreamy, and so melancholically drunken as her.

When she had eaten, and they had opened a skin of wine for her, Caora played for the crowd in the commons. At first they had listened for fear of interrupting a blue-robe, but as the harp introduced an air of their own village, they paid attention. When her voice took up the words, they could think of nothing else: they had never heard their own songs performed with such talent.

Later, as she was drinking, the innkeeper spoke to some of the villagers, three men and a dog.

"Who is she, Ólachán?" one man whispered, as he scratched the ears of the dog at his feet.

"She is Lady Caora, Reo, and she is our Steward." It was good news, and he told it as good news, although to lie about someone so important still frightened him. "The Mentor has sent us a Steward, like we asked."

"How does she know our songs?" asked Ordóg, a younger man with red hair.

"It is as if she were the Lady herself," Reo added. Ioraí, the largest, nodded.

"The Lady taught her," the innkeeper quickly explained. "She is the Lady's Favourite, she tells me." He added "She's my relative, a second cousin, removed once. Her parents moved to the City, years ago."

"So she is young, a Novice?" Ordóg asked.

Ólachán tried not to let his nerves show. "What did you expect, Ordóg? Lord Miotal? Lady Damhánalla? This is not Port Teorainn, you know."

"Hush," said Ioraí. "She's starting again."

Ólachán told everyone about Caora, and the word spread quickly. But when his guests had gone home, and they were getting ready for bed, his wife Beatha spoke to him.

"You never told me about your cousins in Ceatha, Ólachán," she chided. Then, when she saw his face, she stopped, went over and took his hand. "What is the matter?" she coaxed.

"It's Lady Caora," he explained.

"Is this to do with that nephew of yours who..?"

"It's nothing to do with Colm."

"But she is his sister, is she? Surely that would make her your niece, not cousin. You're related to her through..."

"Beatha, listen to me. It's much worse than that. Lady Caora is a dangerous person."

"Oh, Ólachán, you're far too jumpy. She's probably about the same age as Saonta. And she's far better mannered. The Lady would never have sent us someone who would hurt us, she loves Áthaiteorann too much."

"Beatha, everyone talks about the Lady like that, but think about it. She is just a few years younger than Lord Aclaí; she is older and higher-Rank than the Steward of Port Teorainn. She is Second Oldest, Beatha. You presume she is kind, but nobody living in Áthaiteorann has ever met her."

"Not true, Ólachán. Lady Caora has met her. She's the Lady's favourite, even though I thought she didn't have favourites. And she's your mysterious cousin."

"She is not, Beatha."

"Then why..?" It was Beatha's turn to look scared. "Ólachán, do you realise what trouble we would get in if you have been making up stories about something like that?"

"Wait, keep your voice down," Ólachán begged. "I said it because she told me to say it."

"Why in the world would she...?"

"Beatha, love, think. She knows our songs. She speaks like one of us. She wants people to think she is my cousin, to explain why she seems to come from here."

"Who is she? Why would the Lady send someone who..?"

"The Lady didn't send her, Beatha my love."

"Oh," Beatha replied. She sat, and stared at her knees. "What can we do? So she isn't the Lady's favourite? Does the Lady know she is here, even?"

"She does, Beatha. But if the Lady Herself was here, would that make it all right?"

"I'm not sure anymore. As you said, she is Second Oldest, nearly as high a Rank as Lord Aclaí. If Lord Aclaí was here, it wouldn't be all right!"

He sighed as he made up his mind.

"Beatha, I'll tell you a secret, but I need you to promise me that you won't tell this to anyone. Not your mother, not your sisters, nobody."

Beatha looked injured, but she judged her husband's face.

"I won't," she replied.

"You promise me."

"I promise," she agreed. "Don't you trust me?"

"After that business with Flannbhuía and her ..?"

"I said I was sorry, Ólachán. How many years are you going to remember?"

"This time it's serious, Beatha. This is a secret about the blue-robes, about one of the oldest of them."

"Lord Aclaí?"

"Not Lord Aclaí, which is the one comfort. But it is nearly as bad. I know I said that Lady Caora wasn't sent by the Lady Herself. You see, Lady Caora *is* the Lady Herself."

"Can it be possible?"

"Beatha, you heard her sing."

"Oh. Then what are we to do?"

"Take care of her. And do as she tells us. She told us to pretend that she is her own favourite, and that she is my cousin."

"She doesn't have favourites, everyone knows that. She's never even taken a candidate to Selection."

"We can't argue, Beatha. That is what she asked me to say."

In the morning, Beatha remembered how Ólachán had forbidden her to tell anyone, and reminded her of how "Caora," was one of the Immortals, and how badly, how savagely things might go if her orders were disobeyed.

So before telling anyone, Beatha swore them to secrecy. She told her sisters, and her mother. They in turn swore others to secrecy, before telling them too. So the outcome was that within days of Caora arriving to be their Steward, most of the village was pretending she was a young Novice of the Sea People, and Favourite of their village's most honoured daughter; but they all secretly knew, with fear and pride, that she was the Lady herself, Lady Éirime, their village's long-lost daughter, come home at last.

— 2 —

The City of Immortals

To a watcher from the modern day, looking down on the world of the Sea People, what would have stood out most about that Neolithic planet was the Land of the Immortals: as if the little island that would one day be called Bermuda had been stretched out a hundred miles south and west. Going lower, the island would have become stranger: the landscape was not quite shaped right; the rivers had not meandered in their valleys and cut through flood plains; and most of it was covered in pasture and fields. There were trees, but the trees were planted regularly, in neat rows, like a giant version of the maize that was planted in the fields. There was no wild forest throughout the entire Land of the Immortals. That was no accident, for the feud between humanity and the wild Forest was a thousand years old when Éirime went home.

Halfway up the Land of the Immortals, on a bay facing east, was the City of the Sea People. The City was built on a hill, around which a river wound on its way to the sea. The river and the sea formed a harbour, and the harbour was filled with boats, large and small. Most of them were flimsy structures, no more than rafts made of logs or reeds lashed together, made to withstand the ocean by Words of Power: what sea trade there was always came to the City, so of course the traders' boats were made using the arts of the Sea People.

Over the river there were two crossings: one spanned the river at the top of the harbour, and the other was on the harbour walls, the gap into the haven bridged by a wooden walkway counterweighted with immense stones, that swung up when the ships came and went. This artifice could have been assembled by hordes of slaves, working with rollers, levers, and ropes, but that was not the way the Sea People did things. The landward bridge led out through the fields to the Grey Gate, a great stone arch that led to other worlds.

On the outer side of the river's curve, by the fields, the houses were made of sun-dried brick, with roofs of reed thatch. Here maybe five hundred

23

dwellings stood: five hundred families of ordinary people drawn by the first City humanity made. Five hundred dwellings would look to a modern visitor like very little, although at night he would recognise things like the lighting in the streets. In the Stone Age, it was a great thing, the pattern of all future cities.

On the inner side of the river's curve, the wooden bridge and the stone walkway of the breakwater entered the stone walls that marked the outer perimeter of the City on the Hill. To enter through either the Land Gate or the Sea Gate was to enter the world of the Immortals. Except during certain celebration days, ordinary men could not enter either gate without the permission of the Sea People. Some came and went without question: the servant girls and eunuchs who served the City of Immortals.

Looking closer, our watcher would have seen the Sea People: among the men and women carrying and working, crossing the bridge with their animals upon their errands, he would have been able to see the Selected, visible in their turquoise blue cloaks, the mark of their office. There, within the outer court, was the Great Hall, the largest building in the world in those days, with space for a thousand men to sit and eat. Here was where City met world, on the first day of the year, when the world brought the best of their young men and women to see if they would be judged fit to cross those bridges for good: to be judged beautiful, intelligent and courageous enough to be Selected to become one of the Sea People; and for a very few, the ones with skill, good friends and sufficient luck, to become one of the Immortals.

But this was not the end of the year. That would not be for months: it was not long after the Summer Solstice, and the hot, drowsy days of the Month of Darkness had come. It was not yet Harvest, but the Celebration of Midsummer's Day was a memory.

Within the wall of the City there were other walls, concentric rings like the layers of an onion, each enclosing a smaller space higher on the hill. The outer layer, enclosed by the outer walls, included the Great Hall and also Novice dormitories, teaching halls, servants' quarters and kitchens, simple long buildings, made of stone and thatch.

Within this part, enclosing the higher part of the hill, was another stone wall which enclosed the Court of the Veterans. This space was for those of the Sea People who had mastered the basic skills of their order, who had served their apprenticeships in the Forest, and were seeking to master Immortality. They lived here in various houses, individually or in small groups: not families, for the Sea People did not marry; but sometimes friends, bound together by bonds of shared danger in the Forest. For here lived the people who had given their lives in service of the City and the Sea People, and if they did not soon learn the Immortal Breath, their lives would be over. Here the blue cloaks wrapped around shoulders that stooped and heads that were grey or white. Within this space dominated by old age was the next wall, again incorporating the higher part of the hill: age besieged the Court of the Immortals, but there was no place for grey hairs and wrinkles within it.

The Court of the Immortals enclosed only a small space, yet the buildings were palaces of stone and plaster: great buildings, immortal architecture to reflect the immortality of their inhabitants. But there was only a handful: the Immortals who lived here could be numbered on a man's fingers. For most Immortals accepted that precious gift as their reward for one lifetime in service to the Sea People and, when they gained Immortal Rank, they Retired and went out into the worlds, into the Forest, to live among ordinary people and keep them safe.

Within the Court of the Immortals there was another wall, though. This last wall enclosed the top of the hill, the Court of the Favourites. Here were the two-roomed cottages of the Favourites, each the exact dimensions of the others. There were a few individual buildings used by the Mentor: the House of Power, a pyramid of glazed bricks; and the House of Records, with a red tiled roof. At the summit of the hill was the Mentor's House. The City was his creation, his great work, and he had lived there from the start of its millennial history, since he raised the Land of the Immortals from the ocean. It was fitting that the City should enfold and gather around him, for he and the symbol of his authority were the source of the safety that allowed that first, now forgotten, human civilisation to flourish. There he was in his room, behind the balcony window with the curtains that were always closed; that symbol of authority around his neck. He looked young, a small, pale man with dark blond hair. His appearance was quite ordinary, apart from his green eyes, but he was almost the oldest thing on this island. The oldest thing in the Land of the Immortals was on the table before him, yellow-white in the dark room: the eleven-centuries-old skull of a twelve year old boy.

All the rest of the Court of the Favourites was given to formal gardens: fragrant blooms and mature trees, a fountain, paths that led nowhere, trysting spots. A cypress grew by the wall and in its shade was one such secret place. It could not have been seen from the rest of the Court of the Favourites, because of the tree, and it could not have been seen from the Court of the Immortals, below, because of the wall. From the air a watcher could have seen the stone seat, just big enough for two, worn by the many lovers that had sat there as a thousand years of history had gone by. But that day, a pretty woman sat there, alone, eating her midday meal, and looking down at the life and industry that bustled in the harbour, far below her.

The woman was tall and thin with thick curly hair, the colour of honey, reaching down over her shoulder-blades. The hair contrasted with the blue of her cloak. Her tunic was also blue, silk, and woven so the iridescence of the silk reflected many shades of blue and green. Her face was pale, but shaped by ancestors from all over the planet: not something unusual for a modern observer, but in that day, a mark that said that her family were from the City for many generations. Her eyes were sometimes blue, sometimes green. That her dress showed the same shades was not an accident: but it was something that few would notice without looking at her carefully, without staring into her eyes. There were not many people whose Rank would have permitted them to safely look her in the eye, and on that day, all but one of them was within the Court of the Favourites.

This was a place of calm for her. It was a lovers' place, she knew, but she loved it most when she could sit there and be alone, ignore the surrounding games of politics and power. But this time, she heard voices. She felt frustrated by that, felt that they were invading her quiet space. She listened for the voices, trying to decide if she should give up and come out, or see if they came to her. She concentrated on the sounds, hoping to recognise the approaching invaders of her calm.

When she heard the first, deeper voice, she smiled and turned, half rising. But then she heard the other voice and a look of irritation crossed her face as she sat down again. But, judging from the closeness of the voices, it was now too late to escape: the only exit was the way they were coming in. So, rather than be caught trying to escape them, she sat and waited.

"Grandniece," Miotal greeted her. "Eibheara."

The two men came out into the shade of the cypress, so much bigger than when Miotal had first sat in its shade. Eibheara reminded him of how she had been as a girl, as if she had never really grown up, as if she wasn't really an Immortal. Her parents had called her Ceathrua, since she was their fourth daughter, born on the fourth day; but she had taught them her name almost before she could talk. When Eibheara made her mind up about something, it was made up.

She turned around, and looked straight at Aclaí.

"How are ye?" she asked. Then, to Miotal, "I didn't know you had returned, great-uncle. What brings you back to the City and who has brought you into the Court of the Favourites?"

She was reminding him that he was not one of the Mentor's favourites, like she was, but was only here by Aclaí's invitation.

"Aclaí asked me," he told her. "He said he had things he wanted to say to me. Perhaps we should leave you in peace."

She looked at Aclaí.

"Stay," she said. "If you don't mind."

As Aclaí approached, she moved over, making space for one more. He sat down, and Miotal went over to the wall and perched on that. Seeing her close to Aclaí, on the seat that was designed for two and only two, he felt a pang of jealousy.

But Aclaí was there for a reason.

Miotal asked, "What was it that you wanted to talk about, Lord Aclaí?"

"It's Éirime," Aclaí replied.

"You must know it is Éirime, uncle," interrupted Eibheara, impatiently. "Everyone is talking about it. She is still a Favourite, although nobody knows why. She walked away from the City. She rejected everything we have here. She might as well have spat in the Mentor's eye as she left."

Miotal was only half listening: he was watching Aclaí's face. He knew that there would be emotions behind that mask, but he did not know what. Perhaps it was good that Eibheara was here: she would draw out Aclaí's thoughts, and tell Miotal the parts that Aclaí would not. He always felt more from Aclaí's touch than from his face, but they weren't touching. The seat he had hoped would hold them together as they talked was being used by Eibheara to keep them apart.

"The Mentor let her go?" Miotal asked.

"He did," Eibheara replied. "She had been asking to go for years, but last ten-day he said she could go. She picked up her things and walked out there and then. She didn't say goodbye to anyone. She wasn't even at the Evening Meal."

It was useful information, but Miotal wished Aclaí would talk and wished Eibheara would be quiet. He looked straight at Aclaí.

"How can I help?" Miotal asked, hoping the simplicity of the statement would convey what he could not convey with touch.

"When an Immortal leaves," Aclaí said, briskly, "we should look at the things they used to do, to see if any of them are Traditions that should be kept alive."

Miotal and Eibheara both knew that. Éirime was the first Favourite to leave the City, but not the first Immortal: and for an Immortal to choose to leave the City after staying so long was unusual. For an Immortal to leave suddenly was bound to leave matters to be resolved. The Traditions of the City came from the habits of the Immortals who lived there. But what traditions came from Éirime? Miotal tried to remember.

"The only Tradition I remember that centred on her was addressing the newly-Selected Novices at the start of the year." As he spoke, Miotal looked quizzical. "I never understood why she did that. She never seemed to care about the Selection process, but she went and spoke to them every year." He seemed to dismiss it as an oddity. "She's a strange person."

"I know what she was looking for," Aclaí growled.

"Oh," Miotal answered.

He seemed to understand then. He looked at Aclaí, glanced at Eibheara and looked back at Aclaí. Eibheara felt like she was an outsider, that there was some kind of unspoken understanding, some secret between Aclaí and her great-uncle, something that they would not or could not share with her. She hated that.

"I will take that responsibility," said Aclaí. "Somebody should. It's a good Tradition."

"She was reassuring, Aclaí," replied Miotal. "I can't see you being reassuring."

Eibheara felt him react, and it gave her a shock that he should feel something.

"I will have to learn," Aclaí said. "It will be good practice." He looked at Miotal, and could see that he was not convinced. He swore: a dirty phrase not unusual in the City, but it was very unusual for Aclaí to show such passion. "Look, Miotal, if you don't understand what she was looking for, with all you know, what chance is there that anyone else does?" He breathed a moment, what Eibheara recognised as Immortal Breath, a source of calmness. "It's a good Tradition. If she doesn't come back just to do it, then somebody else needs to do it. And I don't think she is going to come back, for that or anything else. I don't think she will find what she is looking for, but she has Retired."

He looked at Miotal, and Miotal remembered how their long day and night tracking had ended.

"She's not coming back," Miotal agreed.

"Well, we must assume she won't be looking anymore," Aclaí grumbled. "Which means someone else should look. It could be important."

Miotal came over from the wall and placed a hand on Aclaí's shoulder. Eibheara saw the gesture, and it reminded her of how her father would place his hand on her mother's shoulder, when she was upset. To her it seemed oddly out of place, for a man to touch another man like that, but she knew they were close. She saw Aclaí's head move, just a tiny fraction, towards Miotal.

After a few moments, Miotal replied, "Then you should do it, Aclaí, or you should tell someone else what she was looking for."

"She never told anyone, either. I think she kept the secret for a good reason. I will continue her search and, if I find it, then you will know."

Caora woke up. Her head was stuffy from drinking wine and cider, but no more than most mornings. As she breathed the Immortal Breath that was a part of her morning ritual, she felt the hangover start to clear. She remembered she was home first and then she remembered the suspicion they had felt towards her blue robe. She would have to do something about that. But first she would do something about breakfast. She got up, put clothes on, singing the Words of Freshness as she shook her hair. Then she went down to the commons.

The commons was the main room of the inn and occupied half of the building: above them the thatch was blackened by smoke and stone walls surrounded a stone floor. The shutters were open now, letting sunlight in, illuminating the trestle tables, benches and stools. A few merchants ate breakfast while their boats were prepared for the last part of their journey to the mountains, but most of the space was empty.

As Caora was drinking the last of her breakfast she had her plan sorted out. She put down the mug, then went to the middle of the room, over to the hearth stone and sat by it. They had not lit a fire yet but Beatha had swept it ready. Caora had a small knife on her Silver Cord and with a tiny tug it was in her hand. The blade and handle were both of the greenish Metal and she unfolded the blade and locked it. The handle was about the size of her finger and the blade about three quarters of that.

Holding it like a pencil, she began to scratch Words of Power into the stone, carefully: not because she found them hard to remember, although it had been a long time, but because she knew that if the knife slipped she might easily lose a fingertip. As she worked, she was aware that travellers in the commons were watching her, wondering what she was up to. Her hands trembled this early in the morning, and it would be embarrassing to bleed in front of them while she struggled to remember any Words of Healing.

By the time she was done, Ólachán and Beatha were watching too. She carved the last bit, the codicil that drew Power from the House at Ceatha. She had almost carved the codicil that drew Power from the Red World, but here on Anleacán, it was probably too far away to work. Then she reached into the wood basket and took out a branch. The Words of Power she sang were simple enough, a short little phrase invoking a Manifestation of the Great Principle of Fire, and suddenly the branch was burning. She put it on the hearth stone, and watched the smoke. It rose true and out of the hole in the roof, carried by the smoke guide she had carved on the hearth stone.

Beatha came over and spoke to her, awe in her voice.

"My lady," she said, "what do we owe you?"

"I enjoyed playing here last night," Caora replied, "but the smoke got in my eyes. Now it won't. If ye'll let me play again, then that will be my reward."

"My lady, you can play here any time you wish. My husband says you are his kin, and anyway, playing as beautiful as yours cannot help but attract us more custom."

When she had done all the hearthstones in Ólachán's inn, Caora went across the river to the well. She sat by the well and carved more Words into a rounded stone the size of her two hands in a fist.

While she was carving, a girl came out to fill a pitcher. The first thing Caora saw about her was her eyes, which were the same shade of green as the Mentor's. Her skin was pale and freckled, especially on her little upturned nose. Her hair was the colour of red gold. The girl's body inside her woollen dress was thin and bony; she was not quite a woman, but Caora could see that she would be soon.

The girl was also shy. She seemed to want to speak, but she didn't. Caora looked up at her.

"I won't be long," she said.

"I can wait, my lady," the girl replied, in a tiny voice.

Caora was scratching the codicil for the Ceatha Power, to complete the work.

"Almost done," she said. Then she looked up. "I'm Caora. What is your name?"

"My name is Eala, my lady," the girl replied. "People call me Eile, though. I am a twin, and my sister is much more popular than I am."

"There," said Caora, "It's done."

Caora dropped the carved stone into the well: there was an audible plop as it landed. Then she let down the bucket to draw the water, and drank a little. It seemed the Formula had worked. She offered the bucket to Eala.

"Try it," she said.

Eala tried it.

"It has no flavour, my lady," she said, pulling a face. "Where has the taste gone?"

"Bad water causes sickness, Eala. The well water is clean now. Clean water has no taste. Fewer people will get sick now."

"My father got sick. Duille the Healer said that was bad water."

"What happened?"

"He died, my lady." Eala looked at her, an intense green gaze that reminded Caora of the Mentor again. "Will what you've done to the well stop people dying?"

"Everybody dies, Eala. But it will stop some people dying before they should."

"Why are you doing it?" she asked.

"I am the Steward for Áthaiteorann, by the Mentor's order. It's my duty to take care of people, to stop them getting sick."

"We have a healer, my lady. Duille is our healer."

"I am sure Duille will be happy to be less busy. Purifying the well and carving smoke-guides on hearths will stop many people from getting sick."

"What is a smoke guide, my lady?"

"It's not easy to explain. Let me show you. Show me where you live."

Eala showed her to a one-roomed cottage, extended years ago. There was a red-haired boy there, playing outside. There was no-one else, and Caora was suspicious.

"Who else lives here?" she asked, afraid this Eala was an orphan, bringing up her little brother alone.

"Mammy and my sister are out getting firewood. I'm looking after Spideog," Eala replied, indicating the boy.

The resigned way the boy looked back showed Caora that he didn't appreciate being looked after by his older sister.

"That's good," said Caora, relieved to hear that she still had a mother.

Eala watched as Caora swept ashes from the hearthstone, got out her knife, and began carving the Words. As she worked, she hummed, and then began to sing softly to herself, the cook's song that Eala's mother often sang at their hearth. Eala's first thought was surprise that a Lady of the City should know one of their own village songs, and her surprise grew as she listened. Mammy was always a little out of tune, but Lady Caora, seemingly without thinking about it, was the best singer Eala had ever heard.

It didn't take long, as their hearthstone was soft, Caora now had steady hands, and the Words were clear in her mind. Soon she was ready, and she lit a small fire. The hearthstone in Eala's house was not under the smoke hole, because the roof was in two parts, so the smoke rose up to the roof, then flowed neatly across and out of the hole.

Eala watched it and then she blew gently to see how that disturbed the smoke. It didn't, of course. Then she put her hand in the smoke, and tried to waft it. Finally she blew on her hand and, as she was blowing, she put her hand into the smoke. Caora watched her experiments, seeing her intelligence and her curiosity.

Eala said, "It separates the air, doesn't it? Can anything get the smoke out?"

Caora reached her two hands into the smoke, cupped them, and pulled them out. When she opened her hands a curl of smoke was released.

"It doesn't have much force behind it. You couldn't suffocate yourself with it. If you put your face up to it and blew hard, that would blow the smoke out."

"It's wonderful," she said. "How does it work, my lady?"

Caora smiled, enjoying this strange young woman's company.

"The Words on the hearthstone are a command to the Great Principle of Air. The Ceatha House provides the power and the Words tell the Principle of Air how smoke should flow here."

"The Principle of Air, my lady?"

"There are five Principles that control what form matter should take: Earth, Water, Air, Fire, and, well, the other one doesn't normally occur in nature." She looked at Eala, who seemed to be following it, and not to be bored. "Think of water. What form does water take when it is cold?"

"It becomes ice, my lady."

"And when it is hot?"

"It becomes steam."

"Those are three forms that water takes. Ice is solid like Earth, water is liquid like ... Water, and steam is gaseous, like Air. If you got it still hotter, it would change form again, and glow, like Fire."

"And the form that doesn't occur in nature, my lady?"

"If you heat water it turns to steam, but if you squeeze steam it turns to water. If you do both enough, it becomes something else, a fifth form of matter. Humans only encounter this fifth form with the aid of Words of Power. You can't make a pot strong enough to contain that form of water."

Caora watched young Eala think about these things. "Smoke becomes fire sometimes, when it comes out of hot wood. Is that the same thing?"

"It is a similar thing."

"Is that the thing that keeps the clouds separate from the blue sky?"

"The clouds are separated by the normal rules of Air. These Words change the rules, just in a little column over the hearthstone."

"Why does this ... Great Principle of Air take any notice of your writing, my lady?"

Caora looked at Eala, surprised at the good sense of the question.

"The Words are written in ... I suppose you could call it their mother tongue. They ignore the normal speech of humans, but there is a language the Universe uses. That is the Words of Power."

"How did you learn all these things? How did you learn Words of Power, my lady?"

"The Mentor teaches these things at the City."

"Could I learn?"

"Anyone could learn how the world works, the philosophy of nature, although I don't think anyone is teaching it outside the City." Eala watched Caora consider that as she said it. "But," she added, "only the Sea People are allowed to learn Words of Power."

"Could I be one of them?"

"Why would you want that?" asked Caora, slightly scornfully. "Why throw away..?" She hesitated. "Why throw away your life to learn a few stupid tricks?"

Eala didn't know how to answer that, so she didn't.

"How do we repay you, my lady?"

"You don't have to."

"Mammy says that all debts must be repaid."

Eala could see that she hadn't thought of that.

Caora pondered for a few moments, and then said, "I will be staying at the Songbird for a while. If your mother wants to repay someone, get her to repay Ólachán for a little of the hospitality he is showing me. I'm going to be a while at the Songbird, until I find somewhere to live. But only give him a little, mind: there will be others helping."

"I will tell her, my lady."

Caora got up, and looked down at herself. She was sooty where she had leaned on the hearthstone, her hands were black, and Eala could see smudges where she had brushed her hair from her face. Then Caora sang an odd little snatch of song, strange Words that seemed to reverberate in Eala's head, like a language she had forgotten. Suddenly, Caora was clean. Her linen dress was white again, the marks on her face were gone, even her fingernails were clean. Only her blue cloak seemed unchanged, but it had not been affected by the dirt.

Eala watched as she carved a few more symbols into the doorway, and into the shutter, then Lady Caora got up to go.

"I have lots of other houses to visit, Eala. I want to visit the whole village. Thank you for your company, though. You are a clever, inquisitive girl and it has been fun to talk to you."

"Thank you, my lady," Eala replied, gravely.

Eala hoped she would be able to talk to Caora again soon. But they would not speak again for more than a year.

— 3 —

The Other Twin

It was the Month of Light. The travellers who came into Ólachán's inn
were cold after their long journeys and looking for hot food and the warmth
of a fire. Caora was in her favourite corner in the inn, playing idly. She
hadn't really got to play a whole song, but she was playing with the music,
rather than playing music. A mug was on the table, her harp was in her
hand, and she could smell food. She was about as happy as she could be.

The place was starting to fill up, people were starting to notice her, and
soon they'd be expecting her to play for them. Nobody would actually
insist, although they might ask very nicely. Her blue cloak did get her
some respect, of course. In this place, where travellers came by, strangers
who wouldn't know who she was, she was glad of the peace that her blue
cloak brought.

She looked up from the harp; Leathar had arrived. He came over to
her, uncovering his drum.

"Good evening, Lady Caora." His words were respectful but he talked
to her like a friend. "Can I get you another drink?"

"That would be kind. Thank you."

He put down his drum near her and went. Fuiseoga came in too and
came over.

"Lady Caora," she said. "Is Leathar getting you a drink?"

"He is getting one, thank you. Sit down."

She sat. Leathar and Fuiseoga had at first been suspicious of her blue
robe but their shared love of music had helped the three of them build a
friendship over the last year. Without saying anything more she took out
her pipe and blew the note she knew Caora needed. Caora heard the note,
and sang the Words, then picked out a chord on the harp. That was one
of the few uses she had for her Words these days: tuning her harp. She
laughed silently to herself, wondering what the point of it all had been.

Leathar came over with the drinks. He sat on the other side of Fuiseoga
and passed the mugs over. The place became quieter as people noticed

35

they were sitting together now. Leathar put down his mug, wiped his lip, and picked up his drum.

"The Hare in the Spring, my lady?" he suggested.

Caora looked at Fuiseoga. She seemed pleased with the suggestion and Caora smiled her agreement back at Leathar. He counted the time, and they began playing.

They were halfway through "The Grasshopper," when a young woman burst through the door and ran through the dancers to the musicians. Caora was absorbed completely in her playing – "The Grasshopper," was a very fast piece, and needed good fingering, especially with all the flourishes she liked to put in it, and Leathar had responded to her showing-off by doubling the beat. The dancers were flying around, the young woman stumbled on someone's foot, and crashed into the table, upending it and the drinks on the players. Caora was shocked. Quickly she pulled her harp out of the way. She jerked her Silver Cord and her sword was in her hand. Her training, so long ago, had her wheel off the stool and spin on her knees. She felt her armour appear over her body. One hand held the harp; the other held the sword, blade horizontal, point forward, edge up, guarding her head. She felt Metal scrape stone under her knees. "Find the target, you stupid girl," Iolar had shouted at her, in those first dreadful days when she had learned to hold a sword. "Quickly, before it kills you!" Her sword was ready, the hilt up by her ear, the blade protecting her head, the tip looking for the target.

The young woman looked up. She had never seen a sword: she had never even seen Metal. The closest equivalent in her world was gold, used for the finest jewellery and by the merchants for barter. But this was the thousand-times-more-rare Metal, used only by the Sea People, which she had only heard about but never seen. Her own knife was flint, knapped skilfully to keep the edge keen. Like all flint blades it was fragile and, since her family was poor, it was small, about the size of two of her fingers side by side.

But in Lady Caora's hand was a knife as long as her arm, a straight blade, edge uppermost, that tapered back to a point over the last hands-length. And, looking down from the blade, Caora's body was completely covered in the same green-tinted Metal. All the gold that the girl had ever seen would have fitted in the palm of her hand. To see enough Metal to cover someone was a sight out of an impossible dream. It was then, realising that Lady Caora had come out of the stories she heard about the legendary people of the City, seeing the great gap between Lady Caora and a village girl from Áthaiteorann, that she first believed this shining apparition could save her brother's life.

Caora realised she had overreacted. Ólachán's guests were staring at her in fear. Her sword-hilt and her helm both showed her Rank, for those that had the knowledge to read them, but the sword-blade and the cloak would have been enough. The only person who did not show fear was the golden-haired young woman, who struggled up from the upended furniture. Caora thought she recognised those green eyes.

"Lady Caora," the young woman squealed, breathlessly. "Spideog has a fever and he's having fits. Duille the Healer says he'll die before we can get to Port Teorainn and that it's too big a Healing for someone of your Rank, but please try anyway."

Her fear was for her brother's life: she was not afraid of Caora's blue cloak.

Caora handed the harp to Leathar, and lifted the visor of her helm.

"All right, Eala, I'll try and help your brother. You never know, I might know more of Healing than Duille thinks."

She put the sword in the scabbard, and then reached her hand to help the young woman stand. She tried to think: what healing Arts could she remember? It was a long time ago: these days she used the Immortal Breath and that was enough for her. The Immortal Breath could cure a hangover, and that was the worst she needed these days. She hadn't used Healing since she used to walk the Forest. When a village boy had broken his arm, the summer before, she had used the Creation Power, but it made her feel that the Mentor could see her. She would have to use Words, if she was to avoid that, and it was a long time since she had used Words for healing. On the other hand, her body remembered how to fend off an attack, even if it was a frightened child. Maybe she would remember Words.

The young woman led her out of the place, pulling on her hand.

"Please be quick, Lady Caora."

Caora carefully curved the fingertips: the climbing-blades weren't very long, but they were Metal like the rest of the gauntlets, and would easily have sliced the girl's hand open to the bone. What was she thinking of, taking up her sword in the inn? She remembered the Mentor's voice, telling her what she had been thinking – nothing at all. Her emotions ruled as they always did. How could she even be an Adept, let alone the second Oldest? She had reacted to the girl and to her fear. The girl was no threat, but her fear was a monster.

They reached the bridge. Caora took her hand from the young woman's, stripped off her gauntlets, and lifted the helm over her head. She threw them and the scabbard-belt over the bridge, as they ran across it, and they heard the splash. She would have to get them back, but they were on her Silver Cord. Spideog's family would be frightened enough without her marching in with her sword on her hip. They would be twice as frightened if they could read the Rank on her sword, as she suspected Duille might: and that would never do. It would be bad enough that she would be wearing armour, but there was no time to remove it, it seemed. She pulled her cloak to her. That would at least cover some of it.

"Won't you need those, Lady Caora?"

"I can get them when I need them, Eala. They'll be in the way. There are blades on the fingertips of the gloves."

The girl hesitated a moment when Caora spoke her name. But then she said, "Can you save him?"

"I think so. But we'll have to see."

They went into the little hut. In one glance Caora took in the scene in the firelight: the red-haired boy, shivering and flushed on the bed and his red-haired mother beside him, holding his hand, fear on her face. By the fire, an older woman, grey haired, boiled a pot whose steam was filled with herbal scents. On the other side of the boy, bathing him with cold wet cloth, was a girl identical to the one by Caora's side.

The grey-haired woman, Duille, looked around as Caora came in.

"It is a brain-fever, Lady Caora." She turned to the other twin, bathing the boy, trying to cool his fever. "That's enough, Eala," she said. Then she showed Caora the rash on the child's body. "It has gone into the blood," Duille said. "It is beyond my art, and we cannot get him to Port Teorainn in time."

Face to face, she would never directly question Caora's competence. But of course, she was right. If the fever had gone into the brain and blood, it was unlikely the child would ever get well, even if she could stop the fever. He might lose limbs; he might never think or move properly. There were Words that could do it, but they were beyond the ability of who she was pretending to be. Caora sat by the boy, and Duille spoke again.

"Perhaps you have a Flyer, my lady, and can get to Port Teorainn quickly?"

Caora was not going to go and argue with Miotal, and anyway, she had come on an old, borrowed horse, now on permanent loan to Ólachán: she had no Flyer. But she liked the twins, with their eyes like the Mentor's: so she was not going to let Eala's little brother die. She didn't have the Words that Miotal would have used, but she could remember more powerful Words: the Words of Restoration. It was all she could remember: probably because she had learned it most recently. She thought back, cleared her mind, and began to sing the Formula.

It was hard work, but exhilarating, as she felt the Breath-Power, shaped by her Words, surge from her fingertips and into the child. She rarely

voiced Words of this power, these days. As her strange song reached the
end, Spideog suddenly sat up.

"My headache's gone, Mammy," he said, "but I'm thirsty." Then he
looked around. "What are you doing here, Lady Caora?"

"Eala ... not Eala, Geana said you were ill, but you seem to be all right
now."

He looked over at Geana and Eala, holding hands, their green eyes
round. One of them nodded agreement: in the flickering light of the fire,
Caora couldn't tell them apart.

"Did you make me well?"

"I did."

"Thank you, my lady," he replied. He looked around. "Why is it dark?"
he asked. "Have I been asleep?"

"I think you have." She got up. She didn't want a big demonstration of
gratitude, so she began to make her excuses. "The child needs rest," she
said, "and I should leave you alone with him."

"Thank you, Lady Caora," said Flannbhuía, his mother. "We will not
forget this. I will talk to you about this tomorrow."

"I'm supposed to be the Steward, Flannbhuía. It's my duty, nothing
more." She laughed, trying to make it a light matter. "I can't spend all
my time in the inn, playing music, however agreeable it is."

"We will talk about this tomorrow," repeated Flannbhuía, seriously.

"But now the boy needs rest." Caora opened the door. "Duille, will
you walk with me?"

"Thank you," repeated Flannbhuía.

Duille gathered her things, and followed Caora into the night.

"What did you see?" asked Caora.

"I am not sure, my lady," she replied. There was a great deal more awe
in Duille's voice than Caora had heard before. "I did not recognise the
Formula of Words you used. I have seen Lord Miotal work before, and for
something like this he would use the Purification of the Blood, my lady."

Caora laughed again. It felt good, to use Words of Power to actually
help someone.

"I would have used the Purification of the Blood if I had remembered
it. It was a long time ago I last saw it used. I'm a singer, not a healer."

"Did you use a Restoration, my lady?"

"What do you know about the Restoration? Have you seen a Restoration used before?"

"I've heard about it, from my aunt in Port Teorainn."

"Miotal uses Restoration?"

"He doesn't, my lady. Lord Aclaí was visiting, and Miotal asked him
to use the Restoration on one of his servants who had fallen from the tree

when picking apples. His back was broken, and he couldn't use his legs. His sons had to carry him."

"Then it is too much for Miotal to use?"

"My lady, I imagine it is. She described how everyone in the room had felt the Breath-power as he had spoken the Words of Restoration."

Caora was not going to convince Duille that it wasn't Restoration, so she changed the subject.

"I hear that you have been telling the villagers how limited my abilities are, making it plain that you consider the healing powers of a young Adept to be far less than that of a village healer of your years."

Now Duille was frightened. "Are you going to kill me, my lady?"

"What?" For a moment Caora's face registered disgust. "Of course I'm not. I just want you to promise me something."

"That I won't say these things anymore? I won't, my lady: I can see that your powers are far more than I expected."

"That is the opposite of what I want you to do."

"I don't understand, my lady."

"I want you to carry on telling everyone in the village that you have better healing powers than a young Novice. You do, you know. You have studied one thing all your life. No Novice of the Sea People is going to know more."

"But you are not a Novice, are you, my lady?"

"That is not what I want you to tell them, either."

"I still don't understand, my lady."

"What Rank do you think I am?" Caora asked.

"You must be higher Rank than Lord Miotal, my lady, or you wouldn't be able –" She stopped. Caora saw her face change. "You are the Lady Éirime, lady. The Shepherdess, which is why you call yourself *Caora*. You are Nineteenth Rank."

"I am. But I don't want to be. I want to be Caora, to drink ale in the inn and play music, like I used to when I was Caora's age and younger, to have fun and, occasionally, to help out when a Steward should."

"You were Caora's age over a thousand years ago, my lady."

"I am younger than that, Duille. The Mentor is barely over a thousand years."

"You are still an Immortal, my lady." Duille frowned. "Why are you telling me this?"

"Because you are not stupid and you would realise it soon enough, after tonight. Because I'd rather you went on telling the village how you are a better healer than me, rather than telling them who I am." She stopped at the bridge, looking down at the starlight on the river. "I couldn't bear

the way everyone would treat me if they knew who I was. I left the City
to get away from being Éirime."

"As you wish, my lady."

"When you call me *my lady*, there used to be a superior tone."

"I am so sorry, my lady," she answered.

"Try again."

Then Duille realised what she was asking.

"I am sorry, *my lady*," she said.

"Thank you, Duille." She turned from the water and looked at her in
the darkness. "You know, your healing arts might be improved by the
sorts of tools and drugs a blue-robe could obtain for you. If you were to
visit quietly, when nobody was watching, I might be able to help you with
things."

"Herbs, my lady? Do you keep *pennyroyal*?"

"I don't keep anything," Caora replied. She couldn't even remember
what *pennyroyal* did. "But if you have a little, I can make it into a lot."

"Thank you," she said.

"Bring it around tomorrow. And remember, Duille. Remember to forget."

"I will. *My lady*."

They parted at the bridge and Caora went back to the inn. She sneaked
in the back, stripped off her armour, smoothed down her linen dress, then
used the Silver Cord to get back her equipment from the river. She shook
the water off them, then stowed them in her wooden chest. Softly she sang
her Words of Freshness, to take the stink of fear off her body, and she went
down into the commons, to have another attempt at "The Grasshopper".

Eala was out walking with her sister, Geana. It was a fine day, even though
it was winter: the light had returned but the warmth hadn't which, their
mother said, is how the Month of Light got its name. They were both
wrapped in sheepskin against the cold, but the brightness of the sky was
reflected on the river. As they walked, it was easy to believe that the winter
was over.

At home, their mother was concentrating on looking after Spideog, who
had been healed by Lady Caora the previous night. Geana and Eala suspected that Spideog was perfectly fit, but was enjoying the attention.
Geana was a little annoyed that, when she had been ill, there had not
been as much fuss. She had got well on her own but Duille had said that
Spideog would die before morning. With the relief, nobody really minded
that he was the centre of his mother's attention.

Geana had been sent to get Lady Caora, and that was what she was describing as they walked along the riverbank towards the hillside pastures.

"When I got into the inn, I fell over and tipped the table over them. I banged my head." She lifted her golden fringe to show the bruise high on her forehead. "And I fell under the table when it tipped. When I got up, Lady Caora was wearing all her armour and waving her sword around."

"What happened?" Eala asked.

"I think I made her jump. She was concentrating on the playing and she didn't expect someone to spill ale on her."

"You split ale on her?" Eala squeaked. "You spilt ale on the Steward?"

"A whole mug of it."

"Don't you remember how frightened Mammy was when she found out that Lady Caora had visited me? How long she spent telling us how dangerous she was, how we should be polite, and how it was safer not to talk to her?"

"Oh Eala," Geana replied scornfully, "if I didn't talk to the people Mammy thinks I shouldn't talk to, I'd never have any fun. She worries far too much."

"Geana," she said. She stopped walking, took her sister's hands, and faced her. "Sister, at the First Day of Spring in Port Teorainn, last year, one of the servants spilt a few drops of wine on Lord Miotal's grandniece, the Lady Eibheara. She used Words of Power to light a fire in the servant's entrails and he burned to death right there by the table."

"That's Lord Miotal and his family. Everyone knows what they are like."

"At the Night of Light in the City three years ago, Beatha's cousin from Ceatha, I think his name was Colm, was kissed by a girl from the City. She had a boyfriend, also a blue-robe, and there was a fight. It was in the street somewhere, not within the walls. I think the blue-robe was Sixth Rank. Certainly he was a Novice, no more. He cut Colm with the sword. Colm bled to death there in the square, over a kiss he didn't even ask for."

"That was three years ago. It must happen rarely if you have to think of someone's cousin in the City, and three years ago."

"It's not rare, Geana. It happens all the time. The only reason we never hear of it is because, until Lady Caora came here, we never saw a blue-robe. Blue-robes don't come to Áthaiteorann. All we get is traders, going from the sea to the mountains and back. She might seem a bit dizzy and harmless, but Lady Caora is a blue-robe and that makes her dangerous."

"She could be dangerous, I suppose, if she'd wanted to. She had her sword and armour on, quicker than blinking. If I'd been a wild animal instead of a clumsy girl, she would have been able to kill me, just like you said. But I wasn't. She wasn't angry with me at all. I just surprised her, because she was engrossed in her playing."

"I mean it. We are supposed to show respect to the blue-robes because they are dangerous people."

Geana looked back and Eala could see that she wasn't listening.

"Eala, sometimes it's like I've got two mothers, not one. You're supposed to be my sister, not my mother. Nothing happened. Anyway, why would Lady Caora save Spideog and then kill me?" Geana took Eala's hand and started walking again. "You worry too much. Lady Caora is not like that. She's just like us, but with a blue robe on." Geana smiled and added "And she doesn't have a mother who won't let her go to the inn."

"That's not just Mammy: Beatha doesn't like young people in her inn. We can still go to The Sun."

"The Sun is full of old men talking about the weather and how it will affect the harvest. It's boring."

"Ordóg is there."

"I'm bored of Ordóg. He's so stupid. It's all very well for a boy to want to kiss, he kisses very well, but he's just so dim. I have to explain half of what I say to him, and he just stares at me and tells me how pretty I am. It's like having a pet, not a boyfriend."

"Geana, you should be nice."

"Why? Do you want him?"

"Don't be silly, Geana!" Eala answered.

"You didn't mind on the Night of Light, when we swapped names," Geana suggested, mischievously.

Eala blushed. It had only been a few days ago, just before Geana had come down with the sickness she had given to her brother: she had been very sick, although her life had not been in danger.

"He does know how to kiss," Eala admitted.

"Don't you want to do more than kiss?" teased Geana.

"I don't know, sister," she replied. Then she added, "but you shouldn't say bad things about him."

"Oh, I haven't said anything to him. I'm just so bored of Áthaiteorann. I want someone I can really talk to."

"You've got me, you've got Mammy. Can't you talk to us?"

"I couldn't talk to Mammy about Ordóg, could I?"

"Maybe you should. It might be better than having to tell her you're pregnant. You know she only nags us because she's worried about us."

Geana ignored the slight.

"Even so, she hasn't been anywhere. Neither have you. The only person from Áthaiteorann who has seen places is Lady Caora. So either I could talk to her or I could talk to the visitors who come through the Shepherdess. But Mammy won't let us visit the Shepherdess and Lady Caora lives in there. She plays her music there, she makes friends there, and she never comes out unless something needs doing, or someone is sick. It's not fair." Geana waved her hands, frustrated. "When I went in yesterday, everyone was dancing. Lady Caora was playing the harp and she's better than anyone."

"I know. Remember what she was like playing the dances last Midwinter Night?"

As she spoke, Eala remembered: Geana had danced with Ordóg until midnight, when Mammy had insisted she went to bed. But Eala had sat and watched and listened to the musicians. She had almost not minded that she had nobody to dance with. One of their friends, Saonta, had stolen a wineskin; Saonta, Eala and their friend Eilite had hidden from their mothers and stayed up all night, like adults, listening to Caora and remembering. They had talked about boys, and how bad they were, but Eala had remembered her father.

Eala continued, "Or what about the time we sat at the riverside by the bridge, and listened to her play, last summer? She is so talented. That's probably why she stays at the Shepherdess."

"You mean because she's called *Caora?* Or because of some old legend?"

Eala realised she had said too much. It was always like that when she tried to keep things from her sister.

"It's more than a legend. I heard Ólachán and Beatha talking about it in the Sun, when they came down to trade wine for mead. The Shepherdess – the Lady, I mean, not the inn – is real, and if you went to the City, you could meet her. She's a real person. She's supposed to be Twenty-Sixth Rank and over a thousand years old. Ólachán says she taught Lady Caora to play the harp. That is how she knows our songs."

Geana was thinking, hard. Then she said, "She couldn't be more than a thousand years old. That's impossible."

"Why not?"

"Well, work it out. What is today?"

"The Fifteenth Day of Light."

"But what's the year?"

"It's Eleven Twenty-One, of course."

"In full?"

"It's the one thousand one hundred and twenty-first year of the Sea People." Now Eala was thinking. The twins had loved to play with numbers when they were younger, but their mother had taught them no more than basic arithmetic. "But that would still give her over a hundred years to be

Selected."

"Nobody who was Selected that long ago is still alive. Anyway, when did the worlds meet?"

Eala knew the story of the worlds meeting. It was the starting point for their history: the day the Sea People had come to their world and brought them civilisation.

"It's Two-Fifty-Five," she said.

"It isn't. It's Two-Fifty-Four. Two of two of two of two of two of two of two of two, less two. That's how I remember it. Two-Fifty-Five was the first Selection that anyone from Anleacán could have seen. So how old would that make the Shepherdess?"

"Two-Fifty-Six is what?" Eala thought a bit more. "Oh, so it is. That makes remembering the date easy: 'Two of two of two of two of two of two of two of two, less two'. But that would still make her..."

"Eight hundred and seventy, plus however old she was when she was Selected. So more than eight hundred and eighty, but maybe less than eight hundred and ninety. Less than nine hundred, anyway. She certainly can't be a thousand."

"Well, I'm sure we can have an argument about it on our nine hundredth birthday," replied Eala, with a trace of sarcasm.

"The way we could do that would be to put on blue robes of our own," replied Geana, encouragingly.

"Geana, you've lost your senses," Eala protested. "There is no way we could be Selected."

"Why not? Everyone says we're pretty. Nobody in the village can do numbers like we can; nobody can understand what we talk about except Mammy. If we're clever and pretty, maybe the Mentor would Select us." She poked Eala, teasing her. "Anyway, if that's what it takes to find you a boy..."

"Geana!" Eala protested. Then she argued, "Clever and pretty for Áthaiteorann, maybe, but in the City there will be many people who are better. You've seen how beautiful the Sea People are, when Lady Caora has made the Visions for us." She remembered the reluctance on Lady Caora's face and how she had not watched the images that came from the City. "Anyway, look at Lady Caora. Haven't you seen what is in her face when she's engrossed in her playing? Or haven't you understood why she was ready with her sword when you spilt ale on her?" Eala looked at Geana and she worried, not that this scheme might be impossible but, that it might be possible. "Lady Caora is not like us. She's hurt and she's scared. All the time, she's grieving inside, or waiting for something terrible to happen."

Geana could see it was true. Reading people's faces to see what was in
their hearts was the twins' secret hobby and Lady Caora's heart was one
they had spent a long time watching, if only from a distance.

"But what's to be scared of? What if it's just that she's a nervous
person?"

"A nervous person couldn't perform the way she does."

"You don't know that, Eala. The voice she uses when she is singing fills
the place but, when she is talking, she is as quiet as a mouse. She hardly
raises her speaking voice above a whisper. It is like she has two voices – it
is like she is two people."

"Geana, listen to me. Being a blue-robe isn't all about Words of Power,
or living at the City and having people call you *my lady*. Three quarters
of young people who put on a blue robe don't live the first year. So the
chance that you'd live through it is one in four. The chance that we'd
both live through it is one in sixteen. Even if we were Selected, which we
wouldn't be, fifteen chances in sixteen we'd one or other be dead before
the year was over."

"But we could take care of each other," Geana replied. "That would
improve the odds. Anyway, she's grieving inside, like Mammy was after
Daddy died. We don't have anyone to grieve over except each other and
we'd take care of each other, same as we always do."

"Her grief isn't like Mammy's, Geana. Her grief is like Fleánna's."

Geana didn't immediately reply to that. When the twins were little
girls, before they were allowed out of the village on their own, Fleánna
had been caught walking along the river, much as they were doing, but
later at night. Travellers in a boat had seen her and attacked her. She
had come into the village, screaming and crying. It had been years ago,
before Lady Caora came to the village. Nobody would tell Geana and
Eala what exactly had happened to Fleánna but, although her body had
healed, her mind had not. She would not go out after dark; she would not
find a husband; she would not even be alone with a man, although she
was in danger of becoming an old maid. Fleánna was a cautionary tale
to the girls and young women of Áthaiteorann, another reason they were
not allowed in the Shepherdess. The Shepherdess was full of travellers,
strangers from out of Áthaiteorann, and strangers were not to be trusted.
As Geana thought about it, she realised that Eala was right. Whatever had
happened to Fleánna, something like that had happened to Lady Caora.

"Maybe it happened before she was Selected," Geana suggested. "Maybe
she put on a blue robe to help her not be scared. Imagine what would happen if those travellers attacked her."

It seemed unlikely to Eala that someone who had been attacked like

Fleánna had would want to go to the City and seek a blue robe. Fleánna hardly left her cottage, especially after dark. But anything was possible.

"Maybe she did," she conceded. "But if she did, it didn't help her, did it?"

"It did. No traveller can hurt her."

"But she is still scared, Geana."

"Lady Caora is less than ten years older than us. Maybe she needs more time to get used to being a blue-robe."

Without thinking, Eala answered, "She is much older than that, I'm sure."

And straight away, she regretted it.

"Why do you think that?" Geana asked.

"While you were gone, Duille was talking to Mammy. You know what she is like: Duille may be a good healer, but she heals with her hands, not her words. If she thinks someone is going to die, she just comes right out and says it. She told Mammy that there was no point in getting Lady Caora, unless Lady Caora had a very fast Flyer and used it straight away. She said that she knew what a low-Rank blue-robe could do and all she could do was waste time."

"Well, she was wrong, wasn't she?"

"Think, Geana: why was she wrong? Do you remember what her face looked like after Spideog sat up? She couldn't believe it. But she was scared of Lady Caora then."

"What does that mean?" asked Geana. But then she saw it.

"It means," said Eala, a little slowly, "Lady Caora is a higher Rank than Duille thought she was. Maybe as high as Lord Miotal."

"Of course she isn't as high a Rank as Lord Miotal."

"There's no *of course*, Geana. All we know is that she was able to do something that Duille thought beyond her; something she thought Lord Miotal would have to do. That means she is higher Rank than Duille thought, so her Rank is somewhere between the two."

"That doesn't mean it has to be between the two: her Rank could be higher than Lord Miotal's. But it won't be."

"It can't be much lower. She must have the Sixteenth Rank, at least."

"Why?"

"Because she looks so young. She has to be an Immortal."

Geana thought that through. "So she's a newly-Retired Immortal: less than eighty years old, probably, but still enough to make Duille frightened. But why choose a boring place like Áthaiteorann?"

"Beatha said that her family was here. She's Ólachán's cousin, or something."

"Do you think that, if we ask her, she'll take us to the Selection?"

"Not that again, Geana. If she's a newly-Retired Sixteenth Rank, she probably wants to stay away from the City."

"Maybe she could introduce us to the Shepherdess."

"Please just leave that. Think of Fleánna. Do you want to end up like that? We still don't know what made Lady Caora grieve. Until we find out what caused that, I don't want to go to any Selection. I don't want to be laughed at for being ugly and stupid, either." Talking about Fleánna had made them both uneasy. "Let's go back home. And please, Geana, stop talking about Selection."

"Can we at least find out about it?"

Eala knew that there would be no peace until they did.

"We can find out about it. But let's talk about something else."

When they got home, Spideog was outside with his friends. He had got bored of being the invalid and was playing a noisy game with sticks for swords, pretending they were blue-robe warriors. It seemed Caora's over-reaction at the inn last night had been talked about and the children were inspired. Flannbhuía was standing in the doorway, watching him, overjoyed that he was alive, but remembering how quickly he had fallen sick.

"Hello, Mammy," said Geana. "Can we talk?"

"Of course we can," Flannbhuía replied.

Eala could see nervousness start to appear in her face, but also relief. She was worried, probably about Ordóg. Eala wasn't the only one who had been waiting for Geana to announce she was pregnant, she guessed. Flannbhuía stepped back out of the doorway, making space for her daughters to enter. They went in.

They sat down around the fire. Eala saw the smoke rising, then sliding along under the roof. For a moment she remembered Lady Caora sitting by the hearth, the day after she had arrived. Geana started the conversation, of course.

"Mammy, do you think we could ask Lady Caora to take us to Selection?"

Eala watched her mother's face. Her first emotion was disbelief, but a moment later, she could see there were other expressions there. She could see disapproval, but she could also see pride, and something more calculating.

"Perhaps when ye're older," she said.

"How old do you think Lady Caora is? If she is an Adept now, how old was she when she was Selected?"

Eala realised that Geana knew she must be an Immortal and was pretending to her mother that she wasn't, to make it seem that Caora had been little more than a girl when Selected. It was like Geana to do that and like their mother to see through it.

"I doubt she is as young as she looks, Geancacha," replied Flannbhuía. "Ye saw how Duille was surprised at her abilities."

Eala was irritated by her sister's attempt to deceive her mother.

"Mammy," Eala said, "we know she is older. She must be an Immortal: she looks too young for the Rank she must have, so she must be Immortal. She's probably the same age as Grandfather."

Flannbhuía sighed and thought a moment. "Look, girls, I'm going to tell ye a secret and ye must not ever tell anyone else. I know ye're not gossips, except to each other, but I still need ye to promise ye will keep this secret."

"I will, Mammy," said Geana, straight away.

Eala didn't like being told to keep secrets, when she didn't know what secret she was keeping. But she trusted her mother.

"I will," she said.

Flannbhuía began, "Do ye know who the Shepherdess is?"

"Who, Mammy, not what?" asked Geana. "You mean the woman from Áthaiteorann who became a blue-robe, nine hundred years ago?"

"That woman, Geancacha. The Lady Éirime. She is a real person, a blue-robe of Nineteenth Rank. She's the second-oldest Adept: she's barely younger than Lord Aclaí. She is nearly as old as the Mentor, and has been one of his Favourites for years."

Eala added, "We think Lady Caora is Lady Éirime's Favourite. We think she taught Lady Caora the harp and our village dances. At Sneachta's wedding, she played almost all of them. The only one she didn't play was the Song of the Bride."

"You don't know she wasn't taught it, Eala," objected Geana. "She just slipped away and left Fuiseoga to play for that. Some people were joking she had too much ale. I heard them whispering."

Eala remembered it. Caora had not slipped away; she had fled. She knew the song, but she couldn't bear to play it, or even to hear it. Eala had wanted to go after her, to comfort her, even if it meant missing the Song of the Bride, but she hadn't dared be so familiar with a blue-robe, not after her mother's warnings.

"That's a good guess, Eala," said Flannbhuía, ignoring Geana's interruption. "But it's not right. You know that Lady Éirime went to the City nearly nine hundred years ago, and you've been told that she never returned. But that last bit is not true, not anymore. Lady Caora is not Lady Éirime's Favourite. Lady Caora is Lady Éirime herself."

Eala reflected that it wasn't often that Geana really didn't know what to say. So she got to speak instead.

"How do you know, Mammy?"

"Beatha told me, months ago. Seeing Duille's face yesterday just confirmed what I already knew. I guess nobody told Duille. Duille wasn't born in the village, and you wouldn't want to tell a secret like that to an outsider. Ólachán recognised her when she first arrived. She thought we'd forgotten her: as if Áthaiteorann would forget the Shepherdess!"

"But Ólachán says he is related to Lady Caora, that they are kin," objected Geana.

"They are," Flannbhuía agreed. "They are descended from her older brother. Ólachán is her great, great – I don't know how many greats you get in nine centuries – great grandnephew. He's always known it and that is why his inn is called the Shepherdess." She seemed to be musing. "Funny that she should walk in there, of all places, when she first arrived."

It didn't seem strange to Eala. "Ólachán's family have always lived north of the river. She was trying to go home. It was probably the closest building to her home."

"Eala, I guess you are right. That seems even stranger, like someone from an old story had come to life and –" Flannbhuía stopped. Someone was at the threshold. She got up to go to find out who it was.

"Remember Fleánna," whispered Eala to Geana. "Do you still think she's getting used to..?" But her mother was showing the guest in.

It was Lady Caora. Lady Éirime, just a few years younger than Lord Aclaí. The Mentor might as well have walked in. They stood up.

"You said you wanted to talk to me today, Flannbhuía. If you are not too busy."

"We are not too busy, my lady. Will you have ale with us?"

"That would be kind."

Caora sat down near the fire and pulled back the hood of her cloak. Sitting like that, she really looked, to someone who didn't know better, as if she was only a couple of years older than Geana and Eala.

While Flannbhuía busied herself finding mugs and drawing ale, Geana spoke.

"I promise I will not tip it on you, Lady Caora. I am sorry I did so yesterday."

Over Caora's shoulder, Eala could see her mother's horrified face, her head turned, and the mug dangling perilously in her fingers, forgotten. She had heard about Eibheara and the servant, it seemed. Knowing Caora's age and Rank just made it worse. But Lady Caora reached over and touched Geana's arm, a gesture of reassurance.

"That's fine, Geana," she smiled. "Neither of us was paying attention and you had more excuse than me. I am sorry if I frightened you with the sword."

"You didn't frighten me, my lady. I was under the table: I didn't see you draw it."

"That is good. I frightened a lot of Ólachán's guests: the inn is almost empty now." She laughed "I frightened myself most, I think. I really wasn't paying attention at all."

"It seems so strange, that anything should frighten an Adept of the City, my lady."

"When I was your age, shortly after I was Selected, I had to go into the Forest, to keep monsters away from people. That is what the Sea People are mostly for: keeping monsters away from people. I went with Adepts from the years above which helped keep me safe. It also meant that we went deeper into the Forest than a newly-Selected Novice normally would. I'm not a very good Adept – I don't have much courage – but the standard was very low in my Selection, and so the Mentor was left with me. Sometimes when something makes me jump, I think back to the Forest." She looked up: Flannbhuía was offering her a mug of ale. "Thank you," she said. "When I was first at the City, being frightened was the thing I felt more than anything else. Frightened, and lonely. Sometimes that comes back. As I said, I'm not a very good Adept."

Now it was Eala and Flannbhuía's turn not to know what to say: if the Lady Éirime was not a very good Adept, who was? But Geana felt no such concern.

"If you are not a good Adept, my lady, what would that say about the rest of us? You were Selected: only the cleverest and prettiest are Selected. How stupid and ugly must we seem to you?"

"You are certainly clever and pretty enough to seek Selection, if that was really what you wanted. I think you are courageous enough, from what I saw yesterday. You two may be more clever and pretty than I am but, much more, you have courage. Courage is what I never had, Geana. That is why I am no good as an Adept." She looked at Geana, and saw her enthusiasm. "But why would you want to? What boy or girl would really want to give up their life for that?"

"You did, my lady."

"When I left home and went to the City, I had no idea what was going to happen to me. I hadn't been told I was going for Selection – I didn't even know what Selection was. They told my parents they would return me that evening. I spent every day afterwards wishing I hadn't gone. The first day I could, I came home."

"When was that, my lady?"

"Geana, you know when I came home. It was the last summer."

"Oh," said Geana.

Eala could see Geana thinking about the City being a prison; about being trapped there for nine hundred years, while everyone you knew aged and died. Maybe she was remembering what Eala had said about Caora and Fleánna.

"We are in your debt," Flannbhuía said to Caora. "As you know, my lady, I am a widow. But widows have pride: it is often the greater part of what we have. How can I pay my debt to you?"

"Another mug of your ale, perhaps?" suggested Caora.

"You are mocking us, my lady," Flannbhuía replied.

But she reached for the mug. Caora did not let go. She put her hand on Flannbhuía's hand.

"I am sorry, Flannbhuía, I don't mean to mock you. I find this very hard. Everyone says 'how can we repay you?', and they mean it, I know they do. But I don't want to be repaid, I just want to be like everyone else. When I left Áthaiteorann, I was a girl, younger than these two, and that is what I remember. I don't feel like some Lady of the Sea People that everyone should fear. I want people to like me. I don't want them to be in my debt."

Astonishingly, Eala could see her mother's face set. She had just told Eala that this woman was barely below Lord Aclaí in Rank. Everyone knew that when an Immortal visited villages and was slighted, all that was left was smoking ruins. And here was the second Oldest of the Immortals sitting before their hearth. How could she dare to be stubborn to her face? But Eala could see it coming. She thought please, Mammy, let it go, let it go and then, before her mother could speak, she found herself speaking.

"Lady Caora, everyone in the village pays their debts to each other. Even girls as young as us. Would you permit me to repay? Spideog is my brother. I have much more time, though, because I don't have a family to take care of. Mammy works hard taking care of us. I will work hard, too, at whatever you want me to do."

All three were looking at her. It was Geana who responded first, though.

"It is true, Lady Caora, we will both pay the family's debt, if you will permit us."

Caora looked up. "Will that satisfy your pride, Widow Flannbhuía?"

"It will, my lady."

Eala could see relief on her mother's face. She realised that she didn't know her mother as well as she thought she did. Flannbhuía looked down at the table, at Caora's hand on her own.

"Would you like that ale, my lady?"

"Thank you."

Caora took her hand away and everything was normal again, or as normal as it could be with a blue-robe sitting by the hearth.

Flannbhuía brought the mug back.

"Do you know what you will do with them, my lady?"

"I don't know now, but I will think of something. I rather think the exertion will be between the ears, if you don't mind. I think I would like to see if we can get some knowledge into those pretty heads."

Eala realised and, at the same moment, saw Geana realise: she meant for them to be apprentices. That meant they might learn about the Sea People without going to the City. Eala thought that was wonderful. But it was her mother who answered.

"It is not up to me to mind, my lady."

"I promise I will take care of them." She put down the mug and got up. "This really is good ale, Widow Flannbhuía. I have never tasted better and I have tasted a lot of ale. Thank you for your hospitality." She turned to Eala and Geana. "You two I will see tomorrow morning, but not too early."

With that she stepped to the doorway, lifted the hood of her cloak, and was gone. Flannbhuía sat down heavily on the bed. Geana went over, sat by her, and put an arm on her mother's shoulders. Flannbhuía looked at Eala.

"She is nearly a thousand years old and she doesn't know what ye both know: that debts should be paid."

"We don't know how old she was when she was Selected, Mammy. She said she was younger than us. She might have been too young to really know that."

"Why do you always have to go trying to be understanding? Your heart is too soft and one day it will get you into trouble."

"But it could be true, Mammy."

"It could well be true. But it is certainly true that your soft heart will get you into trouble."

— 4 —

Apprentice

Geana was the first of them to go into the Shepherdess. She had been in before, at least. Both girls knew that they were not supposed to be there, normally, but both knew that this time they were instructed to by the Steward. That was the perfect, unassailable excuse.

They had packed a bag each. Flannbhuía had concluded, as they had, that they were meant to be apprentices. That meant that they would be expected to live with their teacher, learning from her. They did not know it was true, and if it was not they would go home again in the evening, but both of the twins hoped it would be. The only real education in their world came from the City, and they both craved education.

The commons were much quieter than they had been the night before last, when Geana had burst in. Trestle tables were out, and a few travellers sat around, eating breakfast and talking amongst themselves. There was a fire on the hearthstone, and Beatha was there, in a woollen dress and leather apron, distributing hot smoked pork to her guests. She looked over at them as they came in.

"What do ye girls want?" she challenged, suspiciously.

"Lady Caora asked us to meet her here," Geana replied. It was true and it was beyond argument. Geana's tone was a tiny bit triumphant.

"Well, sit over there then and be quiet. She's not awake yet."

They obediently went over to the table she had indicated. Eala was nervous and she could see that Geana was nervous too, although they reacted to it in different ways. Eala had never been in the Shepherdess. For her it was a forbidden place and looking around the room, at the stones of the floor, the plaster walls, the smoke-blackened beams, at the rough tables, she felt a tiny bit disappointed that it should be so ordinary. The smell of the place was the same as the Sun: stale drink, cooking food, and smoke. Geana could see what she was thinking, as she looked around.

"This place is much livelier in the evening," Geana said, as if being there for less than a hundred breaths had made her an authority. But Eala did not want to argue. "Come on, Eala," said Geana. "Look where we've got to. Apprentices to the second-Oldest of the Sea People. We'll get our blue robes yet."

"We don't know that we will be apprentices," said Eala. "I never heard of a blue-robe taking an apprentice." She could see that Geana knew she was right. "Besides," she added, "I still remember Fleánna."

"You worry too much," replied Geana. "I think that the problem is how old she is."

"How can it be a problem with age? Do people get more scared as they get older?"

"Well, it's not her age, it's that she was born a long time ago. If she was Selected only two or three centuries after the Sea People first started, then she will have gone to the City when it was still filled with savagery. She won't have seen civilisation, like there is today."

"You have no way to know that," replied Eala.

"Shall we ask..?" Geana suggested, and then noticed Eala was staring over her shoulder.

She turned around. Lady Caora had arrived.

Caora stood at the door to the commons. She looked half asleep and was wrapped in her cloak as if it were a blanket. Beatha got up as soon as she saw her, went to the taps and drew a mug of something. Caora came over to them. "Good morning, my lady," Geana said to her.

She sat down next to Eala and leaned forward, putting her face in her hands, massaging around her temples and eye-sockets. Eala thought she could smell drink. Beatha came over, the mug in her hand. Caora looked up as she took it. "Thank you, Beatha," she said.

"It is nothing, my lady. Are these girls bothering you?" she asked.

"I asked for them to come here," she replied, verifying Geana's story. "I also asked them not to come too early."

Eala could see from her expression that Beatha didn't think it was early: people who had animals would certainly have been up some time and Beatha had to have breakfast ready for her guests. But Beatha didn't contradict Lady Caora, whatever she thought.

"Do you want breakfast, my lady?" she asked.

"Maybe in a while," Caora replied. She drank a good part of the contents of the mug and then put it down. Beatha hurried away. Then Caora turned to Eala and seemed about to say something. Then she seemed to think better of it.

Instead she asked, "Do you sing? And which one are you? Are you Eala?"

"I am Eala, my lady," she replied. "Everybody sings, though nobody sings as well as you sing."

Eala was suddenly afraid that Caora might want them as apprentice musicians, and she knew that she didn't have the talent to do that.

"Don't worry, Eala," she said. "I'm not expecting ye to become entertainers. But I have a song I'd like ye to learn."

"All right," said Geana.

Caora's harp was in her hands. She hadn't reached for it, and it had been nowhere in sight, but suddenly it was there, on the table. Geana's eyes were wide: it was real magic. Eala saw that Caora didn't look at them, to see how it affected them. To her, being able to have things in her hand when she needed them was just a normal thing. She sang Words, language that Eala didn't recognise but which she felt she should know: a phrase that echoed in their heads, like a forgotten language from forgotten dreams: and Eala remembered how Caora had made herself clean, last summer in their mother's cottage.

Then Caora began to play.

The song was simple like a children's rhyme. It sang of a river, an ocean and a bird; a seed in the sunshine; and many other things. It was simply a recitation of odd objects, joined together by rhyme and melody. However, they listened as she sang it and enjoyed her voice. When she stopped playing, Eala noticed that the commons were silent. The travellers had all stopped talking to listen to her.

She looked over the table at Geana.

"Do you understand my song?" she asked.

Geana looked puzzled, thinking it must be some kind of riddle. Eala could see her worrying it in her mind and, guessing that if Geana gave up it would be her turn, she worried over it too.

Looking for more time, Geana asked, "Can we hear it again, my lady?"

Caora played and sang again. Geana still did not understand and neither did Eala, but part-way through the song, she noticed that one of the travellers thought he did. The traveller seemed to find it amusing. He had a broad smile, like someone who knew a secret.

When she was done, Caora asked Geana, "Well, can you tell me?"

"I can't, my lady," admitted Geana.

Eala was looking at the grinning traveller. She could see him looking and wondered what it was about him that made him able to understand it. He was an old man, well wrapped in furs and leather against the cold of the Month of Light. He had a heavy leather pack, with rolls of something in it. His gloves had no fingertips and his bare fingers were stained. He was a ...

"Is it to do with writing, my lady?" asked Eala.

"It is. How do you know?"

"Over there is a traveller who understands it, my lady. I think he is a scribe."

Caora looked over at the direction she was looking. The traveller looked away.

"Are you a scribe?" she called over to him.

He looked up, worried that she might be addressing him.

"I am, my lady."

"Can you explain my song to these two girls?" she asked.

"I can, my lady. The things in the song are the pictures that scribes use for writing. The river begins with Aw, at least in the accent of the City; the ocean with Ah; the bird with Ay; the seed with Sh; the sunlight with S; and so on. If you learn the song, you know how to write." He watched her, to make sure she approved of what he was saying. "I never heard it before," he added. "If my teachers had known it, I think it would have saved me from some beatings, my lady."

Caora laughed. "When I learned to write, I was rather older than that."

"My lady, don't all Novices learn to read and write?"

"They do now..." she answered and stopped.

Hearing it, the girls remembered that she was pretending to be far younger than she actually was. But was she really older than writing?

The scribe continued, "Do they teach it at the City of the Sea People, my lady?"

"I made it up myself," she replied. "It was the only way I could think of to remember."

"Would you teach it to me?" he asked. "I have apprentices at home. That is, if it is not something that belongs to the Sea People, of course."

"It does not belong to the Sea People, scribe. I don't believe anyone else knows it but me. Come over here and I will teach you as I teach the girls. You shouldn't take long, as you already know the words."

He came over and pulled up a stool. Eala could see how nervous he was about being so close to a blue-robe, but the song fascinated him. He learned it in two repetitions and then could sing it back. Then he had to go: his boat was packing up, ready to take him upriver to the mountain villages. But he got out a sheet of leather, in payment, and carefully copied out the pictures named in the song. He gave this leather and some spare sheets, along with some ink, to Caora.

It took Eala and Geana more attempts to learn the song. But they had their materials and their lessons began.

Geana had promised Eala that she would not keep asking Caora about Selection. She kept her promise for more than a ten-day, which was longer than Eala had expected.

During that ten-day they had settled into their new life. Since they were apprentices, albeit apprentices in a very strange profession, they moved into Caora's home. All that meant is that Ólachán found another pallet for them to sleep on and put it in the room by the hearthstone. They found it odd to be away from their mother and brother, but they had each other and they knew that they were not eating at their mother's table, which helped her to make ends meet.

Caora was a strange person to live with. The twins knew that she sang to entertain people, but what they quickly learned was that she sang all the time. Even when she was busy with something else, she would be humming, whistling, or tapping a beat. They had realised that some people must find it intensely annoying, although of course nobody would dare complain about her behaviour, because of her blue cloak. Watching the people around Caora, they easily identified the few who were irritated by it. They tended to avoid her.

As soon as they had moved into her room, they realised another thing about her: she hardly ever seemed to sleep. She would fiddle with her harp, sudden bursts of beautiful melody in between her doodling, and they would doze off to the music. When they woke up, she would be still doodling, or doing some sort of odd breathing exercise, or she'd be out walking. They realised eventually that she did sleep, but only for a couple of hours a night. Being young, they needed to sleep for nine or ten hours a night and rarely noticed that Caora had slept. The only time they saw her fall asleep was when she had been drinking especially heavily.

Then the girls would put her to bed and speak in whispers, as their mistress snored behind her curtain, until they fell asleep too.

Eala was woken up by Geana turning over. Sunlight was shining through the shutters and Caora was sitting on her bed, fiddling with her harp. Geana sat up, her golden hair a wild mess. Eala looked over and fumbled around to find the comb: her own hair would be the same. Outside, the birds were singing and she could hear them running on the roof, fighting.

"Girls, do ye know the date today?" asked Caora.

Geana answered, as she normally did.

"It's the First Day of Planting, my lady."

"What happens on the First Day of Planting?" asked Caora.

"It's not a Celebration Day: the Celebration Day in Planting is the Third ten-day, so in twenty days time. The time between now and the Day of Planting is spent planting, my lady." Eala listened to Geana's jumbled explanation, thinking how obvious it was and trying not to laugh. Geana was not fully awake.

Caora asked, "Would yere mother let me release ye both to help her?"

Eala knew Geana would prefer not to be involved, since planting was hard, physical work, but Eala knew that their mother needed them. She spoke first, before Geana could accept the excuse.

"I don't think she'd let you release us, my lady, but if you gave us a few days off, we could lend a hand. She could put our help to good use."

"All right then, ye two. After breakfast ye should go to yere mother and come back in time for the evening meal."

"Are you sure you don't need us, Lady Caora?" Geana asked. "After the Day of Planting there is only a ten-day of winter left and then we are into the Lost Days. You will be called on to celebrate a lot, all the way up to the First Day of Spring. And anyway, my lady, your nativity is the First Lost Day of Winter. You should celebrate that."

Caora was staring at Geana.

"How do you know my nativity, Geana? What makes you think I was born on the First Lost Day of Winter?"

Eala spoke quickly, to try and repair the damage.

"I think it's my fault, my lady. I've confused her. I told her that your Sponsor's nativity was the First Lost Day of Winter and I think she's misunderstood."

She could see Caora think about it a moment, and look somewhat relieved.

"How do you know my Sponsor's nativity?" she asked Eala, more mildly.

"Everyone knows, my lady. The Lady Éirime was born in this village, this side of the river. That is how this house got its name. Everyone remembers her. The whole village is proud of her. If nobody tells you, it's only because they are afraid to talk to a blue-robe about someone so important. They're afraid of being too familiar, my lady: of saying the wrong thing."

Caora shrugged. "Ólachán mentioned it when I first arrived. If he named his inn for her, he would have remembered her. I didn't know everyone knew her nativity. Do people care that much about nativities in Áthaiteorann?"

"We do," replied Geana. "If you have friends or loved ones, you remember their nativities. We would like to remember yours, my lady," she looked over at Eala, who was afraid that Geana was jumping back into the trap. "We would, wouldn't we, Eala?"

Caora saved Eala the trouble of replying. "All right," she said, "when is your nativity, Geana?"

"The Seventeenth Day of Midsummer, my lady. Duille said I was born in the Rising of the Cat, she was born in the Rising of the Bride." Geana added, thoughtfully "Whatever that means, my lady." It was a question, and a hint.

"It means you were both born in the morning, after dawn but before midday, and that you were born first." Then Eala saw Caora look to her a moment, as if she was going to ask her nativity, then think better of it. Instead she asked, "Do you mind sharing your nativity?"

"I'm used to it," Eala said. "I've been sharing it for all my life."

"Well," said Caora, "so am I."

Eala watched her, watching for the little hints that gave away that she was lying. Lady Caora was Eala's mentor: she wanted to learn how Caora's feelings appeared on her face and in her movements.

"I share my birthday with my Sponsor," said Caora.

Well, Eala thought, that was a clever lie.

"So Geana was right?" she said. "You were born on the First Lost Day?"

"I was," replied Caora, "and so was Lady Éirime."

Eala, still watching carefully, was astonished to see something in her face. Caora still didn't believe either answer, even though Eala knew it was true. Eala also saw something in her face, some reflection of that same grief. Why would she be hurt by remembering her nativity? Eala was concerned they were going into an area of Caora's life that might carry too much hurt.

"Would it be too familiar for us to help you celebrate your nativity, my lady?"

"It would not, but it is too much of a coincidence that I share my nativity with my Sponsor. I would prefer that ye did not tell other people."

Eala understood that, although she thought Caora would be surprised if she knew how many people knew. But they agreed that they would not tell.

Then Caora turned it into a mathematics problem, perhaps knowing it would distract them.

"How many people do you need to get together to make it more likely than not that two of them share a birthday?"

Eala thought about that. It was hard. She guessed they needed a number that made itself into the number of days in a year. Well, twenty twenties were four hundred, but there were only three hundred and sixty days in a year. Eighteen was six threes, six sixes were thirty-six, and three threes were nine, and nine thirty-sixes were three hundred and thirty six, so eighteen was too small –

Geana spoke, interrupting her train of thought.

"Nineteen, my lady."

"Not quite, Geana," said Caora. "It's a few more than that: the number is twenty-three. I know what you've done: you've looked for a number that squares to three hundred and sixty. But you've forgotten that there are two people sharing the nativity. One person can't share a nativity, so there have to be at least two people for any chance at all. Then you add each person in turn and work out how much extra probability you get."

She began to explain the mathematics of probability and of permutations and combinations and the twins were soon engrossed.

Eala and Geana were walking to the well. Geana carried the bucket, Eala walked beside her. Geana had asked Caora why things floated, and in response they had been sent to get water.

"It's too hot for fetching water," Geana said.

She was right: it was a hot day, late in the Month of Life. The sky was a clear abyss of blue: at the horizon a pale blue, at the zenith a darker colour. A few white clouds wandered aimlessly, as if lost in all that space. The trees were still and the heat seemed to make everything lazy, even the bees.

"It will be hotter coming back," Eala warned. "The bucket is heavy when it's full."

"I don't know why Lady Caora doesn't just explain things. She expects us to figure it out for ourselves."

"It's a better way to learn, sister. And we don't just learn the answer to the question, we learn how to answer other questions."

"Do you think that's what they do at the City? Fifty Novices all filling buckets?"

"I don't know. I doubt Lady Caora knows. She hasn't been a Novice for more than eight hundred years. She doesn't want to think about the City, anyway."

"You don't know that. She's upset by her memories, but..."

"Geana, sister, she's not just upset. She's *paralysed* by her memories. She drinks all the time, from the moment she wakes and late into the night. I've heard Beatha talk about how much she drinks. She says that Lady Caora should be dead, that it is only because she is Immortal that she is still alive."

"I know. But she doesn't forget even when she drinks. You can see it in her face. It's only when she's singing or playing that she really forgets."

"And she hardly ever stops singing and playing, either," Geana added. "But you still don't know that her fear comes from the City."

"What about the stories we hear of the others? Lord Aclaí, Lord Miotal,

Lady Eibheara? Why do you think people are scared of them? I bet they
are as hurt as Lady Caora, they just show it in cruelty instead of song."

"Like when we talked to the bullies?"

"Like that. They hurt people to forget that they were hurt themselves."

"But Eala, sister, that doesn't prove that the City is a bad place. Lord
Aclaí is Oldest; but those others are nearly as old. Back then the City
was small and the Forest was huge. People lived in caves, with no Words
of Power to help them. If someone wanted to kill you, nobody stopped
them. And the Forest was everywhere with monsters attacking all the
time. Anybody born then would grow up scared."

"Lady Caora says that when she was a girl, Anleacán wasn't like that.
So she didn't grow up in savagery."

"But she also said that she had to go deep into the Forest. That she
was the only one who survived from her year."

They had arrived by the well, and Geana put the bucket down and
began to draw water with the pitcher into the bucket.

"But Lady Caora never says the City is a good place."

"She never says–"

"Eala?"

They both looked up. A girl of about their own age was approaching,
being pulled by a big, hairy dog, one of Reo's dogs. They both recognised
her, Geana with embarrassment. Eilite was a little blonde, whose brown
eyes made her stand out among the fair people of Áthaiteorann. She loved
dogs, but Reo's dogs were huge, and Eala could see she was not in control.
This dog was hot and thirsty and as soon as she saw the dog coming over,
Geana let down the pitcher to refill the trough.

Eilite saw Geana pouring out the water and so did the dog.

"Slowly, Arracht, slowly," Eilite protested, but the dog ignored her.

It put its head into the stone trough and began to lap noisily. Eilite
looped the lead over the rail and sat down heavily. She was breathing hard
from keeping up with the dog.

Geana idly scratched Arracht behind his ears. One ear moved, and his
tail wagged, but he was not going to be distracted from the water.

"You're a fine boy, aren't you?" Geana told him.

Geana didn't talk to Eilite: she found it too uncomfortable and so she
would leave that to Eala.

Eala looked at Eilite. "That's one of Reo's dogs? How does he get them
to be so huge?"

"He breeds the best dogs in Anleacán. He thinks he can make one big
enough to hunt a wolf." Eala could hear the admiration in her voice. "He
has the Gift, Eala," Eilite added.

"Well, if I don't see you with Reo, it's with Reo's dogs. Are ye both getting serious?" she asked.

She was delighted to see Eilite smile. After the business with Ordóg, it had been a while since she had smiled. Eala remembered Eilite with Saonta and with her sister, back before things had gone wrong.

"That is something I wanted to ask you about," she replied.

Eala could see she had news.

"Well?" she asked.

"He's asked me to marry him."

"That's great," Eala answered. She could see relief on Geana's face too, as she felt a little freed from her guilty conscience. "I hope you said you would."

"Of course I did."

"Well, congratulations to ye both."

Eala got up and hugged her. Geana got up, came to within an arm's length, and stopped there.

"May ye have many grandchildren and many years and love one another for all of them," she said. It was a formal well-wishing, one Eilite and Reo would be hearing a lot as their news got out. Seeing Eilite's suspicion, Geana added: "I really mean it."

Eilite seemed to understand at last.

"Thank you, Geana," she replied. Then she added, "I hope we can be friends again."

"I would like that," Geana replied, relieved.

Eilite took her hand. Geana knew people well enough to know that wasn't the end of it, but she knew also it could be a new beginning.

Eala asked, "How many people know?"

"My parents know. Reo's father knows. I don't know if he's told anyone. I was telling ye because I was going to ask ye a favour."

"Whatever you want," Geana said.

Eala would not have promised so much, but if Geana and Eilite were going to be reconciled, then there was a time for Eala to mind her own business.

"I wondered if you would ask Lady Caora to play for us."

"Of course," replied Geana. "When is it?"

"We were thinking of the Midsummer Celebration," replied Eilite. "Weddings are best on a celebration and it'll help Reo remember the date."

"It might help, anyway," Eala answered. "Reo can be absent-minded."

"We can ask her," said Geana.

Eala was concerned about one thing, which seemed to her more important than minding her own business.

"What did you want to do about the Song of the Bride?" she asked.

Geana and Eilite both looked at her, both surprised.

"I think I was expecting to sing it," replied Eilite, not understanding.

Eala could see from Geana's face that she understood very well. Eala thought how to explain. She didn't want to intrude on Caora's privacy too much, but she remembered how Sneachta's wedding had hurt Caora. Then she had an idea.

"Have you heard it said: 'The Sea People do not marry'?"

"I've heard it. Why?"

"I don't think you should ask Lady Caora to play the Song of the Bride."

"Oh," said Eilite.

Eala could see her take this in. Eilite's problems with Geana had been about marriage. Eilite had always wanted to be married. Last year she had thought she was about to be married to Ordóg, before it had all gone wrong. She was trying to imagine what it would be like to be forbidden from marriage and Eala could see that she didn't like it.

Then Eilite asked, "Is that what happened at Sneachta's wedding?"

"I don't know," Eala replied, thinking that she couldn't be certain, even if she could make a very good guess.

"It's not something I'd have thought of before," Eilite mused. "The Sea People seem to live such wonderful lives, but it can't be so wonderful to live hundreds of years and never get a husband." She spoke more quietly, aware that what she was saying was disrespectful, maybe even dangerously so. "I think I pity her, poor thing. Does it hurt her very much?"

"I think she tries not to think about it," replied Eala.

"So she won't want to play that, will she? Will she be all right to play for a wedding at all?"

"I think she will. She likes to help, you know that. And she does love to play."

"But not the Song of the Bride," Eilite continued. "Well, I'm a better singer than Sneachta. I think it always sounds better if it is not accompanied, if the girl can stay in tune. I'm not Lady Caora, but I can manage to sing one song without her."

"Then we'll ask her for you," said Geana.

"Thank you," Eilite replied.

"Is it still a secret?" asked Eala.

"Until we have an answer, it would be better," she replied. "People will want to know when."

"Of course," said Geana. "I'll get you an answer as quickly as I can."

Eala and Geana went back to the Shepherdess with the water. But when Caora saw them return, she wanted to hear their news.

"What happened?" she asked.

"We met Eilite," replied Geana.

"How is she?" asked Caora, not knowing anything about the problems between them.

"She is happy."

"That's good. She's not been so happy over winter, has she? Sometimes the darkness can make people unhappy."

"It's more than summer that's cheered her up. She's going to marry Reo."

"That's nice," replied Caora. "Wasn't she going to marry some other boy, last year?"

"I don't think he loved her," Eala answered. "He went off with another girl."

"He might have loved them both," suggested Caora.

"He didn't love either," Geana replied. "Anyway, she asked us to ask you to help."

"Why didn't she ask me herself?" Caora was hurt, Eala could see.

"She's known us since we were little girls," said Geana. "She's only four months younger than us. We grew up together."

"And I'm a scary blue-robe," said Caora, bitterly.

"My lady, people know what you are, and they know how old your Sponsor is," replied Eala. "I believe that Lady Éirime is like you, not like Lord Aclaí, but nobody here can be sure of that. If Lord Aclaí came to live in the village, then you'd see how terrified people would be. People here care for you very much, but they know you are not like them, and they are cautious."

Caora put her fingertips on her breastbone.

"In here I'm the same as them," she said, sadly.

"I know, my lady," replied Eala. "If you spoke to her, I'm sure she'd ask you. But she doesn't want to bother you. She's afraid to intrude."

Caora looked at her, and then stood up.

"All right," she said. "Let's see."

Eala hoped she was right. But it was too late to do anything else but find out. Eala put down the water.

"Geana, will you lead us?" asked Eala.

Geana led them out of the inn, across the bridge, to the house Eilite shared with her parents. Her father was outside, chopping wood with a heavy hand-axe. He looked up as they approached; saw Geana and Eala, then Lady Caora. He got to his feet.

"My lady, how can I help you?"

"We were looking for Eilite," Geana said.

"She's with Reo, Eala," he said, looking at Geana. He looked nervously back at Caora. "You could try Reo's house, my lady."

"Thank you," said Caora.

"It is nothing," he replied.

Geana led them, along the river, to Reo's house. As they left the village, they heard Reo's dogs begin to bark. Arracht came tearing out, straight towards the three of them. Reo emerged, just too late to call him back, as the dog ran up to Caora. She didn't sing any Words but she moved from her hip, and her arm and wrist moved slightly in an opening spiral. It was as if she gathered something from the air by her side, and then threw it towards the dog. The dog skidded to a halt, then turned and ran, yelping. It had not come closer than three paces to them: even Reo could see that Caora had not touched it. But as she looked at Caora, Geana could feel that same power that she had felt when she had spilt drink on her. She could see that Eala was frightened. It was the first time she had really felt that Caora was someone to be feared.

Arracht ran back, tail between his legs, and hid behind Reo: a ridiculous sight, as Arracht was a massive dog. Eilite came out of the cottage and looked at Arracht.

"Whatever scared him like..?"

She looked up, and saw the three of them. She took Reo's arm, held him.

By the time Caora had walked over to them, she was back to normal, it seemed.

"Congratulations to ye both," Caora said.

"Thank you, my lady," said Reo.

Arracht held his head low and looked at her, the whites of his eyes showing for just a moment, and then he slunk into the house. Geana looked at Eilite, who spoke to Caora.

"My lady, I wanted to ask you a favour."

Caora smiled, encouraging her to ask.

"Well, actually I wanted to ask you two favours." She let go of Reo's arm. "One of them I'd prefer to ask alone, if you wouldn't mind."

Caora stepped away from the twins. They watched as Caora sang Words of Power and then she spoke to Eilite, but there was no sound. Eilite looked back, spoke in reply, but again, they could hear nothing.

"What is happening?" asked Reo.

"There's a wall between us that stops the sound," said Geana. "It's a blue-robe thing."

"So they can't hear us either?" asked Reo.

"They can't."

"You're Geana, aren't you?"

"I am."

"I know you're trying to repair your friendship with Eilite. She cares about your friendship, or she wouldn't be willing to forgive you."

"I know. I never meant for her to be hurt like that."

"Don't hurt her again." He spoke mildly, but it was a warning.

"I will try my best."

Caora and Eilite returned, ending the discussion. Eilite spoke.

"Lady Caora has agreed to play for our wedding."

The Chamberlain sat alone in his room at the top of the Hill, in the Court of the Favourites. He tried to spend some time every day alone, working on his experiment, but he didn't always get time: the demands of his position on the Hill took time away from him.

But he couldn't simply come off duty and return to his experiment. He also needed to clear his mind of distractions. If his mind was too busy with other thoughts, these thoughts would drown out the thoughts that arose from the experiment. Even when he did his best to clear his mind, the thoughts he had would affect the communications he received.

He was thinking about Midsummer Day. In the City, the Sun rose and set every day, but among his own people the summertime was a time when the Sun never set.

In the summer the Sun shone for months, day in and day out. His people lived in tents of leather. They hunted, fished, and enjoyed what life had to offer before the Sun set and the winter came again. The tribes would come together, share stories and news, make trades and exchange gifts, and parents would find wives and husbands for their sons and daughters. And if he returned, to walk tall among them, his family, his tribe, his people would all be proud of him.

Thinking of his family made him think of his younger brother, who nagged him about Selection every time he went home. It was all he talked about. And ... the thought came: *if you bring him to Selection, he will be dead before the Sun rises after winter.*

The Chamberlain thought at first that he had imagined it, that his own worries were intruding in the process. But he answered. Can't we keep him safe?

Perhaps you could, the thought replied, *but you won't.*

The Chamberlain knew that there were many dangers for a Novice, and that most of those Selected for his Year were now dead. But most of them hadn't had a brother on the top of the Hill. So he thought: Why not? You could tell me what to do to keep him safe.

I could tell you, the thought replied, *but you will not follow my advice.*

He remembered the other prediction he had obtained, about the first ten-day of the New Year. It was something he wanted for his brother, as he had had it for himself.

He will die, came the thought, unbidden.

But the Chamberlain saw the opportunity, even if he wasn't sure of the source. He was sure of his own position, though. He was sure that his own power in the City would be enough to keep his brother safe. Especially with the prophecy.

As the days of the Month of Flowers went by and the Day of Midsummer approached, the twins noticed that Caora kept giving them the slip. At first they had noticed her absence, then they realised that she was deliberately going. Finally they resolved to follow her and when she realised they would not let her slip away quietly, she sang Words of Power and vanished in front of their eyes.

She was always back in time for the next meal and, knowing she was evading them, they accepted that they had no duty to be with her. Eala persuaded Geana to go back to their mother's house: there was always useful work to do there and Mammy liked to see them.

Finally the Day of Midsummer came. On Midwinter's Day, the people of Áthaiteorann danced all night, and on Midsummer's Day, they danced all day. Geana was the first awake. She looked over at Eala and she listened to the sound of the rain on the roof. Then she looked over at Caora's bed. She wasn't there.

"Wake up, Eala. She's gone again," said Geana, prodding her sister.

Eala looked up, her green eyes bleary.

"What's gone? It was right here a moment ..." She looked around, as if noticing her surroundings for the first time. "Is it raining?"

"Torrents of it," said Geana. "Caora's up already. I don't know where she is."

The twins got up as quickly as they could. As they were getting up, Caora came back in, a mug in her hand.

"Come on, girls, there's no time to waste. We have to save the day."

She sang Words of Freshness over them and they came with her, one holding each of her hands. They went out back, avoiding the commons, and away on to the riverside path. The river was swollen, muddy, the surface troubled with eddies and turbulence. The girls both had sheepskin jackets, rubbed with beeswax to keep the wet off their bodies, but the rain got into their hair, which hung down on their cheeks and into their eyes, sending cold water trickling down their necks. As she felt it, even Eala envied Caora's blue cloak.

They went up the riverbank, beyond the waterfall, to the high pastures.

"What are we going to see, my lady?" asked Geana.

"We're going to see Reo and Eilite married. But first we have to save the day."

Caora found a place on the pasture, away from the trees.

"This will do." She drained off the mug, gave it to Eala. "Let's clear up this mess," she laughed. "Let's make it shine."

She rubbed her hands together and then she began to shout, a high clear voice holding one note. She was not shouting, she was singing, as loudly as her magnificent voice allowed her, singing Words of Power to the leaden sky. These Words didn't whisper in corners of their minds. These coursed through the girls' awareness, robbing them of the power of speech, robbing them of thought.

She flung her arms up as she sang and Eala and Geana saw the underside of the clouds ripple, like the surface of a pond when a rock is thrown in, but so much bigger. Then, as she continued to sing to the sky, the clouds parted and a shaft of sunlight came down, obliquely, because it was still early morning. They looked down at Áthaiteorann, illuminated, picked out by that great beam of sunshine. The sight made them feel tiny, like insects caught on a table when the shutters are opened. As Caora continued to sing, the blue area in the sky opened, becoming wider, until it spread above them, leaving the storm clouds all around them, on the horizon. Only then did Caora stop singing.

She brushed back her hood, and shook her dry hair. She was smiling, a big broad smile over her face. Eala had seen that look on her face once before, the night Spideog nearly died. She put her arms around both of them, hugging them to her.

"Have a happy Midsummer, girls," she said. "Let's go back and see what is happening, shall we?"

When they returned to the commons, the whole place was abuzz. Beatha came over to refill Caora's mug.

As she gave Caora her drink, she asked, "Was that you, my lady?"

"Was what me?" asked Caora.

"The sunshine? You can see that the rain is falling all around us, but Áthaiteorann has sunshine."

"It has brightened up, hasn't it? It's good. The sun should shine on Midsummer's Day, don't you think?"

"I am sure Reo and Eilite will think so, my lady. I'm sure they will be very grateful for it."

Caora turned to her and the smile was gone.

"Now, Beatha, don't you dare go putting ideas into their heads. I struggle enough with trying to avoid the whole village being indebted to me, without people putting crazy ideas about that I am responsible for the weather. To control weather with Words requires a powerful Formula, beyond all but the oldest of the Sea People. I'm not the Mentor, Beatha. I'm not even Lord Aclaí."

Beatha looked at her, not quite willing to let it go.

"Is it something your Sponsor would be able to do, Lady Caora?"

"Enough, Beatha," she replied. "Believe what you will, but don't get anyone thinking they are indebted to me. And don't spoil a lovely day. We're both going to be busy."

"As you wish, my lady," she replied, and she turned away.

Caora finished the mug and went over to Leathar and Fuiseoga.

As they walked, Geana asked, "Is that something only the oldest of the Sea People can do, my lady?"

"Look, I meant what I said. I hate having people indebted to me. Can't I just make people happy for one day?"

Eala said, "I think Beatha just wanted to thank you, Lady Caora."

"I know, Eala," Caora whispered.

Then they were with Leathar and Fuiseoga and that was the end of that conversation. They went out over the bridge, to the clear space before the Sun, where the dancing always happened. They took their seats under the roof.

Leathar looked up at the sky.

"Do you think the rain will return, Lady Caora?"

"It won't, I'm sure of it."

Leathar eyed the horizon suspiciously. "You are sure?"

"I am sure. Let's not worry about the weather, let's just enjoy it."

They did enjoy it. Reo and his friends arrived soon after and Caora, Fuiseoga and Leathar played music for them, as the crowds gathered. Eala went over to Eilite's house, to see how she was getting on. They had been friends since they could first walk: Eala belonged with her today. Geana stayed close to Caora, taking care of her. She was aware of Ordóg standing alone, watching her, and she realised as she felt his gaze that the consequences of her guilt were not over yet.

Then Eala was at the other side, over by the great oak, waving. Geana leaned over to Lady Caora.

"They're ready," she said.

Caora looked up at Eala. Then she looked at Leathar. Leathar looked at the others and checked they were ready to play. Then he beat the time, and they began.

Reo started, and looked around. The crowd watching drew apart and the first of the girls came in. Among them was Eilite, in a long dress of red silk. Geana could see it in the faces of the girls and women watching:

how had Eilite and Reo afforded to get her silk? Reo was staring at her, and so was Ordóg, she saw. Eilite came in like a queen and walked over to Reo and his friends. There she stopped. The music stopped and there was silence. Caora put down her harp, took up her mug and leaned back in her seat. Eala looked over to make sure she was all right. This was where, in Sneachta's wedding, things had gone wrong.

But the musicians didn't start. Instead, Eilite began to sing unaccompanied. Eala could see that Caora was taking an interest in what she did, the way she took an interest when the twins were trying to do something she had taught them. And, as Eilite sang the Song of the Bride, Eala heard how her voice had improved so much. She didn't sing like a girl, she sang like a woman, her voice powerful enough that she did not need instruments. She realised Caora had been training her. That was where she had been going when she was evading them.

Geana sat near Caora, as close as she could without appearing over-familiar with their Steward. She could see how Caora was hurt, even now, but she could also see how her interest in her pupil was stopping it from overwhelming her. So she drank, but not too much, and at least she could stay there and watch and only those who knew her would notice.

Then Reo took Eilite in his arms and everyone cheered their approval. Leathar called for them to drink to the new couple and the cheers continued. Eilite hugged her new husband. Then Leathar looked over at Caora and Fuiseoga and he marked time for the dance the bride had requested.

The Hall of the Novices stood at the bottom of the Hill: a structure of irregular stone blocks carved to fit minutely together. The stone walls supported a roof of stone slabs, but reinforced with paper-thin lintels of Metal. Here and there in the roof and walls, blocks and slabs of quartz had been introduced, to allow light in. The Metal support allowed it to be bigger than any other building in the dominions of the Sea People: fully ten paces wide and thirty long. At one end there was a raised platform and, at the other, double doors made up the full width and height of the far wall.

The Sea People sat on benches and ate their evening meal at trestle tables. The Favourites were around the Mentor's table on the raised platform, looking down on the rest: their appearance was that of a collection of young men and women from all around the world, but to those that knew, they were a group that included the best part of four millennia of experience. They all looked to their leader, looking for his love and approval. He was a young-looking, rather plain man of average height, with short sandy hair and striking green eyes.

A clear space existed in the middle of the hall, before the table where the Mentor and his Favourites sat, but either side was a sea of turquoise blue cloth: cloaks on the shoulders of diners from all over the world, united in their service to the City.

Among the diners, servants came and went, providing food and drink. They also came from all over the world and, like their masters and mistresses, the servants were attractive. But although beneath their blue cloaks the Adepts wore all manner of clothing, according to their own origins and the fashions of their patrol groups, all the servants wore the same uniform: a wide strip of pale yellow linen, with a slot in the middle for the head, covering front and back and tied with a cord around the waist to make a simple tunic. It was a design of cloth woven without stitches or fastenings, unchanged in a thousand years. Some of the younger servants were shy, and cautious as they moved, aware that as they bent or leaned their bodies might be exposed. But the older ones did not worry about it, being used to their positions among the blue-robes.

As the servants cleared the tables after the Evening Meal, the Mentor looked up. He knew that there was some sort of entertainment planned for the evening and he waited to see what it was.

The great doors opened and he watched drummers come in, tall dark folk from the great continent to the east of the City. They wore jewellery, carved wood and gold in their hair, around their necks, on wrists and ankles. But instead of clothing, their upper bodies were painted in bright colours. The Mentor had not been offered music since Éirime had left and, although he appreciated the sensitivity, he missed seeing young people dance.

The drumming began: music of a sort, but no melody, all rhythm. The drums were very expressive, their pitch changing as the beat throbbed through the hall, a deep loud rhythm that could be felt in the belly. And then, with a long cry, ululated with the tongues of the drummers, the dancers appeared.

They were dressed in little more than paint, and the dance they danced was utterly wanton, filled with shaking, thrusting and gyrating whose significance was unmistakable. The dancers were in pairs, a boy with a girl, each moving exactly in time with the others.

The drummers quickened their beat and the dancers went faster and, as they did, each boy and girl drew closer, until they began to touch in their movements. The dance of boy and girl were not identical: they complemented each other, so that, if they danced a little closer, they could have danced as he penetrated her. The Mentor saw the dancers react to the proximity, saw their almost-naked bodies aroused. He glanced around for a moment and saw that almost everyone else in the hall was noticing the same thing.

As the pace quickened, the dancers were touching, and pressing against one another. Then, after a few breaths of that, the drummers stopped and the dancers stopped with them. The whole hall roared its approval.

The Chamberlain was by his side.

"What is it?" the Mentor asked.

"Did you like this dance, Mentor?" he asked.

"I did, but I wanted to see how long it would go on, how far they would go."

"Two of the Novices know this dance."

"Oh, really?" The Mentor was interested. "Are they from the same place?"

"The girl is. She has been teaching a northern boy. When they dance, they go further than that."

He looked up. "And you have got these dancers ready at the top of the Hill?"

"I have, Mentor."

"You're a good Chamberlain," answered the Mentor.

He got up to lead the Favourites up the Hill and everyone in the hall rose with him. He leaned a little closer to his Chamberlain.

"Let us meet this couple, then," the Mentor said.

Eala came into their room, carrying the lamp, and Caora and Geana followed. Geana was limping a little: her feet hurt from the dancing. Caora was unsteady, but no more than usual, and she was smiling.

Eala wondered about it, but Geana asked instead.

"You are happy, my lady. Do you think the day went well?"

"It did, Geana. You spoke to Eilite, didn't you?"

"Why do you say that?"

"I expected to get the usual problems about debts when I tried to help her, but she didn't make a fuss. She said that you owed her a favour. Did you?"

"In a way, my lady."

"Was it your idea to get her to sing unaccompanied?"

"In a way, my lady."

"Well, you're not telling me everything, are you?"

"I'm not, my lady. I did something bad. You've helped me make it up to her. Thank you for that, my lady."

"You are not in my debt, Geana. Because I've been helping and because it's all been in the preparation, this is the first time in a very long time that I've enjoyed a wedding. You did that. Ye girls are manipulative, I know, but I have never benefited from it like this. That puts me in your debt, Geana, more than you can know. So, what can I do to repay you?"

Eala was shocked and upset at how that turned out. She didn't think that Geana's indiscretions with Ordóg and ill-treatment of Eilite should result in her being offered a debt by Caora. But what happened next was worse.

"Well?" prompted Caora. "Whatever you want."

Geana said, "Take us to Selection, my lady."

"What do you think this Selection will be like?"

Liús looked up. He looked across the courtyard, to the fountain in the centre of the Court of the Favourites, where Eibheara sat in the fading light with her friend, a thin, dark-haired woman with pale skin, whose Sea-people beauty was all-but-hidden by her short hair and her scruffy appearance.

Liús spoke. "I don't think it will be very different to last year's, Lady Eibheara. The Traditions of the City don't change much from year to year."

Éise was sitting beside him on the bench, as dark as he was fair, holding his hand.

She added, "What do you think it will be like, Lady Eibheara? Do you expect anything out of the ordinary?"

"I don't think it will be any different *for me*," Eibheara replied.

"What do you mean?" asked Liús.

Eibheara laughed, and Liús knew she was laughing at him. But he didn't understand the joke. Eibheara's companion, Cathúa, spoke.

"She's referring to the threat each new Selection brings to us." Cathúa looked directly at Liús. "And particularly to you, Favourite. With every new Year, there is the chance that some purple Novice will arrive who will attract the Mentor's attention and be brought up the Hill to join us."

"Why is that particularly threatening to him, Lady Cathúa?" Éise asked.

"Because he is *the* Favourite," Eibheara answered. "Few are sent down from the top of the Hill, but being *the* Favourite is a precarious position." She smiled, and there was cruelty in her smile. "It's not something you will understand."

Éise had been brought to the top of the Hill at Midsummer, but with Liús: she was a favourite, but not the Favourite. Éise squeezed Liús' hand and he squeezed back. They both understood that he had no fear: they would rather be just two favourites and neither be The Favourite. But they knew that Eibheara didn't know that and they were glad of it. It had been a difficult and potentially dangerous three months.

From the darkness, Aclaí spoke.

"It happened to you, Eibheara," he said.

"And to you, Aclaí," she replied. "I bet you're glad she's Retired."

"Are you glad that he Retired, Eibheara?" He laughed. "Or perhaps you arranged it."

Eibheara laughed back. "It's always nice to help people get what they want. He wanted to go. I helped him."

"Do you still hear of him sometimes?" asked Éise. Then she added, "Who has heard of Lady Éirime since she Retired?"

"She's not someone you'd fail to hear, is she?" commented Cathúa.

The rest of them laughed, but Aclaí said, "We won't ever hear from her again."

Cathúa looked concerned.

"Her breath?" she quietly asked.

"Her breathing is so strong, she will out-live us all. But she will never return to the City," explained Aclaí.

Cathúa looked reassured.

"I miss her," she said.

"You are not the only one," Aclaí admitted, before turning away from the conversation.

After that Eibheara looked in the direction of the Chamberlain's room.

"I wonder what he does in there," Eibheara mused.

In his room, the Chamberlain tried to ignore the laughter outside. The Selection was tomorrow, and he knew his brother was already in the City. He couldn't get the thought out of his head, and he wanted to learn more. There was a lot to worry about, but he cleared his mind.

This Selection will change everything on the Hill, the thought came suddenly, surprising him.

For me? He thought.

For everyone, it answered. *But most especially for you.*

Because of my brother?

One of the new Novices should be Favourite within a ten-day. This Novice will force the Mentor to make a chain of decisions and, if he makes the wrong decision, the City will fall.

How long?

That is up to the Mentor. The chain of decisions starts at the Selec-

tion, but it could go on for centuries.

The Chamberlain laughed to himself. So I'll have reached Immortal Rank and Retired by then, he thought.

You will not leave the City until the new Favourite does.

Is this about my brother?

If you want to save your brother, you must call the Initiations in strict order of status.

Uninitiated Novices don't have status, he thought. That makes no sense.

They do not have status, but their Sponsors do.

The Chamberlain thought about that. Well, if the prophecy was going to come true, if the Mentor made a purple Novice Favourite within the first ten-day, then he would likely be the first one Initiated. If the Chamberlain only brought one purple Novice in the first ten-day, then it would have to be the one he chose. So what were the odds that someone of greater status than him would bring a Candidate tomorrow?

The question was ambiguous. Or at least, he thought, it could be argued. The obvious way to order status was according to Rank. But he was one of the Favourites, even if he was only Twelfth Rank. Not only was he a Favourite, but he was Chamberlain – by that measure, only Liús, the Favourite, was of higher status. On the other hand, there were two dozen Veterans and half a dozen Immortals whose Rank exceeded his.

If he discounted those who weren't Favourites, that left Aclaí, Eibheara, Cathúa – and Liús. If they didn't bring Candidates, he rationalised, then he could put his brother forward first, with safety.

Eala heard Caora get up. She quietly shifted Geana's arm and got up herself. Geana was snoring: she couldn't keep up with Caora's drinking, even when she tried to. She needed to learn to pretend to drink more and to appear to be more affected by it. It was the Second Lost Day of Autumn, three months after Midsummer and, with the harvest in, everyone in Áthaiteorann was relaxing, celebrating a successful summer. The celebrations had taken their toll.

"My lady?" Eala called softly.

"Geana?" came the voice from behind the curtain.

"It is Eala, my lady. Geana is asleep."

"Good," came the unexpected reply. "Will you come and help me?"

Eala was just reaching for the curtain when Caora swept it aside. She was in her blue cloak, beneath it her favourite linen dress, and tall boots. Eala thought of her sister, drunk on autumn wine and how her attempt to keep up with the lighter, more slender Caora left her unconscious. She followed Caora out of the room into the commons. Caora smelt of wine, but her hands were steady, her walk graceful.

"Eala," Caora said, "you don't have to go tomorrow. I promised Geana I would take her, however little I want to, but just because she wants to go, you don't have to."

"I know," Eala answered. "But if I don't go, I will regret it."

"You will regret it more if you do go, Eala. What do you think will happen?"

"We will present ourselves to the Mentor and he will choose Geana. You and I will come back to Áthaiteorann. And then, my lady, I will serve you here, and we will never leave again."

Eala could see in Caora's face that she expected the same.

Caora whispered, "Then why go?"

"Because if she does get Selected and I don't go, my lady, I will always wonder what might have happened." She realised she was in danger of showing her emotions and was glad of the darkness. "And I will miss her, my lady. We have never been parted before. If I am here, missing her, I will know I did everything I could to be with her."

Caora stopped walking. "Eala, you are forgetting what will happen if you are both Selected. It will be easier for her: she has been in love before."

"My lady!" Eala objected. "Just because I am more careful of gossip doesn't mean I have never felt love."

"Eala, I'm sorry. I just thought you weren't interested in boys yet."

"I won't look for a husband until Geana is married. There is no point. I am interested in men, but they are not interested in me. They won't be, not until she is married." Eala shrugged, determined not to care. "Anyway, I have responsibilities. There is Mammy and Spideog. There is you, my lady. I will not turn away from those responsibilities just for a man."

"If I was choosing one of ye for a wife, Eala, it is you I would choose, not your sister." Lady Caora looked away as soon as she had said it, leaving Eala to wonder how drunk she actually was. "If I was a man, that is," she whispered.

"Perhaps you would, my lady," answered Eala, "but men don't feel the same way as women do."

They walked through the commons in silence. Then Eala said, "My lady, you should set the Visions."

Caora sighed. "I suppose I must."

"Beatha will be grateful, my lady."

Eala watched as Caora selected a clear space of wall at one end of the commons, made up the frame and softly sang her Words of Power. The frame became filled with darkness: there was nothing coming from the City yet. But Eala knew they would all be gathered around, to watch her and her sister get rejected.

As they walked into the cool night, Caora looked back.

"I would release you if you found a husband, Eala."

"If you had your way, my lady, you would never have taken us in the first place. Mammy insisted."

"You are right. But I have been very glad of ye both. Ye take care of me. Ye are the family I no longer have."

"I know. My lady, I will not simply go because you released me. I am my mother's daughter, Lady Caora."

"I see that, Eala. Ye both are. There is less difference between ye than you think. If the Mentor chooses either of ye, I think he might choose both. I wish neither of ye would go. I told myself I would never take a Candidate to Selection, before I had been in the City a year. But a promise is a promise. I just hope ye can be strong for each other."

Caora reached the stable, opened the door and sang a song ever so softly to the horses. Old Longeán poked his head out, shaking his mane.

"We will be all right, Lady Caora. Even if we are both Selected, we will be Novices in the dormitory, like you described. We will be strong for each other. Even if the Mentor hurts us, it will only be for one night."

"That one night will break your heart, Eala."

"I know it would, my lady. But could I leave my sister alone and heartbroken?"

The horse came out and Caora tied the halter around his nose.

"My lady," Eala added, "you promised to take Geana once. When you have taken her, if she is rejected, we can come home again. You said that most Candidates are rejected, that most of the successful ones are trained and coached by their own Sponsors. We are two country girls and we are not as pretty as Geana thinks we are. Tomorrow night we'll be back home here, all three of us."

"You are probably right, Eala. I really hope you are right."

"I hope I am right too, my lady. And I will make sure she doesn't ask again."

"Thank you."

Caora whispered in the horse's ear, then jumped up on to its back.

"Shall I come with you, my lady? I know you don't like the City."

"I am not going to the City, Eala. I will go through the Forest, as far as Lorgcoiseaigéan, and get a Flyer there. I will bring it back through the Gate and be back here before dawn. You go back to bed."

"All right, Lady Caora," Eala replied, looking up. "I will see you in the morning, then."

Caora kicked her heels and the horse started to walk.

"Come on," she told it, "you've done nothing but eaten Ólachán's grass all summer. Time to do some work. Time to go back into the Forest."

Eala watched her ride carefully through the orchard, then over the bridge and up the hill towards the wood. They entered the trees and were lost from sight. She turned back to the inn, crept inside and lay down beside her sister.

Geana turned over, and Eala felt her warmth. The thought suddenly occurred to her that she might be sleeping alone the following night. The fear of it prickled at her eyes.

She put her arm over her sister and tried to sleep.

The Selection

"My lord Aclaí," the servant called, "Lord Miotal is at the gate. He has a message for you."

"Tell him he has my permission to enter," Aclaí responded and the servant hurried away.

The Lost Days of Summer were over and it was the First Day of Autumn, the first day of the New Year. The favourites were together at the top of the Hill, dressed in their best, waiting to accompany the Mentor down to the Hall and see the new Candidates. Eibheara looked after the servant.

"I wonder why he doesn't just use the sword."

Aclaí replied, "Why don't you ask him?"

Eibheara's joke from the previous night had been preying on Liús mind, in spite of Éise's reassurances. And, now he had started to notice it, he saw that he was not the only one who was nervous. Rónmór was the most jittery, but everyone had learned why: he had to balance his duties as Chamberlain with his duty as a Sponsor. He had brought a relative along. Then, when Cathúa disappeared, they realised that she was also Sponsoring someone.

Miotal ran over from the gate, leaving the servant behind.

"Éirime is here," he said, a little breathlessly. "She brought Candidates."

Liús didn't think he had ever seen Aclaí lost for words before. It was Eibheara that broke the silence.

"So, what are they like?" she asked.

"Two girls," Miotal responded. "They're not pretty, but they are very alike. I guess they are cousins, but they look as if they could be twins."

"Why couldn't they be twins?" asked Éise.

"Because the Mentor decreed that only one Candidate is permitted per family," replied Eibheara. Then she laughed. "But in a little village like she Retired to, everyone is one family."

"Is it all right for Rónmór to bring his brother to Selection?" asked

Éise.

"The Mentor decreed that there would only be one Candidate per family," Eibheara replied. "But Rónmór is not a Candidate anymore."

"Why doesn't the Mentor like too many from one family?" asked Éise.

"Cathúa would know," answered Eibheara. "There are several rules and Traditions about Candidates. She seems to know them all, even if the reasons are lost in time. She spends her time reading archives, after all – and if the reason is not in the archives, she will ask the Mentor."

"Not about everything, my lady," Innealta said. "I don't see how she could know about the forbidden names."

For a moment, Eibheara scowled.

"Why wouldn't she know about the forbidden names?" asked Éise.

"Because the forbidden names are going to be people who offended him. Even she is going to be cautious enough not to ask about that," Innealta replied.

"She knows some of them, at least," answered Éise. "She told me about Iolar."

"I was the one who told her about Iolar," answered Aclaí. "And Iolar didn't offend him. He hopes Iolar will come back and doesn't want another person called Iolar on the Hill."

Since Rónmór wasn't there, it was Toirneach who directed the servants to ring the bell. The Mentor came out and the conversation ceased as they walked down the Hill.

"You didn't bring Candidates this year?" the Mentor asked Aclaí quietly.

"I didn't, Mentor," answered Aclaí. "But Éirime did, apparently."

"Éirime is here?" Aclaí saw the Mentor smile his surprise.

"She is, Mentor. And she has brought a couple of girls with her."

As they entered the hall, the musicians began to play. To their left was the raised platform on which the Mentor and Favourites normally ate, now occupied by the musicians. To their right, there was the crowd: almost all of the blue-robes that lived in the City and at the front of the crowd, the row of Candidates and their Sponsors waited.

About half the crowd were like the old Sea People, thin and dark-haired, but fair of skin and eyes. The other half were from all over the world, with all skin colours and face shapes represented. The first in the line, closest to the door, were young-looking, soft-shaped people with the eye-fold that showed they were from the Great Ocean: Rónmór the Chamberlain, and a young man who looked like him.

"Mentor," Rónmór greeted them, "this is Léaró, my brother."

The Mentor talked to young Léaró, but Liús could see that he was distracted. Next to Rónmór was someone that Liús recognised, but had never spoken to: the Lady Éirime. In front of her were two young women, with reddish blonde hair and green eyes. The two women were each holding one of Lady Éirime's hands, which seemed very familiar for two peasant girls accompanying the Second Oldest.

Perhaps the Mentor thought the same. He turned from Rónmór and his brother.

"Éirime," he said, "have you finally brought me Candidates?"

Liús expected her voice to be powerful, but it was hardly more than a whisper.

"They wanted to come, Mentor. They talk of nothing else."

The Mentor looked at the girls.

"Is this true?" he asked.

"It is true, my lord," one of them replied, confidently.

The other smiled and moved her head in agreement. The Mentor looked back at Éirime.

"They are pretty enough," he told her, "and they are twins, which is certainly different. I don't think I have ever Selected twins before."

Liús could see surprise on Eibheara's face, but he didn't know what else: was it curiosity, was it anger? But the Mentor was laughing, delighted with them.

"But," he continued, "do they have the brains to learn here?"

"I think they do, Mentor," she replied. "I think they will make good leaders, too."

The Mentor reached down and, with a big gesture, he took out his sword and held it before the girls. The blade was Metal, as long as his arm, and sharp like a razor. He held it, threatening, testing their courage.

Both girls stood still, looking him in the eye, refusing to cower, but then the one who had spoken moved forward a tiny bit, her head high, the point below her chin, as if she was defying him to cut her. Liús, knowing that the Mentor had killed Candidates before, thought she was taking a huge risk. He was sure he could see the fear in Lady Éirime's eyes.

But the girl had judged the situation right. She was not being threatening, but eventually, as she crept forward, the Mentor must move the blade or she would be cut. He laughed and put it away again. He took her chin in his hand, and moved his face close to hers. Liús could see she had aroused his interest.

"You have courage and it is either foolishness or wisdom." He was smiling, amused, not cruel. "What is your name, child?"

"Geana, my lord," she told him, unafraid.

The change was as rapid as any Liús had ever seen in the Mentor. He snatched his hand away from Geana's face as if she had burned him, then swept the hand around and struck her with the back of it. Her head whirled around in a cloud of red-gold hair and she fell to the floor. His hand now had the gauntlet of his armour on it – he had pulled the Silver Cord as he swung – his arms went up and the sword was there again, appearing at the top of the movement. He was about to cut her in two. But the other girl was there first, in the way.

She had stepped in as he raised the blade, half-reached to his wrists, and he held its descent before it cut her. She flinched, terrified, but she did not move. She looked at him, eye to eye. His eyes were filled with anger; hers were pleading for her sister's life and her own.

Éirime watched, her breathing held, waiting to see if he would kill them. The other girl's instinct was perfect: if she could hold his attention for a moment longer, she knew he would grant her plea. But if he didn't calm down, they would both die.

He breathed out, and lowered the blade a little.

"What is your name?"

"Eala, my lord."

Liús imagined that he heard a tiny sound from one of the women with them, but he was not sure if it was from Éise or from Eibheara. The Mentor spoke again, and his tone made them all cringe.

"Among twins, one often leads and the other follows. Which of ye leads, *Eala*?"

She looked down at her sister. Geana was looking up, her face cut and bleeding, her hair and clothes disarrayed, her eyes unfocused. Eala looked at the Mentor again, and met his eyes.

"She does, my lord," Eala said.

"Not any more," he told her and turned away from them both.

He tossed the sword to the ground, near them, and it bounced and skidded on the floor, scattering chips of stone, the ringing sound making Éirime jump. Liús remembered then what Lady Éirime must have forgotten. The first and oldest of the forbidden names was Geana.

When The Mentor had walked around the whole hall, he came to the raised section at the front. There was a pause and then he began to name names. Eala was called, Geana was not.

Then, when all the names had been called, he announced, "Ye are the one thousand one hundred and twenty second cohort of the Sea People. Come and learn."

As they walked away up the Hill, all the new Novices but Rónmór's brother were led to their new dormitories. The favourites talked amongst themselves. Cathúa and Rónmór were both happy: their Candidates had been Selected. But Éirime had not walked up with them. She had stayed behind with the other twin, the one that had nearly died. Liús heard Eibheara whispering to Éise.

"I can't believe there are villages where people really call their second twin *Eile*," Eibheara laughed.

The newly selected Candidates were led away and Éirime was left with Geana. She took her out of the hall, sat her down on the Flyer, and lifted her head to see her face. Her cheek was cut and swollen, her lip was split, and one of her back teeth was broken. Éirime quickly sang the Words, touched her, and the bleeding stopped, her skin was made whole, and the bruising disappeared.

"Is the tooth hurting you?" she whispered.

"It doesn't hurt, my lady, it's just rough." Her voice was shaking as much as the rest of her.

"I'll fix it when we get you home, then. I'm not going to sing a Restoration in the Court of the Novices. But tell me if it starts to hurt."

She looked around her and realised that several people were coming over to speak to her. She had been gone from the City too long, but she didn't want a social meeting, especially not with Geana hurt and shocked. Especially when it was all she could do to keep the tears off her own face, when she was so in need of a drink. She sat next to Geana, and the Flyer rose.

As they left, Éirime looked behind her. Several people watched her go, people anxious to see her. But she caught the eye of one other: the Lord Aclaí, looking back as the Favourites left the Court of the Immortals. She could not tell why he was watching her, but he was watching her with great interest. His gaze always made her feel uncomfortable, but especially at a Selection. This was the first Selection she had chosen to participate in and she was afraid of what he might be thinking. She guided the Flyer down the slope, away from the Hill.

The flyer took them rapidly through the City, through the Gate, and away into the strange grey space between the worlds. Away from the eyes of the Sea People, Éirime let her own mask slip and the tears came.

She swore, ugly words describing an obscene act, and added, "I thought he was going to kill ye both."

Geana leaned over and put her arm around Éirime, an action far too familiar for a villager to their Steward, let alone to an Immortal, a Favourite, or an Adept of the Nineteenth Rank. But Éirime leaned towards her, and rested her head on Geana's shoulder.

When they had both calmed down, and the rolling countryside of their world was blurring past, Éirime spoke.

"Did you notice how they reacted to me?"

"I saw it, my lady," she replied.

"You don't need so much of that 'my lady' now. We're nearly home."

"Among the Sea People, I saw you are a very important person. You walked past the servants running the Selection, hiding the Rank shown on your sword-hilt, but when the blue-robes saw you had come in, they wanted to come over and fawn on you."

It was true, and Éirime was impressed that Geana had noticed. Éirime knew she would not have noticed, on the day she was Selected.

Geana went on, "The Mentor recognised you, he knows you well: you have had business in the past." She waited for Éirime to affirm it, until she could see it in her face. "You're a Favourite, I guess."

"I was a Favourite, Geana. I gave it up to be the Steward of Áthaiteorann."

The implications of it were beginning to sink in.

"You have more influence at the City than Lord Miotal at Port Teorainn, or Lady Damhánalla in Áthaiminn." She thought more. "But then you're older than them, aren't you, Lady Éirime?"

"What did you call me?"

"Lady Éirime. I know you're supposed to be her Favourite. But if you were her Favourite, she'd have met you in the hall. Besides, the Mentor called you by name. He wouldn't mistake you for your Sponsor, would he?"

"You were expecting to see her in the hall?"

"I wasn't." Then she thought and corrected herself. "I was, but only because I arrived with her. I knew you were Lady Éirime before we went this morning."

"You guessed?"

"My mother told me. She swore us both to secrecy, and then she told us."

"How did she find out?"

"I don't know. But the whole village knows, my lady. I never understood that Lady Éirime would be so important in the City, but of course it makes sense. You're nearly as old as Lord Aclaí, but you were a favourite too."

"I was Selected only a few years after he was." She laughed a bitter laugh. "I replaced him as The Favourite. He never forgave me. Did you see how he looked at me as we left?"

"My lady, you know him better than I do."

"Geana, tell me what you saw." Geana saw the eagerness on Caora's face and heard it in her voice.

"I saw longing, my lady. He misses you."

Éirime laughed again, a moment of scorn. "That's not possible," Then with more sympathy she added, "Lord Aclaí has complete control of his emotions. He can make you think he is feeling anything, when he's actually feeling something completely different. His emotional control is why he has lasted as long as he has in the City, among the Favourites. He plays people, snares them with offers of friendship, and binds them to him with a pretence of love, all to advance the influence of Aclaí." She pondered, looking a little worried. "I've been trying to work out why he would give me such a look, what he's trying to achieve." Her face registered her confusion. "But I'm sure it is not good."

"You know him better than I do, my lady," Geana repeated. "I will ask Eala when she comes home."

"Lady Eala."

"Oh, of course. She's been Selected. Mammy will be so proud."

The emotions playing across Geana's face were hard to follow, she changed so quickly.

"Anyway, Geana, you must be careful. You might know who I am, but you must not give it away."

"I will be, Lady Caora," she replied. "Why Caora?"

"My mother was a shepherdess. I always wanted to be a shepherdess."

As the Flyer descended towards the village, there was a crowd waiting. They had watched the Selection in the Visions, and they already knew the story before the Flyer had landed. Flannbhuía hurried over to see. As she did so, Éirime realised that her secret was out: Geana had noticed the Mentor call her by name. But the villagers didn't seem to be reacting any differently to her. Perhaps Geana was right, and they all knew.

Geana's mother hugged her daughter, and then wanted to look at her face.

"Are you hurt?" she demanded.

"I am not hurt now, Mammy. He cut my face with the glove, and I banged my head, but the Lady made it all better on the way home."

Except for the tooth, she thought – but that is only chipped, and anyway, it's a only back one and it doesn't hurt. Her mother couldn't see it.

"What made him angry?" her mother asked.

"I think it was my name," Geana answered.

Éirime thought: maybe she was right. She had been wondering what it was that had triggered the anger in the Mentor.

"Don't be silly," her mother replied. "You are a Geancacha and so is your sister. Ye are like two peas from a pod."

Geana flinched a little: she hated the name her mother called her. But she kept it out of her voice.

"I don't think he minded my nose, Mammy; he minded the name. I don't know why, but that was it, I'm sure of it."

Éirime could see that she might be right. She sifted through all the people she had known in her centuries at the City. Had anyone else been called Geana? She couldn't think of one. She would have to ask Cathúa. Cathúa would know. But she was being asked something.

Geana was speaking. "I don't think I can go to another Selection. Do you still want me to serve you, my lady?"

"Do you want to, Geana? Yere debt is long paid."

"Of course I do, my lady."

"Are you sure? A girl of your age should be looking for a husband, surely."

She saw Geana smile, a tight movement of her mouth.

"I don't want a husband, my lady. And I have caused enough heartbreak looking." She looked back at Caora and, as she did, Caora felt that Geana could see through her eyes right into her head. But all she said was, "I would prefer to serve you, my lady. If it pleases you."

When things had calmed down in the evening, Geana followed Caora back to their room, carrying the harp and the pipes. She didn't think her mistress could carry them safely. Caora often drank a lot when she was playing and Geana missed the first warning sign, the way that she started to pick songs that were sad, that told of loneliness and lost love. They were hardly the right songs for a celebration of Eala's success, or even for the Celebration of Autumn, but it was too late by then.

The next sign was when her playing started to suffer. By then she could barely stand and Geana quickly got her out of the commons, before too many people noticed. Geana knew that Caora wanted the village to be more familiar with her, but it didn't seem to Geana that having them laugh at Caora for her drunkenness was the best way to do that. When they were back in their room, Caora sat on the bed and Geana pulled back the curtain and lit the fire.

Eventually Caora spoke. "I'm sorry you've had a disappointing day, Geana."

Geana put down the tools she was using on the fire and came over.

"I am not so sure it has been disappointing, my lady. I've learned a lot. I hope Eala is happy. I am scared for her, I think."

"Eala is strong. I think she will be all right in the end," Caora replied.

"Is the Mentor always so mean?"

"It is not right to judge him, Geana. Everything about us, all the things we take for granted, they were not true when he was a child."

Geana remembered arguing the same thing to Eala, about Caora. It seemed strange to hear Caora arguing it about someone else. Geana thought about how she felt about Caora and wondered how Caora felt about the Mentor. Caora chattered on regardless.

"We were all brought up to rely on civilisation to keep us fed, to keep us warm, and to keep us safe. Us Adepts go beyond the limits of civilisation, into the Forest, and see how the universe hates humanity. When he was a child, there were no Adepts, there was no City. There was no light, there was no Visions. Children grew up sickly, with smoke in their lungs. There were plagues and famines, and lots of people died. And there was the Forest, right by people's homes. Nobody went into the Forest to find monsters. Every single person, man, woman, child, all spent their whole time waiting for some nightmare to come out of the Forest and kill them all.

"The Mentor spent his boyhood on an island bare of wild trees, because it made the attacks less likely. He took charge of that nightmare in his own bloodthirsty way, pushed back the Forest, and created a safe space for civilisation to grow. But for all that we are civilised, he remains what he was before he made things safe: a savage. When he was a boy, killing someone because their name offended you was something that happened all the time. And he still has to protect humanity from the Forest. The Power of the Words is a very dangerous thing and the Power of Creation is worse, so he uses Words to bind the Novices to him. We promise our hearts to him and his Words make that promise impossible to break. Once it happens, your heart is bound to the Mentor, forever. It's like being in love, but also like becoming married. That is why the Sea People do not marry: we are already married, to the City."

Geana saw that Caora was shaking and she put her arm around her. It surprised her to see Caora's reaction to what she was saying: every girl in the village knew about the Sea People, about the Initiation. If we all know about it, she thought, why is it upsetting this blue-cloaked lady? But she couldn't say that.

"That is what he will do to Eala tonight?"

"Probably not tonight. There were about fifty Selected today and he will take their hearts one at a time, during the year. But Eala is strong and she has a wise head. She must be loyal to the City to be trusted with the Powers, but her wise head will keep her from being too upset." Caora's eyes were reddened and her face streaked with tears as she looked up at Geana. She brushed the tears away, like she might brush a midge off her face. "You shouldn't think that because it upsets me so much, that it upsets everyone. It doesn't. I just wasn't a good Candidate, that's all."

"Then why were you Selected?"

"I was Selected by mistake."

Geana remembered them lined up and wondered how someone could possibly be Selected by mistake. She couldn't see it.

"But Eala wasn't Selected by mistake?"

"She wasn't. Her Selection and mine were completely different. She went there expecting to be Selected and wanting it, just as you did. I didn't want it. I wasn't trying to be Selected. But I got Selected by accident. I wasn't ready for it at all."

"How could you be Selected by accident?"

"I was mistaken for a Candidate when I wasn't one. It wasn't what I wanted from my life, so it was a shock for me. It wasn't like being married for me; it was more like being raped."

"But you still ended up loyal?"

"I still ended up with my heart owned by the Mentor," Caora replied, as if she was talking about something that happened to someone else. "I'm not really loyal. I've made my excuses and come home and, when the chains on my heart tug too hard and tell me to be loyal, I play music and drink too much instead." She looked at Geana. "They were tugging hard today: look at me. I promised myself I would never see him again. But you mustn't think it is the same for Eala. She is there because she wanted to be: she will be happy."

Geana sat next to her, trying to make sense of all of this. She knew that Caora was talking so freely because she had drunk so much, but also she knew that she was drinking so much because meeting the Mentor had upset her. Looking at Caora's face and listening to her voice, Geana was not sure she was telling the truth, or the whole truth, but it was hard to tell, when Caora was so upset. She knew that something that was marriage in one place could be rape in another and that a large part of the difference was how welcome it was. She remembered Eala had compared Caora to Fleánna and she had guessed that Fleánna was raped. But that didn't mean that Eala would end up as unhappy as this.

Clinging to this thought, she asked, "So for most it is like being married?"

"It is like becoming married: like a wedding night, if you like." Geana knew that much already. "But it is not being married. The Sea People do not marry." Caora looked blearily at Geana. "I'm upsetting you with this, giving you all sorts of wrong ideas. Let me tell you about the Legend of the Wife instead."

"All right then," replied Geana, not sure what relevance this would have, but happy for Caora to distract herself.

"The Legend of the Wife says that, when the Mentor was a young man, he had a wife. If it is true, I never heard confirmation and I certainly never knew anyone who would dare ask him. The earliest chronicles of the City are in the Power Language and they are locked: but the legend says that The Wife disappeared shortly after the City was founded. She was one of us – one of the Sea People – and from his own village, of his own age. All the stories suggest that she was beautiful: love personified. Most times I've heard it told, they said she had red hair. If she were still alive she would be the highest ranking Adept, a quarter-millennium older than me or Aclaí."

"What happened to her, then?"

"If she existed, she doesn't exist now. The story says that she ran away and that he never found her. The story also says that the reason he takes hearts but never gives love back is because he misses her. Whoever made the story up was obviously not a Favourite of the Mentor: he does give love back, in his own strange, savage way."

"What does this have to do with Eala?"

"Well, Geana, the Sea People have studied the power of precognition. We know that some people sometimes see things that will happen in the future, along with things that have happened in the past, or are happening in alternative worlds and realities. For various reasons, which I'm way too drunk to explain, this thing can never be reliable. It is barely reliable enough to test, let alone reliable enough to use. But precognition does exist and many people with an aptitude for it have suggested that the Wife will return."

"What would that do to the Sea People?"

"Well, it depends what is meant by her returning. If she existed, and if he still cared about her – both sound unlikely, but they are vital elements of the story, you see – if both of those were true, given that he is the Mentor and has both the City and the Key of Creation at his disposal, then he would have found her. He hasn't found her, so either she is dead; she never existed; or he doesn't care about her anyway. But if he does care about her, she might be able to balance the inequality between him and the rest of us Sea People."

"But if she's dead, how can she return?"

"She can't return. Necromancy is a forbidden Art and there is no afterlife."

For a moment, Geana wondered what an *afterlife* could be.

"But," Caora continued, "if the precognitives have anything, I think it might be that someone might be born who is capable of taking her place. Someone strong, someone clever; someone beautiful; someone good at understanding people and dealing with emotions and someone with a wise head to anchor her when his storm takes her heart. Before I Retired, I made it a project to look out for such a person among the Candidates."

"Did you ever find them?"

"Not before I Retired. Now nobody's looking." Caora laughed. She really was drunk, laughing and crying at the same time. "But here is the funny thing. I thought it might be you."

Geana didn't know what to say. She knew Caora was drunk, but was that loosening her tongue, or was she simply rambling? She thought to herself: how could I be all those things?

"That's not right," Caora continued. "I think it might still be you. She might still be you. You might be her. I have this feeling, like a certainty inside me, that the Mentor reacted so badly to you because he recognised you as her, that you could become The Wife."

"Why me? What about Eala? She is wiser than me, you know that."

"You lead, Geana. Eala follows. You've had boyfriends, she hasn't. Nobody looks at her when you are there."

"That is the tiniest difference and maybe wisdom makes up for it. Anyway, it's not true. If you watch us closely, all it means is that I'm in the front. 'The ox doesn't guide the plough, the ploughman does.' Eala makes the important decisions. Do you remember when we offered to serve you? It wasn't my idea. Oh, I talked quickly, before people noticed, but I was trying to catch up. Eala is the leader when wise heads are called for. Perhaps Eala can do it, my lady."

She turned around, expecting a reply; but Caora was just staring at her. Her stare was glassy. She made an indistinct noise, then another.

Then she said, "I need to lie down for a moment. Keep talking, I'll listen."

She closed her eyes, and moments later, she was noisily snoring. Geana gently took Caora's boots of, and arranged her cloak and the blankets over her.

When Geana had laid down herself and blown out the lamp, she realised that the blankets were unnecessary: Caora's cloak would keep her warm without. But it was too dark, and Caora would be all right. The cloak would keep her cool, as well as warm. Eala would be sleeping under another cloak, just like Caora's. She would be warm, too. That thought comforted her.

She did not feel warm, though. It was the first night in her life that she had the bed to herself. When she had been a little girl, she had shared with Eala and her parents. Then Spideog had come and things had been a little more crowded. Even when she had begun her apprenticeship Eala had been there. She was sure she would sleep better alone, but only if she could get to sleep. With no-one to hug, she couldn't imagine how that would be possible.

She lay there, thinking about Eala and about what Caora had said. Geana knew about boys. She knew what to do to make a boy notice her. Of course she had tried to be noticed. But it didn't make any difference if boys noticed her, not Eala: she was not there. And anyway, she knew she couldn't be The Wife: what Caora had called "leadership" she knew was bossiness. Eala was better at leading because Eala was cautious whereas Geana rushed into things, and Eala was gentle when Geana was stubborn. Nobody could be bossy and be a perfect wife, certainly not to the Mentor. But she had always told herself (and never admitted to anyone else) that Eala would make the better wife of the two of them: less bossiness and more wisdom was the best thing in a wife. So it couldn't be her, but maybe it could be Eala. And if it couldn't be her, Eala would be better alone, without her being a distraction.

The Mentor had not reacted badly to her, she knew, but to her name. He had liked her, had desired her, before she told him her name. As her train of thought began to break apart into the chaos of dreaming, she wondered about the Mentor's wife: about her name. What was her name?

Geana was awake. There was darkness around her and her mind was full of fading dreams: Eala in the darkness and bad things pursuing her. She heard Caora breathing, the measured breathing of Immortality and then her voice softly singing, almost whispering Words of Power.

Sudden, soft light illuminated the room, making Geana blink. Caora got up, came over and sat by her.

"Geana, you were crying. What is it?" she asked.

"I think I was dreaming."

Geana realised her face was wet. She must have been crying. All she could remember, though, was the bad dreams.

"Do you remember what it was about?"

"It was about Eala. She was being chased by bad things, by monsters. There was a skull, with something bad in its eye-sockets."

Caora flinched at the description.

"Sounds like a bad dream to me." Caora held her.

"They will send her into the Forest, won't they? And she will be chased by bad things, won't she?"

Caora didn't really know what to say. "The Forests aren't as dangerous as they were when I was a Novice. Iolar's Forest People do most of the work these days. The Novices see some danger and they understand the relationship between the City, humanity and the Powers of the Great Principles. They need to know that. Their duty – our duty – is to keep the rest of you safe."

"But she might already be dead in the woods?"

"She won't be sent into the Forest for a month or more; not until she's had some training. Before she has training, I'll speak to her."

"How?"

"When they give her a sword, I will be able to speak to her. The hilt of the sword carries words from one of us to another. The words are cold and it's no substitute for proper speech, but she can tell us what she is doing, and tell us that she is all right." Caora thought, resolving herself before making a promise. "If she calls for help, I can go out and rescue her. I've done plenty of time in the Forest and I am Nineteenth Rank, Geana. I can help if she needs help."

"I miss her," said Geana and suddenly the tears came again, prickling at her eyes. "I'm cold without anyone to sleep with, and I can't sleep, so I lie awake and miss her."

Caora didn't reply. Instead she gently took Geana's hand, pulled her to her feet, and over to her own bed. Geana felt she was trespassing, but the bed was warm where Caora had slept.

"My lady..." she began to protest, but not too hard.

"Geana, I was born and raised in a hut smaller than your mother's house: our family lived in a space smaller than this room. I didn't sleep alone until I was Selected for the Sea People and I hated it. I always have. Now I have no family to sleep with. They are all dead, centuries dead and I'm cold too." She climbed in next to Geana, extinguished the light with a gesture. "If you would trust me, be my family, I would be happy."

Geana thought that Caora did not feel like Eala and she didn't smell like her either. Caora smelt of honeysuckle and wine, but Eala smelt of Eala and Geana. But she did trust Caora, if it was really all right to hug a blue-robe. Then she remembered that Eala was a blue-robe now, so it had better be all right. She laid her head on the pillow, next to Caora. Caora's hair was softer than Eala's, and not as ticklish, and being straight, not wavy, it didn't poke unexpectedly into face or ears. Geana kissed Caora, where her shoulder met her neck, as she would have kissed Eala. She felt Caora tense a moment, and then relax. So she relaxed too and, again, she

was dreaming.
    This time there were no nightmares.

— 6 —

Novice

The Adept spoke. "Novices, I want two groups. If ye lived in the City, on my right: if ye lived in the country, on my left."

They had followed the Mentor and his Favourites out of the Hall of Selection and up the hill upon which the City was built. Then they had turned aside at a gatehouse in the wall, remaining in the Court of the Novices, while the Mentor and his Favourites passed on up, along with the first boy that he had talked to in the Selection.

Eala followed the country group, obediently, as did maybe three-quarters of their number. The less than a dozen who were from the City were taken away and the rest were led into one of the long buildings she was to learn were dormitories. As she entered the doorway, she heard water and smelt steam and strong herbs.

The Adept directing them shouted, "Form a line this way," indicating a long trestle table.

At the table stood five servants: three women and two tall men with smooth arms, legs, and faces, like women. The servants were dressed like all the servants on the Hill: a broad strip of linen with a hole for the head, hanging down front and back, and tied with a cord at the waist to make a short tunic.

The Adept spoke again. "We will teach ye what washing is and get the beasts off ye."

The first five in the line were handled by the Adepts for a moment and then sent to the waiting servants. The servants took combs and knives and began cutting the first Novices' hair, then painting their scalps with some purple goo.

Eala didn't want her hair cut. It was hard to keep it nice, at least without Caora's help, but she liked it. The Sea People were supposed to be good looking and her hair was her nicest feature, she thought. One lad stood forward.

"I have brought no beasts with me."

97

"None of ye country children know how to wash or to take care of yerselves," their guide replied.

"I am favourite of Lord Rian," the young man asserted. "In Lord Rian's household, we do not have *beasts*. But we do have good manners."

The Adept guiding them let the rebuke go by: he knew who Lord Rian was, even if Eala didn't.

"Come here," he said.

When Lord Rian's favourite was by the Adept, the Adept held him a moment, one arm around his waist and a hand lower down, and said Words of Power. The young man flinched as he was held. Then he was let go.

"Go on then," the Adept said. "Go find the Novices from the City."

Eala saw her chance to keep her hair.

"I am favourite of the Lady Éirime."

In the silence that followed everyone was looking at her, Veterans and Novices alike. Even Rian's boy had stopped at the door, looking back. But someone must have remembered the Selection: it was only a short while ago that she had thought Geana would be killed.

"Well!" he exclaimed. "You are someone to keep an eye on, then, aren't you? Does anyone else claim to have been brought here by Immortal Rank, or even," he fixed his eye on Eala, "by Favourites?"

Nobody else volunteered.

"Well, get on with it, then."

The servants continued cutting the other Novices' hair. But the Adept looked over at Eala.

"Come here."

She went over. The Adept put an arm around her waist and the other hand he laid on her belly, below her navel. He muttered Words and, before Eala could register surprise that he didn't sing them, there was a sudden pain, like a period pain but all over in a second.

"What are you waiting for?" he said. "Off you go then."

She went out, following Rian's boy, rubbing her belly. What would she do here, away from home, if her period started? She couldn't exactly ask her mother for help. Caora had never told her what they did in the dormitories: but Caora never had periods. Rian's boy was talking. Eala looked over at him: an earnest young man with sandy-brown hair and blue eyes.

"Are you really Lady Éirime's Favourite?" he asked, awe in his voice.

"Well, I think my sister is her favourite. But she did bring me to Selection." She then admitted, "We did keep nagging her."

"Ye kept nagging someone of her Rank? Ye are braver than me."

"Lady Éirime isn't like that. Anyway, I'm Eala. What is your name?"

"I'm Lách. I thought having a Sponsor of Immortal Rank would help me get by." He still couldn't believe that Eala was sponsored by Éirime. "Anyway, what happened to your sister?"

"The Mentor didn't like her, remember? I thought he would kill us both."

"I couldn't see: I was at the other end of the hall. But I saw the sword. Did you think he would really have killed ye?"

"I think so. He was so angry."

"Do you know why?"

"I think it was her name. I want to ask Ca ... Lady Éirime when they give us swords."

"You'd just call her up? Lord Rian told me not to call, that he would be too busy to chatter to Novices."

"She didn't say I shouldn't. I think she was expecting both of us to be Selected. I know I thought that if it was just one of us, it would be my sister. But we're twins and people are always mixing us up. If people can't tell us apart, then you'd think the Mentor would have chosen both or none. But he didn't like her name." Eala realised how upset she was. "It's so stupid, that a name should make all that difference."

Lách looked scared at what she was saying.

"You think the Mentor's choice is stupid?"

Eala hastily replied, "I didn't say that. My mother's choice of name for my sister might be stupid. If she'd known, I'm sure she'd have called her something different."

"What is she called?"

"Geana," Eala replied. "Mammy called her Geancacha, and she shortens it, of course. But it could as easily have been me: we both have the same turned-up noses. Mammy says that she only chose that name when she saw us for the first time."

She could see it in Lách's face.

"What is wrong with the name?" she asked.

"Nobody ever calls a child who is going to be a Candidate by any name that sounds like *Gean.* I thought it was a superstition but, if ye both nearly got killed for it, it must be more than that. Didn't Lady Éirime tell yere mother when ye were born?"

"Lady Éirime only came to our village a couple of years ago."

"She didn't warn ye about your sister's name before bringing you? Your sister could have changed her name, if she really wanted to be Selected."

"I don't think Lady Éirime had anything to do with Selections before we nagged her to take us. I don't think she knew."

"She must have been to one Selection, at least."

"I suppose she must. But it was a long time ago. We think it was about nine hundred years."

"Of course, she's the second Oldest."

They arrived at the dormitory. It was a long, low building, half buried, so the roof and windows were just at the height of the ground outside. There were steps leading down to the doorway. Beds went either side of it, against the walls, eight on each side, with a space to walk between. All beds on the left but one had new Novices sitting on them, but only one bed on the right was occupied.

"What do ye want?" asked the Adept who was supervisor of the dormitory.

"We were sent here," said Eala. "It's because we've got Immortal Sponsors, I think."

"All right then. Were ye Closed?"

"We were," Lách replied.

"The two beds there and there," the supervisor pointed.

They went where they had been indicated. Eala had never seen a bed like these: a raised platform like a table, but with some sort of big cushion on it. On the big cushion was a piece of cloth, a blanket maybe, of a brilliant turquoise blue colour. The Adept showed her how to wrap it around her shoulders, over her head, and then he said Words of Power. The material crawled on her shoulders, around her neck, and it fitted her. The material on her skin was cool, even though it was thick as a blanket.

The supervising Adepts told them to wait and left them. Lách turned to Eala.

"Look," Lách said, "blue robes on our shoulders. We've done it, you know."

The girl on the bed the other side of Eala said, "I remember you from the Selection. Your Sponsor was Lady Éirime, wasn't she?"

She held out her hand. She looked more like Sea People: black curly hair, but blue eyes and pale skin stretched over lean cheekbones.

"I'm Rósa. What is she like, Lady Éirime? Is it true that she can sing well?"

"She sings more beautifully than anyone I've heard, even on the Visions. She sings when she's walking, she sings while she's reading, she sings all the time. Every morning she'd wake us up by singing and every night her singing is the last thing I'd hear. We've been serving her since the Month of Light last year." Eala realised that her vision was blurring. "I miss her, and I miss my sister."

Rósa looked at her and Lách saw her scorn and he spoke up for Eala.

"She's homesick, can't you see?" Lách said. "My Sponsor was either too distant and ignored me or too close and watching me: but hers was nice to her. And she expected her sister to be with her, either both rejected or both Selected. If it wasn't for her name, she probably would be."

Another boy came over from the other side of the dormitory. His skin was brown, darker than anyone Eala had ever spoken to, and his black hair was like sheep's wool.

"I saw that. My great-aunt talks about the history of the City all the time. She was talking about it even during the Selection. I thought we were going to get into trouble. She's my Sponsor: the Lady Cathúa."

Eala wiped her eyes and looked up. "What did she say?"

"She said that the problem was the name. There has never been someone Selected with a name that starts *Gean*."

"That's a superstition," said Rósa.

"It isn't. Lady Cathúa is the record-keeper for the City. She has looked at all the records of Selections, back before Lord Aclaí was Selected, back as far as when writing was invented and before. Nobody has ever been Selected who was called *Gean*. It's one of three names that have been forbidden since the City was new. She thinks that some *Gean* long ago did something dreadful."

"How could she have read records from before writing was invented?" asked Rósa, scornfully.

"The earliest records are written with Words of Power. So you have to be careful when you read them, in case you attract the attention of the Great Principles or elemental powers and the roof blows off your library or monsters come or something. She's been trying to transcribe the earliest records into the human tongue, for the last hundred years. Some are secret, locked in the House of Power by the Mentor but, even with unlocked records, she has to do it a little at a time in case she stumbles on some Formula of Words. It's dangerous work, even for an Immortal. She thinks that one day she'll find the story of the legendary *Gean*."

"I see why the Mentor asked you if you talk too much," sniffed Rósa.

"That is because Lady Cathúa always wants to ask him questions," the boy replied. "She told me."

Lách reached a hand to the boy.

"I'm Lách," he said. "I don't think you talk too much. Lord Rian says that knowledge is the most powerful thing an Adept can possess. Even the Words are knowledge, which he says proves it. I wondered if the name had to do with the Legend of the Wife."

"I'm Cabairí," the boy said, quietly.

"So even your mother thinks you talk too much?" Rósa laughed.

Cabairí ignored her and turned to Lách.

"Lady Cathúa has wondered if it has to do with the Legend of the Wife, too."

"The Legend of the Wife?" Eala asked.

But she never found out what the Legend of the Wife was, as the Adepts returned.

"Take yere robes and come along," they were told.

As they did so, they heard a bell being sounded, away at the top of the hill. Outside, Novices like them were being led out of all the dormitories, converging on the Hall of Selection. But also down the steps from the Court of the Veterans, blue-robed figures were walking. Everyone was gathering in the Hall.

Inside long tables had been set out and the raised platform at one end had seating for about a dozen people. Their Adept led them to the other end of the hall from the raised staging and suggested they took seats. They sat down: Rósa on one side of her, with Cabairí the other side. Lách sat on the other side of Rósa. Opposite the main entrance, where people were coming in, there were servants with big pots. They could smell food.

The sound of the bell stopped and everyone got to their feet. The new Novices took a moment to realise what was happening but they hastened to catch up.

"What are we waiting for?" Rósa whispered.

From the other side of her, Cabairí replied, "The bell is rung by the Chamberlain in the Court of the Favourites. When it stops, it means the Favourites are coming down with the Mentor."

Rósa was quiet after that. They waited a while, uncertain because they did not know what it would be like. Then they saw shadows at the doorway, then the Mentor entered, walking with a young man that Eala did not recognise. Immediately after them Lord Aclaí entered with the black-haired, rather chubby man that Caora had spoken to before the Selection – Rónmór, Eala remembered – and behind him someone Eala recognised as Eibheara, Miotal's grandniece. They were the start of the Favourites, a procession in pairs, with their blue cloaks. As they entered their presence seemed to fill the room and Eala could see how everyone else stiffened. The Mentor and Favourites took their place at the table on the platform. There was an empty place. The Novice who had gone up was among them and he came down and stood with the other Novices at the table with Eala and her companions. It was Rónmór's brother. Eala thought he looked a little shocked and she wanted to reassure him.

The Mentor sat down, and everyone sat down as he did. Then he spoke. "Today I have a few announcements." Eala could see that the entire hall was interested in his announcements, hoping for something. "First I will name the Candidates that were Selected. He began naming them. Eala's name was called about halfway through. He added, "One of them, Léaró, is ready for First Rank. Léaró, raise your hand so people can see you."

The boy who had come down with them raised his hand and people looked around. He looked down at the table as he sat.

The Mentor continued, "One other Rank will be granted tonight: to Rónmór, Thirteenth Rank."

The woman beside Rónmór nudged his arm, evidently congratulating him. Eala wondered if they had both been given Rank because they were brothers. And then, she couldn't help it – like a hollow feeling in her belly, she missed her sister.

"That will be all," said the Mentor and they all sat down.

Servants took food out, first to the top table, then to the tables nearest it, and so across the hall. That left the new Novices waiting a while.

During the meal Cabairí and Rósa argued and, on the other end of the table, a girl called Abhainne told her new friend Nóiníne about horses. The two of them had the Sea People look, like Rósa, and Eala thought Abhainne in particular was very pretty, the way a blue-robe ought to be. The only horse in Áthaiteorann was Ólachán's: that had been given to him by Caora. Before Caora came, Eala had never seen someone from Áthaiteorann ride a horse. Horses belonged to travellers, and to blue-robes. But Abhainne, selected that day, had lived with horses all her life. This, Eala guessed, was how Tírcapall had got its name.

Caught between Abhainne's bragging and Rósa arguing with Lách and Cabairí, she turned to Léaró. He ate in silence and Eala could see his sadness: she guessed he was wondering if he had done the right thing, just as she was. She asked him about his home and as he described it, he seemed to forget his sadness. She heard about how they followed some sort of big deer over their plains but, now it was the winter months, the Sun was falling in the sky and soon they would be living in houses made of ice, under the river of cold fire they called the Sun's Wind.

When the meal was over, Rósa and Cabairí walked back to the dormitories and Léaró and Eala followed. It was a short walk to the dormitories and they were soon by their beds, unpacking a few belongings. Eala had brought very little, warned by Caora that almost everything she needed would be provided, but some of the others had brought big bags.

Abhainne and Nóiníne unpacked dresses and compared them and their styles. Then Abhainne found a small leather bag and from it she removed statues, unglazed clay figures each about the length of her hand. She looked around at the space above her bed, then she chose a spot where the wall let one of the beams of the ceiling through. She lifted out a stone, to make a space for them, and arranged them where they could look down at her.

"Ancestors?" asked Nóiníne.

"They watch over our household. This one is my great grandmother and this one her sister, my great-aunt. The other one is the Lady of Summer. Our Lord of Winter is at home, watching over my parents."

"Oh," Nóiníne answered. "In our family we keep our ancestors in ourselves." She rubbed her belly. "Their bodies give our bodies strength. It took a long time to make Grandfather tender enough to chew, mind."

"I've heard of that," Abhainne told her. "But the Tírcapall people make images of themselves before they die."

Eala didn't understand at all. Cabairí looked at her, then at Abhainne.

"They're clay statues," he said, puzzled.

Abhainne looked around. "Well, of course," she said, rolling her eyes. "How do your ancestors look after you, wherever it is you come from?"

"My great-aunt Cathúa is in the Court of the Favourites."

"We don't all have blue-robes in our family, you know," she answered, annoyed.

"Actually, you do. Your family has you. But I wouldn't keep those where anyone can see them."

"If they can't see us, they can't watch us. Don't you know anything about the dead?"

"The dead are dead," answered Cabairí. "Peasant superstitions don't change that. You're not here to teach peasant superstitions, you are here to learn the truth."

"How can they possibly know something like that?" Abhainne asked, looking around.

Most of the others were giving Cabairí hostile looks: they clearly believed as she did. Eala didn't understand the issue but she could see that it was important to all of them. She kept her peace.

But Cabairí knew no such discretion. "In the language of Words of Power, you can talk to someone wherever they go, even deep in the Forest, if you know them well enough, if you know the right Words to name them. That is how the sword-hilts work. Do you think nobody's tried talking to someone who has died?"

"You stupid boy!" snapped Abhainne, "Nobody here believes what you are saying." And Eala could see that she was right: only herself and Léaró seemed to doubt her. Abhainne continued, "We are all watched by our ancestors and we all have our different ways of honouring them. It doesn't matter what some old woman told you, even if she is a blue-robe. Blue-robes don't know everything."

Eala saw that most of Abhainne's audience were no longer looking at her but were instead looking at the door. She looked around herself, and saw the supervisor of their dormitory standing in the doorway.

The supervisor came in and walked over to Abhainne. "This *some old woman* is Lady Cathúa?"

Abhainne looked frightened, and Eala was more frightened for her. She suspected Abhainne had not yet realised that this man could kill her without any sort of retribution.

Abhainne answered, "If blue-robes know everything, my lord, why would they still be researching?"

"Research is directed by the Mentor, girl. Death is not something researched anymore. If the City believed the dead could hear us, then attempting to talk to them would be Necromancy: a forbidden Art, and punishable by death." He allowed himself a smile. "Luckily for you, foolishness is not something we normally kill Novices for. We allow the Forest to do that." His smile vanished. "So, girl, were you practising necromancy, or foolishness?"

Abhainne was smart enough to answer, "Foolishness, my lord."

He reached up and the three little statues were in his hand. Eala saw the helplessness on her face.

"Shall we teach you some wisdom, then?"

Abhainne looked as if she would cry.

"It would be a kindness, my lord," she answered.

He dropped the three statues on the floor. Two of them cracked across, and she made a tiny noise. He watched her face as he put his foot on them and, as he did, a shining boot appeared on his foot, part of his Metal armour. He turned the ball of his foot slightly as he ground them.

"Now, all of ye, get to sleep. I don't want to hear any of ye again tonight."

With that he left, his armoured foot tapping on the stones. They all lay down on their beds and Abhainne put the hood over her head and huddled up.

In the morning, they got up, and an Adept called to guide them to the first of their lessons. They were shown into a hall, with benches arranged around, stepped up towards the back so that everyone could see. Eala sat with Rósa on one side and Cabairí on the other. Rósa seemed to want to be her friend but Cabairí, true to his name, would not stop his commentary on the place.

Then the Adept looked out of the door, then back to them, and spoke.

"Get on yere feet, ye miserable lot! The Lord Aclaí is coming to speak to ye. He's the oldest and highest ranking in our Order and if anyone has good advice to help ye survive, it is him. So pay attention and be respectful."

They got up and stood. Eala knew who Lord Aclaí was, of course. She had seen how Caora had seemed to admire him at their Selection but also seemed to fear him. Looking around, Eala could see that she was not the only one in the room who knew who he was. More than half of them had reacted to the name and, of the rest, most of them could sense the atmosphere in the room had changed.

Three senior Adepts came in. The first was a short man, with laugh-lines on his face but a serious expression, with eyes that looked everywhere, and hair as bright red as her mother's. His sword had the crystal in the hilt that showed he was Immortal: the two bands below it showed he was of Seventeenth Rank. The next two Eala recognised as Eibheara, Miotal's grandniece and behind her, big enough to make her look like a little girl, was Lord Aclaí.

He looked them over. Nobody else in the room dared to speak. Eala tried to read his expressions, his body language. She could see he was thinking of violence, of death but, looking closer, she could see that this was a mask. Beneath it he was concerned and something else too. He was searching for something.

"I am Aclaí. I was Selected for the Two Hundred and Forty Sixth Year, over eight hundred years ago. I sat in this room then, with twenty-two other children much like ye."

Eala didn't think of herself as a child but, compared to Aclaí, she supposed she must be.

"All the rest of them are dead. Only three of us were still alive to see the next Selection. Today, the odds are a bit better than that but, of the forty-nine of ye, less than a dozen are likely to survive to next year's Selection." He stopped and seemed to collect his thoughts. "There is only one Year where every single Candidate survived to the next Selection. It has only happened once and I don't believe it will ever happen again." Then he looked at them, again, searching for an answer. "If any of ye think you know what ye are doing here, and why ye have been Selected, raise a hand."

Many hands went up. Eala was trying to remember what Caora had said about it. She knew she had been told, but she couldn't remember. So she kept her hand down until it came back to her.

Aclaí pointed at a rather keen girl on the front row.

"What is your answer?" he asked.

"We are here to learn the Words of Power, to become powerful."

"That is the answer I expected. Most of ye have come here from yere parents' homes and yere parents and family do things for ye without expecting ye to pay them back. Nobody else in the world will do things for ye without a good reason. They won't teach ye Words of Power because they want ye to be powerful. They will teach ye Words of Power in exchange for yere service, yere obedience. The Mentor will take yere obedience from ye, soon enough. Whatever Power ye will attain – and given how short most of yere lives will be, most of ye will attain very little – whatever Power ye attain will be bought at a high price. If any of the rest of ye were going to give this answer, put yere hands down. I want hands up for those with another answer."

Most of the hands went down. There were about three left, including that boy, Léaró. Aclaí turned to him.

"What do you think we are here for?"

"We are here for the Mentor, to satisfy his whims," he replied.

Eala saw Léaró's face redden, then saw that he fought to control his tears again. Aclaí bent over him, said something to him very quietly and placed a hand on his shoulder. Eala was not sure what he had said, but she could see that it was not frightening, it was reassuring. In that unguarded moment, she could see that other feeling, that concern, and still that he was looking for something.

Then he stood up, impatiently.

"We are all at the Mentor's command: but the Mentor's rule gives us the structure to achieve what we are here for. What is that?" He looked around. There were no hands up. "Does nobody know? Many of ye have been Sponsored here, guided and groomed by Adepts. Ye don't know why ye are here?"

And Eala remembered and raised her hand.

"You, red-hair," Aclaí said, pointing at her. "What are we doing here?"

"My Sponsor said that the Sea People's work is mostly keeping the monsters of the Forest away from humanity, Lord Aclaí."

"Who is your Sponsor?"

"She calls herself Caora, Lord Aclaí. She is the Steward of Áthaiteorann."

"Do you know what name her mother called her?"

"I know what they call her here in the City, my lord. But I never met her mother."

"You didn't. I am the only other person living who did. What is your name, child?"

She wasn't going to argue with what he called her, even if she was a grown woman back home.

"I am Eala," she answered.

He looked at the rest of them.

"Eala here has been told the reason. The City is here to teach Adepts to keep the monsters out. The Universe is full of monsters that want to destroy humanity and they come to us through the Forest. When I was yere age, the only thing to stop the monsters was us. Now, we have created monsters of our own, to protect humankind. Our monsters, the Forest People, keep us safe, mostly. But we are still needed to guide and lead the Forest People and that is what ye will do. Ye will go into the Forest, to find the monsters there and to prevent them from attacking humanity. It is dangerous work and most of ye will meet a violent end at the hands of these monsters. We can heal almost anything, if enough of yere patrol survives to bring ye home, but raising the dead is necromancy, which is a forbidden Art: when ye are dead, that is the end of ye."

He looked around to see if they understood. The frightened faces told him that they did.

"Most of ye will have thought the City is a place of power, both the Words of Power and power over men. It is these things, but first ye need to survive it. If ye are still with us this time next year, ye will have a chance to start to learn more. After a few years, yere Forest Service will take up less of yere time.

"A lot of us, when we have attained the Eighth Rank and so completed the Forest Service, simply Retire at that point. Only a few try for high Rank. If ye are smart, pay attention to yere lessons and get some luck, ye might one day obtain Sixteenth Rank. Perhaps one of ye will obtain Sixteenth Rank before ye die of old age. One lifetime is barely enough. If ye do, almost every Sixteenth Rank Retires within a ten-year of being given the Rank. Many don't even wait a ten-day. Most of the Veteran Ranks are hoping to learn Immortality, so they can win back the life that they gave up to come here. When they Retire, they end up like Eala's Sponsor: Adept in some place far away from the City, almost indistinguishable from the low-rank Retirees.

"There are a few of us that don't want to win back some former life. For some of us our life is the City and the Mentor and that is all we want. We are very few. Foscúil and Eibheara here are two, I am another. I am not telling ye it is a good thing for the City to be yere life but for us it is true and we are some of the highest Ranks you will meet.

"Perhaps one of ye will be chosen to be one of the Favourites. You don't choose to be a Favourite, you don't win it like a Rank. It is simply something that happens and you have to accept it and the consequences of it. Grant of this is completely up to the Mentor. Only one Favourite has ever Retired. She is the second highest Rank, and the second Oldest. Don't expect to emulate her," he warned, looking at Eala, "even if you are Sponsored by her.

"What I am saying is that yere place in the City is dangerous; ye have to pay attention and learn if ye are going to survive; after a few years most of ye will go home but, if ye want to try Immortality, ye will probably die here in the City, of old age. This is all the life of the Sea People has been for as long as I have been alive and of course it will go on like this for many years more.

"That will be all. Foscúil here will take ye to the Hall of Swords, where ye will learn the craft most likely to save yere life. It is not the Power of Words, whatever ye might think. Eala and Léaró, wait behind."

Foscúil led the others from the room. Eibheara and the dormitory leaders remained behind, until Aclaí turned to them.

"That will be all," he said.

The dormitory leaders went. Eibheara seemed about to wait, but he continued to look at her, and she went. He turned to Eala.

"Did Éirime tell you why she wanted you to be Selected?"

"I don't think she wanted me to come to Selection, my lord."

Eala was embarrassed. She had started to realise that all Caora's warnings were done for a good reason.

"So why did she bring you? Surely she saw something in you?"

"We nagged her, my lord. My sister wouldn't talk about anything else."

"Your sister with the unfortunate name?"

"Geana, my lord."

"For your own good, Eala, do not speak her name here. You will have a hard enough time surviving the first year anyway, without provoking the Mentor to kill you."

"As you wish, my lord. It was my sister with the unfortunate name that Lady ... Éirime was bringing really. I came along but she is the better leader, or whatever else it is that Lady Éirime saw." Eala could see the disappointment in Lord Aclaí's face. "I don't even know if she saw anything in my sister, Lord Aclaí. She warned us both not to come but she warned me more; that might be simply because she didn't believe that ..." she had almost said her name again, "... that my sister would listen."

"Then I won't keep you, Eala." She could see the disappointment on his face, still. "Off you go, the Hall of Swords is waiting."

The Novices filed into the room. At the front of the room, there was a tapestry hung up, with the forty-nine symbols of speech on it. Eala sat towards the front, since she was on familiar ground here: she had already learned them.

The teacher banged his table, and they all paid attention. "Today ye learn how to write. These forty-nine pictures are what ye use to write. We'll start with yere names. Who is first?"

Eala met his eye: she had been exchanging notes with Geana and Caora all summer. He pointed at her. "Freckles, what is your name?"

"Eala," she replied. "Bird for Ay, hand for L, and ocean for Ah."

"We have an expert, Novices. That makes my life easy. I will come and sit on your chair and you can stand here and explain it to the rest of us."

Again Eala realised she had drawn too much attention to herself. But Caora had warned her that she should accept challenges as far as possible without being disrespectful. They were there to learn leadership. She got up and stood next to him at the front of the lecture room.

"May I have your pointer, teacher?" she asked him.

He seemed surprised, but he shrugged and gave her the pointer, then sat down. She turned to face them, while he watched, disinterestedly.

"Writing is quite easy, really," she told them. "You just draw the pictures that sound like the thing you are trying to write. There are only a few hard bits: remembering to use a the-circle for Uh; an eye-on-the-peak for Rd; and remembering which pictures to use. You need an Old City accent to remember that the river is Aw. But today it's easy, because the pictures are up here. Let's try some." She pointed at the river. "What is this picture of?"

A few voices answered, "A river."

"And what sound does a river start with?"

Some bright spark piped up, "Aw!" in a clear City accent, and the others chimed in.

"So," she asked "how many of ye have names that start with an Aw?" she asked. Then she remembered one. "Abhainne," she said, putting a little of the City into her accent, "you have your first sound." She pointed at the pictures next to it. "And here is the ocean, and here is a bird." She looked back, to see that they understood. Then she pointed to the river, the ocean, the bird. "Aw, Ah, Ay," she said, putting the City into her accent so they could hear more clearly.

She moved on to a more easy sound, so she pointed at another picture. "What is this?" she asked.

"It's a fire," they replied, easily.

"What sound does it start with?"

Most replied Tch but she heard some indistinct sounds and even a Th from a few.

So she pointed them at the picture of the wave and asked them about that sound. Most of them realised that the Tch of a fire and the Th of a wave were different, although she saw that the ones who were struggling were the ones that had come a long way to the City and had strong accents. She realised they were trying to learn to speak a new language at the same time as learning to write. That must be hard, she realised, and she got a glimpse then of the uncomfortable fact that she wasn't the most intelligent in her year-cohort. Never mind, she thought.

"Who has a name that starts with Tch, and who has a name that starts with Th?"

Some had. Now she was making progress.

So she selected the next two pictures together: the Gu-for-goose that started Geana's name, and the Gw-for-spear that might be confused with it. And that is how she did it, slowly, watching who understood and who did not. Her practice with Geana at spotting what people were thinking turned out to be very useful: she soon had them all able to write their own names. The teacher let her continue while he wandered around, looking at their writings and suggesting corrections. She had most of them reciting the song that Caora had taught her to learn the pictures when they heard the sound of the horn being blown outside, to end the morning lectures and call them to eat.

The proper teacher stood up.

"Learn to draw yere names before the next lecture, not forgetting that all creatures face towards the start of the line. If ye have time, ye can learn some of these pictures: this tapestry is always in this room. Ye don't have to use Freckles' strange song if ye think it is too much like a nursery rhyme for Sea People to sing. Off ye go." They all started to get up and, in the noise, the teacher looked down at Eala. "Not you, Eala. I want to talk with you."

Eala waited as they filed out. Now she was in trouble again. She pushed the pointer back at the teacher, aware of the likelihood that he would beat her with it. She tried not to let her fear show, looking up at him and smiling at him in what she hoped would be a friendly but respectful way. Caora had taught her that if she cowered, it would make things much worse. The teacher took the pointer and the way he held it made her more scared.

"Eala, by rights I should put you over this bench and give your bottom a beating that would make you weep like a child." He waited a half-second to see if she would react and she tried very hard not to. "I don't think I'm going to, though, even though I really ought to. Do you know why?"

"I don't," she replied.

"The first reason is because you just about avoided arrogance. You came very close but you didn't quite get there. The second reason is because you really are a good teacher, especially for some country girl who only arrived at the City two days ago. You are a good teacher because you are a good leader, albeit one who seems to lead with far too little dignity." He chuckled in his chest. "Nursery rhymes to learn the letters?" He shrugged. "It's also worth knowing who taught you to write, of course: your Sponsor might be someone important. Who is he?"

"She is the Lady Éirime," said Eala, flinching inside as she remembered the effect this news had on everyone else she had told.

The teacher slapped his leg with the pointer, chuckling more.

"I see that your Sponsor certainly might be someone important. Did she used to beat you? Did she tell you that you would be beaten here?"

"She didn't beat us at all. My father had done enough of that when we were young." Eala was embarrassed and, with her fair skin, it showed in the pink of her cheeks. "But she told me that I would be beaten."

"And so you will, I'm sure, especially if you behave like that in all your lectures."

"I'm sorry," she offered, deliberately looking down, "I didn't mean to be bad. Ca ... Lady Éirime told me that the Sea People wanted to train leaders and that leaders should step forward and lead. She said that was the second most important thing I should remember."

"Well, that's advice coming from one of the oldest and highest-Ranked of the Mentor's Favourites. You'd do well to follow it, if you want to follow in her footsteps. But I think, pretty as you are, you will follow her advice walking, not sitting down. I must be soft, passing up an opportunity to dispense such a richly deserved punishment."

Eala could see that he didn't want to hurt her because he was angry with her but because he would enjoy it. Looking at him, quickly, when he looked away from her eyes, she saw the explanation, not in his head or shoulders, or his eyes, but distorting the clothes over his lap. She thought of Fleánna and suddenly she realised that the heat of her embarrassment was spreading over her face and neck, unstoppable. He wanted to beat her because he wanted to rape her. She didn't know if he was allowed to, or if he would dare, and not knowing made her far more frightened than she was of the beating.

The teacher spoke again: "I guess if Lady Éirime is your Sponsor that explains the song. Anyway, what was the most important thing she taught you?"

"She told me that I should always do what I knew to be right, no matter how dangerous or difficult that might be," Eala replied, hoping that if she could steer the conversation away, she might avoid the danger.

"That is also advice from the second Oldest, so I wouldn't argue with it," he replied, although she could hear that he didn't think much of it at all. "Anyway, Eala, you needn't be afraid I'm going to beat and rape you, however much fun it might be. I'm teasing you, because I like to see you blush, and I like your courage. You don't avert your eyes and the courage in your eyes reminds me of the Mentor. So I'm going to do you a favour instead and hope you remember who did it for you."

"What favour?" she asked.

"The fellow who schedules the Mentor's evenings is a friend of mine. I'm going to speak to him and get you in the Mentor's bedchamber soon. Since you're not a City girl, chances are you wouldn't be scheduled until next summer and by then you might be dead. When I get you in I'll ask again and you'll not mind so much." He stared at her, and she could feel his eyes appraising her body. "With a bit of luck and enough of that sort of look, you might even be a favourite."

"How will that help you?" Eala asked. "Chances are I'll not survive until the summer anyway, if the odds we've been told are right."

"You might still die in the Forest, Eala, but Favourites don't tend to end up doing the most dangerous errands. Do you really think all errands are as dangerous as each other or that they are assigned randomly?"

She hadn't thought of that at all but, of course, it made sense, in the strange logic she was learning applied here. "But why would it matter to you?"

"I might want a favour in the future."

"Just ask, then. I –" Eala stopped.

She was feeling an odd tingling sensation, and it seemed to be coming from her sword. She looked at it. The hilt was undecorated as she was not Initiated but there was a pattern of light around it. The pattern suggested the jewel in a claw mount, and below it, she could see four bands of green.

"What?" she wondered.

"It is your sword hilt," the teacher explained. "Someone is trying to get your attention."

"Sword hilt?"

"They're Nineteenth Rank," he explained. Then he added, "Put your hand on the hilt," as if explaining to a small child. "But first remember I'm going to do you a favour." And he gathered the pointer and left.

"I'd like to eat lunch in my room," Caora told Beatha. "I'll come down afterwards and play for your guests but there's something I have to do first."

"My lady, do whatever you wish. Shall I bring something up for you?"

Caora looked over at Geana. "Would you bring..?"

"Of course, my lady," Geana smiled.

Caora took her hand a moment, interlaced their fingers and squeezed them. Then she walked away. Beatha watched Caora go and then turned back to the cooking.

"Are you sure you know what you are doing?" she asked.

"What do you mean?" Geana replied.

"You know what I mean, Geana," Beatha said. "What would your mother say?"

Geana laughed. "She'd be relieved. Lady Caora isn't going to make me pregnant, is she?"

Beatha shook her head: Geana could see the disapproval on her face.

"If Lady Caora wanted you to be pregnant, she could sing a song and you'd have twins."

"And what is wrong with twins?"

"I have the answer in front of me, Geana. I don't know how your poor mother copes."

"Our mother is proud of us, Beatha."

"I'm sure she is. And I'm sure she's sick with worry. You've always played with fire in your relationships, with that no-good Ordóg and everything else, but Lady Caora is far more dangerous than you can imagine." She turned back to the pot, and stirred it. "And your sensible sister away at the City." She ladled out stew for Geana and Caora, and handed it over. "Your mother might be proud but I don't know how she sleeps at night."

"We're not children anymore, Mistress Beatha," Geana answered, as she left.

If there was a reply, she didn't hear it.

Caora was in the room, sitting on their bed. One hand rested on the hilt of her sword, which was between her knees, still in the scabbard. Between her fingers, Geana could see some sort of glow, some phosphorescence, covering the jewel-in-claw that made up the hilt.

Geana put down the bowls by the bed. Caora looked up.

"Geana," she said, "sit by me."

When Geana sat, Caora took her hand and placed it carefully on the sword-hilt, before she took her own away.

are you still there

Geana nearly dropped the sword.

"What? Who is that?" she asked.

lady caora The words had no inflection, no tone or voice at all.

"I'm Lady Caora's ... I'm her ..." Then Geana remembered the warnings about telling strangers she was an apprentice. "I'm her maidservant," she offered.

sister

"Eala? Is that you? I can't hear anything, there's just the words."

it is a horrible way to talk

"It is. I can't hear your voice at all."

are you well

"I am. I'm still serving Caora. People haven't stopped talking about you."

theres not much to say

"Have you learned any mighty Formula of Words?"

nothing at all came the expressionless answer. *i have learned to hold a sword and some things about words of power but not one formula*

"It sounds very exciting."

then it sounds far better than it is

"Sister? Are you homesick?"

i am came the empty words. *but there will be excitement soon i expect*

"When they send you into the Forest?" She looked over, anxiously, at Caora.

lady caora has promised to come out and rescue me if i need it

"That's good." She glanced over. "Will you call often? I want to hear all your news."

i will try answered the words. *the city is full of rules and one rule is that novices do not bother immortals*

Geana wondered at the significance of that, then realised.

"But Lady Caora is our friend."

she is also second oldest and third in rank after lord aclaí and the mentor

"She said that you should call as much as you want."

Geana looked over, Caora was silently agreeing.

its hard sister came the reply *i remember that caora is like aclaí or foscúil or even the mentor*

"Have you met them?"

lord aclaí came and spoke to us after selection but the mentor i have not spoken to since you did

"What is Lord Aclaí like?" Geana asked. Then, as she saw Caora's face, she regretted it.

he is big and scary was the answer *but i believe he is secretly a good man*

"I believe so too," Geana agreed.

i should go i am missing lunch

"All right. I love you, sister. My lady."

i love you too

Then Geana noticed that the sensation of the sword-hilt under her hand seemed to change and she knew the magic had gone. She looked up at Caora, then took her in her arms.

"Thank you," she said.

"You're welcome," Caora whispered back. "I promised we would talk when she got her sword."

"You did, my lady. But I didn't know I would be able to talk to her too."

Rónmór was talking but the alien thoughts cut across everything. *We need to talk*, the thoughts came, unbidden. He looked at his friend and the friend looked back at him.

"Is it your sword-hilt?" he asked, glancing down. "I should..."

"Not exactly," Rónmór explained. "But I have to go. I will see what I can do about this friend of yours."

"Don't forget."

"I won't. But I have to go."

Rónmór turned away and hurried up the Hill to his own room, in the Court of the Favourites. He walked in, shutting the doors behind him and sat down. I'm here, he thought.

It's her, the other thought answered. *She is the one.*

So what do I do? Other than my duties, of course?

She will need your protection. I have shown you the shadows at the heart of the City.

Everyone needs protection from that, he thought. Nobody knew and, the way things were taught at the City, none would ever know. What was special about one Novice?

I told you about the Mentor's decisions. They will be around her.

"Decisions?" he said out loud.

She will need your support and protection, until he decides if she should be a friend or an enemy.

Then Rónmór's suspicions of his experiment came flooding up. He didn't want someone to be the Mentor's enemy. What if they hurt the Mentor? If she can hurt the Mentor, he thought, it would be better to cut her head off now.

How can she choose to be his enemy when she is Initiated? came the answering thought.

Very well, he thought to himself and his strange ally. I will have her Initiated, and then she cannot be his enemy.

Initiation

At the evening meal, after the Mentor had finished his announcements and began eating, Rónmór came down from the top table and over to where Eala, Rósa, Lách and Léaró were eating. Léaró looked up at him and then put his head down.

Rósa hissed at Léaró, "Who is that?"

"That is Rónmór," said Léaró. "Thirteenth Rank. He is in charge of the Mentor's chambers. He's my brother. I really don't want to talk to him."

But Rónmór didn't want to talk to Léaró. He looked straight at Eala.

"Are you Eala?" he asked.

"I am."

"Stail mentioned you to me. Come with me."

Eala got up, wondering who Stail was. She picked up the bread she had been eating. She had missed lunch: even if she had to leave the pottage, she wasn't going to be hungry. She then realised that Stail must be the writing teacher. Over her shoulder, she saw Rósa give her a look of pure jealousy. But Léaró would not look at her. Rónmór led her up, into the Court of the Veterans.

As they went through the gate, he spoke.

"You're pretty, you know. You don't need to be nervous. It'll be all right." Eala couldn't think of any answer. "Come on," he said, "smile, at least."

"I'm sorry," Eala replied. "My Sponsor didn't do well at Initiation, I think: every time she talks about it, I can see bad memories. She says she was not suited to it. Her problems might not affect me, but I still feel, well, apprehensive."

She couldn't say scared. Caora had warned her not to show fear.

"You have nothing to worry about," he said, smiling at her. "There can't have been much wrong with her Initiation: Lady Éirime was Favourite a very long time. The Mentor still speaks of her with nothing but fondness."

They were entering the Court of the Immortals, going higher up the hill that the heart of the City was built on. Eala could see the whole City behind her, light and shadows in the twilight, the first of the street-lamps already lit and, behind it all, the sea. She still didn't know what to say and all she had to go with her confusion was the advice to be brave and to appear cheerful. She breathed deeply, as she had watched Caora do so many times, and it did make her calm, she found. From the Court of the Immortals, they went up into the Court of the Favourites. Eala looked around at the tall pyramid of the House of Power, at the Mentor's House on the top of the hill and at the other cottages, about the size of her mother's house but each identical with the others, in a circle around the fountain. But the building to which Rónmór led her was behind these – a larger construction, of sun-baked bricks.

"Let's find you something to wear," he said, as he led her in.

She had been told that, if the Mentor liked her, things would be easier.

In the building was a servant, tall and soft like they all were and wearing the same uniform. All around, on racks on the walls, there were brightly coloured clothes.

"Hello, pretty lady," the servant greeted her with a child-like voice. "I think you need green silk to match your eyes." The servant stood up and found a silk dress among the clothes hung up. "How do you like this, my lady?"

It was a shiny material and Eala liked it very much, although it seemed more the length for a comfortable shirt than a proper dress. She took it but she turned away to put it on, wrapping her cloak around herself to hide from Rónmór and the servant. A moment later and she had put it on, but she was shy of how much of her legs it showed. It didn't seem to fit right on her shoulders and breasts, either.

Rónmór spoke Words and touched the dress at the neckline. Again she felt that strange crawling on the material, as it shifted across her. Now it fitted. The servant brought her a mirror, a sheet of shining Metal, and showed her. The mirror was slightly tilted, closer to her feet than to her head, so that she appeared to be looking up at herself, tilted at an angle away from her. She saw herself looking pretty, but she realised the dress was much too short. It didn't cover her legs: it didn't even reach them, and looking like that, she was glad that at the City they had been given underwear.

"Should it be this short?" she asked.

"That is perfect," said the servant. He turned to Rónmór. "Don't you think so, my lord?"

"It is good. Do you have anything that matches for her feet and for her hair?"

The servant found a ribbon, stretched it over her forehead and down behind her ears to the back of her neck. The servant's hands were soft, like her mother's or sister's. Then came sandals of white leather, which she put on herself, unwilling to have anyone bend down in front of her. There were earrings and a pendant necklace, with large, dark emeralds suspended from gold wire. Looking in the mirror that was leaning on the wall, she could see that for once, if you ignored the freckles on her nose, she almost looked like a pretty woman. She wished that they could see her like this in Athaiteorainn but she would have liked the dress to be a little longer.

Then the servant leaned over her, and sniffed.

"Lavender," the servant said, and turned away to find some.

Eala asked, "Do you have honeysuckle?

The servant turned. "Honeysuckle, my lady?"

"It is traditional in my village."

"Let me see."

After some rummaging in a chest, a small bottle was found. Eala picked up the scent as the stopper was removed.

"Thank you," she replied.

She took it and began dabbing the strong perfume here and there. When she was done, she handed back the bottle and Rónmór led her to the Mentor's chambers.

"One last thing," he said. "Don't fall asleep in the Mentor's room. Leave before you fall asleep. Nobody is permitted to sleep in his room, not ever."

And with that, he left her there.

She sat on the bed, waiting. The room was richly furnished, with tapestries on the walls, wood on the ceiling, a fire on the hearth-stone. Brackets on the frame and door were ready to receive bars. She could not see the bars but the brackets were made of Metal. The bed sheets were silk, a rich feeling against her legs as she sat there. Near the door there was a harp: did the Mentor play? That was the only thing in the room that might have been personal.

But the tapestries depicted scenes of young men and women wearing little or no clothing. Some of them were having sex. By the bed was a table, with the pitcher of water and bowl she might have expected, washcloths, towels, and a vase of yellow chrysanthemums. But also she saw a goad, like the drovers might use on cattle, but of skilfully braided leather, oiled. She felt sure it would be used on her and she hoped she would be brave enough.

She realised how old this building was, that Caora must have sat here once, and she looked back at the harp. Caora had been hurt because she had cowered, she always said. She remembered her conversation with Stail, before the midday meal, and realised that the lesson had proved to her that Caora was right: if she led and avoided arrogance, she could also avoid a lot of hurt. But she needed to be calm.

She went over to the harp and sat on the stool by it. Caora had taught her and Geana to play, although of course they were never going to be as talented as their teacher. Still, playing calmed her nerves, if only because she had to concentrate to avoid mistakes. She had to concentrate so hard, she could forget that she was in the Mentor's bedroom, that her dress was too short and that the goad was on the table beside the bed.

The door opened and the Mentor came in. She stopped playing.

"Carry on," he said, and sat on the bed.

She started again, at the beginning of the verse. It was a slow dance: she would never be able to attempt something like "The Hare in the Spring" and she wasn't going to try in front of such an audience. She was aware that the harp was between her knees and, with a dress that short, she had no dignity at all. The Mentor watched her, seemingly enjoying her playing. She didn't think she was that good.

When she was done, he spoke again.

"Scared?" he asked.

"A little, Mentor." She hoped it didn't show too much. "I don't know if I will please you: I don't really have any experience to help me here."

"You're Éirime's girl, aren't you?"

"She is my Sponsor, Mentor."

"Did she tell you anything about Initiation?"

"She said I should try to show leadership and initiative and be brave."

"Come over here and sit by me," he said.

She came over and, as she got close, she realised that although he was wearing the blue cloak, he was wearing little else beside. She could also see he was aroused by her. He made space for her, beside him, next to the table.

"It's all right," he said, "I won't hurt you."

She glanced at the goad, forgetting to check his eyes before.

He noticed, and added, "They always put out the same things. Sometimes Novices need it. I don't think you will, Eala, not tonight."

"I'm not used to that, Mentor. At home, children are normally punished by their fathers, but my mother is a widow and we have no father. We try to be good anyway."

"I'm sure you do. Did Éirime teach you to be afraid of Initiation?"

"She never told me there was anything to be afraid of, Mentor. She was afraid of it, but she told me that it was because she was a bad Novice, not because there was anything for me to be afraid of."

The Mentor asked, "But?"

"But what, Mentor?"

"You are only telling me half."

"I suppose she's only experienced her own Initiation, Mentor, so she still has doubts. She keeps saying she was a bad Novice. Was she?"

"She is one of my favourites and, since she has left, I miss her." Looking at him, Eala could see that he did and that surprised her. "We didn't start well. The year she was Selected, the standard of Candidates was very bad, and it made me angry. She didn't get to know me at the best of times, I'm afraid." He looked at her, looking in her eyes. "I don't want to make the same mistake with you."

Eala thought of her sister, lying on the floor of the Selection Hall, bleeding, and of the sword over their heads.

"She says she made mistakes, Mentor. I will try not to make the same mistakes."

"What mistakes?"

"I will try to learn what you have to teach, to become a leader."

"Oh," the Mentor replied, thinking. Then he said, "I have heard that there is a tradition in your village, a song that a young woman sings when she is newly married."

"There is, Mentor."

"Can you play it on the harp?"

"I haven't been taught to play it. I could sing it, any girl from my village could, but my playing would not be good at all."

"Will you try?"

"If you will forgive me, I will. I have never tried to play it before."

Eala got up to fetch the harp and, as she did so, she remembered Caora not playing the song at Sneachta's wedding. The fear was rising again. She brought the harp over and sat by it on the bed. She thought about the notes, and had a go at playing. She picked out the melody, fumbling for a moment, then she thought she had it. It would be easier to pick out chords and let her voice do the work. As she did so, the Mentor laid his hand on her bare thigh and slipped his fingers inwards and upwards. She found it distracting, but not unexpected, and she tried to concentrate on the playing and ignore the heat she could feel on her face. His hand was touching her, her clothing pulled aside, his thumb somewhere intimate and his fingertip below, somewhere worse. She concentrated on the strings.

"Now sing it, Eala."

She began to sing, although it was hard to sing while playing a tune she had never played before. She wished she had practiced; she could have guessed that he might ask her to sing this, but she hadn't known there would be a harp in his room. As she started the second verse, he whispered Words of Power and suddenly her body was flooded with sensation, pleasure so strong it shocked her like pain, radiating from the two places where he was touching her. Her breath was knocked out of her and her singing stopped. With his other hand he caught her neck and head as she slumped backwards, laid her gently back on the bed, all the while letting the savage, spasming feelings course from his fingertips into her body, blurring her vision and taking away her mind.

When he could see that she couldn't sing like that, he moved the harp aside with his free hand, lifted her knees, and took possession of her body there on the edge of the bed. He looked down at her, her face red and damp, her nose and mouth clutching for breath, her hair sticking to her forehead, and her eyes closed.

"Open your eyes, Eala," he said, "look at me".

Her pupils were wide, her eyes black with a tiny green rim, not focusing properly. He made sure she could see him before letting go of her and of himself.

When he was done, he let her catch her breath, seeing the emotions playing on her face. She was clearly his: those Words of Power always worked. But what to do with her next? He was aware that whatever he did with her, Éirime would hear.

She spoke: her voice sounded like she would cry, but she didn't. The quavering might just be the result of what he had done to her.

"I am sorry I didn't finish the song, Mentor."

"That is all right. You can finish it another night. You go to bed now. You have a lot to learn in the morning."

"As you wish, Mentor."

She tried to get up, staggered, but steadied herself. She took the harp back to the corner of the room, then picked up her cloak, and wrapped it around herself. She couldn't see the missing piece of clothing anywhere and her dress was certainly too short without it. She went to the door, watching him for signs of approval as she did. She opened it and stepped into the doorway.

"Thank you, Mentor," she said.

"For what?"

"For being kind."

"Go to bed," he told her.

She shut the door behind her and walked out. Rónmór was waiting.

"Is everything all right?" he asked.

"I think so. He's not angry, if that's what you mean."

She heard her own voice, still shaking.

"That's good. Go get some rest," he told her.

"Good night, Rónmór," she said, "thank you." She wondered why she wanted everyone to like her tonight.

"Good night, Eala."

She walked out into the night, cool on her face and calves. She felt soiled, dirty, and she wished she knew Caora's Words of Freshness. As she walked down through the Court of the Immortals, she hoped her hood would cover her embarrassment and she tried to walk in a dignified way, hoping nobody would notice her.

When she got back to the dormitories, the others were in bed. She found her way to her own bed, found the bowl and pitcher, and tried to clean herself up in the darkness. She dressed quickly and climbed into bed. She thought everyone was asleep, but as she pulled her cloak over her, she heard Rósa.

"Well, what happened?" she whispered.

She didn't want to talk.

"I was Initiated by the Mentor," she whispered back, hoping the whole dormitory couldn't hear.

She looked over at Rósa and saw her eyes staring back, gleaming in the darkness. Rósa was scared.

"Look," Eala whispered, "it's not bad. It's a bit frightening, but it doesn't really hurt or anything."

Eala felt uncomfortable at the lies. She saw Rósa looking reassured.

"It feels nice, in a scary sort of way," she continued. "But it's also very tiring and I really need to sleep."

"All right," Rósa whispered back, "but you have to tell me everything in the morning."

"Good night, Rósa."

"Good night, Eala."

She hid her face in the hood of the cloak and thought about what she felt. She felt upset and, as she thought of it, she felt her eyes flood. But what had upset her? It wasn't what he had done to her. That was embarrassing, but she was a woman now, not a girl: it was time she grew up a bit. The thing that was hurting her was how quickly he had dismissed her when he was done. If she had not stopped singing, would he have let her stay? She remembered the scent of him, and the way his face looked like a boy, even if he was a thousand years old. She remembered how, when it was happening, she had seen his eyes and wondered if he would weep, if she would comfort him. And, oddly, she had noticed that his own nose was lightly dusted with freckles.

She knew he wouldn't have let her stay. She wanted to sleep with him, not here in this dormitory, in an empty bed, with Lách snoring on one side and Rósa dropping off on the other. Nobody was permitted to sleep in his bed, she reminded herself.

Then she realised: there was probably nothing special about her Initiation. Chances are every newly-Initiated girl felt the same way and there was no space in his bed for everyone. Then she thought of Léaró, of where the Mentor's fingertips had touched her and she realised it wasn't just girls. If she wanted to be his wife, then all of the Sea People must want to be his wife, from Lord Aclaí to the youngest Novice. *The Sea People do not marry*: she understood it now. She had thought of the wedding song, and she knew why Caora couldn't sing it and why she had been drinking so heavily at Sneachta's wedding. Caora was weaker than they were, more emotional, for all her Rank and age. And when she closed her eyes, she imagined herself standing with the Mentor, as her husband, and she knew it could never happen.

In the darkness, Rósa watched Eala's shape under her cloak and saw it begin to shake as Eala silently cried.

After the midday meal, they were led into lectures. The little woman giving the lectures had dark grey hair, a long nose, red-brown skin, and deep black eyes, with the fold of eyelid that showed that she was from the Great Ocean. As well as her cloak and sword, she wore a heavy necklace of turquoises.

"I am Féileacána, and I am Eighth Rank, which means I have survived my tour in the Forest. None of ye have been in the Forest and most of ye will not survive it. If ye want to get to be like me, ye should listen.

"Most of ye will think that the lecture ye should most pay attention to if ye are going to survive is sword-craft. Well, that is not true. The lecture ye should most pay attention to is the one concerning the Great Principles: these lectures. The Great Principles are what the Language of Power is based upon and even what the Power of Creation is based upon, if any of ye ever last to the rank of Immortal and beyond. So we will talk about each of the Great Principles, and ye will take notes and commit them to memory before the lecture in three days' time. If ye don't have them memorised and I catch ye, it will go hard with ye. But I won't kill ye. If I don't catch ye, then the Forest *will* kill ye."

She showed them a big tapestry, a diagram of circles, each with the name of a Great Principle, both in common language and in the Power Language. The circles were joined together with straight lines, to make a big, strangely symmetrical web. The straight lines described the interrelations between the Great Principles. They duly copied them all down.

"The most important Great Principle for the City is the Great Principle of Creation. It is the thing that gives all else form and it is one of the great powers that makes the City of the Sea People what it is. The Manifestations of Creation are the source of the breath to drive the Words that make everything work. Everything, from a great Flyer to the glowing pebble that lights some peasant's hut, is powered by trapped Manifestations of Creation, on the Red World in the sky, or for some distant other universes, like Anleacán, by their own House of Power.

"The Great Principle of Creation, the mother and father of all those Manifestations, was tricked by the Mentor into taking an inanimate form. And there it is: the pendant around his neck is one of the greatest and most powerful Great Principles, now a power-slave to give the City whatever we want. If any of ye reach Immortal Rank, ye will be permitted to access the Key of Creation and learn to alter reality without using Words."

So Eala was copying and Féileacána was talking: something like, "– so that brings us to this duality here. They are called *Good* and *Evil*, but it is a mistake to think of *Good*, particularly, as like the fairy-stories yere mothers used to tell ye when ye were children. Real human morality is all relative – yere ideas of what is good and evil come from the way yere parents taught ye and the way they lived. Now ye are here, good is doing what the Mentor commands and evil is the opposite. But these Great Principles are not the same. Remember, all the Great Principles hate humanity.

"Anyway, this one is called 'Good': never mind the name. It is –" and Rósa nudged Eala.

Eala looked up. Rónmór was there, at the door, looking over at her. Féileacána acknowledged him with her eyes, and, when he nodded, carried on giving the lecture. He didn't make a fuss, he just waited for the lecture to finish. Then, when they were dismissed, he went over to Eala.

"The Mentor has asked for you," he said.

Her heart leaped and Rósa looked at her again. She told herself she was being foolish: even if her heart was full of mad dreams about marriage and children, she knew it would simply be a repeat of a few days before. She followed Rónmór out.

As they walked up to the Court of the Veterans, he said to her, "Less nervous now?"

"Hardly nervous at all. Did he really ask for me?"

"He really asked for you. He's been talking about you. He thinks you are pretty and he thinks you will be a good Adept. He likes you."

"Why?"

"I guess it is because you are pretty and you are nice to people. You're different to most candidates, Eala."

"My mother says I have a soft heart and it gets me into trouble."

"I don't think your heart is soft. Have you done much sword-craft?"

"Hardly any. We have barely learned not to cut our fingers."

She shuddered as she said it: Rósa had sliced off half her hand trying to put her sword back in her scabbard. The Adept teaching the sword had pressed the severed part back where it belonged, said Words of Power, and her hand was perfect again, but Eala still remembered it. It wasn't the only injury Eala had seen in the sword-hall, but since Rósa had been her partner that day, she had seen that one close up: close enough to be splashed when Rósa's blood had sprayed out.

"You will get better. Anyway, there are two ways to protect yourself when fighting with the sword. One is to wear armour. But I saw Lord Foscúil give a sword-craft demonstration: two Veterans attacked him with swords, when he was wearing no more than a shirt and kilt. They just couldn't hit him. He could hit them, though. Every time they attacked him, he simply walked out of the way. He didn't run or anything, he just walked and laughed and hit them on the head."

"I can't imagine that."

Lord Foscúil was widely known to be a superb swordsman and was often away researching some sort of military matter for Aclaí on Anleacán. Eala, being a Novice, had never seen him fight – she had only seen him on that one day when Lord Aclaí had inspected the Novices.

"Maybe not, but I don't think your heart is soft. I think most of us have hearts that wear armour, but your heart is like Foscúil: it dodges, and it parries, and it just can't be hurt."

She laughed, amused by the image, however unlikely.

"My heart can be hurt, Rónmór. I'm not some ancient warrior inside."

"I've seen a lot of purple Novices Initiated. The Mentor has put me in charge of his bedchamber for three years now. You shouldn't underestimate yourself."

They had arrived at the Court of the Favourites and went to find something for Eala to wear. She still had the little green dress she had worn a few days ago, but it was so short she wouldn't wear it. If she knew the Words to change it, maybe she would – or maybe her mother could let down the hem the two-fingers-width that would be enough to make it wearable. But it and the emeralds were hers now: nobody had asked her for them to be returned.

She looked around for herself, rather than letting the servant choose for her. She found a turquoise-blue skirt and shirt: the shirt was shiny silk, like her green dress, but the skirt was made of linen, dyed to match. It would go well with her cloak, she knew. The skirt was folded and would cover her hips and the tops of her legs: it simply laced with ribbon, wrapped around her waist once and halfway around again. He could unwrap it, or lift the corners of the cloth, or just rumple the whole thing up. He wouldn't make her his wife, but they could have fun, like Geana had with her lovers, and maybe he would remember her at least.

When she was wearing it and her cloak was on, she looked at Rónmór.
"Will he like it?"

"I think so."

The servant brought her three turquoises on a gold chain and smaller turquoises as earrings. She wondered where they got all this jewellery. She recognised it was the work of craftsmen, but they seemed to have such a lot. There were also clips to gather her hair behind her ears. Behind her left ear the hairclip was fastened to the stem of a paradise-flower: a bloom she had only glimpsed in the Court of the Favourites. The curved bloom fitted well over her ear and they put her hair to one side to balance the shape. She could smell the perfume.

They waited a short while, then Rónmór went down with the Favourites to the Evening Meal. The servant led Eala to the Mentor's room, to wait.

"Oh that Eala! She is terrible," laughed Rósa. "We had a girl like that in the Low City. I met her in our scribe class. When the ships came in, she would go down to the waterfront to watch them. The boys would come off the ships and she'd always end up speaking to them. She was always saying 'I don't understand what you are doing to me', but it always ended up the same."

"She got pregnant?" Abhainne suggested from over the other side, and the whole dormitory roared with laughter. Spéire threw a cushion at her: they had been fighting with cushions only a moment before. Rósa laughed as much as any.

But she explained, "The thing was, all her innocence was an act. She did it because the boys liked it."

"That's the thing to do," agreed Abhainne. She lowered her voice, still uncomfortable with the over-familiar disrespect Rósa seemed to have towards the City, "But the problem is, how to get *the* boy to notice you in the first place."

"I think for that, you need an important Sponsor," answered Rósa. "That gets you up there early, so you can attract his attention before he's bored of the year."

"Or before you die in the Forest," suggested Nóiníne.

"Important Sponsors don't just get you up the Hill early, Nóiníne," Abhainne answered. "When the Forest assignments are made, they'll keep you safe."

"It's a bit late to choose your Sponsor, Abhainne," answered Rósa.

"Maybe it is, but it's not too late to choose your team for Forest assignments. If your patrol includes the Candidate of someone important, they're not going to send you somewhere dangerous."

Abhainne glanced over at where the two boys were reading. "So *that's* what you see in him?" Abhainne asked.

"Hush," she answered. "He hasn't noticed. Don't tell him."

Cabairí looked over Léaró's shoulder. Léaró was reading, ignoring them, his lips moving silently as he tried to work out the symbols, and Cabairí was helping. Abhainne shook her head.

"Boys!" she muttered. Then she thought. "Hey, maybe when she comes down from the Hill again, I should ask her out. You collect the boys, I'll collect the girls."

"You prefer girls?" Rósa asked. "I hadn't put you down as one of those."

"Preference doesn't come into it," answered Abhainne. "It's all about how important their Sponsors are. I'd sleep with a horse if it would get me out of Forest service. You heard Lord Aclaí. I intend to survive the year." She sat down on the bed beside Rósa. "Anyway, she's not quite as ugly as a horse. But I'm surprised someone as high Rank as Lady Éirime didn't make her more pretty before bringing her."

"What do you mean?" asked Rósa. "Do you mean painting her face? Covering over those freckles?"

"Something far more drastic than that," answered Abhainne. "The high-Rank Sponsors can change the bodies of their Candidates: make their features more regular, or re-shape their bodies."

"Did that happen to you?" asked Rósa.

"I didn't need it. But ..." she lowered her voice, looking around "...lots around here did."

"Maybe they got it wrong," said Rósa. "Eala has been called back and, even if you don't think she is pretty, the Mentor must like her. Perhaps after hundreds of years as a Favourite, Lady Éirime knows more about what the Mentor likes than we do."

"Well, Rósa, if it turns out he likes ugly girls, we're in trouble."

"There are always the Immortals. We could be someone else's favourite."

"We have to get Initiated first."

Sitting in his room again, she was less nervous, at least until he came in. Then her emotions spilled over and she was afraid she would lose all her calmness.

"Good evening, Mentor," she said, hoping she was keeping her emotions out of her voice.

"You're pretty tonight," he said. "Have you been looking forward to being here?"

"They only told me tonight," she said, "but I wanted to please you."

"I told you I wanted you to finish the song."

"You did, Mentor," she replied, "but I didn't think it would be so soon."

"Didn't you believe me?"

"I believed you, Mentor, but there are forty-seven purple Novices and maybe four hundred more Novices in the City, about fifty Veterans, and six Immortals. There are ten favourites among them. All of them have a better call on your time than I have. Even the other purple Novices have a better call on your time: they need to be Initiated and I don't. If we all take turns, you should call on me sometime around the Day of Life, next year."

"Did you want me to call on you before then?"

"I did, Mentor," she said, trying to keep the eagerness out of her voice. "But I have no right to expect it."

"You are well trained, Eala," he said, "better than I would have expected from Éirime. All right, take your cloak off and get into bed."

She had hoped they would have fun, but it wasn't that much fun. He put pillows under her belly and then treated her as she had guessed boys would have been treated. It only worked if she relaxed and she wasn't much good at relaxing. It hurt and he kept getting frustrated with her. In the end, he held her down and used the goad and then, when she was crying, it worked better, although she didn't know why. After that there was pleasure intermingled with the pain: not the shocking, consuming pleasure of the Words of Power he had used on her, but enough to take her breath away and re-open the wounds on her heart.

Afterwards she lay there, her body as weak as she had felt the last time. Her skin was tingling where he had beaten her and she felt sore where he had entered her. He lay next to her, his breath close by, and she knew, looking at his face, at the shape of his nose, at the eyes that reminded her of her sister, that she still loved him very much. Too much, she suspected. His hand was on her hip, stroking the marks the goad had made.

"What do you want, Eala?" he asked her.

"I want to please you, Mentor. I'm sorry I wasn't good at relaxing."

"Very few are, at first. You did all right." His hand came up and stroked her hair from her cheek. "To say that you want to please me is the sort of answer that a Sponsor teaches their Candidate to say. What do you really feel?"

"Will you be angry if I say?"

"It depends what you say. I will be angry if you say nothing, or if you don't tell me the truth."

She thought of how to explain what she felt without making him angry. "We are taught that the Sea People do not marry."

"What about it?" he asked. His tone suggested a little danger.

"Well, Mentor, I think I understand why. The Words of Power you used last time, they have left me in love with you. I can only assume you do the same to every Novice. The silly peasant girl I was a few years ago would want the thing any silly peasant girl would want if she was in love. But I am one of the Sea People now. As I said when you first came in, I can see that there are five hundred people like me. So if you want five hundred people in love with you, then you must want them to feel that way to serve the City and the Sea People better. So I want what you want. I want to serve the City and the Sea People better."

"That's a very clever answer, Eala. But what about the silly peasant girl? What would she want?"

"She would want a husband, Mentor. But you don't need five hundred wives, do you?"

He smiled: humour was a dangerous trick, but it had come out right.

"I don't need five hundred wives, Eala. Do you think I need one?"

"It is not for me to say, Mentor. I can see that for you to have a wife would upset a lot of people here. But it seems that if you did choose a wife, you'd choose one of the Favourites, one of the Immortals. You wouldn't choose some not-yet-first-rank girl with a flower in her hair, who needs a beating to get her to relax."

"If I did choose a wife, you might be surprised what I would choose. But I'm not going to choose a wife. You guessed why the Sea-People do not marry and it was a good guess: maybe half right, better than most purple Novices could do. I learned the whole reason before Aclaí was born. Aclaí is a few years older than your Sponsor, you know?"

"I know, Mentor. She told me. I figured out that you couldn't marry anyone and, if you could, it wouldn't be me. So I need to please you, maybe have some fun too, and forget being a peasant girl. I'm sorry if it wasn't fun, but I'll learn. I won't let any peasant ideas spoil it, not for you or for me."

"I'm sure you won't, and we'll have fun. I assumed you had been well trained, although I was surprised that you had learned so much from your Sponsor. But you have figured most of this out for yourself, haven't you?"

"I have, Mentor."

"Will you sing for me now?"

She began the song. He slid his hand down, between her legs. She wanted to open her knees wide, to encourage him, but at the same time she wanted to squeeze them together, to keep him out. But she did neither, just concentrated on the singing while trying to ignore the words. Then, at the end of the verse, he whispered the Words of Power again, and she couldn't sing anymore.

He let her recover, and said, "Carry on."

She carried on, but now as she recovered, she felt the words more keenly. By the time she had reached the end of the song, her eyes had overflowed.

"How are those peasant ideas doing now, Eala?"

"I am sorry, Mentor." She turned her head away from him. "Give me a moment, please," she said.

He heard her breathe, then she wiped her eyes and turned back. She was smiling again.

"You are a good girl," he told her. "Off you go."

"Eala?"

They were leaving the lecture, Rósa and Cabairí ahead of her. She turned around.

"Léaró." She could see he wanted to talk but that he was embarrassed too. "Shall we go somewhere quiet?"

"If it pleases you," he answered, obviously grateful.

They took food away and found a bench that was unoccupied. As they went, Eala heard Rósa say something to Cabairí, something that might have suggested they could be in love. She walked on rather than respond to it, aware of Léaró's discomfort. They sat down.

"Is it about the Day of Selection?" asked Eala. "About Initiation?"

Léaró agreed. "I hate my brother," he said.

"Why? Didn't he explain it to you?"

"He told me about Initiation," agreed Léaró, embarrassed. "But he ... he dressed me as a girl. Why did he do that?"

"I don't know, Léaró. I don't know the Mentor well. Maybe your brother chose what was best for him and for you."

"I don't want that." He looked frightened. "It's all right for you, you are a girl."

What's wrong with being a girl, Eala wondered, but didn't say.

"If the Mentor thinks of me as a girl," Léaró continued, "he might change me into one."

"Maybe that's what the Mentor likes."

Léaró looked at her with a moment of scorn. "Do you think Lord Aclaí dresses like a girl for him?"

Eala couldn't imagine that. "Maybe not. I doubt that Lord Aclaí could make a convincing girl, at least not without the Words of Shaping, or Illusion. But maybe that's what the Mentor wanted that night."

Léaró seemed to understand that.

"Rónmór said I should be Initiated within the first ten-day. He said I would be the only one Initiated this ten-day."

"Oh. But I was..."

"You were," he agreed. "But he told me that it would only be me."

"It's not his decision, though. If the Mentor tells him to bring another, what can he do?"

"So I was supposed to be good enough for the ten-day and he asked for another?" asked Léaró. "I think that might be worse."

"There has to be more than one Initiation each ten-day, Léaró," Eala replied. "There are only thirty-six ten-days in the year, and there are forty-nine of us."

"Lord Aclaí said we'd not all survive the year."

"But most of the Initiations ought to occur before the Forest service starts. How can we gain Rank without Initiation?"

"I suppose. But the City isn't run for the Novices, Eala."

"It isn't. But dead Novices don't do the City any good either. Between now and midwinter there are nine ten-days. If we all get Initiated, that ought to be five every ten-day. Even if we're not Initiated by Midwinter, you'd still expect more than one each ten-day."

"I suppose," agreed Léaró. "So why was Rónmór so sure about the first ten-day?" Eala saw the embarrassment come back. "And why did he paint my face, like a girl who ..?"

"I don't know what the Mentor likes, Léaró. When I was with him, he seemed to want a peasant girl from Athaiteorainn."

"Rónmór painted freckles on my nose, Eala." He stared at her face a moment. "Do all the girls from Athaiteorainn have freckles?"

"Lady Éirime is from Athaiteorainn and she doesn't have one freckle. The Mentor misses her."

"Lady Éirime is the singer? The Mentor didn't ask me to sing."

"He asked me," answered Eala. "I'm not a good singer. He asked me to play the harp and I'm a rotten harpist. But he wanted Athaiteorainn songs."

"Then what is my brother trying to do to me? Humiliate me?"

"I don't know, Léaró," Eala answered. "I really don't. But I am sure that your brother is trying to take care of you. There are so many things that we don't understand about the City. The City is a very strange place and the Mentor is someone from a very different past. Léaró, he's over a thousand years old. We don't know what he's seen, what he's done in that thousand years, but your brother must have a pretty good idea or he wouldn't be Chamberlain. You should trust him. And if you want to know, you should ask him."

"I'm not going to ask him," Léaró answered. "I'm never going to speak to him again."

After the midday meal, as they filed into their first Words of Power lecture, Abhainne watched as Eala sat down. She hoped that Rósa would give way after their talk yesterday and leave her with Cabairí, but it was Eala that came in late, with the other Favourite-sponsored Novice, the Chamberlain's brother. Cabairí had already sat down with Rósa and Lách on either side, but Eala avoided them and sat down on her own. Léaró sat one side of her, and Abhainne moved quickly, and sat the other side of her. Nóiníne and Spéire sat on the other side.

"You got in late last night," Abhainne offered as her opening move.

"I was walking," Eala answered. "I needed to think." She looked around at Abhainne, then said, "Do you think we will learn anything useful today?"

Abhainne was a little scandalised. "Of course we'll learn useful things."

"That's not what I mean," Eala explained. "I mean: will we know any Words of Power by the end of the day? There is so much I need right now."

"Impatient to be able to summon elemental fire on your enemies' heads?"

"I was more thinking of the *Words of Freshness*. Or the *Plaiting of the Silver Cord*. The things that blue-robes take for granted."

"I don't know much about what blue-robes take for granted," answered Abhainne. "How do you?"

"My Sponsor uses Words all the time and it's the little things she uses. I haven't needed to bathe since Spring: I forgot to bring a comb. Every day, Lady ... Éirime would sing the Words of Freshness over us, and we would be ready to start our day. I miss that."

"Sing?"

"Lady Éirime sings her Words of Power. I haven't heard anyone else do that since ..."

The Veteran in front of them banged the table. "Today is the day ye've all been waiting for. Today ye learn yere first Words of Power: a thing called the *Binding of the Silver Cord*."

He reached out his hand, up where everyone could see it, and closed his fingers. As he closed them, his naked sword was in his hand, the tulip-shaped end of the hilt by his wrist, with two heavy bands beside it. The Novices gasped.

"The sword is bound to my hand using the Words and I can make it appear in my hand by thinking of the gesture of holding it. For sword practice, we bind the sword to our hands in several ways. Look."

And he raised his other hand and the sword flicked from one hand to the other without crossing the space in between. Then it moved rapidly around, left hand, right hand, point up, point down, silently and quickly as blinking. After a few breaths, the sword was gone and, as they wondered, the Veteran shifted his hip and the sword-hilt poked out from under his cloak.

They roared their approval. As the noise died, he spoke again.

"The *Silver Cord* is a vital part of sword-craft, allowing us to draw and cut faster than we would be able to otherwise and to throw the sword when we need. They will tell ye the primary positions and grips to use in the Hall of Swords and ye should use the *Binding of the Silver Cord* to bind the sword to yere bodies in all six primary positions. But today, ye'll learn not to forget yere books and pens.

"Now, how much have ye learned about Great Principles?" He looked at a crowd of blank faces. "Oh well. A living body has various elemental fluxes associated with it and the different levels of the elemental fluxes are joined by a central current of elemental power, the thing we call the *Silver Cord*. The gesture that makes the object appear is recognised by the flow of this elemental power that is associated with movement. When ye are more experienced, ye will be able to make the elemental power flow without needing to actually move yere bodies. But by then ye will be well on the way to Immortal Rank ... if any of ye survive that long."

When the lecture was over, Eala walked back to the dormitories, to bind the rest of her gear onto her Silver Cord. Abhainne, Nóiníne and Spéire came down with her and watched as she worked her cloak onto her shoulders and into her hands.

"Why into your hands?" Abhainne asked.

In answer, Eala reached out her hands, and after a few attempts to make the gesture, her cloak was in her hands, not on her shoulders. She dropped it on the bed.

"See?" she asked.

"You bind it to your shoulders to put it on and to your hands to take it off?"

"Or to my hands if I want to fetch it but not wear it."

"Where did you learn this?"

"Watching Caora. That is, Lady Éirime."

"It must be wonderful living with a blue-robe," said Spéire, shyly.

Eala seemed to stop and think about what answer she could give. Then the bell began to ring for the Evening Meal and Eala jumped up.

"We must go," she said, and hurried to the door, leaving her gear on the bed. "Come on," she added.

Abhainne came, bringing her cloak. As she did, she saw Eala's cloak appear on her shoulders. They found their way into the Hall of Novices before the bell stopped and Abhainne followed Eala as she sat down beside Cabairí.

The Favourites came in, a procession through the doors, the Mentor leading them. As the doors closed behind them they walked across the middle of the hall and up to the table on the platform. As the Mentor stood a moment, Eala noticed that there was a gap to his right, where Liús, the Favourite, normally stood. Eala looked for Liús: he was standing further along, five seats on, between Lord Aclaí and Éise. Cabairí nudged her.

"Liús has moved," he whispered excitedly, "and there's another place set. That means the Mentor will announce another Favourite."

"I don't mind, as long as he gives me my Rank," whispered Eala.

Cabairí was about to reply, but one of the older Adepts gave them a glower and he was quiet. But Eala could see the excitement elsewhere. Others had noticed.

The Mentor began to speak. "I'm not going to keep ye from yere food for very long tonight." Not that anyone cared about food. "I am going to announce one Rank."

Eala knew which one that was. It was hers, since she hadn't been at the evening meal last night, she had been waiting for him in his chamber.

So when he said, "Eala is First Rank," she was not surprised. Then he added, "She is also my new Favourite."

Her mind filled with confused ideas but she didn't react. Cabairí nudged her hard.

"Go on! Quick! Go up!" he hissed at her. "You have to go up!"

She looked around. Everyone was looking at her. Cabairí was surprised and happy for her, Rósa's expression was indescribable. She looked up: the Mentor was looking down at her and she could see he was waiting for her to come to him. She walked over, between the tables, past the crowds of curious faces, up onto the stage. Somehow she got up without stumbling. She took her place between Rónmór and the Mentor and they sat down. Around the hall, the talk started. The Mentor turned to her.

"Are you crying?" he asked her.

"I'm happy," she replied.

She was happy, she knew, but she couldn't believe how much joy and sorrow could intermingle without either diminishing the other.

"But no peasant ideas, Mentor," she added, hoping it was true. "It's just an honour and so unexpected. You've taken me by surprise."

"Good. You are pretty when you are surprised. I shall have to surprise you more often."

She half-stood, turned around to face him, and reached over to kiss him. He reached up to her as she did it, held her, and kissed back. She just wanted to hold him. She lifted her knee over his leg, to reach him closer.

After a while, he whispered to her, "One surprise each: we're even. We need to talk to you about the protocols of being Favourite."

"I'm sorry, Mentor," she whispered back.

She moved her head away from his and saw that he was happy, amused. She also heard that all the conversation had stopped. With his help, she transferred her weight back to her own chair. The Mentor looked around.

"I've finished announcements," he told them, laughing, "ye can eat yere food and talk amongst yerselves."

The silence quickly turned to a buzz of conversation. She looked across the mostly-smiling faces and saw Rósa and Cabairí arguing about something, probably her. She also saw she had left her cloak on the seat between them. If she was to leave with the Favourites, she'd need her cloak. Concentrating, she pulled on her Silver Cord, and it was in her hand, under the table. Cabairí caught the movement in front of him, then looked over at her, happy for her.

She looked over to see how Liús was. He was looking at her in astonishment and, thankfully, with no malice. But as she looked over she accidentally made eye contact with Lord Aclaí, who was staring at her with curiosity and something that might have been suspicion.

And she looked back to where she had been sitting, to the empty space between Cabairí and Abhainne.

— 8 —

Favourite

Eala lay in the darkness, listening to the sounds of the night, but trying to concentrate. She could hear insects and birds, the wind in the trees, and talk, in soft voices. She wondered who was speaking.

Walking up the Hill beside the Mentor, he had taken her hand, in front of everyone. With his hand holding hers and with his kiss on her lips, she had expected to be led to his bedroom. But she had, instead, been shown this house and given a servant, Luchóg, who she guessed was no older than her. Then they had left her alone to wonder if she had made a mistake.

She would not think about that now. Just when she thought she had worked out who everyone was in her dormitory, she had to remember a new set of names and faces. And if she got mixed up between Nóiníne and Abhainne, neither of them could turn her into some species of insect.

She closed her eyes and tried to summon each face as she thought of their names. Aclaí and Eibheara she had no problem remembering. No girl from Anleacán would forget them. The other Immortal was Cathúa, someone who made Eala curious. She had the dark-haired, slender beauty of the old Sea People but she didn't bother with it: her clothes were unflattering; her black curls were cut short. She looked more like a boy than Miotal did.

The fragrance of the night was drifting through the shutters: breaths of honeysuckle, jasmine, roses, borne in on the clean air of the sea. The shutters were open because the night was so warm and because of the faint mustiness of the room. The flies couldn't get in: a simple carving on the window frame saw to that.

So the Veterans. There was Rónmór, the Chamberlain. She could remember him, he was rounded, chubby like his name, with soft brown eyes. And he was so odd, with his strange way of looking at things. There was Innealta, small and golden-brown. Like Rónmór, she had the little fold in her eyelids that they said came from the shores of the Great Ocean. And there was Toirneach, who spent his time sculpting his body into dark brown muscles. Which left the Novices, Liús, Éise and herself. She tried

137

to remember how Éise, a girl as dark as Toirneach or Miotal, but with seductive...

She heard the sound again, like an animal in distress, destroying her concentration. Eala sat up. It was almost completely dark, but a little moonlight shone in, highlighting the room in grainy monochrome shapes. She could see her bag, her clothes and her armour on the table by the bed. The sound came once more and suddenly she realised what it was. Somewhere nearby, in one of the other houses, a woman was slowly edging towards orgasm. And she didn't mind who heard.

Eala wanted to wash and she needed light. How was she supposed to do this? Of course, nobody up here in the Court of the Favourites would have to worry about trivial things like light or washing. But the servant who had brought her clothes had said she should call if she needed anything.

As she went over to the doorway, she heard her own name. The voices were talking about her.

"...And homesickness," the voice continued. "All purple Novices are the same, at least for the first few months."

"What I don't understand is what a purple Novice is doing up here, anyway. And why she isn't crying in there yet."

"Hush, Eibheara. She's asleep. Don't you remember how much sleep you needed at that age?"

Eibheara's answer was a little quieter, at least, but Eala could still hear clearly enough.

"I can't believe Éirime brought twins. Everyone knows that nobody brings more than one Candidate from a family in a year. So how does she get away with it? Éirime gets away with so many things that nobody else ought to."

"She didn't get away with the name. Do you really think he would have killed them?"

"I think he was teasing them, Cathúa. If he'd wanted them dead, they'd have been dead there and then."

"I suppose they would," answered Cathúa.

"You're the one who collects stories. What is wrong with that name? Why is it forbidden? The oldest three –" and there was another, louder moan. "Liús!" she called, not shouting but her voice carrying clearly. "Just finish her off so we can all get some sleep!"

The other voice, Cathúa, answered with nothing but giggles, and Eala tried not to laugh out loud. Then, when she thought she had composed herself more, she opened her door.

They were sitting by the fountain, clear in the moonlight. Eibheara wore a silk dress that the moonlight shone through, highlighting her own shape.

Cathúa was wrapped in a woollen blanket. They were both drinking from pottery mugs. They looked around as Eala came out.

"Good evening," said Cathúa.

"Good evening," Eala replied.

Any reply they gave her was lost, as the moans reached a squealing crescendo, and Cathúa gave in to her laughter.

"She does it for attention," commented Eibheara, looking in the direction the noises had come from.

Cathúa was laughing, but she added, "She is catching up, Eibheara. She has been forbidden him since he was made the Favourite. Now she has him back."

"It's true," Eibheara agreed. "Do you know, she's the only one living at the top of the Hill who has never been *the* Favourite?"

"The Mentor hasn't been Favourite," answered Cathúa.

Eala tried again.

"I'm Eala." She smiled her best smile, moved a little closer. "I think that makes me the new kid."

"I think it does," replied Eibheara. "Last ten-day you were nothing more than a peasant. I guess you haven't learned the Words of Light yet and I can see and smell that you haven't learned the Words of Freshness. You only have one thing in common with us. Do you know what that is?"

Eala could think of several things but she was sure they weren't what Eibheara was thinking.

"You could tell me," she answered. Then she added, "My lady."

"You have ambition or you wouldn't be here. Your ambition must be powerful stuff. You're not particularly pretty; you're not particularly smart. All you've got is the Mentor's sentimentality about your Sponsor. But the Mentor won't be sentimental about you. He has seen a lot of ambition in his centuries and he plays with it before it's discarded. Do you think you'll still be here in five years' time?"

"I don't know," Eala answered. "I didn't expect any of this. I don't know why I'm here, or how long for. Not long, I expect."

"I expect not long either, Novice. When you go back, you don't want me as an enemy."

"I don't want anyone as an enemy, my lady."

"Then you need to be careful."

Eibheara looked at her in disgust, then walked away, back into her own house.

"Don't mind her," said Cathúa, unconvincingly.

Eala didn't know how to reply. Cathúa smiled awkwardly, then spoke her Words of Freshness and touched Eala's hand. She felt the crawling sensation of it on her skin, then knew she was clean.

"Thank you, my lady," said Eala.

"It's nothing," answered Cathúa, shyly. "Good night."

She got up and left. Eala returned to her room and found the servant there.

"Do you need help, my lady?" asked the servant, in the high voice their name suggested.

The servant was small, fair, and a little chubby and Eala was very glad not to have to wear something as humiliating as the short, sideless little tunic that servants wore. But Luchóg had brought Eala's bag up, and seemed to be trying to be helpful.

"I was told you might need help bathing," Luchóg offered.

"I'm fine now," Eala answered. "Lady Cathúa helped me with the Words of Freshness, Luchóg."

"Then I should go," answered Luchóg. "I'm glad you don't need..." Luchóg hesitated, "that is, my lady..." A deep breath, and a frightened look, then, "I'm sorry, my lady. I just meant that ... I haven't been doing this long and I seem to be doing it all wrong."

"Don't be afraid," Eala answered. "I haven't been doing this long either. As Lady Eibheara reminded me, I was a peasant a ten-day ago and I still feel like one now. I won't tell if you don't."

Luchóg seemed even more flustered by this, but grateful not to be in trouble.

"May I fetch you a lamp?"

"Please do," replied Eala, and the servant hurried to fetch it.

When the lamp was lit and on the table, Eala sat on the bed and her eyes were drawn to the tapestry. A river flowed across it, from right to left, over a waterfall near the right, between some little stone-and-thatch houses. There was a ford and an orchard. Sheep were in the foreground, and mountains on the right-hand side. She was thinking how the colours reminded her of home and the waterfall, where they went walking with Caora, and the river path. If you put Ólachán's House by the orchard, and made the ford into a bridge ...

"Is that my home?" she asked.

"It is Lady Éirime's home village, my lady. Lord Aclaí gave Lady Éirime the tapestry soon after she came to the Court of the Favourites. The tapestry is very old, my lady."

"Then it is my home village, too, even though it has changed. Lady Éirime is from our village. She is my Sponsor."

"I heard that, Favourite. Maybe that is why you were given this room."

"Maybe it is."

Eala looked around. Luchóg had brought a pottery mug with the lamp.

"I brought this for you. It's the drink the Favourites drink in the night-time. Or at least most did. Lady Éirime drank wine, day or night."

Eala took the mug.

"You served her?"

"My mother did. I have only been on the Hill as long as you have, my lady."

Eala realised how homesick she was and wondered what poor Luchóg felt.

"Do you miss your family?"

"I don't. My mother works in the kitchen these days. I see her every day, when we are not on duty."

"I see," replied Eala, a little envious.

She raised the mug. She had thought it was warm milk but she realised it smelt nothing like milk. She sipped and the taste of it was wonderful.

"What is it?" she asked.

"It's from a tree," Luchóg answered. "The fruits are brought over the sea from the West, then pounded and heated. The fruit is red but the oil it produces is brown and rather bitter. The oil is added to milk and honey. I don't know what it tastes like, but it smells wonderful and all the Favourites like it."

"I like it," agreed Eala. "Thank you for bringing it. My mother gave us hot milk when she wanted us to sleep but this is much better." She yawned. "I need to sleep now."

"Call if you need anything, Lady Eala," replied Luchóg, at the door.

"I will. Thank you."

Luchóg looked shy.

"Lady Eibheara is wrong about you, my lady. You are very pretty."

"You shouldn't say things like that, Luchóg," Eala answered. "The shutters of these houses are very thin and you will get yourself in much more trouble if you make Lady Eibheara your enemy. But thank you for the thought."

"It's nothing, my lady."

"It's much more than nothing. But don't say it anymore. Good night, Luchóg."

"Good night, my lady."

And Eala was left alone. I'm like an old maid, she thought. She took the warm mug and sat up to finish it. An old maid with a dutiful family to take care of her, even if they left her alone at night.

She looked up at the tapestry and wondered what was happening to Éirime and her sister, back in Áthaiteorann.

* * *

Eala could go to lectures given at the Court of the Favourites, but nobody at the Court of the Favourites was giving lectures in things like reading and writing or in other elementary subjects. She asked Rónmór and he told her it would be fine for her to go down to the Court of the Novices and attend their lectures. Apparently, anybody could: the Novice lectures were available to everyone.

Eala didn't need to learn reading, of course, but she did need to learn other things. One of those things was the natural world and their first natural world lecture was the following morning. Eala went in with everyone else, conscious that lots of people were watching. Rósa was the first to speak to her.

"Well, you never told us that would happen!"

"I never knew."

"I told you," said Cabairí. "If she'd known she wouldn't have just stood there with her mouth hanging open."

"You always have to be clever, don't you?" replied Rósa. She turned back to Eala. "Anyway, your mouth was open when you sat by the Mentor." She was giggling. "Or at least it was when you sat on him."

Eala was embarrassed at that. She now knew she had broken protocol, but also that there was a reason for the protocol: to prevent jealousy.

"I was confused, Rósa. He surprised me so much, I didn't know what I was doing."

"You seemed to know what you were doing to me. Are you really in love with him so much?"

"I am. That is what the Initiation does."

She looked at Rósa, realising that her own intense feelings were overwhelming her empathy and making her insensitive. She would have to watch that.

"Rósa," she said, "there's nothing to be afraid of."

"Not if you're Favourite, maybe. How are the rest of us supposed to feel?"

Léaró interrupted. "We all feel it. That is what happens; what you accept when you put on the blue robe. It's the thing that binds the Sea People together. Without Initiation there would be no loyalty. With no loyalty the City couldn't protect us from the Forest: it would just be Adepts fighting, trying to get their own piece of the world. Do you want to Retire already?"

"I don't," Rósa argued. "But how do I make the Mentor notice me?" She stared at Eala.

"I don't know," Eala answered, feeling guilty. "It's nothing I did, unless it's knowing a few Anleacán songs. He said he missed Lady Éirime."

A man walked into the lecture hall, a veteran Rank.

"Quiet!" he shouted. A moment later they were quiet. "Good morning, Novices," he said. "Good morning, Favourite."

For a second Eala was looking around to see where the Favourite was. This was going to take some getting used to. But the Veteran was still speaking.

"In these lectures ye will learn about the worlds that are commanded by the City. So, how many of ye think ye grew up crawling around the outside of some ball in space, like wasps on apples? Raise yere hands."

Cabairí raised his hand, and so did Léaró. Perhaps three or four others did.

"Oh dear," the Veteran said. "I can see we're going to be fighting ignorance here." He pointed at Cabairí. "You, boy, are we going to have a problem with ignorance?"

"I don't think the problem is as bad as it seems, my lord." replied Cabairí. "Not everyone here was born on this planet." He looked at Eala. "Take the Favourite: she was born on Anleacán, which is a flat world in space: she was a wasp on a leaf, not a fruit."

The Veteran stared at Cabairí a moment, surprised: then he began to laugh.

"All right," he chuckled, "not all of ye are ignorant. Who wasn't born on this world?"

Eala raised her hand and three others did too: one of them was a girl from their own dormitory. Eala could see that none of them were from Anleacán: they were all too dark. They must come from other worlds.

The Veteran pointed at her and said, "Favourite, how did you come here?"

"At Idireatarthu, in the south of Anleacán, there is a Gate. My Sponsor took me in a Flyer to Idireatarthu and through the Gate. There is a path in a sort of grey place, which leads to the Gate to the north of the City."

"The Grey Paths join the Gates and connect the other worlds that are under the City's dominion. Most of the worlds are accessed through the Sky Gate, which is on the other side of the world, in the mountains. But the older gate, the City Gate, is near here and that leads to Anleacán." He looked back at Eala. "Is that the only way you came here?"

"My Sponsor got the Flyer from Lorgcoiseaigéan: she rode through the Forest and somehow that took her from the woods near our village to the Watchtower in Lorgcoiseaigéan, which is on this world. I don't know how that works, my lord."

"All forests are one Forest, Favourite. You have heard of great principles in Féileacána's lectures. There is a principle of Forest: the Great Principle

of Forest is all around us and any woodland can lead you into the Forest.
The wilder that wood is, the easier it is to walk into the Forest. Anleacán
is not easy to walk to from the Forest, but if your Sponsor is Lady Éirime,
it is not impossible. The woods here in the Land of Immortals are kept
tame, cut and cultivated, to make it hard to connect to the Forest. That is
why Lady Éirime came to Lorgcoiseaigéan, instead of coming to the City."
He looked around the rest of them. "Do any of ye know why woodland in
the Land of Immortals must be kept tame?"

"Monsters," answered Cabairí. "Elemental Forest has many monsters in
it and they hate humanity and the City. The woods are tamed so nothing
can walk onto the Land of the Immortals."

"That is correct," the Veteran replied. "The Ocean is our moat, to
keep them out." He looked at them all, the laughter now gone from his
face. "The shapes of this world, or if you were like the Favourite the world
ye grew up in, are the less important thing ye will learn here. The most
important thing ye will learn is the paths in the Forest, that join the various
strongholds of the Forest People to the Watchtowers and so to our world.
If ye only learn one thing in my lectures, learn those Forest paths. Soon
they will send ye on patrol into the Forest and if ye get lost in the Forest,
ye will die."

It was midday and Eala was walking down to the Court of the Novices and
the eating hall, after a hard lesson with the sword, still shaking with fear
and exhilaration.

She found them already eating and talking. She put her bowl down,
Rósa shuffled nearer to Cabairí, and she sat on the end of the bench,
opposite Léaró. Lách was speaking as she sat down.

"Favourite," he acknowledged her, then continued, "it's not two days,
anyway. In two days the first lots will be drawn for the Forest patrols, and
there are over three hundred Novices. There are four of us: Eala, you're
good with numbers."

"If there were three hundred Novices, the chances that one of you will
be picked for the first pick would be four in three hundred – one in seventy-
five. A little bit more for each pick after that – four in 299, four in 298, four
in 297 – because there are fewer names in the pot. But there are actually
nearly four hundred and fifty Novices, so the chance is nearer one in one
hundred and fifteen and a quarter. Slightly more for each patrol because
the ones picked are no longer in the pot. If there are five patrols picked in
a day, you'll come up every other ten-day."

"What is a quarter of a chance? They teach you numbers in the Court of the Favourites?" Rósa asked, with a little scorn. "I can't believe you are so good at something so boring."

"I am not nearly as good as Lady Cathúa," answered Eala, glancing a smile past her at Cabairí. "Anyway, my mother taught us, then Lady Éirime taught us too."

She thought that Geana was probably better at mathematics than her now, since Lady Éirime would be teaching her that, not wasting her time with sword, or Forest lore, or the Words of Power.

Rósa was still speaking, but now Cabairí was the subject of her playful scorn. Eala looked beyond them, at the girls at the other end of the table. They looked away from Eala, clearly thinking Rósa and Cabairí were too silly to be blue robes. Eala wondered what they would think of Liús and Éise, if they saw them at the top of the Hill.

"Far away," agreed Léaró and the others laughed.

"I'm sorry," answered Eala. "I really was far away. What did you ask?"

"Rósa asked what you were doing for the Day of Death. Lách asked what you do in your village. It's what we were talking about before you arrived – did we have to spend all our time studying for Forest service, or did we have time to get costumes for the Day?"

"It's quite a small Day in our village," answered Eala. "I think it's bigger in the City but I don't know why, or what people do. Rósa, you're from over the River..." a girl at the other end of the table looked around as Eala spoke "...what do you do for the Day of Death?"

"We dress as ghosts and frighten people."

"What are *ghosts*?" asked Eala.

It seemed that everyone spoke at once. Then Rósa's voice prevailed, as it normally did. "I *know* the City teaches us that we shouldn't believe that our ancestors are watching us but who here actually believes it? Over the River, the people of the Low City don't revere their ancestors, don't believe in their ancestors, but they're still afraid of them. But most of you do, don't you?"

"I do," replied Lách. "It's what my parents believe and it's what I've been taught to believe all my life."

"I'm afraid of them too, sometimes," admitted Léaró. "My brother says that I should believe the City but I have seen the spirits of my ancestors in the sky. My grandmother talks to them. But my brother says there is a current of fire that blows from the Sun and that what we see is the wave of fire where that current flows around the Earth. But that is not what my grandmother says. Not what *his* grandmother says." He lowered his voice. "And when he looks in the sky on Midwinter's Day, I don't think he believes what the City teaches."

"I believe the City," answered Cabairí. "At home they tell stories of ancestors and carefully bury the dead to keep them from returning, too. But Lady Cathúa knows better about many things and she says the dead are nothing." He looked at Eala, the one who hadn't spoken. "You have been taught by Lady Éirime but you must have customs in your village. And she came from the same village and must know your customs better than most. Even if you don't believe what you were taught as a little girl, you can still tell us what it was, can't you?"

"I was taught what I believe now," answered Eala. "Nobody in Athaiteorainn believes in these *ghosts*. When people die, that is the end of them. My father died, when we were girls of just nine summers, but my mother took our hands and led us away from the funeral pyre and that was the end of him."

"*Cac agus fuil!*" swore Lách. "What a bleak way to bring up your children. Is your whole village like that?"

"The whole of Anleacán is," answered Eala. "How else would they be? It's the truth and we were taught the truth from when we were small."

"Perhaps Athaiteorainn is *enlightened* now," answered Rósa. "The Low City is the same. But if you asked Lady Éirime what it was like when she was a girl, she would tell you a different story."

"She would not," answered Eala. "She tells me the beliefs of the village are almost the same. She even knows all our songs, all our oldest stories. Anleacán has always had this view of the world. Anyway," she continued, knowing the excuse was weak, "all the places you come from believe different things: it is a matter of chance that one land happens to believe the truth." Then, before they could realise how unlikely that was, she said, "What will you do, then? Follow City custom and dress as dead people?"

"I have a mask that looks like a skull," Lách replied.

Eala knew the diversion had worked.

Eala watched the servants decorating the Court with skulls and snakes, with toadstools, bats, wasps and spiders. The Day of Death was that night and everyone seemed to be enjoying the anticipation. Lord Aclaí had a visitor, which took him down the Hill to the Court of the Immortals but the rest of the Favourites talked about their preparations for the Night. Rónmór helped Eala turn her idea into a Formula of Words.

She tried it on Luchóg first: the little servant came into her room, saying, "Do you need help with your costume, my lady?"

"I think it will be fine," answered Eala. She had chosen a pretty dress, linen and silk in a pale green, and high boots that she knew the Mentor would like.

Luchóg looked at them. "They are pretty, my lady. But..."

"But they are not scary?"

"Well, my lady, they aren't."

"I know. Let me show you what I will do."

Eala said the Words that she had devised with Rónmór's help. She looked at her hand and saw the bones, animated as she wiggled her fingers. Her hair was on her shoulders, just as it always was, but she knew she could turn and her face was nothing more than a skull. She looked over, facing Luchóg.

"How is this?" she asked.

Luchóg looked around, Eala's dress still in hand, and screamed.

"It's all right. I'm still here. All that has happened is that my flesh is invisible. Give me your hand."

She took Luchóg's hand in her own and Luchóg felt the warm flesh instead of the hard bones.

"That's very scary, my lady," Luchóg admitted, voice shaking.

"You see, I want to wear a pretty dress. The hem of the dress reaches past the boots and I have the gloves, too. I think the effect will be stronger for being dressed prettily. Let us see."

She shrugged off the tunic she was wearing and put the dress on. Luchóg seemed less shy about her undressing tonight: the horror of her appearance obviously cancelled whatever Luchóg normally felt. But Luchóg was less and less embarrassed about serving her as the days had gone by. Eala turned away, looked over her shoulder and saw Luchóg shudder.

"You see? The only problem is, you can't see me smile, can you?"

"I can, my lady. Your hair is visible, and so you still have eyebrows."

"Of course I do. I'd forgotten eyebrows. Do they look all right?"

"They look fine, my lady. Fine and scary, I mean."

"Good. Let's go and see if the Mentor likes them."

Eala went out into the courtyard. The Mentor was there and he stared at her.

"Eala?" he said, wondering.

"Mentor?" she asked.

"It is you, then. What did you do?"

"It is a variation of the Words of Concealment, Mentor. My flesh is invisible but my bones are visible. Do you like it?"

He stared at her, and she tried to read his face.

At last he smiled and answered, "I think it is utterly hideous. I like it very much. Will you teach it to me? We could match."

Eala was delighted, for all the incongruity of teaching Words of Power to the Mentor. When they were both done they walked down, hand in hand, to the Evening Meal on the Day of Death. Eala kept looking around at the stares of the other strange beasts in the hall, but the Mentor kept looking at her.

Aclaí didn't follow the Favourites all the way back up the Hill. He was at the back of the line and, when they got to the Court of the Immortals, he turned aside. It didn't take him long to reach Foscúil's house.

The servant said, "They are inside, Lord Aclaí," and stepped aside to let him enter.

Miotal was sitting on a couch with a girl, thin and bony even for one of the old race of Sea People, with pale skin and black hair. She smiled, looking him directly in the eye.

"Damhánalla," he greeted her, "are you enjoying the Day of Death?"

"I always enjoy the Day of Death, Aclaí," she answered. "You know that."

Miotal made space for Aclaí on the couch, between him and Damhánalla. Aclaí sat and he took Damhánalla in his arms. She felt frail and he knew just how light she was, how easily he could pick her up and sit her on his lap. She was like a child, hardly heavier than she had been when he had first met her. She smiled at him.

"May your next year bring you every happiness, little girl," he told her.

"So you remembered my Nativity Day?" she said. "You always do. The Mentor didn't, I'm sure." Then her smile disappeared and her face was serious. "I haven't spent my Nativity Day at the City in ... it's more than six hundred years, Aclaí. Why have you brought me here tonight?"

He relaxed his hold on her some, still with an arm around her but letting her move away more.

"Damhánalla, today you have lived seven hundred and twenty-nine years. Miotal has lived six years and four months less than you; Foscúil has lived a century or so more than you." He looked around at the three of them. "You are Third, Fourth and Fifth Oldest. And you are here and the Second Oldest is not."

"I don't live here, Aclaí," Damhánalla answered.

"Neither of us do," Miotal said. "We don't belong to the City. We belong to Aclaí."

Damhánalla didn't admit it but Aclaí felt her move closer to him again.

"That is not why you are here," Aclaí said. "The Immortals are the strength of the Sea People and you should take notice of what is happening here."

"Like Éirime?" asked Miotal.

"Éirime is gone," Foscúil explained to Damhánalla.

"I noticed that it was quiet," she smiled.

"So have a lot of others," said Foscúil. "So has the Mentor." He wasn't smiling, for once.

Aclaí added, "Just because she is gone, it might be a mistake to assume she is not involved." He looked back at Damhánalla again. "What did you see that has changed in the six centuries you have gone?"

She frowned.

"It's certainly not how I remember it," she said at length. "I don't know what has changed. The Mentor has changed, I think."

"What changes do you see?"

"I think he's more contented, more relaxed. The Favourites cling around him more," she said, "especially the younger ones." She looked in Aclaí's eyes, seeking encouragement. "Cathúa and Eibheara seem the same, and you, of course. But the young ones seem so ... familiar with him. Especially the other skeleton."

"That skeleton," Miotal asked, "was that Eala?"

"That was Eala," Foscúil confirmed.

He was her sword teacher, and knew exactly how she moved.

"What's she like?" asked Damhánalla.

"She has good courage," said Foscúil, "but she is too gentle to be a good warrior."

"She'll need good courage if she keeps pushing herself forward like that," Damhánalla remarked. "I am surprised the Mentor allowed her to be that over-familiar for so long. How does she get away with it?"

"I suspect it is her Sponsor," answered Miotal. "Éirime brought her."

"Éirime never brings Candidates," objected Damhánalla. "When did that happen?"

"She brought two of them," answered Aclaí. "This last Selection. Eala is a purple Novice – and she is Favourite."

"That's quick," she replied.

"She was Favourite on the Fifth Day of Autumn. I think the Mentor is trying to send Éirime a message." Aclaí smiled, a humourless smile. "I cannot imagine what would have happened if he had Selected both of them."

"Both?"

"Éirime brought twins," Foscúil explained.

"That's not allowed," objected Damhánalla. "They'd be from the same family: brother and sister."

"Sister and sister," clarified Foscúil. "I don't think Éirime knows much about the Traditions of Selection. She was never really interested." He smiled. "She brought one with a forbidden name. One of the first three forbidden names."

"Oh. And that is why he didn't Select both?"

"Presumably," offered Aclaí. "The two of them looked identical to me, like they had come straight out of the Room of Replication. But the other one is called Geana and so she had to go back home to her parents."

Damhánalla frowned. "I think her father is lucky to have her back at all. I've seen Candidates killed for far less."

"The Mentor misses Éirime," Aclaí explained. "I don't think he would kill a girl she was fond of, right in front of her. He wants her to return and she has enough bad memories of the City Hill without adding that. He was on best behaviour with her watching. And now it seems he is on best behaviour in front of her Candidate."

As he explained, he felt Miotal's thumb stroke his fingers.

"And you think this girl, this Eala, is allowed to be over-familiar because of her Sponsor?" Damhánalla asked.

"I think so, Damhánalla, but I think it is more than that. I've been watching new Candidates ever since Éirime left, because I was looking for the thing she was looking for, the fulfilment of a prophecy."

"You think it's this Eala?"

"I think it might be her sister. I think Eala has caused enough mischief on her own, but I think that ... Eala misses her sister, you can see that, and she is not confident on her own. That hampers her. It was the sister that spoke to the Mentor first. I think we got the wrong twin. I think Éirime was searching the purple Novices and, when she had Retired, she brought a Candidate along because she spotted what she had looked for all those years. Then the Candidate she brought was rejected."

He led her into the room, and called the servants to bring the mirror from the Wardrobe House to his chamber. There he undressed Eala before it and had her undress him. Then they made gentle love watching themselves in the mirror: two skeletons clinging together. The contrast between touch and vision seemed strange to her and rather off-putting, but she could see how the Mentor loved it. Then she closed her eyes and it was easier.

Afterwards, as they lay there sleepily, she turned over and started to get up.

"I should go," she told him.

"Stay, Eala."

"I will fall asleep, Mentor. I have had too much wine and I need more sleep than you."

"Then fall asleep. I won't mind."

She climbed back into the bed, trying not to look at him, put her head on his shoulder and felt his skin on her face.

She said, "If you want me to go, you'll wake me up?"

"I want you to stay," he answered.

"Thank you, Mentor," she replied. She nearly added the word "love", but she remembered to keep silent. A moment later, she was asleep.

She woke suddenly, in the growing half-light. She had been pursued through the forest by a skull that wanted to kill her. She knew it wanted to tear her flesh.

The Mentor was sitting on the bed, naked and looking at her.

"Are you all right?" he asked.

"I am a bit confused, Mentor. I wake up slowly."

She remembered not to say that Geana was the same, even though that was how she knew.

"You were having a bad dream."

"I was dreaming about skeletons and skulls, Mentor. I don't think it's hard to understand why."

"Of course," he answered. "You must think I am strange."

"I don't mind, Mentor."

"You had your eyes closed most of the time."

She looked at him, embarrassed and surprised that he should be so perceptive. The only people she knew who might have guessed would have been Geana and maybe her mother and she was glad that neither had been there.

"Your hair was still visible," he explained.

"I thought it would be more effective with hair," she answered.

Then she realised what he was saying.

"You could see my eyelashes?"

"Of course. I thought the Words might have made your eyelids transparent from inside but they didn't. I tried. You had your eyes closed. I am a savage from long ago, Eala."

"If we are civilised, it is because you have allowed us to become so, Mentor. We have no right to judge you."

"People still judge, if they have the right or not. You are very understanding for someone so young."

"I am an adult, Mentor."

"Do you even have twenty summers, Eala? Few women of double your age would have learned to accept what is different. Even up here in the Court of the Favourites there are some thirty times your age that lack your flexibility."

"I do my best, Mentor. I'm sorry I kept my eyes closed."

"It's all right."

He looked around, then found his blue cloak on his Silver Cord.

"I will call the servants and have them bring breakfast."

Quickly Eala found the white linen dress that she kept on her Silver Cord and said her Words of Freshness. As she dressed, he took down the magical wards that protected the room, and lifted the bars from the door. When he opened the door she was by his side. Several faces looked around: Rónmór looked horrified, Cathúa looked curious, and Eibheara looked triumphant. Then the Mentor's hand found Eala's and Eibheara's triumph turned to anger.

"Where is Aclaí?" asked the Mentor.

"He is in the Court of the Immortals," replied Éise.

"He is with Lady Damhánalla and Lord Foscúil," added Liús.

"Lord Miotal was with them too," added Toirneach.

"Mentor, I could fetch them," offered Innealta.

"Please do," said the Mentor. "It would be nice to have breakfast with you all. And Innealta, you may tell Miotal, Foscúil and Damhánalla that they are welcome too."

"I will, Mentor," she answered and hurried to the gate, down to Lord Foscúil's house in the Court of the Immortals.

Rósa watched the Favourites leave the hall and looked at Cabairí.

"So now they draw the Forest assignments," she whispered. "Still confident about the odds?"

"I'm confident about the odds," he answered. "Perhaps a bit more nervous about us."

"Hush," answered Léaró. "She's going to start."

Feileácana took the bag with the names on and spoke.

"There are four patrols tonight and four more tomorrow."

She reached into her bag and drew out eight slips of wood. Nobody in their dormitory had been called. Two first-year Novices were in the following day's patrols, but they were in Stail's party, who were mostly Veterans.

"See?" said Cabairí. "The odds are good."

Lách spoke. "Léaró, when we are called, will you ask your brother to help?"

"I wouldn't ask," replied Léaró, "and he wouldn't help anyway. He could get my name off the lists altogether but he won't. He once told me that the favouritism in the City is wrong."

"Easy for him to say," answered Rósa.

"Lady Éirime convinced him," answered Léaró.

"And look at her Candidate," came a voice from further down the table. "She's not on the lists, is she?"

Rósa turned around.

"Abhainne, Lady Éirime hasn't spoken to her since she was Initiated."

"Perhaps not, but she must have spoken about her. Favourite in five days? That's never happened before. And I heard she is sleeping in Lady Éirime's room on the top of the Hill. Hey, you people are her friends, Rósa – why don't you get her to get you easy assignments?"

Cabairí answered, "There is nothing special about it. Anyway, Abhainne, you must know someone. You are Sea People by blood: your voice and look says Lorgcoiseaigéan. I bet you have a dozen relatives here on the Hill."

"I am not from Lorgcoiseaigéan," answered Abhainne. "I am from Tírcapall. You must be deaf if you think I sound like someone from Lorgcoiseaigéan. There is a man in the Veterans who is from the same village as my cousins. We haven't spoken. It's not the same as having Lady Cathúa for a great-aunt."

"Lady Eibheara's family are from near Tírcapall," said Rósa.

"Is that true?" asked Abhainne.

"It's true," answered Cabairí. "Her father was Watch-keeper of the Grey House in Lorgcoiseaigéan but her mother's family came from Tírcapall."

Abhainne sniffed. "The Watch-keepers are Forest People."

"They are now. Lady Eibheara was Selected five hundred years ago," answered Rósa.

"Four hundred and ninety-seven years ago, Rósa," corrected Cabairí. "Lord Aclaí appointed him Watch-keeper after he failed Selection. He was an Anleacán person."

"I see," answered Abhainne. "Well, even if you lot are too principled to try and escape Forest service, we're not all so stubborn. Good luck." And she got up. "Come on, Nóiníne," she said to her companion, and they left.

Eala saw Cabairí in the Court of the Favourites and she went over to him.

"What are you doing here?" she asked.

He was scared, she could see.

"Initiation," he said.

Eala was relieved: it was about two months since the last Initiation – hers. So that would make her, Léaró, and Cabairí, out of forty-how-many? She was afraid for the other Novices and vaguely she had felt that it was her fault.

"It'll be all right," she answered. "Lady Cathúa spoke for you."

"Léaró didn't think it was all right," Cabairí answered.

"Hush," soothed Eala, "Léaró is the Chamberlain's brother. But don't worry about him. You will be explaining to them that it's not so bad before midnight."

"Not tonight," said Cabairí. "Lách drew a patrol. I should be with them, but I'm here instead."

"They'll understand," Eala reassured. "It'll be –"

Rónmór came over. Eala touched Cabairí's fingertips, then watched him as he was led away.

— 9 —

The Forest

Three young Novices rode through the Forest, in the dying twilight. They rode carefully, no more than a walk, looking around them. They were in full armour beneath their cloaks, their swords loosened in their scabbards, ready to fight. From time to time, the rider at the front, Léaró, looked at a map. When he looked up, he frowned.

As Léaró went behind the tree, the horse shied, he flailed a moment, and landed hard on his back. Fortunately the ground was soft and his armour was well-fitting. When he had his breath back he sat up. Rósa was looking down at him, scornfully.

He got to his feet and found the map in the darkness. He looked around for the pony, but it was gone. He groaned to himself and rounded the tree on foot. Rósa and Lách tried to follow, but Rósa's horse stopped. Léaró could see the animal's nostrils flare and its eyes roll.

"Come on, you useless lump of dog meat!" Rósa grumbled.

But the horse was going nowhere.

Lách tried to ride around, but his horse would not go either.

"Come on," he encouraged. But it was no use. He got down, awkwardly, falling the last part but somehow keeping his feet. "What's the matter?" he asked the horse. "Are you scared?"

"They've given us the most useless nags they could find," said Rósa.

"If you hadn't argued with that watch-keeper..." Léaró grumbled.

"If you had spoken to your brother, they'd have sent us somewhere better than this."

"This isn't helping," said Lách.

And he softly spoke the Words of Light, looking on the ground to see what spooked the horses. The ground was soft and black and here and there he saw something glittering. He took off his gauntlet and, reaching out, he touched one. It was sharp. He put the gauntlet back on and dug it out carefully with the blades on the fingertips.

It was an arrowhead, roughly moulded like clay, but it was Metal. He held it up.

"Look at this," he said, showing it to the others.

Léaró came over and picked up another.

"Careful," Lách warned, "they're sharp."

"Of course they're sharp," Rósa scorned.

"Do you know what this stuff is?" Léaró asked, lifting a long spike.

"It's Metal, of course," answered Rósa.

"Not the Metal, the stuff it's in. This is the spoor of an animal. A carnivore – a hunter."

"How can that be?" Rósa replied. "It would have to be..."

"Bigger than a white bear," Léaró agreed.

"Much bigger," said Lách. "My people are fishermen, Léaró. We don't have big predators on our island. How big is this one?"

"Too big. But I'm more worried about what it eats," said Léaró. "It looks to me like its last dinner was armed with spears and daggers."

"If it was, it didn't help them much," Lách added.

"This is all very interesting," said Rósa sarcastically, "but can we get on? Once we've finished this patrol we can get back to civilisation."

"We're supposed to collect any Metal we find."

Rósa eyed the dirt suspiciously.

"You have got to be joking..."

"Éise?"

"Come in, Innealta," Éise replied.

As Innealta came in, Éise indicated that she should sit down.

"How are you?"

"I'm well," Innealta said. She looked around. "Liús isn't here, is he?"

"He's gone off to speak to some Novice. Something about horses."

Éise didn't attempt to hide her boredom with horses.

"Good. It was you I wanted to talk to, really."

"Oh, really? Good gossip?"

"Sort of," Innealta agreed, warily. "I wondered what you think of Lord Aclaí."

"Ah." Éise looked over at Innealta, at her awkwardness. "That's not something I normally discuss in front of Liús. He's sensible, mostly, and he knows that I couldn't touch him while he was Favourite..."

"...But it's easier to handle boys if you don't tell them too much?"

"That is it." Éise let her teeth show in a wicked smile. "Lord Aclaí is a gentleman but one with a firm hand." The smile became more feral. "In other areas he is even more firm." Éise saw with satisfaction that Innealta blushed. So she added, "What did he do to you? Or propose to do to you?"

"Well," Innealta began, and then she stopped, and took a breath. "You remember when I went to fetch Lord Aclaí from Lord Foscúil's house?"

"The morning after the Day of Death?"

"That's it. Well, when I went there, Lord Miotal insisted that I should deliver the message myself. And, when I went in, I could hear..."

"People having sex?"

"Lord Miotal insisted I went and told Lord Aclaí myself. I didn't know what to think. I couldn't believe it; he's kind to servants, but this servant girl, he was, you know..?"

"He has a firm hand. The servant probably liked it. Blue-robes are all Initiated but you don't have to be Initiated to have a taste for that. Many of the servants do too."

"You?"

"Not since Liús was Favourite. Liús is too much in love with me anyway: he is always gentle and afraid to hurt me. It's not always gentleness you want, is it?" Éise watched Innealta look away. "Did he take you in hand, Innealta?"

"He never touched me. He made me watch, that is all."

"Made you?"

"He said that, if I asked to leave, he would use the Truthful Aura on me."

Éise laughed, not unkindly. "So he didn't touch you, but you watched, and wished he would?"

"I ... the *servant girl* he was disciplining: I found out after she was Lady Damhánalla. I really did think she was a servant. She is Fourth Oldest, Éise, and I watched him humiliate her. I could have got in terrible trouble."

"I doubt he would have let you get into that kind of trouble. Lord Aclaí plays rough but it's all play. I am sure his friends are the same."

"How would you know that?"

"I'm sure he wouldn't let one of his friends turn on you just for being there. He'd have warned you off. You wouldn't want to get on the wrong side of Lord Aclaí but he plays fair."

"Are you sure?"

"Sure enough. Look, if you want him, just ask. If he was playing with you that way, he will probably agree."

"Éise! I wouldn't dare."

"You would. And you will."

* * *

"Didn't we pass that willow already?" Rósa asked.

"Probably," answered Léaró. "The landmarks are all burned and trampled. You can see there's been some sort of forest fire in this valley."

"So we're lost. Some good you are as a Forest-walker."

"Cabairí is our Forest-walker. I'm not so good at it." Rósa made a scornful noise, so Léaró added, "Perhaps you would like to lead."

"I can't do as badly as you're doing," she answered, coming forward and taking the map.

Léaró fell behind, but Lách stayed at the back. Rósa led them the other side of the willow, into the water, and they splashed through the cold wetness for a few tens of paces.

"Up here," she said, moving some brambles to reveal a little animal trail.

"Aren't these human footprints?" asked Lách.

"We know patrols come this way quite often," answered Rósa.

Léaró thought that Sea People wouldn't patrol in bare feet, but he kept quiet: he had experienced enough of Rósa's sharp tongue. She had been complaining about the patrol ever since Lord Rónmór had taken Cabairí away and, it seemed, blamed it on him. And everyone else, including the watch-keeper. Couldn't she see that he had no way to control his Veteran-Rank brother?

His thoughts were cut off by Rósa screaming.

"Get back!" she yelled. "It's an ambush!"

He did as he was told in an instant, without thinking. He turned back and withdrew, hid in the cover of some bushes. He saw Rósa run back, and behind her, things that looked like they belonged in the deep sea, not in the Forest.

Then Rósa put her foot in a hole, and crashed heavily to the ground. She cringed a moment as she expected the things to grab her and tear her apart, but they ran on, past her, into the Forest, as if she was invisible. For three breaths they flowed past, running, hooting strange screams, their skin rippling in different colours as their camouflage tried to keep up with their movement.

But even if Lách closed his eyes against the sight of the gelatinous skin, the tentacles, the inhuman eyes, he could not close his nose against the smell of them: the smell of rotten fish.

Then they were past and Rósa lifted herself up a little, and looked after them, astonished she was still alive.

"*Cac is fuil!*" she laughed. "Those things scared the life out of me."

"What do you think they wanted?" replied Lách, putting his head out of the bushes and looking around.

There was a fog flowing out of the trees, and as it came towards them, they smelt its fetid odour: not of fish but of bad eggs, and something else, something sweet, something dead.

Léaró got up and walked around, picking up the spears and other gear that the strange creatures had dropped in their flight. The spears were tipped with Metal.

"Look at this!" he exclaimed. "I wonder if..."

Then the fog exploded with a dull thump. Rósa was thrown to the ground by the shock of it. When she looked up, Léaró was running around, his hair on fire, screaming.

"Use your cloak," she shouted at him. "Use your cloak to put out the flames!"

She didn't have a chance to find out if he understood. She just saw a shadow move among the trees, as if a mountain had woken up, and then a head like a snake, as big as a horse, struck out. She saw teeth gleam a moment, a tongue flick and great eyes as big as her head, yellow, glittering. One crunching snap, and the head was gone, back above the trees. Léaró was gone too.

She climbed out of the hole, realising it was a footprint, and circled around, looking for Lách. She wanted to get going, but she wouldn't leave him. He was crouched under a bush, his hand on his sword, calling for help.

All Rósa could think was – how can we get rescued if they don't know where to send the help?

Eala woke up. It was in the middle of the night, and she thought she heard someone at the door.

"Eala," came a whisper.

It was Rónmór.

"He wants you."

"Now?"

"Now."

Eala took her robe, and went out into the courtyard. Cathúa and Innealta were sitting by the fountain, talking quietly to Aclaí. Eala wondered if Innealta was attracted to Aclaí, and wondered if he knew. The three of them watched her as she hurried to the Mentor's room. She called at the door.

"Come in," he said.

She went in, feeling like she was trespassing: nobody went into his room after he had slept. He was sitting on the bed.

"Come here."

She sat beside him, close enough to feel the warmth of his body.

"How can I serve you, Mentor?" she asked.

"I want you with me in the night watch, Eala."

"You are always alone in the night watch, Mentor. Even Lady Éirime said you never wanted company then."

"I find that I want your company. Come and spend the night watch with me."

"Tonight?"

"Any night I ask you. No questions."

"I will, Mentor."

Next day Eala had a full day in the Court of the Favourites: in the morning Lord Foscúil was teaching sword and in the afternoon Lord Aclaí was teaching Forest Walking. Eala knew she would need both skills when she ceased to be Favourite and went back to being a Novice and, anyway, she daren't snub Immortals. But she wanted to know if Cabairí was all right, after hearing him weeping the night before; and she wanted to know how Lách's first patrol had gone. So, while the other Favourites ate around the fountain, she slipped away and down to the hall in the Court of the Novices.

She spotted Cabairí and went over to him. He would know where the rest were. She remembered how much Initiation had upset Léaró and how much she had felt. She wondered how he would be.

"Hello Cabairí," she said.

He moved slightly to face the chair she was going to take.

"Are you well?"

"I'm sore, but not unwell," he replied.

She could hear that he was worried too and she wondered what had happened. There had been no reports of bad behaviour.

"Where are Rósa and Lách?" she asked, "Have you seen them?"

"Nobody has. Rósa, Lách and Léaró didn't come back. I am afraid something awful has happened to them."

"Have you spoken to the Leader of Patrols?"

"The Leader of Patrols lives up in the Court of the Veterans, Eala."

She had forgotten that he had no right to go up there.

"Shall we go up together and ask?"

"Let's do that," he replied, eagerly. "I'm not hungry anyway."

She could see, looking at the food in front of him, that he wasn't. He was worrying too much. Luchóg would bring her food any time she asked for it: there were no fixed mealtimes for her.

"Come on, then," she said.

They got up and left the hall together. As they went up into the Court of the Veterans, he said to her, "I was hoping you would come down to eat. It was either you or Lady Cathúa and I wouldn't want to bother her. Nobody seems to care about a Novice patrol."

He was right: the lives of Novices were simply not important. Eala had learned that over the three months since she had joined the Sea People but she didn't like it. She couldn't tell him that, though.

"We will see what we can learn," she said.

They went into the house that the Leader of Patrols used. Eala had never been there before and, of course, neither had Cabairí. The Leader on duty looked around. He was old as only a Veteran can be old: woolly grey beard and hair against wrinkled, dark skin. He recognised Eala.

"What can I do for you, Favourite?"

He didn't recognise Cabairí and he didn't acknowledge him. Eala always felt uncomfortable about the way such senior Ranks showed her deference for what seemed to her such a frivolous position. But Cabairí needed her help.

"I am trying to find out what happened to a Patrol of Novices that were out last night," she said.

"Friends of yours?" he asked, as he reached for the written journal of last night's activities.

"They are," she replied.

"Well, let's see."

He opened the journal and skimmed through the entries, his lips mouthing the words he was reading.

"Féileacána was Leader of Patrols last night. She takes good notes." He continued looking down the page. "Here we are. Novice patrol: the only one unaccounted for last night. Looks like they ran into something bad. There is a call for help but they didn't tell her the location. Probably lost: it happens with Novice patrols all the time. The notes describe them as 'walking tentacles': probably Greater Manifestations of Chaos. Doesn't say how many, just 'lots'. She tried to raise them afterwards, up until dawn when she handed over the watch. Your Novices might turn up but I wouldn't spend a lot of time hoping." He looked up from the notes, and saw her expression. "I am sorry, Favourite."

"Is there anything can be done?" she asked, suspecting she knew the answer but hoping she didn't.

"They were lost, so we can't send another Patrol to see what happened to them. We wouldn't know where to send them and the Forest is deep. I'm sorry. Perhaps the next patrol that goes that way will find something.

It depends how lost they were."

She thought of Rósa, saw her in her imagination, and she realised she was losing control of herself.

"Thank you, Patrol Leader," she said, formally and she led Cabairí out.

Outside the door was a bench and she sat on it. She put her head down and breathed deep, the way the Immortals did when they wanted to be calm, the way Caora did. But the breathing came out all sobs. She thought, incongruously, of how Rósa had been frightened of Initiation and of how their Initiations had saved both her and Cabairí. Thinking of that made her think of Rósa and that she would never see her again. She couldn't bear it, this place, she just wanted to go home.

She must have cried out: she realised she was surrounded by people. They were talking to her, or about her, or something.

"Did he hurt you, Favourite?" she heard someone ask.

"I didn't do anything," she heard Cabairí's frightened reply.

She looked up. Veterans had gathered around them. Cabairí was standing, but it was hard to see what was happening to him, as there were people standing in the way, separating them. But she could see they were handling him roughly.

"Hey!" she called. "Leave him alone! He didn't do anything."

They looked around at her shout. She pushed her way through them, and they gave way to her. Standing by him, she told them off.

"We're upset because our friends are lost, people ye don't care about because they're too low-Rank, and ye make yere judgements and interfere. What were ye expecting? Favour from the Mentor for protecting his Favourite from the last of her friends here?" She looked at them all, aware that they were worried about what she would say to the Mentor, but that they weren't listening. "Ye were all Novices yerselves and ye lost friends in the Forest. Has life here really scarred ye so badly that ye can't remember what that feels like?"

With that, she took Cabairí's hand and led him out of the Court of the Veterans, down to the dormitory. She saw her old bed, now stripped and empty, until the next Selection. Either side were beds for Rósa and Lách, soon to look the same way. A couple of girls were sitting at the other end of the room and they looked around at Eala. She wanted to say something to them, wanted to tell them something about what she had seen. But she had no words and she knew that they could no more hear her than the Veterans could. Cabairí sat on his bed.

"I have to go," she told him. "Lord Aclaí is giving a lecture."

It was about the Forest, she knew, and she knew she would be learning things that might have saved Rósa's life. Cabairí looked up at Eala.

"I never told her how I felt," he said.

"I'm sorry," she replied, holding his hand. "I'll come back when I can."

She let go and left the room. She hurried up the steps to the Court of the Favourites, and, as she did, she suddenly realised what Cabairí had not told Rósa. But they had argued constantly, she thought. Then she realised how stupid she had been not to spot that and how Geana would have laughed at her for missing it. Perhaps she should have swapped names with her sister and gone home with Caora. She hurried on up, all the way up to the Court of the Favourites. Lord Aclaí was already speaking but he broke off as she arrived.

"Good afternoon, Favourite," he said to her and she felt every bit of the Ranks and age that separated them.

He stood quietly while she found a seat. Rónmór moved over and she sat on the bench beside him.

"So, can anyone explain to me the technique they were taught to walk the Forest?" Aclaí looked at her. "Favourite? Can you help us?"

"I haven't been taught Forest Walking, Lord Aclaí." She tried to keep her voice steady, but she couldn't do it.

"So if you are taken into the Forest and your guide is killed or injured, how will you get home?"

"I wouldn't know how to get home, Lord Aclaí."

She knew she was not following Éirime's advice and leading, but she couldn't help thinking of Rósa, Léaró and Lách.

"Even favourites go into the Forest. Don't you consider this a serious matter?"

Something about his tone was too much for her to bear.

"I consider it a serious matter. Last night three people went into the Forest and didn't return. You have never heard of them because they are only Novices but they were my first friends here at the City. Their names were Rósa, Léaró and Lách." She heard some noise from Rónmór, by her side but she was not going to let him stop her. "They came here with hopes, people at their homes cared about them, they had family, mothers, but the Forest just swallowed them up. They got lost. You see, my lord, I do know this is serious."

Instead of replying to her defiance, Aclaí spoke to Rónmór.

"Rónmór, what is the matter with you?"

"Léaró is my brother, Lord Aclaí."

She could see Aclaí thinking, but she did not know what he was planning. She expected it to be a punishment but his face was unreadable to her.

Instead he said, "I think today we need to do some practical work. Favourite, go down to the Leader of Patrols. Take your sword. The rest of you, come with me."

Eala gathered her cloak, found her sword on her Silver Cord, and walked down the stairs to the Court of Veterans as she buckled the sword on. The others seemed to be taking a walk in the garden. As she entered the Court of Immortals, her sword-hilt tingled and she realised she was being called. The light on her sword-hilt indicated the claw and jewel and two wide bands: Twenty-Second Rank. Nervously, she put her hand on it.

are you there yet cold words asked.

"Nearly there, Lord Aclaí," she replied.

when you get there you will need to find the leader on duty when your friends were lost

"As you wish, Lord Aclaí." Then, although she thought it might be too familiar, she added, "Are you going to find them?"

i am going to try

"Thank you for that. I am sorry I spoke out of turn in your lecture."

i only picked on you because i thought you were being lovesick came the reply. *think of this search as my apology it will be good for the favourites to be taken out into some real forest work* Then, before she could answer, the words continued *have you found the leader yet*

"I'll do it now."

He was gone. She went back into the building. The Leader of Patrols had changed: now it was a woman she did not recognise, with a flattish face, dark hair and a broad nose.

"What do you want, Favourite?" she asked.

"Lord Aclaí has asked me to come down here. He has just taken a Patrol into the woods. He wants me to find the Leader who was on duty last night."

"That would be Féileacána. I will call her for you."

She grasped her sword, and Eala could see her lips moving slightly as she formed words to send. Then she put the sword down, and spoke.

"She's coming. Lord Aclaí is calling."

She went back to the sword. As she was doing so, Féileacána entered, already speaking.

"Blátha, why can't I eat in peace one day at ..?" She looked at Eala. "What are you doing here, Favourite?"

"Léaró is Rónmór's brother. Lord Aclaí is looking for him."

"Who is Léaró?" she asked. Then, thinking on, "Was he in that Novice patrol that got lost last night?"

"He was. Lord Aclaí told me to come down here and find you. I don't know why."

"Lord Aclaí can track through the Forest, like a hunter stalking a deer. He will want me to read out my notes from the journal and will want you

to relay them. If I know Lord Aclaí, he will probably use the Words of
Shared Mind." Eala's sword began to tingle again. "You might find that a
bit strange." She made a cynical noise. "Or he might have sent you down
here to avoid taking a purple Novice out into the Forest. In which case
you just need to stay out of the way."

Eala placed her hand on the sword-hilt.

"Lord Aclaí?" she asked him.

are you there yet

"I am and Féileacána is here too. She has the journal."

good girl stay there in case i need you

"As you wish, Lord Aclaí," she replied. But he was gone.

She watched Féileacána working the sword-hilt, guiding Aclaí, and she
watched Blátha, the Leader of Patrols, working her sword-hilt, taking notes
of the other patrols in the Forest. After a long, boring wait, Féileacána
got up, replaced the journal and spoke to her.

"He says you should go back up to the fountain in the Court of the
Favourites and wait for him."

"Does he have any news?"

"Not good news, Favourite. They tracked where they had gone, but
nobody's survived. The Forest Warriors found the monsters that attacked
them at first light." Then she added "I'm sorry." Eala saw that she meant
it, that not all Veterans were beyond caring. Féileacána added, "But at
least you know."

"Thank you for your help," replied Eala, woodenly.

Then she left and made her way back to the Court of the Favourites.

When she got there she was alone. The other Favourites had not got back
from the lecture. She went to her room, left the door open so she could
hear them return, or if the Mentor should look for them. Then she took
out her sword.

First she thought of Cabairí. She didn't know what she would say, but
she knew that if she worried about that she would say nothing.

eala asked the cold words.

"Cabairí, I persuaded Lord Aclaí to go on a search for Rósa."

are they dead

"They are. I'm sorry."

at least we know came the emotionless words. *was it hard for them*

"I don't know. Lord Aclaí has not returned yet."

well let me know what else you find out the answer came *you didnt
have to do this you know you are a good person eala*

"She was my friend too."

i know but I wasnt thinking of the search you didnt have to call and tell me Then he must have added *you dont have to come down and mix with us novices*

"You are my friend, Cabairí. There isn't enough friendship among the Sea People. We should hold on to what we have."

There was a long pause, and she guessed he was weeping, remembering that they had fewer friends now.

Then *i find this hard because I cant hear you i cant hear what you are feeling it doesnt seem like eala at all all i can hear is this coldness* and she knew what he meant. *come and see me when you can eala*

"I will. I have to call Lord Rian and then see if I can find Rósa's parents."

you dont have to do anything like that

"I do, Cabairí. I don't have to do it for the Sea People, but I have to do it for myself. Wish me luck."

good luck favourite he replied. And she let go of the sword-hilt.

She found it harder to get the sword to reach Lord Rian, because she had never met him. But she kept concentrating on the name and, in due course, she felt the sword-hilt work.

who is this what do you want

Of course all the sword-hilt told him was a name he didn't know, and her Rank. The sword-hilt robbed his words of any emotion, but she could tell he was irritated from the phrases he chose.

"Lách is dead. I thought you should be told."

who is lách

Eala couldn't believe it.

"You sponsored him this year."

then he was a novice novices often die

"Will you tell his family?"

why should i Then he added, *i have too many that im sponsoring to go around visiting every time one of them dies they knew that it was likely before i took him on*

"He was my friend. I would like you to."

and why should i care what you would like novice

She had no idea what he was actually thinking, of course. He could be simply irritated with the interruption or he might be using the pretence of irritation to hide anything else. But she could use an approach she knew would work.

"I am the Favourite of the Mentor."

the mentor has chosen a second rank for a favourite

"The Mentor has chosen a first-Rank for the Favourite, Lord Rian. He announced my Initiation and named me Favourite with the same breath.

That was on the Fifth Day of Autumn. It has caused a bit of a stir."

i can imagine and she knew she had his attention. *and you are asking me to do this as a favour*

That was the price of using her position, of course.

"As a favour to me. Thank you. Please, my lord, be nice to them. They've just lost their son."

i can be nice favourite

"Where do they live?"

they live in gainmheach his father is bradán the carpenter he makes boats

"Thank you, Lord Rian."

dont thank me until you know what favour i ask in return

"What is that?"

i will tell you when i know favourite And he was gone.

After Lord Aclaí had returned and the lecture was over, Rónmór found Eala. Eala spoke first.

"I'm sorry, Rónmór."

"It happens," he said. She could see how upset he was. "I have to go and see my parents, to tell them. If I am not back tonight, will you go to the Mentor's chamber?"

"I will, Rónmór. Don't worry about that, I think I can look after him. I wish I could change what has happened. Your brother was a good friend."

She saw how he stood and she put her arms around him. She thought it might be against protocol, but nobody was watching: and if it earned her a beating, she didn't care. He put his arms around her and she knew it was the right thing to do, if it was against the rules or not. And anyway, he knew the protocols, even if she didn't. He held her tight: not how the Mentor held her, or how her mother or her sister or Caora held her, but desperately, as if holding her would bring life to him. She realised he was crying, too, and she didn't let go until it had passed.

Then he was wiping his eyes with the knuckles on the back of his hand.

"You are a good person, Eala. I think you may be the wisest choice of Favourite the Mentor has ever made. If you can't melt his heart, it is because he has no heart."

"I'm not so special, Rónmór. Go on: the sooner you leave, the sooner you will return. I will take care of the Mentor while you are gone."

He went. The Mentor was away teaching the Veterans, so she knew he would be occupied until the evening meal. She put her cloak around her and began to walk down to the City. She walked down the familiar steps to the Court of Novices, but then out to the landward bridge and out of the

gate that led from the Hill to the Lower City. As she passed the gate, she
realised it was the first time she had left the Hill since Caora had brought
her, months before. She had only seen the Lower City from the air, she
had never walked the streets.

It was crowded and it smelled bad. She had never seen so many houses,
crowded so close together, leaving only narrow walkways between them.
There was room for one horse or two donkeys. Fortunately people did not
crowd around her but, instead, stepped aside and let her pass.

She came to a space between the houses. A man had a bench out, with
a little awning above it, and was selling food. Another man played the
harp, adding a sort of jolly air to the place. He was a far better harper
than Eala but she was used to Caora. She went over to the food-seller and
he eyed her with suspicion.

"What do you want, my lady?" he asked.

She almost looked around to see if there was a blue-robe behind her,
before she remembered.

"Not food," she quickly explained. "All I want is to find someone. I am
looking for Rósa's family. I believe her father is a scribe, who makes up
ledgers for ships."

"Then he will work on the waterfront, my lady. I do not know him. I
am sorry."

"Where is the waterfront?"

"That road over there," he pointed, "will take you down to the waterfront. Do you need a guide?"

"I will find it myself. Thank you for your help."

"It is nothing, my lady."

She saw his relief as she started to turn away.

She walked down the other road and it turned to steps, going down.
The smell of the streets started to include fish, as well as everything else,
and between the houses she could see boats. The street ended and there
were stone slabs separating the houses from the water and the ships.

There were many more stalls: fishermen trading and merchants with all
sorts of things they had brought from around the world. She walked up to
a merchant selling huge, fine flints, bigger than her two hands made into a
fist. He looked at her warily.

"What can I do for you, my lady?"

"I am looking for someone. He has a daughter called Rósa and he makes
up ledgers for ships."

"I don't think he works here, my lady. I think the fellow you are talking
about works on the South Wharf, by the harbour wall."

He pointed, over the ships and the sea, not a way Eala could have
walked. She would have to double back through the streets. The merchant

saw her look over.

"Would you like me to get my arrachtumair to guide you?"

She wondered what an arrachtumair was.

He added, "It is no trouble, my lady. It's just standing idle: the ship is unloaded." He stood up, looked down at one of the ships, and called through cupped hands. "Fómhara," he shouted, "Stir your lazy – whatever you have that's lazy – and come and help this lady." He turned back to Eala. "I hope you don't mind that I call it by a name, my lady. It is just my way. I think it is kinder to it."

"I don't mind at all," said Eala, intensely curious to see what he was talking about.

One of the ships he was looking towards shifted, as some large weight moved in it, and then the arrachtumair emerged. At first Eala thought it might be a small cow, seeing the thick hair on the brown hide. But what got up was shaped like a man, at least in having legs and a head. The face looked very human, like one of the monkeys she had seen in the trees of the Hill, but the ears were still incongruously cow-like. The arrachtumair stepped to the back of the boat, then slid over the side. Eala thought it was graceful, for all its ugly bulk, because it seemed to just flow into the water.

She saw the wake as it moved below the surface, gently rocking the nearer boats, then a brown, furred hand came over the edge of the wharf. The palm of the hand was bigger than both her feet together and there were three fingers which ended in nails made of black hoof. As she watched, the hand and arm thickened, flesh shifting and bulging under the hide, and then another hand appeared next to the first. Both swelled until each was three times the size and the body came over the edge. As it did, gill slits on either side of it poured out filthy water and then closed up. The eyes now looked like fish eyes, big and watery, but they blinked, and then they looked like the brown eyes of a cow or a dog. The mouth changed shape a little and the body seemed to grow legs and feet. As it came over to the stall, the merchants and the crowd made a path for it. It stood before them, twice Eala's height. The mouth closed up, shrank, and opened again. Eala wanted to run away from it. She wanted her sword in her hand. It stank from the harbour water and it was huge, bigger than a bear. She had realised that it did not have a form, it chose the form that suited what it was doing.

The mouth and face were now almost of human proportions.

The merchant said, "Fómhara, take this lady to the South Wharf. She doesn't know the way. You know how to be polite to someone like her, don't you?"

"I do, master." The voice was all wrong for a thing of that size. Eala had expected a deep growl, but it had a high voice, like a child. "It is this way, my lady," it said. "Would you like me to carry you? Or would you like to take my hand?"

She didn't want to touch it.

"Lead me, Fómhara," she said. "I will keep up."

When they were out of earshot of the merchant, Eala spoke again.

"Forgive my curiosity, Fómhara, but what sort of thing are you?"

"You know, my lady," Fómhara replied, "I am an arrachtumair."

"I don't. I've never met an arrachtumair."

"The arrachtaíumar are made by the Sea People, my lady. I was made on the Hill."

"I've not been here very long, only a few months. Before I was from the country. We haven't been taught about things like you yet."

"There is not much to teach. We are made of animals and we are servants. We can make any part of the animals which were in us, or any of the animals we eat, if they are not long dead when we eat them."

"So you grow parts of a fish to walk underwater?"

"I grow gills and fish-eyes," the arrachtumair replied.

"And you grow a mouth and throat to talk to me?" Eala had a horrible, sickening thought as she was asking.

"I do."

"What animal do they come from?" she asked, thinking that she knew the answer.

"I always had them," replied the arrachtumair. "They came from my mother."

Now Eala knew she was right and she tried not to let her revulsion show.

"You remember before?"

"I remember, my lady. Fómhara was the name my mother gave me." The creature extruded an arm, pointing along the street. "The South Wharf is here, my lady. By your leave?"

"Thank you, Fómhara," she said. "Before you go, how old are you?"

"I am three hundred and," the arrachtumair was quiet, and although she could see little body language, she guessed it was counting, "three hundred and twenty six, my lady."

"How old were you, when they ..?"

"I was seven summers, my lady," it replied.

"Thank you," she said again. "You may go."

The creature walked over to the water's edge in two strides, then half-leaped, half-flowed over the edge. She stood staring at the water, wondering what it must be like to be that creature.

After she had stared a bit, a voice asked, "Are you all right, my lady? Can I help?"

She looked up. It was a merchant selling pottery.

"I'm sorry," she said, "I was just thinking. I am looking for the father of a girl called Rósa, who was Selected this year. I think he is a scribe."

The merchant pointed.

"The fellow over there in the red and white woven cloak, he is a scribe, and has a daughter called Rósa. His daughter joined the Sea People, my lady, and he never stops talking about it. I think he might be your man."

"Thank you," she said.

"It is nothing."

She went over to the man he had pointed out. He was old and balding, but she could see Rósa in the shape of his chin and nose. He was talking to another man, dressed in the thick stitched skins that sailors wore when they came from the northern ocean. The sailor nudged him and pointed at Eala. He turned around.

"That's not her," he said to the sailor. Then as Eala approached, "Can I help you, my lady?"

"Do you have a daughter who was Selected this year?"

The sailor said, "He never stops talking about her, my lady."

"I have," the other man said. "She is called Rósa. Do you know her, my lady?"

"I knew her. She was my friend in the dormitory."

"Has something happened to her?" he asked, now concerned.

"I'm sorry," she said. He looked so stricken, so devastated, she reached out her hand to touch his arm.

"How did it happen?"

"She was in the Forest."

"I understand," he replied. "She died protecting us?"

"That is what the Sea People do."

She didn't see why it was important, but she could see that it was important to him.

"Will you come and tell my wife?"

She agreed and he led her through the streets, to a large house. He went in and led her in. His wife saw her and her eyes grew big. She ordered a slave-girl to fetch food and drink.

Her husband stopped his wife and held her hand.

"This is Eala. She is in the same dormitory as Rósa."

"I was assigned there, but now I sleep elsewhere. I am Mentor's Favourite." Both of them looked at her in amazement. "It's not important," she added, wishing she had not said it, but still not wanting to make it hard for them to find her, to contact her. "Rósa was my friend," Eala explained.

"I see, my lady," replied the wife. "Well, how can we help you?"

"I'm sorry but Rósa was lost in the Forest."

"She is dead?" asked her mother.

"I'm sorry."

"We knew it was dangerous," her mother stated. "We have other children."

Eala for a moment thought she was utterly emotionless but then she remembered her own numbness when she had first realised that her father was dead. The woman did not have any way to express what she felt, even to herself.

"She died protecting us," said Rósa's father. "Didn't she, my lady?"

"That is right," Eala agreed.

Looking at them, she realised that now she had told them, now she had spoken for the Sea People that had taken their daughter, they needed to be left alone to grieve.

"I would like to help. Rósa was my friend. If I can help you, come to the Gate of the Novices and ask for Eala. Everyone knows who I am."

"That is too much, my lady," said Rósa's father.

"I mean it. Don't think of it as a debt you have to repay." She thought of her mother's stubborn pride with Caora, which had brought her here. "It is because Rósa was my friend."

"Thank you for telling us," Rósa's mother said. "I didn't realise that someone would come and tell us. That's a kind thing for the Sea People to do."

"I am intruding," Eala replied, and she turned to go.

"Thank you, my lady," said Rósa's father.

When she returned to the Court of the Favourites, she spoke the Words of Freshness, to take the smell of the City off her. Then she made herself pretty for the Mentor, all the time thinking how she was learning to seem happy when she wasn't. Or rather, she realised, to make the happiness visible and the sadness invisible. It still amazed her how she could feel both at once and how the two emotions just walked by each other, without the slightest recognition or gesture of acknowledgement.

— 10 —

Time to Remember

"So you're going, are you?"

Eala looked up when she heard Rónmór's voice.

"I am, Lord Rónmór. I should go back for the Midwinter Festival."

"So many people leave at Midwinter. Eibheara and Aclaí are going to Port Teorainn to be with Miotal. The highest Rank here is going to be Cathúa." He smiled dryly. "She is going to be with him on Midwinter's Night. I will spend Midwinter's Night in a hut made of snow, with a wind outside that would freeze you solid. But I think I'd rather that to all the questions that Cathúa will ask."

"I don't think the Mentor minds," Eala laughed. "I think he likes to be asked things about his life, things only he can remember. And Lady Cathúa loves to listen. Midwinter's Night is a time for remembering, isn't it? And he won't get a better ear for his memories."

"I hope you are right," he said. "I worry that I am failing in my duty to him."

"I don't think you are. The City celebrates Midwinter's Day. I've seen it on the Visions. So it's not like he will be left alone to remember by himself, is it?"

"The face the City shows in Visions is not the same as what actually happens, Eala."

"But he still won't be alone, will he?"

"He won't. I'm going tomorrow, on Midwinter's Day and I'm coming back the morning after. I will be with my family but I will not leave him alone too long."

"I'll have to ride. They might give a Flyer to the Favourite but I've never flown one. I won't be there until tomorrow night. I do not ride well."

"Won't Lady Éirime collect you?"

"I haven't asked. She doesn't like coming to the City. I can use the sword-hilt when I get to Idireatarthu. She will come and get me, I am

173

sure."

"I see. Will you let me take you home and bring you back?"

"You would have to go to Anleacán, then back to the City, then on to the north. I couldn't accept such a big favour, Lord Rónmór, you know that."

"But if it gave the Mentor another day and a half with his Favourite, it would be my duty as Chamberlain. I always feel that so many favourites going away for so long at the celebration days is not right. It would not be a favour to you, it would be part of my duty to the Mentor."

"Is that really what you think?"

She had come to the same conclusion herself, but she also cared about her family and about Caora. She hadn't spoken to them since she had been named Favourite because she wanted to tell them in person. But she felt guilty that she hadn't spoken to them and she didn't want to miss Midwinter's Day in Áthaiteorann.

"How many times do I have to tell you how much he cares for you?"

"I'm an ordinary girl, Lord Rónmór. In my mind, I'm still a peasant."

"I know. So does he, I think. That is why he is attracted to you. Lady Éirime was the same but she didn't have your warrior's heart."

"So you keep saying."

"So I keep saying. I say what I believe. So, may I take you and bring you back? And it won't be a favour to you?"

"You may."

Eala heard someone outside her door. She was tired: the Mentor had kept her awake until well after midnight, until in the end she had been unable to keep conversations straight in her head or keep her eyes open. She didn't remember how she got back to her own bed.

She stood up, uncertainly. She was naked and the evidence of the night before was on her leg, dried and flaky. Her cloak was on the bed, though: it had been keeping her warm and it was clean, as it always was. She gathered it around her and went to the door.

It was Rónmór, with his bags, wearing his cloak, but also tall boots and gloves both made of leather. He had trousers and jacket of the same material and the jacket had a fur lined hood.

"I am sorry," she said. "I overslept."

"I am not surprised. You were in bed well after midnight and you are a Novice still. I have left you as long as I could."

"How did I get back?"

"You don't remember? The Mentor brought you out and put you to bed." He laughed, remembering it. "I think he used the Words of Strength. He was carrying you like a baby, wrapped in your cloak. You looked a strange sight."

"Was he angry?"

"Quite the opposite. I think he liked to do it."

She was relieved to hear that, even if it was humiliating to be carried out of his chambers. At least he had not carried her out naked and asleep.

Rónmór continued, "I will go down to the Court of the Veterans and get a Flyer. I'll ask the servants to put you together something for breakfast. Are you packed?"

"I was packed yesterday morning. Luchóg will get me something. All I need to do is clean up and get dressed."

"All right. If you wear something comfortable, you should be able to sleep on the Flyer."

"Thank you, Lord Rónmór."

When she was up and dressed she went out, Luchóg carrying her bag. She was sipping something hot from a mug when she saw Rónmór arrive. He brought the Flyer straight up and over the wall, into the Court of the Favourites, and put it down by the fountain. She went over and Cathúa came out of the House of Power and went over too. They got to the Flyer at the same time.

Rónmór took Eala's bag from Luchóg and put it on the luggage space of the Flyer.

"Lady Cathúa," he asked, "will you be all right with the Mentor while I am gone?"

"Rónmór, it will be no problem. We are normally together on the Midwinter Festival. It's like a Tradition."

"Thank you, my lady."

Cathúa turned to Eala.

"Eala," she said, and looked awkward.

What have I done? Eala wondered. Then suddenly Cathúa hugged Eala, holding her tight.

"You come back to us safe, Eala of Áthaiteorann. We need you here. We need you here very much."

She turned away, quickly, and ran back to the House of Power.

Eala watched her go, wondering. She put down the empty mug on the rim of the fountain, knowing the servants would collect it, and stepped on to the Flyer. When she had sat down, Rónmór spoke and the Flyer lifted off and flew away to the north. She saw the whole City beneath her and the Grey Gate ahead.

"Rónmór, what was the matter with Lady Cathúa?" she asked.

"I don't know. I think Lady Cathúa is the most intelligent of the Immortals and she sees lots of things. But she is shy. She prefers the company of dead people to living ones. She's now the only favourite at the City. When she spoke to you just then, the only Sea People in the Court of the Favourites were the two of us, her and the Mentor. If you want to know Lady Cathúa, you have to get her on her own. It's certainly an experience. She might talk endlessly about history but she can be very insightful." He looked away from her, down at the Grey Gate. "Flyer, follow my gaze."

They started to plunge down towards it and Eala could hear the wind about them.

"Where does she go when she disappears?"

"Researches, she says. Perhaps Lord Aclaí knows."

The Grey Gate suddenly grew large and they were through it. Around them was the vast greyness of the Space, with a line of wagons and walkers snaking away beneath and before them. That was what Rónmór followed, although Eala could see the faint glimmering of the Grey Road that they were following.

"Flyer, follow the Grey Road," he said. Then he turned back to Eala. "I imagine she sees what I see: that you are good for the Mentor. He has been different this year and you are the reason."

"Rónmór, I know you think I am wonderful but please don't, not this early in the morning."

They flew in silence. Eala realised she had hurt him.

"I'm sorry, I'm just tired," Eala said. "You didn't deserve that."

"I think I do. Everyone here has high expectations of you. It must get wearying."

"It does, but it's not their fault, is it? Or is there some secret conspiracy going on?"

She expected him to laugh, but he didn't.

"I haven't heard of a conspiracy. But lots of the Immortals keep secrets." He looked out at the wagons of the merchants, winding along the Grey Road. He seemed to her to be listening to some voice that she couldn't hear. Then he looked at her. "Sometimes Immortals will do things that won't make sense to you."

"Like Lady Cathúa or Lord Aclaí going away some days?"

"It is not just going away. Sometimes Lady Eibheara behaves oddly. It is almost like she has an evil twin." Eala saw the thought occur to him that he hadn't chosen the best analogy. "Anyway, she is not herself. Later, when she is back to normal, it is as if she has no memory of it."

Eala remembered that, when she and Geana had swapped names, keeping stories consistent was the hardest part. But people didn't normally notice – they were too wrapped up in their own lives and didn't seem to spot outrageous gaffes on the sisters' parts.

But Rónmór was still speaking.

"Do you know about the Prophecy of the Wife?" he asked.

Eala wondered about the subject change.

But she replied, "Is that like the Legend of the Wife?"

"I guess so."

"That's something to do with my sister's name and why she didn't get Selected."

"Well, that is part of the story. Certainly nobody ever gets Selected if their name sounds like 'Geana'. Some link that with the Legend of the Wife, though. If you ask Cathúa, she'll tell you that it's not proven. And grumble about the oldest records that the Mentor keeps secret."

"The Legend of the Wife isn't prophecy, though, it's history. So what is the Prophecy of the Wife, then?"

"Well, the Legend of the Wife is that there was a wife when the City was young. The link to your sister's name would be, I guess, that either she was called Geana or that his favourite pet-name for her was *love*. The first is not impossible, the second is not at all unlikely."

"Assuming it's likely him having a wife, anyway."

"Well, the prophecy is that someday someone will come and replace her and he will be married again. Some versions say that it will bring about the end of the Sea People."

"Well, we were taught that prophecy can never be reliable. Something about information selection."

"That is right. Cathúa says that everything is connected together, entangled, even the impulses in our brains that we think are random. It's not that we cannot sense anything about the world, it's that we sense everything about all worlds, past, present, and future – and that we cannot choose what our brains pick out from all that."

"They taught it in naturalism using mathematics. Your explanation makes more sense."

"It's not my explanation: it's Cathúa's." Eala remembered Cathúa explaining it and wondered again what Cathúa actually believed. "You could, she thinks, make reliable prophecy with the Great Principle of Creation."

"Because the Manifestations of Creation work by directing that entanglement?"

"Exactly. But we couldn't build it and make it work for the Sea People while the Mentor has the Great Principle of Creation hanging around his neck."

"That would be a problem. The Manifestations hate us and that is

probably why. Anyway, we know it is not trustworthy but do you set any
store by it?"

"I didn't, not until I met you. And don't be sure that all the Manifestations hate humanity." He looked over at her for a moment, before looking
back at the horizon. "Anyway," he continued, "Some people spent a long
time looking for the Wife. Lady Éirime was one. She used to search the new
Novices for the Wife. That is why you have caused so much excitement.
You and your sister are the only Candidates she ever Sponsored. And now
everyone can see the effect you're having on him and lots of people think
you are the Wife."

"More likely Geana was the Wife, and he's rejected her." She laughed,
but there was no joy in it. "Does the Mentor know about this prophecy?"

"I don't know. I doubt anyone would tell him, to his face. But that
doesn't mean he doesn't know. Why?"

"Because if he knows it, and believes in it, he might also be looking."

"I suppose he might. Why does that matter?"

"Because if he is looking, then the first time he meets a girl he really
likes, he might imagine it was her. Imagining it was her would make him
believe it was her and act differently to her and so on."

"Making the prophecy come true?"

"Until he realised that she wasn't what he thought she was. What the
prophecy says she will be. Then, bad things."

"What if she was?"

Rónmór looked away, again, and saw the Gate of Anleacán in the distance, at the end of the line of traffic below them.

"Flyer, follow my gaze."

They began to descend, quickly, towards the Gate. A moment later and
they were flying up, through heavy rain.

"Which way now, Eala?" Rónmór asked.

"Go north. There are mountains in the way. The other side of the
mountains is the Road of the Sea People. It goes north and east, straight
to Áthaiteorann. Lord Aclaí extended it north beyond Áthaiteorann to the
Midsummer Palace, but we won't be going that far."

"Good. Flyer, go north. Keep us clear of the ground but also clear of
the cloud, as far as possible. Ground clearance is more important than
cloud clearance." He turned back to Eala. "There. Will you recognise the
Road of the Sea People from the air?"

"Maybe. Look, Rónmór, I'm not The Wife. This is sounding like the
Eala is Wonderful Song again."

"I'm sorry. I don't believe you are The Wife. I believe that you might
turn out to be her, but that depends on the Mentor. He has a choice. I

hope he chooses you: if I were him, I would."

She looked over the edge of the Flyer. Great mountains were marching through breaks in the clouds and the wind and rain about them went one way and then the other. The air around them was tremendously turbulent.

Eala was silent a moment, thinking about the mathematics of information. She tried to estimate the amount of information in the Universe and to compare it to the amount of information that the brain could process. It seemed impossible that the brain could ever find any meaningful prophecy: the amount of information was simply too great. But she knew that intuition was not always a good guide to numbers.

Then the clouds broke, or they moved below them, and Eala could see the forest to the left, the Forest House of Maoineas and, through the trees, she could see the Road. She pointed it out.

"There it is. Follow that."

She looked back at the House of Maoineas. It was much bigger than Áthaiteorann and there were various large, strange structures she could not identify at this distance. It was soon lost from sight.

"Flyer, follow the Road of the Sea People."

The Flyer continued north for a while, then as Eala was wondering if it would, it curved to the right, and they followed the Road.

"Eala?" he asked her.

She looked around at him. He seemed to think better of saying something.

Then he said, "What do the people of Áthaiteorann do for the Midwinter Festival?"

"They do the same as everyone else on Anleacán. The whole village builds a great Midwinter Fire. There is dancing, food, and lots of drink. Then when the fire dies down and it gets too cold to dance, they gather close around, and people remember the things they have done in the last year and the things they will do in the next. Finally, unless it burns all night, people go to bed." She looked down, at a village on the road. "See, that big pile by the river? That will be the Midwinter Fire."

"I see it. It must be strange to be able to stay outside on Midwinter's Day."

"What do your people do, Lord Rónmór?"

"There is no Midwinter Day where I come from. The sun last set in the Month of Death, and will not rise again until the Month of Light."

"Because your world is a ball. They told us about that in naturalism lectures. What is it like? Isn't it depressing to have no sun for three months?"

"It can be depressing. But it works both ways. The sun stops setting

in the Month of Life and stays up until the Month of Darkness. Summer
is a day that lasts three months too. In that time, you feel like you could
do anything."

"So what do you do on Midwinter's Night?"

"We stay in houses made of ice and we remember with our families. If
the wind is quiet and there are no clouds, we can get up and look at the
Sun's Wind, which blows above our sky. It is amazing colours, never still.
The superstition among our people is that the breath of our dead blows in
that wind." He looked out, not at her. "That will be hard. This year, we
will be remembering Léaró. If we see the Sun's Wind, Grandmother will
point up at the sky and say she can see Léaró there."

"The superstitions of peasants are comfort, Lord Rónmór. You should
not belittle them. It is in us all to yearn for immortality."

"Immortality doesn't mean living forever, Eala. Some day it will be me
but there will be no grandmother to point at the sky and say she can see
me."

"Some day it will be all of us, Rónmór. But from what I've seen, the
peasants are better at living a happy life than those of us who have put on
a blue robe."

"You are right," he said, still staring out. Then he pointed. "That big
building over there: is that the Midsummer Palace?"

She looked out too. She could see the building in the haze, half a day's
walk north. But looking down between them and the building, she could
see the river and the road. Where they crossed she could see the bare little
trees of Olláchan's orchard by the river and next to it must be the Songbird
and Shepherdess. She felt it in her chest. How could she miss it so much
and not know? It was as if her homesickness lived in a secret place, and
only came out now.

"That village there, that is Áthaiteorann. See the house that's got two
roofs, next to the pine tree? My mother lives there."

"Flyer, follow my gaze and land," he said.

Again, they began to descend and slowly the village grew in front of
them. She saw the toy buildings become real buildings, she heard shouts
in the wind, and she saw people running out, pointing up at them. A
small figure with bright hair stepped out of the house. It was her mother,
she knew, even at this distance. She waved and her mother waved back.
Suddenly they were below the trees and what was remote seen from the
air became immediate and she felt like they were flying instead of sitting
and watching. A moment later, they were on the ground before the house
where she was born. Eala got up and ran to her mother, unable to stay
away a moment longer. They embraced. Rónmór could see the others, all

staring at him, wondering what to make of him. He gathered Eala's bag and got up to follow.

"May I take that, my lord?" a red-haired boy asked him.

"It is Eala's bag," he told the boy, letting him take it.

"I know, my lord," he replied. "I am her brother."

The boy walked towards the house, staggering under the weight of the bag. Rónmór looked around and saw Eala come through the crowd. But it wasn't her: the girl he could see had a green wool dress and a sheepskin; and Eala had her cloak and the blue silk dress that the Mentor loved so much. Behind the girl was the Lady Éirime. They came over.

"Rónmór," said Éirime when they were close, "did you come all this way to bring Eala home?"

"It's my duty, Lady Éirime," he replied. "I am still Chamberlain."

The girl in the green dress and sheepskin, whose face confused Rónmór so much, looked puzzled at Éirime and Rónmór. But Éirime spoke up.

"Why is it the Chamberlain's duty to bring a Novice home?" she asked.

"Eala is the Mentor's Favourite, Lady Éirime."

The girl who looked like Eala was delighted, he could see. But Éirime was not.

"Poor child," she said, shocking Rónmór. "When did it happen?"

"She was made Favourite on the Fifth Day of Autumn. She was Initiated on the Third. Lady Cathúa thinks it may be the fastest ever."

"There is a butcher in Áthaiminn, who is renowned throughout the area because he can kill an animal so quickly. People think he is the fastest ever."

"Retirement has changed you, Lady Éirime. We were friends."

"Since I took Eala to Selection, I've thought a lot about the Sea People and most of those thoughts have been regrets. That life is in my past, Rónmór. This is my home now. Even that name is in the past. Here I am Caora."

"I understand, Lady Éirime. Caora. I will say goodbye to Eala and then I will go away. I will return to collect her tomorrow."

"Thank you," she said.

They went over to Eala, talking to her mother and her brother. Eala spoke as he came over.

"Mammy, this is Rónmór, the Mentor's Chamberlain and my friend."

"Thank you for bringing her home, Lord Rónmór," she said. "How can we repay you?"

"I did it for the Mentor. I have to go anyway. Eala, I will see you tomorrow. Thank you for your company."

Eala went over to him and embraced him.

"It will be all right, Rónmór," she whispered. "Remember him for me, too."

Rónmór let go of her and went back to the Flyer. A moment later Áthaiteorann was far below and behind him. The Flyer knew the way to the Gate that led back to the City. Anleacán marched below him, but he couldn't see it.

From the City Gate to his home was a journey he did without thinking about it. When he was flying above the ice, he easily picked out the shape of the bay and, from that, the place where his family spent the winter, in the lee of the hills. He saw a white bear, a great brawny monster out on the ice, but he missed the humps in the snow that were his family's winter houses. Then he had to concentrate and, on the third go by, he found them.

When the Flyer was landed, the wind blasted over him, and he pulled his cloak tight around his body. He had no idea which was his parents' house so he went to the nearest dome, to the entrance arch, and called.

"I am Rónmór," he shouted over the wind. "Whose house is this?"

"Lord Rónmór, come in," she called from inside. "I've been expecting you to come here."

He crawled in, and then got up once he was inside. Grandmother Realtaíne was sitting cross-legged in her sealskin coat and trousers, carving a piece of ivory into the head for a fishing spear. She moved aside a little, to make room for him by her. The light of the lamp and the brown of the hangings made the space look warm but he knew it was cold enough to freeze even inside the dome. He wrapped his cloak around him before he sat down, feeling the cold, used to the endless warmth of the Land of the Immortals.

"The ancestors tell me all about you," she told him. "Léaró understands that his death was not your fault. The City is caught in a web of fate and he was just one more fish tangled up in it."

Rónmór thought of the advice his own Manifestation had offered, and wondered how Realtaíne could get the same result, knowing that ancestors were not real. But he didn't say anything.

"You don't want to talk about Léaró?" she asked. "Perhaps you will tell me about the girl who has stolen your heart."

"She has stolen everyone's heart, Grandmother," he answered. "I was hoping to get Sixteenth Rank, Immortal Breath, and then return here to live among my people. But, Grandmother, I cannot leave her. She is so beautiful, so kind, and she is in terrible danger. The day I first saw her, the day she was Selected, the Mentor nearly killed her."

"But you can't make her your wife, can you?"

"The Sea People do not marry, Grandmother."

"It's not just that, is it, my lord?"

"It isn't, Grandmother. She's the Mentor's Favourite."

"Even though he tried to kill her?"

"The City is a cruel place, Grandmother," he answered. "She is too kind for it and I am afraid it will destroy her. She will never be mine. I don't know what to do, Grandmother."

"Lord Rónmór, you come and visit me and it is good to see you. But we both know that you do not need me to tell you what the Ancestors say, when you do not believe in them. And Rónmór, you should ask your own spirit guide."

"The Sea People do not have spirit guides, Grandmother."

"They don't, my lord. But, Lord Rónmór, that means they don't know how to live with a guide."

"What do you mean?"

"To the Sea People, a spirit is something to make into a servant, or maybe an ally. That cannot work, Lord Rónmór."

He looked at her and the Manifestation prompted him. "Then what, Grandmother?"

"You have to obey, Lord Rónmór."

"How can I obey when you won't tell me what to do?"

She looked over at him, and laughed.

"Not me, Rónmór. You need to devote your life to the service of your spirit guide. I will sing a while and you should ask your own spirit guide."

And she began to sing, the tuneless, humming song that led the family's spirit meetings. Rónmór allowed the singing to clear his mind and then thought of his friend. I'm in love with her, he thought, silently. I was only staying for Sixteenth Rank and Retirement and suddenly I'm in love with her.

She needs your help. She has a very hard and dangerous road to walk.

I know. Why do I feel like this, though?

You feel like this because it helps you to take care of her and to help her build her relationship with the Mentor.

How will it end?

How it ends depends on the Mentor. You know that.

But how will it end for me?

That depends on the Mentor, again.

Will she ever be mine? If he rejects her, will she be mine?

She won't. If you remember that, it will go easier for you. If you don't we will still take care of you. We won't let you do us this favour without taking care of you. When this is over, one way or another, I will take you home.

* * *

Eala went back to her mother and they watched Rónmór go back to the Flyer. The Flyer rose into the sky and went away to the south. Geana came up to them and Eala embraced her and then Caora. They were all quiet with her, as if she had changed. Geana spoke first.

"That Lord Rónmór had tears on his face as he got on the Flyer. Why is that?"

Flannbhuía looked shocked, Caora looked guilty and Eala did not know why either of them reacted like that.

"His youngest brother was Selected at the same time as me," Eala explained. "Do you remember he was next to us in the Hall?"

"Oh, so he was," Geana remembered.

"He was. His brother died in the Forest less than a ten-day ago. He is going back to his family and they will be remembering, same as everyone does at Midwinter. His parents are very old. Léaró was certainly their last child. I doubt they will be happy." Eala blinked at her own tears. "Léaró was my friend."

Flannbhuía asked, "Do many Adepts get killed in the Forest?"

"Far too many, Mammy," replied Eala. "I am safe because I am Favourite but more than half of them will die. I made four friends when I first arrived and only one of them is still alive."

"Why are Favourites safe?" she asked. "I've heard talk of Favourites but I've never really understood it."

"It means that the Mentor picks out Adepts he likes. We live separately, we are taught separately. Most Favourites become Immortals, if they stay long enough. Rónmór is one of us, in charge of organising ... certain things." She couldn't tell her mother that Rónmór chose who was to share the Mentor's bed. "So I am taught about the Forest by the Lord Aclaí, who knows more about surviving in the Forest than any man alive. He won't even take me out until he thinks I will be safe."

Flannbhuía knew who Lord Aclaí was: if Lord Aclaí was keeping her daughter safe, she would not be so worried for her.

"So the Mentor chooses the Novices but he chooses some of them for extra tuition?"

"He doesn't choose one every year."

"But this year he chose you?"

"He chose me, Mammy".

Geana interrupted. "He chose you to be the Favourite, not just a favourite, didn't he? That's what Lord Rónmór said."

"He did," she said, feeling uncomfortable about her telling it.

"That means he likes you better than all the others."

Flannbhuía said, "But if he only chose one this year, then of course she is the best."

"Mammy, the favourites are not just Novices. Lord Aclaí is a Favourite, and so is Lady Eibheara." Eala saw her look at Caora and saw Caora glare back a warning. "Anyway, if Eala is the Favourite, it means he likes her better than all of them."

"Is that true, Eala? He likes you better than Lady Eibheara?"

"It is, Mammy. But it's not exactly right, either. The Mentor tends to favour Novices. We have to work hard to learn things and the Immortals tend to be busy with their duties. We need to be close to the Mentor and they don't."

"My daughter is the Mentor's Favourite," Flannbhuía told herself. Eala could see her pride.

Later, when the twins got back to Caora's room, Caora turned on Geana.

"Do you enjoy humiliating your sister?" she asked.

Eala saw Geana look startled, shocked, and then upset.

Eala said, "She doesn't understand, Lady Caora."

"Then you tell her. I'm going to find something to drink."

She went out and left them alone. When Eala looked back at Geana, she saw tears overflow Geana's eyes.

"What don't I understand?" she asked.

"The Initiation of Sea People happens in the Mentor's bed."

"I know that. Caora told me the evening you were Selected."

"Did she tell you what the Mentor chooses Favourites for?"

"She didn't. She's never talked about Favourites."

"Well, the Favourites are the ones who spend most time in his bed. Of the people Selected, about half will die before they ever get to his bed. Léaró was Initiated; Rósa and Lách died before they could. Léaró and Lách had important Sponsors and Rósa was from the City. They would have been Initiated soon, if they'd lived. But the ones the Mentor wants to see more often, they become Favourites."

"So they are Initiated in order of importance?"

"Not exactly. My Sponsor is Second Oldest but Léaró was first to be Initiated because Rónmór chooses who goes to the Mentor's chamber." She didn't want to mention Stail and she wasn't even sure if his intervention had made any difference. "If it was just in order of Sponsor's Rank, I would have been there on the First Night of Autumn, not the Third. Lord Aclaí didn't Sponsor anyone this year."

"So what does that have to do with Favourites? You are Favourite because Caora is high-Rank?"

"My Initiation was early because Caora is high-Rank. But Favourites are to do with the Mentor. He likes me, for some reason: probably because he misses Caora and my Áthaiteorann accent reminds him of her. I'm in love with him, of course, but he likes me back. That is unusual."

"Why is it unusual?"

"All of us are in love with him: that's what Initiation does. Mostly he treats them the way a big man would treat slave girls, at least in bed." Telling Geana that, Eala felt embarrassed. "That is how he treated me at first. That is what Caora meant when she talked about showing leadership and bravery and about hiding our sorrow. I tried to please him, I didn't make a fuss that he wouldn't marry me or anything and he liked me. Caora had given me good advice and I was lucky."

"Surely all Sponsors give their Candidates good advice?"

"Some of them give very little advice. For most of them, the only advantage is to get new Adepts that owe their position to them. Some take care, some just send lots of Candidates. When I called Lord Rian to tell him that Lách was dead, Lord Rian didn't even remember that he had sponsored Lách."

"That's awful, Eala."

"It is. Lots of things at the City are awful. Anyway, Caora is a Favourite. She was the Favourite soon after she was Selected, displacing Lord Aclaí. She probably knows more about it than most Sponsors."

"So why is she angry with me?"

"I am in love with the Mentor, Geana, but I know in my mind, not my heart, that becoming a Favourite is like a reward for being a good whore."

She was really shamed to say that, but she knew it was true, and she had needed to say it to someone for a long time.

"We pretend to be happy and do what he wants us to do, and he rewards us by giving us a lift along the road to Immortality. Mostly that road is too long for us to travel, unless we are Favourites. The only Immortals I've met who are not Favourites are Lords Foscúil and Miotal, and Lady Damhánalla: and they are Favourites of Lord Aclaí, who probably did the same thing for them. For the same price." She looked at Geana, to see how much she understood. "And the Favourite before me was nudged into his position by Rónmór under Aclaí's orders and the gossip on the Hill is that Éise paid for it *that way.*"

Eala sighed, looked up at her sister. Geana was shocked but sympathetic, accepting.

"I just tried to do what Caora told me, and I got chosen as Favourite, but most of the Favourites worked their way to those positions. He's just using me to show Caora that he doesn't have to be cruel. And I'm using him, in return. We are all whoring for Immortal Rank."

"Why does that make Caora angry? She got her immortality."

"Geana, can I tell Mammy that I am a whore?"

Then Geana understood and she held her sister.

"You're not a whore, though. You said you were only doing what Caora had taught you."

"I am, Geana. I didn't know that was what I was doing but I know now and I am still doing it. Caora taught me to do it, because she knew it was what we wanted. That is why she was so ashamed of taking us to Selection."

"What else can you do? Give it up, and Retire?"

"I can't do that. But I can't tell Mammy what it means to be a Favourite either. I'm afraid she will find out and then she will be as ashamed as she is proud today."

"Are you really so ashamed? I have lain awake wishing I could be with you in the dormitories, being in the City. Then I guessed you were a Favourite after you stopped calling and I have wished for that all the more."

"How could I tell Caora that I am Favourite?" Eala asked. "You see how it has upset her? Even when I was here in person, not using the sword?" She looked at Geana, frowned. "How did you know?" she added.

"The Day of Death was quiet: there weren't many merchants visiting. Caora wanted to drink, but I wanted to see the Visions. I thought that if I saw the celebrations at the City, I might glimpse you somewhere in the crowds. She left me alone here. And then I saw you by the Mentor's side and I knew you were Favourite."

"How did you know it was me?" she wondered.

"As if I wouldn't know my own sister's face?" Geana looked at her open-mouthed. "As if I wouldn't know my own face?"

Eala realised that the skeleton illusion had not carried over the Visions, that the Visions saw through illusion. No matter.

"If I wasn't Favourite, I would have been in the Forest with Rósa, Lách and Léaró. If you had been Selected, you would have been there too. I think you would have been Favourite, not me – but the Novices choose their own teams and you'd have talked to Lách before I did. All the paths of *what if* lead to this life, or to death in the Forest, for both of us. Or worse, to a whoring life for one of us and death in the Forest for the other. You'd probably be the whore, and I'd be the chewed bones, but it could be either."

"You're not his whore, sister."

"It is like that, Geana. We are like slaves to him."

"That is not what I saw."

Eala looked at her, thinking. She had never been able to read the Mentor's feelings on his face. She got so confused trying, she had given up before the Month of Autumn was over.

"How..?" she asked.

"It's easy, sister. My lady. His face is easy to read. He is in love with you. Whenever you looked away from him, he looked at you."

"I can't read him at all. How can you be sure, just from one evening on the Visions?"

"He was easy to read at Selection. You read him well, when you ... when you saved my life."

She remembered.

"Then why can't I..?" and she realised. "It's the Initiation, Geana," she said. "I can't read him because I am afraid. I'm afraid of what I will see and my fear confuses me."

Her sister hugged her.

"You'll learn," she said. "Being in love is like that. Remember how hard I found it to read Ordóg when I was trying to catch him? How you had to interpret his face for me?" She looked uncomfortable to remember it, but Eala knew she was right. "But you'll feel better after a few months."

"I think it will take more time than that," answered Eala. "Initiation is much stronger than ordinary love. I can't think clearly about him at all."

"You have all the time in the world, sister. You will be Immortal."

"Maybe."

She looked into her sister's eyes, expecting to see envy. But there was none there.

"You don't mind?" Eala asked.

"I don't mind," she answered. "We may still celebrate our nine hundredth birthdays together, Eala. Caora can breathe Immortality into other people. She's never told any of the Sea People but she can do it."

"I never heard of it. But if she can teach me and if I make Immortal Rank, then of course I will."

"She means to do it herself. We are lovers, Eala."

"Are you happy?"

"I am very happy. Or I was, until I angered her."

"Does Mammy know?"

"She does. What blue-robes do is no business of hers, she tells me. The whole village is the same. The only person who isn't happy for us is Ordóg."

"I can understand that."

"But if Mammy says it about Caora and me, she will say it about you and the Mentor, can't you see?" Eala realised Geana was probably right. Then Geana asked, "You think I angered Caora by mentioning Favourites in front of Mammy?"

"I think Caora is upset because you mentioned Favourites at all. I don't think she is angry, I think she is ashamed."

"So what should I do?"

"Forgive her when she apologises, I suspect. I will go down and talk to her."

"Should I come?"

"I don't think you should."

"All right. I love you, sister."

"I love you, sister. I'll come find you when it's sorted."

She went downstairs. Caora was in the commons, talking to Fuiseoga. Fuiseoga looked up as Eala approached. Eala had seen the effect her blue robe had on ordinary people when she had searched for Rósa's parents, but she never expected to see it in Áthaiteorann, where she had grown up. Surely they knew she was just Eala, whatever she wore.

But Fuiseoga said, "Good evening, Lady Eala. May I get you a drink?"

It sounded wrong to hear that. How could Fuiseoga, who would have boxed her ears for attempting to get drink in the Shepherdess before they became apprentices, be offering to wait on her now? Did a blue cloak really make that much difference? But it would enable her to talk to Caora.

"Nothing too strong, please. I am still not used to drinking."

"As you wish, my lady." She hurried off.

"I can't get used to that, Lady Caora," said Eala.

"Neither can I," she replied.

"You know Geana didn't mean to upset you?"

Caora drank, then she spoke.

"I'm sorry. I don't know ..." she struggled for words. "I guessed something was wrong when you didn't call but hearing you are Favourite has really upset me. If I'd known that would happen, I would never have taken you. I am afraid your mother will be ashamed if she knows the truth."

"I'm afraid too but I don't think she would be. Geana told me about you two and told me that Mammy doesn't mind. If she doesn't mind you and Geana, why would she mind me and the Mentor?"

"It's not the same, Eala."

"I know it isn't, my lady. But how would Mammy ever understand that?"

"I suppose she wouldn't. But I still feel upset by this."

"So do I, my lady. I feel like a whore when I am telling Mammy about it."

"I can see that. It is only Geana who doesn't know."

"Of course she doesn't know. She has no idea what it is like."

"Have I made her unhappy?"

"You have, my lady. I explained it to her. She is afraid you will love her less."

"It's not really her. It's me. I'm just so upset about it. You must be so unhappy."

"I'm not as unhappy as you think. I'm a bit ashamed: Mammy taught us the importance of being married and being faithful. I've been faithful, but not married, of course. The Sea People do not marry."

Fuiseoga came back with a drink for Eala.

"It's mead, my lady, but it's mixed with water. It's what I give Saonta."

Fuiseoga's daughter was six years older than Eala.

"Thank you," said Eala.

Caora said, "We're talking about Sea People things, I'm afraid. If you find Leathar, I will come out and we can play by the fire in a short while. Can you find us seats outside The Sun?"

"As you wish, my lady," replied Fuiseoga.

Eala felt uncomfortable about Caora dismissing someone like that, especially when it was someone she knew. Caora turned to her.

"Shall we talk outside?" She led the way.

Eala followed her out into the cold and wrapped her cloak around her. It was much warmer in the City and she felt how the material kept her warm, even in an Áthaiteorann midwinter. She thought of Rónmór on the ice, in the darkness.

When they could not be overheard, Caora said, "How can you be faithful?"

"I was Initiated on the Third Day of Autumn. He asked for me on the Fourth Day: I missed getting my Rank because Rónmór had me in the Mentor's chamber, not at the Evening Meal. On the Fifth, he gave me my Rank but he also declared me the Favourite." Eala thought and laughed a little. "If you consider Initiation to happen when the Mentor announces it, at Evening Meal, the time between my getting First Rank and becoming Favourite was the time of one breath: the breath he drew between one announcement and the next. Now I am not allowed to be with another man. Even if I'd wanted to be unfaithful, even if you judge the time between the acts, not the announcements, I would barely have had time. The only other Initiated person in the dormitory was Léaró and Léaró was nice, like his brother, and really pretty, but he would never have been a boyfriend. The lecturers could have, but they didn't: I only had three lectures anyway and two of them were given by women. Other than that, I didn't know anyone anyway. And I didn't want to do it, and I don't."

"You had it much easier than I did, Eala. It was more than a month before I was made Favourite. He gave me to the Favourites the morning after my Initiation. They raped me, one after another. I had no choice."

Eala was shocked. "Why would he do that?"

"He didn't think I was a good Adept. He didn't think I was strong enough and he thought it would make me stronger." She drank again. Eala realised she must have been drinking heavily since she had argued with Geana. "It made me more bitter, which probably made him think I was stronger. There was one of the Favourites, in particular, who was very cruel."

"Lord Aclaí?" Eala asked.

Although her instinct told her it was wrong, it was the best explanation for why Caora reacted to him like that, although she could hardly believe it. But people change, even in a mortal lifetime, and Lord Aclaí was hard to read.

"Lord Aclaí was the only one of the men among the Favourites who didn't. I thought he was being kind, because I didn't know him. Now I know that he simply had other plans for me. The rest of them are dead and I haven't regretted it at all. Except the one who was most cruel. He's Retired, I think. He vanished between my Initiation and my being made Favourite. Nobody knows what happened to him but it is easy for Immortals to go into the Forest and make a life for themselves. It was easier then. Iolar was the first Immortal and he made the Forest People."

"Then Lord Aclaí is not the Oldest?"

"Probably not. But they searched for Iolar and never found him. I think the Forest People hid him and they are hiding him still. Did Geana tell you about what happened the night Spideog was ill?"

"About her spilling ale on you?"

"Well, it was cider. But that is what I was thinking of. I thought it was Iolar attacking me."

"Who knows this?"

"Lord Aclaí. Me. Now you."

"You haven't told Geana?"

"I don't want to tell her. I don't want her to imagine you being gang-raped by the Favourites."

"They're not like that anyway, Lady Caora."

"Maybe you're right, some of them. But if he ordered it, they'd do it."

"None of them are like that. You already said that Lord Aclaí wasn't like that when you were young. He might be frightening, but he is not frightening in that way. He's not a rapist: girls beg him." The corners of Eala's mouth twitched. "So do boys. Rónmór is nothing like that. Rónmór is the nicest, kindest person on the Hill, with no exceptions. He should

be surrounded by jealousy and live a great life off all the favours, but he
doesn't. Toirneach is not a rapist and, anyway, he's not interested in girls.
Liús is in love with Éise and she leads him around like a pet." Eala smiled
when she thought of it: their names suggested it should be the other way
around. "That is all the boys," she continued.

"I don't know Liús. The rest I'll concede. But for that you are lucky,
Eala."

"I agree there are bad men in the City, Lady Caora. They're just not
Favourites. That's not the sort of person the Mentor picks."

"He picked Iolar, Eala. He just hasn't picked any recently."

"Maybe he's changed."

"I don't believe it."

Eala could tell from the set of her face that there was no further discussion to be had on that subject. But that wasn't why she was here.

"Lady Caora, I think you owe Geana an apology."

She realised as she said it that she would never say such a thing on the
Hill.

While she was thinking about that, Caora replied. "You are right. Is
she still in our room?"

"She was. I told her to wait for me there. Do you want me to come?"

"I will be better on my own, I think. Eala, I was afraid you would come
back from the City changed into something bad. You went to the City a
very kind person. I am so relieved you have not changed. Rónmór isn't
the nicest, kindest person in the City, Eala. You are. Don't ever let that
change, no matter what they do to you."

"It is Geana who needs your kind words, Lady Caora."

"All right. I'll go."

Eala found she didn't want to talk to anyone, fretting about what Geana
said she had seen in the Visions, so she walked out in the gathering darkness
to see how they were making the fire. But as she walked around, someone
called out.

"Geana?" It was a man's voice.

She turned to the shape in the darkness. Then she picked up a twig.
The voice spoke again.

"Please, Geana, I only want to talk."

She spoke Words of Power, softly, and the twig shone with light. She
held out the light. She saw Ordóg sitting on a log.

"I am sorry, Lady Eala." His face showed fear.

"It's all right. I'm still Eala, not the Lady Eibheara. Is there space there for two?"

He shuffled over, she planted the twig in the ground and sat down beside him. He looked at the light.

"You already have great powers, my lady."

"That is nothing, it's very simple really. There's a trick to it, that's all. It means that people can see that all we are doing is talking: that there is no mischief. It also makes sure they will stay away and let us talk in peace."

"Mischief, my lady?"

"You have a reputation, Ordóg. You wouldn't want gossip and to make my boyfriend jealous."

"You have a boyfriend, my lady?"

"My boyfriend is the Mentor. That is what they mean when they call me Favourite."

"You are right, my lady. I wouldn't want to make him jealous. I wouldn't want to make Lady Caora jealous, either. It doesn't make any difference, really. A blue-robe is a blue-robe and dead is dead."

"That is true."

She looked over at him, waiting for him to tell her what was really on his mind. She knew what it was but he had to tell her, if he was going to.

"I guess that is why Geana won't talk to me," he said, eventually.

"I don't know. I don't think Lady Caora would hurt you for anything you did to Geana, provided you didn't force or hurt her. It might be that Geana doesn't know what to say. She hasn't treated you very well."

"How has she ill-treated me, my lady?"

"She has been false with you. She never intended to marry anyone in Áthaiteorann."

"Did she tell you that?"

"She did."

"When?"

"Years ago. Years before Lady Caora came. Before Daddy died. Lady Caora showed her what she wanted to be but she knew what she didn't want to be since she was a little girl."

"She wanted to be Lady Caora's girlfriend, my lady?"

"She wanted to wear a blue robe."

"But she isn't wearing one and you are."

"I know. Strange, isn't it? I never wanted it the way she did. She was disappointed but then she found something else. I think she is happier than she would have been at the City. I am doing very well at the City but Geana is happier than I am."

She looked at him, to see if he saw what she was saying. His face looked odd, illuminated from beneath by the glowing twig.

"The thing is, Ordóg, the things that make us most happy aren't always the things we most want."

"I daresay you are right, my lady. But even if I say she is never going to marry me, what do I do now? Most of the girls in the village are married."

"What about Saonta?"

Saonta was Fuiseoga's daughter. She had shown little interest in marrying and had a reputation to match Ordóg's. When they had been together, the gossip had been glorious.

"Saonta is pledged to marry Iorai."

"I have been away too long."

"Anyway, Saonta is no virgin."

"Neither is Geana. Come to that, Ordóg, neither are you. Why should it matter?"

Ordóg looked uncomfortable.

"I don't know. I want to marry a virgin."

"Sneachta wasn't a virgin when she married."

Ordóg looked more uncomfortable.

"She wasn't."

"Neither was Eilite. And Saonta was a virgin when you first took her to the woods, wasn't she? I make that four. How many virgins can one man want, Ordóg?"

She thought of the Mentor as she asked him.

"I'm sorry, Lady Eala. I haven't been very nice to the girls that have loved me, have I?" He looked sad, and Eala could see he was thinking. Then he said, "You think I don't deserve to be married."

"I'm not here to judge you, Ordóg."

"If you choose to judge me, my lady, there is nothing I can do."

"I don't choose to judge you. In my mind, I'm still Geana's little sister. But if a boy can want to marry when he is not a virgin, why not a girl?"

"She might have been in love with someone else."

"She might. Have you been in love, Ordóg?"

He stared at the light.

"You are right, Lady Eala. I am not very good at choosing things to make me happy. Geana did to me what I did to so many other girls. If my wife had loved other men before, it would only be just."

"If you had another girlfriend, would you treat her differently?"

"I think I would." Eala looked at him, remembered what he had been like when Geana had first been with him. She was sure he had changed. "But I think I will have to leave the village to find one."

"You might simply wait. How old is Iorai?"

"I don't know I can wait that long."

"You might not have to. You never know what is going to happen."

He looked out at the darkness. They saw light and the flames started to rise. The Midwinter Fire was lit. They heard music as Caora started to play, calling the dancers.

"Do you want to dance, Ordóg?"

"Would your boyfriend mind, Lady Eala?"

"At Midwinter, people dance. If you can keep your hands where they belong, I am sure it will be fine."

"Then I would like to dance."

"Take the light, then."

He reached down and picked up the twig, not sure if it would burn him, and they walked back. The musicians were seated outside The Sun and people were passing hot wine out of the windows. They heard Leathar speaking as they approached.

"This is The Ducks and Drakes," Leathar called out. "Who will lead the first dance?" He looked at the crowd and saw them. "Lady Eala, will you honour us?"

"I will dance. As to honour, I'm still a girl from Áthaiteorann."

"Do you have a partner, Lady Eala?"

"Well," she laughed, "I left my partner at the City. But Ordóg has agreed to help out."

They led out.

"Ordóg has a reputation, Lady Eala," someone called out. She thought it might be Olachán, but she was not sure. It was a relief to hear someone joking, after all afternoon of *my lady*.

"And I have a sword," she called back. "I am sure he will be the perfect gentleman."

There was laughter from all sides. She felt it could actually be the Midwinter Celebration, after all.

Other couples came out and the music began. It was a lively dance and she saw various people watching her. Ordóg was a perfect gentleman, as promised: she was sure it was not just her sword and the threat of the Mentor that kept him well behaved. She saw Caora watching as she played and her mother still proud that her daughter was the Mentor's Favourite. She also saw many who were surprised that she should be dancing and Geana sitting out. She knew she had hidden behind her sister as they were growing up. She knew that behind her back they had called her "Eile", not "Eala"; and look at the Other Twin now. She could see it in their faces and it was a surprise for everyone. The most surprised face, though, was Geana.

Ordóg spoke to her as they went around. "You dance well, my lady."

"Lord Foscúil tells us that the only way to learn sword-craft is to learn to walk properly. I think his sword-craft lessons have helped my dancing."

"I understand, my lady. You don't have to mention your sword again. I won't misbehave."

"I know you will. But it is true. Lord Foscúil is the most graceful person I have ever seen." She couldn't help it: "Am I better than Geana?"

"As a dancer, you are. She used to have more passion."

"That's to be expected," she answered, trying to keep the secrets from showing on her face. "We are not lovers. If you were the Mentor, then I would have passion."

"Do you think I will find a wife?"

"I think you will. First you need to dismantle that reputation. That is what we are doing now."

"What do you mean, my lady?"

"You are showing everyone in the village that you can hold a girl in your hands without grabbing her bottom. The girls in the village will see it."

"I will never convince everyone, my lady."

"You only need to convince one."

"I suppose. But won't they think I am just behaving because you are a blue-robe, Lady Eala?"

"Maybe. They have the contrast, though: they have seen you dance with Geana. What you need to do is to dance with someone else."

"Who should that be, my lady?"

"Let me see."

She looked around at the people watching. Most of them were in couples, who had wandered up to see the dancing. The fire was now well lit and, through the village, firelight mingled with long shadows, as clear as the lights she had seen in the City's streets, across the river. She looked beyond the crowd to the cottages around them. Standing in her doorway, looking over at the dancers, she saw Fleánna. Eala could see that she was torn. She wanted to dance so much, but she was scared. Eala's instinct nudged her.

"Can I trust you to be a gentleman, Ordóg?"

"You can, Lady Eala. Really you can."

"Then dance with Fleánna."

"She isn't here, is she? She always stays in her cottage after dark."

"She is standing in her doorway, watching us. She wants to dance, I can see it. She wants it more than anything. But you be nice to her and, when you are done with her, take her back home. Don't leave her alone in the dark, not for a second. If she starts to get scared, or asks you, take her home, straight away. Don't go into her house, or out of sight of others, even if she asks you. Give her the twig: it will make her feel better."

"As you wish, Lady Eala."

"What are the rules?"

"Don't leave her side. Don't get her alone. Don't go into her house. Walk her home, as soon as she asks or gets scared. Give her the twig. And be a gentleman. You know, Lady Eala, it is as if you were her father."

"Fathers guard their daughters, Ordóg. Some day you will be a father yourself. Will you dance with her under my rules? You don't have to but it will help dismantle your reputation."

"I will, Lady Eala."

When the music stopped, they bowed to each other and people cheered. She went over to the Sun and the crowd around the window parted for her. She took advantage of the darkness to tug her Silver Cord and her sword and scabbard was on her hip. Someone passed her a drink: hot wine in a mug. She sipped it: it was spicy and powerful. She would have to drink it carefully, she thought, or she would be rolling her blue cloak in the dirt. She didn't have Caora's capacity.

Eala stood close by Geana and they watched Ordóg walking past the crowd, the twig glowing in his hand.

"What is he doing?" asked Geana.

"Watch," said Eala.

They saw him talking to Fleánna in her doorway. They argued a few moments, then both looked around in Eala and Geana's direction. Then Fleánna came out of her cottage and over to the dancers. They didn't hold hands, but she was staying close to him. She had the twig, wearing it like a shining brooch on her jacket. Eala leaned over towards the musicians.

"Lady Caora," she asked, quietly, "can we have something for younger dancers?"

Caora looked back, assenting.

Leathar looked at Caora and said, "the Scorpion, my lady?"

She looked at Eala.

"The Scorpion is perfect," Eala replied.

The Scorpion was a dance where the partners held both hands in front of them all the way through: there was no chance of any impropriety at all, because the only part of the dancers that touched was their hands. It was named for the elegant dance of scorpions, who must woo at arm's length, out of reach of each other's stings. But it was a fun dance, because they whirled around, especially with lively musicians.

"The next dance is the Scorpion," called Leathar. "Who will lead this time? Ordóg, you have a new partner?"

"I have," he replied.

The two of them came forward and, carefully, cautiously, took each other's hands, just like two scorpions. Others followed and then Leathar beat the drum, counting a lively beat, and Caora followed with the harp. Then Fuiseoga took up the melody and the dancers swung around.

As the music played, Fleánna seemed to forget herself. And Eala saw that she was a fine dancer.

People were still dancing when the sun rose. Eala's feet hurt: afterwards she felt like she had danced with everybody. Ordóg and Fleánna were sitting on the bridge, the light from the twig on her cloak now pale in the dawn. They were looking down at the river, talking, remembering. Eala could see that Fleánna was upset and Ordóg was listening to her, not judging.

Leathar and Fuiseoga were as awake as Caora: she had sung a song and put her hands on them and Eala had watched the sleep disappear. She recognised that Caora was using the Immortal Breath when she sang and, when asked, Caora had demonstrated on her. The feeling was exciting, a shock: she knew it from Foscúil's sword lessons, among the Favourites, but not from the sword lesson she had done with the Novices. It was an Immortal thing.

She was sitting with her mother, outside their house; Geana, Spideog, Flannbhuía and herself were eating smoked pork that Flannbhuía had taken from the fire inside, and were remembering their father, Flannbhuía's husband. She told them how proud he would have been of Eala. But Eala was still not sure and now Geana did not press the matter.

Eala heard the music stop and looked over at Caora. She was getting up.

"We have to say goodbye to Eala now," Caora called out.

Eala looked up: she could see the speck growing in the sky.

As Caora came over, Rónmór brought the Flyer right down into the space in front of the house. Caora stepped up to the Flyer as he stood, and she spoke to him quietly.

"I am sorry I was so bad-mannered last night, Rónmór. I would like to be your friend, still."

"I am sorry I surprised you with Eala's news, my lady."

"It's a normal thing in the City. I had forgotten that things have changed since I was Eala's age. I am sorry."

"It is nothing, Lady Caora."

He smiled at her, but he looked weary.

"Will you take breakfast with us, Lord Rónmór?" asked Flannbhuía.

"I am needed back at the City. Perhaps another day, when I bring her back."

Caora said, "You can bring her back and stay, Rónmór."

"It is hard to get away, Lady Caora. My duties keep me in the City. But if I can, I will."

Caora's hands idly found the strings of her harp, and the beauty that filled Rónmór's ears was like the memory of unrequited love. Geana came up with Eala's bag. He took it and lifted it on to the Flyer, still amazed to see the two of them side by side.

Geana said, "Please take care of her, Lord Rónmór."

All around her he saw the villagers, her people, and he could see how much they loved her.

"I will," he said to them all.

He had already promised. Eala embraced her mother, her twin, her brother, Lady Éirime, then climbed up beside him. As she climbed up, he realised she was very drunk. He saw her unsteadiness and smelt the wine. He helped her sit down.

She whispered to him, "You see that couple on the bridge?" He could see them. "I did that," she said, as if they only loved one another because of her.

"Flyer, go to the Grey Gate," he said.

The Flyer lifted and, all around them, people waved. Eala waved back. Soon they were up and the village behind them.

Eala said, "Do you mind if I put my head down a few moments? I was up all night."

"Of course you should," he replied.

She lay back and put the hood of her cloak over her eyes. In moments, she was asleep.

As they flew over the City, Rónmór looked down at her, still sleeping, only her golden hair and her funny little nose visible from under her hood. He felt like he had her to himself, there on the Flyer, but knew she did not belong to him. As he guided the Flyer down to the fountain in the Court of the Favourites, he saw two figures come to the doorway of the Commons House. The woman was dark-haired, the man was a sandy blond. He realised from the way they stood that they were Cathúa and the Mentor, waiting for him. He wanted to wake her up, but the Flyer was following his sight and he couldn't look away. As they approached, he kept his eyes fixed on the spot until they were down. Then he looked up. The Mentor and Lady Cathúa were coming over. He stood up.

The Mentor looked down at her. It was too late to wake her. To his relief, Rónmór could see that he was not angry but looking at her tenderly.

"You have tired her out," said the Mentor.

"She tells me she danced all night, Mentor," he replied. "I think she was drinking, too."

"She doesn't have any capacity for drink. I would have expected Éirime's Candidate to be able to drink like she does but it's not true." He looked up at Rónmór. "Who did she dance with?"

"I have no idea, Mentor. I took her home yesterday morning, I fetched her back this morning. In the meantime, she has been in Lady Éirime's care. When I arrived, she was eating with her mother."

"Did you see her dance at all?"

"I didn't."

"Oh well," he replied, a little disappointed, "She should be in bed. She will have a bad head when she wakes up, I think."

He looked down at her, spoke Words of Power, then knelt by her. One arm went under her thighs, the other behind her shoulder-blades and the hand up the back of her neck. Then he lifted her, easily, and her head settled on to his shoulder, the hood still covering her head. She stirred but did not wake.

"Will you open her door for me, Cathúa?"

Cathúa went with him, then came out again a few moments later. Rónmór looked at her.

"How was he, Lady Cathúa?" Rónmór asked.

"He is putting her to bed. He's in love with her, did you know?"

"I guessed it, Lady Cathúa. Did you ever hear of it before?"

"Never. I haven't seen it and I haven't read about it either. Last night, she was all he talked about. It got pretty repetitive."

"Did he tell you he was in love with her?"

"He did. I couldn't believe it."

The Mentor came out, and saw them both.

"She is still sleeping. She must be drunk: she is snoring. I wish I could have seen her dance. Do they still like her in her village, now she is one of the Sea People?"

"They do, Mentor. They treat her with respect, of course, but they love her too. Her mother is so proud to hear she is Favourite. I am sure that if you asked her to dance, she would dance for you."

"Dance with me, Rónmór, not dance for me. Did Éirime play for them?"

"She did. I only heard her play for a few moments. She still plays beautifully."

"She always played beautifully. I don't think I will ever hear her play again. One problem with being immortal is that the past mistakes pile up and up. Don't they, Cathúa?"

"We learn from mistakes, Mentor, or there is no point remembering them, is there?"

"I hope you are right." He seemed to collect himself. "Rónmór, you ought to run that thing down to the store," he said, indicating the Flyer. "And you haven't slept either, I can see, and you've gone a long way, if you've flown to Áthaiteorann twice as well as to your family's home. Flying in the snow is hard. Go and get some rest."

The Mentor watched the Flyer go up, hop over the wall and drop from sight. Cathúa looked back at him, and took his hand.

"Do you want company, Mentor?"

"I want to be alone for now, but thank you for asking. I will come to the Power House and find you that archive we were talking about. But you mustn't tell anyone anything about what we have discussed. I have to work some things out and make some decisions, without the whole of the Hill gossiping."

She looked guilty.

"I told Rónmór that you are in love with her. He knew anyway. I thought he should know, being Chamberlain. He only wants to serve you better."

"I know he does and I'd guessed he knew. I should have told you to be quiet earlier. But no more indiscretions, Cathúa. I mean it."

"As you wish, Mentor."

Suddenly his need to be alone was stronger than ever. He reached for the jewel at his neck and used that to open the record that Cathúa wanted, directly influencing the House of Power, Creation to Creation. He let it fall back into his tunic.

"That record is waiting for you. And you be sure to be discreet about that, too."

"Thank you, Mentor."

She turned eagerly away, and he watched her go. Then he went back to his chamber, before Rónmór came back up the hill to his bed.

— 11 —

The Month of Light

At the evening meal, Aclaí was sitting at the table with the other Favourites, beside the Mentor. He had been talking about getting tribute from the Forest People: he was due to visit Dubhloch. Eala had been listening. She didn't understand most of the conversation but the best way to learn was to listen.

"Why don't you take some of the Favourites?" the Mentor asked him. "It will give them some experience of the Forest and it always looks impressive when more arrive."

Aclaí called over to Foscúil, at the next table.

"Haven't we had some problems around Dubhloch recently?"

"A few. Some patrols have seen evidence of wild adepts, maybe."

A wild adept was a creature of chaos which had the intelligence to learn to use one or more of the power forces. They might have Words of Power, they might have Mastery of Creation, or they might have Powers conferred by Chaos, unguessable and ungovernable. If the rumours were true, it was a danger.

"Any idea what Powers your wild adept may have?"

Foscúil came over and stood by Aclaí's side. "Wild *adepts*, Aclaí. We have seen evidence of Language and Chaos. Mentor, has anything wild been drawing on the Key of Creation?"

The Mentor reached for the chain at his neck and held the crystal in his hand. Eala felt the watching-feeling that she always felt when she saw it, as if hidden eyes were following her movements. She saw that all the Favourites had looked up: not just low-rank Favourites like her but Rónmór and even Immortals like Eibheara. The Key of Creation held a fascination for them all.

The Mentor was staring somewhere that none of the rest of them could see. Then his gaze returned to Lord Aclaí.

"I blocked a wild adept before Midwinter Day. After that, it has been quiet. I think there has been a build-up of watchers, though."

203

Eibheara spoke.

"We can all feel that, Mentor. It's become worse over the last few months."

"Perhaps it is time for a purge of the Forest," the Mentor replied.

"It is past time," replied Foscúil.

"How many houses of Forest Warriors did we lose last time?" asked Aclaí.

"Three," said Foscúil. "But that is what we breed them for, isn't it?"

"I think you enjoy it, Foscúil," said Eibheara.

"Of course I do, Lady Eibheara," said Foscúil. "I am a bloodthirsty pirate. I was raised among the Sea Hounds, remember?"

He was looking at the Mentor, his eyes laughing. Eala could see the humour, that he was making light of some old matter.

"Well, you may go back to your food, Foscúil," said the Mentor.

Foscúil acknowledged Aclaí with a look and returned to his table. The Mentor spoke to Aclaí.

"That Foscúil will be trouble one day," he said.

"That Foscúil is already trouble, Mentor. He was trouble from the day you Selected him."

"I Selected him, Aclaí, but I didn't train him to reach Immortal Rank."

"You didn't, Mentor. But he has been a great asset in keeping the Forest safe. He has trained the Forest People and gained their loyalty. When you Selected him, Iolar's disappearance meant we were losing the Forest People. He has regained them for the City."

"Or he has regained them for Foscúil, or the one who chose him, anyway."

Foscúil was a favourite of Aclaí, as everyone at the table knew.

"All our hearts are yours, Mentor, you know that," replied Aclaí.

"Sometimes it is hard to remember." The Mentor changed his voice as he changed the subject. "Anyway, it doesn't sound like there is too much danger and the Favourites need the experience. Take them with you when you go to Dubhloch tomorrow. It's an easy journey. It will be first time in the Forest for Eala here, won't it?"

Eala woke in the darkness, whispered her Words of Light, found her cloak on her Silver Cord and got up. The night was dark with no moon, just a riot of stars, bright and cold. She saw nobody about but she could see light from the House of Power, from the little lean-to building on the pyramid. She knew Cathúa would be there. She walked across, by the fountain, and called softly at the door.

"Is that you, Favourite?" asked Cathúa.

"It is. I woke up. Are you busy?"

"I am," came the answer. Then more awkwardly, "But not too busy to talk, if you want to talk. Come in."

Eala went in. The whole room was full of books: on shelves, on the floor, on tables and overflowing on to chairs. Cathúa was carefully copying on to a piece of leather, translating from glowing words on a golden sheet. The words she was writing with ink were simple script but the glowing words were the Language of Power.

Cathúa looked at her.

"Do you know how to read yet, Favourite?" she asked.

"Lady Éirime taught me. I have never seen so many books. Did you write all of these?"

"I did. The chronicles of the City's earliest history are in the House of Power but they are not in our tongue. I am copying them and translating them into the human tongue." She looked at Eala, expecting her to be bored, but Eala nodded encouragement. "Nobody wants to read them but I think they should be written down. In case someone wants to one day."

Eala answered, "I would be interested, Lady Cathúa. I know how to read but all I have learned is the notes I exchanged with my sister. Lady Éirime had us practice by writing songs. We learn in lectures, we hardly learn by reading at all."

"There are more books on the Hill than when I was your age, Favourite."

"Then there can't have been very many at all."

"There were none."

"Oh," answered Eala, thinking about that. "Who ... did you invent writing, Lady Cathúa?"

Cathúa smiled.

"I found a way to record the human tongue. I was reading the chronicles and I found I couldn't take notes. It was just so difficult. So I used pictures that sounded like the words I wanted to write. It was simple, really. Anyone could have thought of it."

"I don't think so, Lady Cathúa."

"Well, they could if they had *wanted* to. Most of us don't care for reading even if we are taught how. The Words of Power have their own symbols. Once you have learned Words of Power and seen they can be written, writing the human tongue is an obvious trick."

"Obvious to you, Lady Cathúa. Anyway, would you let others read your books if they wanted?"

"Nobody would be interested."

"If they were?"

"Of course," she answered.

"May I?"

"What do you want to read?" she answered. "I don't have much that is simple, I'm afraid."

"Anything, really. I've been reading for two years."

Cathúa reached over to a pile and picked something out.

"Try this," she offered.

Eala opened the heavy leather, carefully. It was a description of the symbols of the Words of Power, written in human tongue, as if she was in one of her lectures. She read it easily enough: Cathúa's pictures were clearly formed.

Cathúa watched her for a few breaths, feeling the pride that something she had written was being enjoyed by someone else. Then she picked up her brush again.

"Lord Aclaí?"

He opened the door carefully. Innealta stood there.

"What is it?" he asked.

She looked around at the empty courtyard, at the fountain in the clear starlight. She looked back at him, over her shoulder.

"Can I come in?" she asked.

He stood aside and she hurried in, as if she didn't want anyone to see her. She went in and sat on his bed. She was wearing a silk dress, the sort of thing he knew the Mentor liked.

"What is it, Innealta?" he asked again.

"My lord," she said and looked down.

He sat beside her.

"What is it?" he asked.

"Don't you know?"

"Perhaps I do. But you should explain anyway. Is there some question? Some difficulty?"

"Lord Aclaí, when Liús was Favourite..?"

"What of it?"

"What ... Did Éise and you..?"

"Innealta, I'm not going to gossip about Éise."

"I understand, my lord. But ... Do you remember the morning after the Night of Death?"

"I remember it. Which part do you want me to remember?"

"I had a message from the Mentor. I didn't mean to ... interrupt you."

"Are you still worrying about that? I will not hurt you. I told you at the time."

"And what about Lady Damhánalla? I have asked about her, my lord. And I hear she can be ... well, she can be vengeful."

"She also said she would not harm you. She is trustworthy." He looked around to Innealta, sitting beside him. "You have not been worrying about that all winter, have you?"

"I have been thinking about it," she whispered and Aclaí saw the colour in her face. "I've been thinking about it a lot. My lord."

"And what have you been thinking?"

"I've been wondering how ... how a girl might find herself in that position."

He smiled at her.

"If she can't think of any other way, Innealta, she could always ask."

She looked away.

"Rejection is always humiliating, my lord."

"The risk of rejection is always present here on the Hill, Innealta. As is the risk of missed opportunities."

"Very well, my lord."

She looked up at him, searching for something in his face. Then her lips tightened a moment.

"Would you be my lover, Lord Aclaí?" she asked.

"The Adepts come from many cultures and there are many expectations that go with love. What do you expect, Innealta?"

"Nothing, my lord. My expectations died when I was Initiated."

He laughed.

"So did many of ours. But Innealta, I have one expectation."

"My lord?"

"I would like my lovers to also be my friends. At the very least, I don't want to make enemies. Sometimes people are jealous and sometimes they mistake games for reality."

"I understand, Lord Aclaí. But I have been a favourite for a while now. I don't think I will make those mistakes."

"And friendship?"

"I will try to be your friend, if that is what you want."

"It is. What do you want?"

"I think you know what I want, Lord Aclaí. Or at least, I would like you to guess."

"Very well," he answered, and reached out to her.

Eala was stiff, her arms ached from holding the heavy leather book and, through the doorway, the first light was shining. She put the book down and Cathúa looked around.

"I can't finish it, Lady Cathúa. I am too tired. Do you mind if I come back another night?"

"Take it," offered Cathúa.

"It's the only one, isn't it?" asked Eala.

"It is. But you will be careful, won't you?"

Eala remembered where her earrings came from.

"Would you let me take it to the Room of Replication?"

Cathúa thought a moment, looking surprised.

"If you want to, Favourite. I would be delighted."

"I will be back soon," answered Eala, and hurried out. "Thank you, Lady Cathúa."

The Room of Replication was in the Court of the Immortals. It was often busy, but it was before dawn and most people were asleep. Around it she could see boxes and bags piled up, things that had been copied and were ready to be sent. She had seen the merchants bringing things from the City: pottery, knives, farm tools, and clothing. She had often seen that a merchant would have identical pots but she hadn't known why. Her mother's cups with the horses on them must have started here.

There was a Veteran guarding it, on one of the easy assignments that kept him out of the Forest. He saw Eala come down and called out to her.

"Good morning, Favourite," he called.

"And to you," she answered, not sure how much she was entitled to claim. "Lady Cathúa said I should Replicate something but I've never used the Room of Replication before."

"What is it?"

"It's a book."

"Well, that figures. How many do you want to make?"

"How many can I make?"

"As many as you like," he answered. "You start with one, and then you have two. If you operate it again, you have four. And so on. Ten operations make a thousand."

"A thousand and twenty-four," answered Eala.

"You paid more attention in mathematics than I did, Favourite."

"My mother taught me mathematics," answered Eala, realising as she said it why that might be a dangerous admission. "And then Lady Éirime taught me more."

"I thought Lady Éirime cared only for music, Favourite."

"There is a lot of mathematics in music," Eala answered. "Anyway, can I make two copies? As well as the original?"

"Of course," he answered. "You need to operate the Replicator, take one out, and then operate it again."

"If I had two books, could I do them both at once?"

"You could," he answered "but you'd have to take one of each out after the first copy, if you wanted two copies."

"How do I tell the original from the copy?"

"You can't, Favourite. Nobody can. They are identical."

"Is there anything I can't copy?"

"You can't replicate Great Principles," he explained. "And you can't replicate Metal or Crystal, unless you load raw materials into there. Other than that, there is no limit but size."

"Size?"

"You have to get two of the thing into the Room of Replication."

"What about living things? Does it copy living things?"

"It does. People even ... so be careful."

"Oh," said Eala, apprehensively. "Has that ever happened?"

"It happens occasionally. People get in trouble. They Replicated a merchant's apprentice a few years ago. He was stealing and they didn't know he was still in the room."

"How could they tell them apart?"

"They couldn't. He went back home twins. They were quite good about it but I don't know what his ... what their mother said."

Eala laughed.

"All right, I'll be careful. What do I have to do?"

Quickly he showed her how to operate the Room of Replication: it was much like any other artifice of Words of Power and she understood straight away.

"Be careful to be out of the room, Favourite," he warned, when she seemed to understand. "Or you might be twins."

"I am already twins," laughed Eala.

"Triplets, then. Just be careful."

The room was large and the two books looked very small in the middle of the bare floor. But the room was always cleaned, as any dirt or vermin would be copied too. She stepped out of the room, shut the door, and operated the artifice with a gesture. There was no sound or light, no clue to show that anything had happened.

She opened the door again. There were two books in that half of the room and an identical arrangement of books in the other half. She left the door open and retrieved one pair. Once more and she had three of each book. She bagged them and then walked back out.

"I've finished," she said, as she passed.

"Are you really twins, Favourite?"

"Well, I'm half of twins. I have an older sister. Most people can't tell us apart. Even our mother mixes us up sometimes."

"But you were Selected? The Mentor must have been able to tell you apart."

"He didn't like her name," Eala answered. Then, before he could reply, "I have to take these back to Lady Cathúa."

"Of course, Favourite," he answered.

She hurried back up, through the growing light, through the fragrance of the garden.

Cathúa was still writing when Eala returned with the books. She put them down where they could be seen.

"Thank you, Lady Cathúa," she said.

"I'm glad someone's interested," she answered. "So few of us care for reading."

"I don't think people know that they can learn things from books. They don't have the books, so they don't see the point of reading."

"I suppose," answered Cathúa.

"You should copy them all, Lady Cathúa. I am sure other Novices would find them useful."

She could see Cathúa was not sure. But she told herself that, if Lady Cathúa would let her, she would Replicate all the treasure that Cathúa had stored.

Next day the Favourites were sitting by the fountain, gathered around Aclaí and Foscúil.

"When the Mentor talks about it at table, it sounds like the Forest can be walked safely," Aclaí said to them, "But that is pleasant talk at the evening meal. A bit of bad luck in the Forest, a mistake or two, and you will be dead. If you die in the Forest, chances are your body will never be found. Dubhloch is close to the edge of the patrolled area of the Forest and, as we were saying last night, there has been a build-up recently. There could easily be real danger and you might get as much experience as you ever want." Eala knew he was looking at her. "Eala, you haven't been in the Forest before, have you?"

"I haven't, Lord Aclaí," she replied. "My friend Rósa went on patrol just before Midwinter. She got lost and killed. Don't you remember?"

There was no recognition in his face: their fate was obviously not important enough for him to have remembered, even though he had found them. He might have remembered Léaró, if she had mentioned him, but Rónmór was there. Aclaí tried to reassure her, though.

"Well, if you are obedient and pay attention, we should be able to bring you back safely." He looked at Foscúil. "You've taught the Favourites sword-craft recently. How much of a liability is she?"

Eala expected criticism. Foscúil's sword-craft lessons terrified her, much more than the Novice lessons had, and she knew that it showed.

But Foscúil replied, "She is agile and alert and she seems to be obedient and willing to learn. She doesn't panic. There is a lot for her to learn but I don't think she'll step on a snake or anything." Inside, he seemed to be laughing again. He stood closer to Aclaí, looking at her. "You can see she has a touch of the fox's wildness about her and we've started to coax it out."

"You know all about the fox's wildness, Foscúil." Aclaí seemed amused too, so maybe it would be all right. "Has she killed anyone at sword-practice yet?"

"She hasn't got that much wildness or I'd have called you to come tame her."

Eala could see the other Favourites looking uncomfortable at the dis-cussion: it bordered on the forbidden, especially as Foscúil had never been one of them. But Foscúil was Third Oldest, after Éirime, and taught them all sword. Nobody wanted to argue with him.

Aclaí spoke. "We don't want any *fox wildness* today, Eala. We just need you to be quiet, do as you are told, and keep alert." He turned back to Foscúil. "At least when I'm given babysitting jobs, the babies are attractive. Let's go."

They followed Aclaí. He turned back to them and spoke again.

"Single file, please: I want you in reverse order of Rank."

Eala obediently came to the front, behind him.

"Now step exactly where I walk."

He led them out into the Garden of the Favourites, then off the path by the fountain and through some bushes. There was a cedar, then a big rhododendron, all covered with fragrant flowers, that Aclaí had to bend double to enter, and then two pine trees and a willow. They could hear the fountain, Eala thought. The pine trees were tall and Eala realised that they were too big for the Court of the Favourites. Lord Aclaí had walked them into the Forest right out of the heart of the City, right off the Hill itself. Eala knew that the Novices were taken across the ocean, off the Land of the Immortals, to find woodland that was wild enough to enter the Forest. With fear, she realised that if Lord Aclaí could enter the Forest from the Garden of the Favourites, then monsters could enter the Garden of the Favourites from the Forest. The monsters would have to be as skilled as Lord Aclaí: but a monster version of Lord Aclaí was not what she wanted to meet when out walking at night.

The water Eala had heard was a little stream they walked by and then across. The forest became darker and colder. There were more pines, a long valley with slopes that made no sense, and at last they came out by a lake. Eala looked back, briefly: the rest of the Favourites were emerging, single-file, from beneath the branch she had ducked under by the lake shore. In their full equipment, armour, swords and cloaks, she knew they looked impressive. Along the lake shore was the ruin of an old fortification, it's black and broken shapes reflected in the calm water.

"Stop here," called Aclaí. "Make the circle of defence."

It was a swordsman's command. Eala drew her sword and stood shoulder to shoulder with Rónmór on one side and Cathúa on the other. Quickly there was a ring of them with Aclaí and Foscúil in the middle.

"Wait here," Aclaí said. "Cathúa, you are in charge. If we don't come back by midday, or if you see something bad happen, you are to take the Favourites home."

"What about rescuing you?" Eibheara asked. Eala could see that she was irritated at Cathúa being put in charge: Eibheara and Cathúa were both Eighteenth Rank.

"If we're not back then you won't be able to rescue us. Call your great-uncle: he will know what to do. But make that call as you are returning, understand?"

"As you wish, Aclaí," she said, reluctantly.

Aclaí and Foscúil stepped out of the defensive circle and Aclaí reached into his bag and took out a silk cloth. He unfolded it. Embroidered on it were Words of Power and, as he shook it, it stiffened on the ground. It was a Flyer, small but large enough for two or three, not like anything Eala had seen. How convenient, she thought, to keep a Flyer in your bag! Aclaí and Foscúil got on the Flyer and skimmed away among the higher trees.

Knowing Rónmór was right next to her and holding his sword, Eala thought to him. His words, made emotionless by the sword-hilts, were there.

what is it eala

"What is happening?" she thought to the sword-hilt, "Why are they so worried?"

have you seen the ruined castle

"I see it."

do you see how much ivy is growing on the stones There was none. *do you see how well kept the land is around it*

Animals had been kept there recently and the fences were in good repair.

"I see it. But what does it mean?"

i think that ruin is the house of dubhloch Eala looked up at him. The voice carried by sword-hilt might carry no emotion but she could see he was scared.

She looked the other way. Cathúa was scared, too, and she was Immortal

Rank. But then, something that could destroy a House of the Forest People was not something to tackle with two Immortals and a rabble of lower-Ranks who had nothing in common but appealing to the Mentor's lust. She imagined how he would react if no Favourites came home at all. It would be good for the Novices, of course: but not good for Rósa, she reminded herself. Rósa, who had never been Initiated, had died on patrol, maybe something like this.

"We are going," said Cathúa, taking one hand off her sword-hilt. Eala saw the glow fade as Cathúa released it. "Aclaí says it's too dangerous for the low-Ranks. Eibheara, you will go first, and then the rest of you will go in the same order as we arrived. We are going back to the City." She waited a moment for them to take it in. "Now go."

Eibheara broke the circle, and Eala followed her. They walked through the Forest, silently. Eala's fear made her alert, and that helped her to see the process. Eibheara would follow something: a sound of a bird, a bit of trail, a scent, a watercourse, and they would end up in different types of forest that happened to have the same sound, look, or scent. The sound of the fountain that had carried Aclaí out of the Garden of the Favourites had also been the sound of the stream by the pines and the willow. Now, the sound of bees buzzing took them to a warm wood of olives, overlooking a blue sea. Eibheara sheathed her sword. A man was working on the trees, and he looked around.

"My lords and ladies," he said, getting down quickly.

Cathúa was the last to emerge, and she spoke, putting the sword away but leaving her hand on the hilt.

"Where is this?"

Eibheara replied, "This is Lorgcoiseaigéan. I am not Aclaí: this is as close to the City as I can walk."

Half the width of the ocean separated them from the City.

"That's fine," replied Cathúa, "I couldn't get any closer. Can anyone here walk the Forest on to the Land of Immortals?"

None of them could.

"I will call for Flyers," Cathúa said, putting her hand on her sword-hilt.

"Can I bring ye bread and wine, my lords and ladies?" asked the forester.

"You may," replied Eibheara.

Cabairí went into the hall and sat down at the front the way he always did when they were learning mathematics. They already took their seats by habit, sitting in the same place; for most of their lectures, Cabairí was at the front, alone. Perhaps it was a little dangerous but not when his great-aunt Cathúa was taking the lesson.

Cathúa was normally in early and he would get a chance to speak to her. They wouldn't speak about much but they would ask after one another and exchange pleasantries. Some mornings it was the first time anyone spoke to Cabairí.

But that morning she was not there. As it became obvious that she was not going to arrive, they began to talk amongst themselves. Then the talk went silent and he looked around.

Lady Eibheara stood in the doorway. She addressed the nearest Novice.

"You, girl," she said, "What are you doing here?"

The girl looked terrified.

"Waiting for Lady Cathúa, my lady," she squeaked.

"Good," replied Eibheara. "Well, she asked me to come and teach ye. Did she tell you what ye would learn today?"

"She didn't, my lady."

"Well then. So, girl, are you sitting still?"

"I am, my lady."

Eibheara looked around the Novices, obviously disappointed. She pointed at the next one.

"Are you sitting still?"

"As still as I can, my lady," he answered.

Cabairí could see that they had all stiffened. She pointed at Cabairí.

"How about you?" she demanded.

Cabairí remembered they had been learning about motion for the last ten-day.

"I am trying to be still relative to the building, my lady," he answered.

"Good! Someone is thinking, at least. Is the building still?"

"It is moving with the rest of the world, my lady. The world is spinning and –"

"Well done. What is your name, Novice?"

"I am Cabairí, my lady."

"Cathúa told me to look out for you. So tell me, Cabairí, what is the fastest that things can move?"

"It is the speed of light, my lady."

"Good. Now, if you want to know how fast you are travelling, do you have to compare your speed to something fixed?"

"My lady, you can compare your speed to anything, as long as you know how fast that thing is travelling."

She looked around.

"Do the rest of you understand this?"

Fortunately, they had been paying attention to the last few lectures and if any of them had missed the point, they didn't dare mention it.

"Today you are going to compare your speeds to the speed of light. You will form groups and measure the speed of light in different directions. Since the motion of the world is such a tiny fraction of the speed of light, we will be able to see who is good at measuring things and who is not." She took out a sheet of cloth, with Words embroidered on it. "These Words are used to measure a time. You must combine them with the Words of Contingency to measure the speed of light. Measure it north, up, and east, write down what you did, what you found, and what it means. Then, when we are done, we will see how good you are. Any questions?"

There were no questions and she turned and left. Ten seconds later, the place was full of noise.

Cabairí did not enjoy that morning. It didn't take him long to figure out how to use the Words of Contingency and soon he was measuring the speed of light. Nóiníne watched him carefully and, not long after, the rest of them were doing it too. But the Formula would not work.

He was trying to measure the inaccuracies of the Words that Lady Eibheara had given them when Nóiníne stood at the front of the lecture hall and banged the table with her hand. They all looked around.

"Has anyone made this work?" she asked.

None of them had. She looked at Cabairí.

"You're the walking brain," she demanded. "Tell us what to do."

"I think it's a problem of inaccuracy," he said. "The difference we are trying to measure is very small. The rotation of the Earth is about two hundred and eighty times faster than a man can march, and the Earth's journey around the Sun is about seventeen thousand times faster than a man can march. But light travels about one hundred and eighty million times faster than a man can march. So the difference will be one part in ten thousand."

"What about our motion around the centre of the Galaxy?" Abhainne asked.

"Oh," said Cabairí. "If the Sun goes around the Galaxy in one hundred million years – I'm guessing that – then ..." he scribbled some calculations "... that is about three hundred and sixteen thousand times faster than a man marches. It's still one part in six thousand. I don't think Lady Eibheara's Words measure small times with that accuracy. We are measuring a millionth part of a heartbeat."

Nóiníne was scornful.

"Why would Lady Eibheara give us Words that can't measure the speed properly?"

"I don't know," replied Cabairí. "I am varying the distances by a hair'sbreadth to check the accuracy of the time-keeping. But it's fiddly work."

"We don't have that long. She's going to come back and demand to know our results. Can you calculate what result we should get?"

"I've already done that," he answered. "That is what I've just been telling you."

"Then tell us again," said Abhainne. "If it pleases you," she added.

"All right," he said. He got up and walked to the front. "First you've got to calculate the directions. The Earth turns East, and the Earth's orbit takes us –" he pointed over to the horizon "– that way." He thought, frowning. "The Galactic motion is harder. The centre of the Galaxy is," he pointed at the sky, low on the horizon to the East, "Somewhere over there," he swung his arm around, following as best he could the shape of the Milky Way in the sky. "So the Galactic motion must be in that direction."

"So how do we work it out from there?" asked Nóiníne.

"You draw right-angled triangles and measure their lengths."

"I'll show you," said Abhainne and the rest of the Novices huddled together while Cabairí fiddled with his length markers.

When Eibheara returned, she seemed happy, looking forward to getting their results.

"How did we get on?" she asked.

The Novices looked nervous, but she went around them all, getting their results and writing them down where everyone could see. She glanced down at the scribblings in front of Cabairí and didn't ask him. When she had the rest of the results, she addressed them.

"So, it looks like you had good agreement. Would anyone like to tell me what conclusions they reached?"

It was Íona that she chose to explain it. She let Íona explain how the Earth moved through the Galaxy and smiled encouragement as it was explained.

Then she asked, "Does the Galaxy move?"

"I guess not, my lady," answered Íona nervously.

She pointed at Cabairí.

"Does the Galaxy move?"

"I suppose it must," he answered, "but I have no idea how much or in what direction."

"Neither have your peers," she said. "What results did you get?"

"I am afraid I couldn't measure the motion, my lady," he said. "I have determined that the Words you gave us can measure a thousand millionth of a heartbeat, but although that should be enough to measure the Galactic motion, I have been unable to do so."

"Did you measure any motion at all?"

"None that I am sure is real, my lady."

"Did you remember that the Galaxy moves?"

"I didn't think of it – but I have no idea how fast it might move anyway, my lady. I seem to recall that Lady Cathúa told me that all the other galaxies are moving away from us ... so we might be at the centre." Then he added, "That seems unlikely, though."

"It is unlikely. But you measure that we are still?"

"I cannot measure any motion, my lady. But I don't believe that means we are still."

She looked at the others.

"One of you has done what I asked. The rest of you have merely tried to please me. And this will come as a surprise, but it is Cabairí here that has got the correct result. Whatever you do, however fast you travel, when you measure the speed of light, you get the same answer in every direction. Before the next lecture, you can think about the implications of that."

She waited for them to react to that and then she said, "I don't expect Novices to know that. But neither do I expect them to cheat and lie to me. Before next time, each of you but Cabairí here will find a Veteran or Immortal, explain that you were caught cheating and ask them to punish you. I will be checking up to make sure that they have done a good job. Especially if I find the ringleader. Now off you go."

They went. Abhainne stayed behind.

"What do you want?" Eibheara demanded.

Abhainne's courage took a moment to find words.

"Would you be the one who punishes me, my lady? If it pleases you?"

"Why would I do that?"

"I am the ringleader, my lady."

Caora felt the sword-hilt was tingling and she pulled her Silver Cord and it was in her hand. Geana saw the glow on the hilt, and looked around.

"Is it Eala?" she asked. "Is she coming home for the Night of Light?"

"It isn't Eala," she replied.

The sword-hilt showed someone of Fourteenth Rank. It was Rónmór. She suddenly thought it might be terrible news.

lady éirime he asked.

"Is Eala all right?" she replied, forming the words in her head so Geana would not be frightened.

eala is fine i see her happy i wanted to ask you a favour for the mentor

"What favour?" she asked, knowing that her suspicion would be lost before her words got to him.

i am organising a dance here for the night of light i want the mentor to see how happy eala was at midwinter day and i know i cant take him to athateorainn

"You are right, you can't do that. So what do you need from me?"

i would like you to play

"I can't, Rónmór. Did he ask you to ask me?"

not yet

"If he asks you, ask him to remember what happened last time I came to the City to entertain at a Celebration Day."

what happened

"I was supposed to return that evening. It took me nine hundred years to get home again."

im sorry he hurt you lady éirime so is he i believe we will miss your company

"Come and visit when you have the time, Rónmór. But don't bring the Mentor to Áthaiteorann. Give Eala my love and her sister's."

She put the sword back in the chest.

"Who was that?" asked Geana.

"It was Rónmór. Eala's not coming home for the Night of Light."

"You two again," said Foscúil, scornfully. "Are you scared of Immortal Rank, Rónmór? You will never learn how to have the breath of an Immortal when you spend your time practicing with a Novice." Rónmór felt stupid again. He had been trying to help someone. But Foscúil continued, "Or are you in love with her?"

He could hear the other Favourites laughing. The only one who didn't laugh was Eala, who looked even more angry with him. Foscúil looked at Eala.

"Fetch Lord Aclaí, please. Tell him I asked."

Eala put her sword away and walked carefully around the others as they practised. Just walking across the sword-hall during a lesson could be dangerous, even if she was in her armour. Foscúil turned back to Rónmór, and spoke more mildly.

"I thought you were hoping for Immortality, Rónmór. I thought you wanted to get out of here."

Rónmór looked at him. How could he possibly know?

But Foscúil continued, "If that's what you want, you shouldn't be messing around with Novices. Or do you want to stay here forever?"

Rónmór could feel the heat on his face, the shame, the tears he would not shed. He knew that Foscúil knew. But how?

"Teacher?" The voice was deep: Lord Aclaí had arrived.

"My lord," replied Foscúil, "will you help me with Rónmór here? He's getting on my nerves."

"It's a while since we killed a low-Rank at sword practice, Foscúil."

Rónmór could tell they were sharing some kind of joke, but he couldn't tell if it was at his expense. Lord Aclaí saluted them both, then Eala attempted the technique they were learning, with Aclaí receiving the challenge. Rónmór could see that she was terrified but Aclaí was so gentle.

Then it was his turn and the gentleness was gone. He felt he was fighting for his life – and maybe he was.

When they were done, Eala seemed not to be so angry with him. Maybe she had thought he would die, too. They shed their armour, put normal clothes on and said Words of Freshness. Rónmór was so hot and scared, he knew he would be saying them again before long.

Eala found him and asked him, "Do you want to eat?"

He didn't want to eat, he wanted to hide in his room until his feelings passed. But if she had invited him to his own execution he would probably have gone. The servants were bringing up food, as many of the Favourites ate at midday, and they found something to eat and took it into the garden. They walked by the cypress, but Eibheara was there, eating alone, looking out at the harbour. They settled for the bench down by the gate. The bench was small and he could feel where their hips were touching. He wasn't hungry but he played with his food and hoped his friend would give him calmness.

"I thought Lord Aclaí was going to kill you," she said.

He could see that she had been frightened, for all Lord Aclaí's gentleness.

"I'm sorry," she added.

"Why are you sorry?" he asked, not understanding.

"In the Court of the Veterans, before Midwinter, I nearly got Cabairí killed. I was upset and some of them saw my upset and took it out on Cabairí." She gave him that odd smile of hers, when she wasn't really happy at all. "Being Favourite, if I show upset, everyone wants to take it out on someone."

"I don't think it's that, Eala. I'm trying to get my breathing right for Sixteenth Rank. Lord Foscúil is right to goad me like that."

"What does that achieve?" she asked.

"It's training." He looked at her, seeing that she didn't understand. "There are several ways to learn the Immortal Breath. There is Iolar's

Method, which teaches it by practising Words of Power: that is how the Mentor learned. There is Éirime's Method but nobody else uses that. She learned Immortal Breath by singing and it took her just seven years: a fifth of the time that anyone else has managed."

"So why doesn't anyone else try it?"

"Eala, you'll only get one chance to learn Immortal Breath. If you don't learn it in fifty years, seventy at the outside, you'll be dead. Nobody else has ever learned Éirime's Method, because you have to be a singer as well as one of the Sea People. I'm learning Aclaí's Method, through physical fighting, and it's working for me. But it's hard and it's scary. That's what Foscúil teaches in the Court of the Favourites, because it works. You shouldn't let that put you off, though. It'll be years before you have to worry about Immortal Rank."

Eala didn't know what to say to that. Perhaps he was right but she didn't know enough to tell. She tried to make sure she remembered to ask when next she went home.

The hurt returned to her face as she remembered: "Lady Éirime called me last night."

Rónmór understood straight away. So that was it. That was why she was angry with him.

"I didn't mean to upset her, Eala. But I'm Chamberlain."

"I know. I'm sorry. You're such a good friend to me, Lord Rónmór, I sometimes forget you're Chamberlain."

"The Mentor misses her terribly."

"I know," she replied.

Rónmór wasn't sure she did.

"Do you know, before she went, there used to be musicians playing at the Evening Meal. There used to be servants who would dance for him. I was only low-Rank then but all the Favourites knew it had been going on for centuries."

"I didn't know," Eala said. "I never heard of it."

"The day she left, the Mentor stopped it. He doesn't listen to music any more. It's been so quiet here. It used to be that the Court of the Favourites always had music, normally Éirime singing. People miss her voice, you know."

"I know," Eala said. "I miss it too."

For a moment, Rónmór thought that she hadn't been here but then he realised that she was thinking of her home.

"Midwinter second," he explained, "when I brought you back, the Mentor asked about you. He asked about Éirime's playing, and about you dancing. He wanted to be there, I could see it, to dance with you in your village, to dance to Éirime's music."

"I'm sorry, Lord Rónmór. I don't think how hard this must be for you. I don't call Caora as much as I should because I don't want to tell her what is happening here. I want to tell her everything but I can't. Half the time it is as if she were dead. I think that is the best way, to pretend she isn't there. She hates the City. You remember what she was like when you came to Áthaiteorann. That is when she found out I was Favourite. I couldn't bear to tell her, not for three months. She is like that all the time. If I had known it, I would never have come here."

"You regret coming here?"

"I regret what my coming here has done to Caora. If I could find a way to change that, I'd give anything to make it happen."

In the House of Power, Cathúa looked down at the golden sheet. Glowing letters were written there, the oldest annals of the Sea People.

"He was lost in the fog," she translated and Eala wrote it down.

Then she handed Eala the tablet. Eala leaned over and stared at the last phrase in the glowing letters. By changing over for each phrase, they broke the flow of the language, so avoiding the hazard of summoning a Power they did not want. But Eala found the Power Language hard to translate.

"There was a mountain ..." she puzzled, her finger pointing at the glyphs. "Hiding," she added. "In the fog. Or perhaps it is cloud." She stifled a yawn and looked over. "So Lady Cathúa, Seilidí was the last Favourite to die?"

"Unless it was Iolar," answered Cathúa. "Nobody knows what happened to him."

"Who was Favourite after Seilidí?"

"Aclaí," answered Cathúa. "He was made Favourite on the Fifteenth Day of Death, in the year he was Selected. It was the quickest there had been back then."

"Forty-four days. That is quite quick, isn't it?"

"Remember, though, there was no Favourite when Aclaí was chosen. Anyway, the next Favourite beat him. Éirime was made Favourite on the Twelfth Day of Death."

"So there was no Favourite between Seilidí and Aclaí?"

"There was no-one. I think that is the only time that has happened, that the Mentor's Favourite died. Even if Iolar died, he was a favourite, not The Favourite. But he didn't choose another one until someone else caught his eye." She looked at Eala. "You were half asleep but now you've

Venus and the Sea People

woken up. What are you wondering?"

"I'm wondering what he sees when he chooses a Favourite, Lady Cathúa. We all seem to be so different." She looked up and looked Cathúa in the eyes. "Do you know? Have you any thoughts or observations?"

"I don't know. I've collected the data but reached no conclusions. In each case he spends time with them but in each case he does different things." She looked away and Eala wondered if she would blush. "With me, he talked."

"You asked him lots of questions, my lady?"

"I pestered him with lots of questions." Cathúa became more uncomfortable. "There was the ... other stuff, of course, but mostly I asked him things that only he would know, about history and people, and he listened. I don't think that's what the other Favourites did."

Eala thought about what she did. Nothing so complicated, really: she didn't ask him to talk, but of course she would listen if he wanted to talk. Again she felt like she was missing out something.

"What did the others do?"

"Before me, I don't know. Eibheara plays games."

"Plays games, my lady?"

"She pretends to be different people. It used to make my head spin, trying to keep up with who she was." Leaning forward, Cathúa spoke more quietly. "Sometimes it still makes my head spin. Children play pretend-games but when I was little I didn't join in. I didn't understand them and I still don't."

"But Lady Eibheara is one of your closest friends, my lady."

"She is. She is intelligent, you see. Most people on the Hill aren't, not properly." Cathúa seemed to hear herself speaking and added, "That sounds so condescending, doesn't it?"

"I know what you mean," said Eala. "But it's not something I'm going to repeat, my lady." She sighed. "I was lucky. My sister is intelligent too. It must be lonely growing up without anyone to talk to."

"It is. I don't think I met anyone I could talk mathematics to before I came to the City." Cathúa laughed. "If only there was a way to use mathematics to model the way people behave."

Eala was almost going to answer, but she didn't think the games her sister had played with her as children would stand up to Lady Cathúa's relentless logic. And she had already mentioned her sister once – probably too many times.

Instead she said, "What did he see in the other Favourites, Lady Cathúa? How did they please him?"

"Please him?" asked Cathúa and Eala could see her thinking. "Well, Rónmór pleases him. He seems to somehow know what the Mentor wants and finds him the right thing every evening. That is why he is Chamberlain, I suppose." Cathúa shrugged. "I suppose you should be asking him how to please the Mentor, not me."

"I don't know if he knows. People don't always know how their instincts work. Sometimes they don't even know they have them. Sometimes you just do what you do and that works. But if you change something it doesn't work anymore."

"That's not logical," answered Cathúa.

"It isn't, my lady," agreed Eala. "Or if there is logic, it is too well hidden for us to recognise."

"We're back to that mathematical model of people."

"We are."

"You understand people, Favourite. Do you think it will ever be possible?"

"I think it might be. But I don't understand people well enough to be sure. And I certainly need to learn more mathematics. I hardly knew anything before I came to the City."

"Lady Éirime is a better mathematician than most, Favourite. And you have a gift for it."

Eala shrugged. "What about the last? What about Liús?"

"That was a strange thing. He was Favourite but Éise was always there with them. It's like they both were Favourite."

Eala thought about that one.

"It didn't last long, though."

"Less than four months," agreed Cathúa.

"You know, the rules of being Favourite must have worked against them. The Favourite is forbidden any other sexual relationship."

"That's not quite true. If the Mentor allows it, the Favourite can." Again, Cathúa looked away and Eala recognised embarrassment. "If the Mentor orders it, she may have no choice."

"Shall we look at another Record, Lady Cathúa?"

"Are you sure you're not too tired...?"

"I think I can manage one more."

"...only there was one other thing I wanted to ask you."

"My lady?"

"Eala, I don't know what to do to make men notice me. I am thirty times older than you, I guess, but you just do it."

Eala had simply been copying what she had seen her sister do. And she thought it was only ...

"Only for the Mentor, Lady Cathúa."

"That's enough. I know he likes me to ask questions, but sometimes it's as if I am his sister. Will you show me how to make him notice me ... like that?"

"Why are you asking me?"

"Because I think you can explain it logically, Eala."

"I can't create logic where no logic exists, Lady Cathúa."

"But if there is any logic, you can find it. And I really want to know."

They walked into the Hall of the Novices, the Mentor's hand in hers. The hall had been decorated for the Night of Light and the tables moved, to create a large space in the centre of the room. Everyone sat at tables that were by the wall and, from their platform, the Mentor and favourites looked down, across the room, at a collection of musicians.

As they sat, a man began to sing and the band began to play. Eala felt the Mentor's hand catch in hers and she squeezed it and looked around at his face. The Mentor leaned over to Eala, and she wondered if he would kiss her. But he whispered, "Is this your doing?"

Seeing that he didn't mind, she wished it was.

"It isn't, Mentor. I am as surprised as you are. Do you like it?"

"Then I think I know who it is," he answered. "I hope you like it. I was told that at Midwinter you danced. What do they do in your village on the Night of Light?"

"That depends," she answered, carefully. "If you have a husband or wife, you remember them. If you don't, then you remind everyone else that you don't."

"How do you do that?" he teased.

Eala thought about the answers that she couldn't give, about being with her friends while her sister danced with the boys and did the things Eala and her friends had only talked about.

Eventually she answered, "I didn't do much, Mentor. I was too shy."

"Then it was time you had a blue robe. Look at you now. What would you do if you were home now?"

"If I was home now, I would not be free. I am Favourite, Mentor."

"And if you weren't Favourite?"

"I don't know, Mentor. I never had a boyfriend."

She saw him stare at her and then his expression changed.

"Who told you to say that?"

"It's true," she protested.

"You must surely have been the most attractive girl in your village. How many were there? It can't be more than fifty."

Eala said nothing, unable to see how to change the direction of the conversation.

"There is another girl more attractive than you in your village? I should meet her." He looked around at the others on their table. "Why haven't I met her?" he asked. He looked at Aclaí. "You are the expert on Anleacán, Aclaí: why haven't I met the most attractive girl in Eala's village?"

"I believe you have, Mentor," answered Aclaí.

"Eala thinks there is a prettier one."

Eibheara answered. "You have met her, Mentor. I think the other one is no prettier: I doubt you could choose between them. She's just less shy."

Aclaí glowered at Eibheara, but Eala watched the Mentor and saw his face fall as he remembered.

Then he said, "Rónmór told me you danced at the Midwinter Festival in your village."

"I did, Mentor," she answered. "I had been drinking."

"Then you should drink now," he answered, and looked around for the servants. "Bring wine for the Favourite," he told them. "Later, I want you to dance," he told her. Then he looked down at her, leaned closer, and whispered to her. "And don't look so serious, Eala. Tonight you have a boyfriend. If you will have him, that is."

"I will."

At the end of the meal, they did not go up. Instead, the Mentor turned to Rónmór, and asked, "This band, do they know the dances of Anleacán?"

"They said they do, Mentor," he answered.

The Mentor turned back to Eala and quietly said, "Then, if you have had enough wine, you should make your choices. Choose a dance, choose a partner, and show me."

"Will you be my partner?" she asked, even more quietly, knowing he might not.

"I wish to see the Anleacán dances before I try such a thing," he laughed. "Find someone else to tread on your toes. If they are flattened, then I might not trip over them so easily."

"All right," she answered, and looked around. "Who should I choose?"

"Choose the man you would dance with if you were not Favourite," he suggested.

"If I were not Favourite, Mentor, I would not dance."

"They are all favourites and they will dance. Pick one of them."

She looked them over. Toirneach was watching with little interest, but she knew that would make him safe. Liús was arm-in-arm with Éise, making no attempt to hide his chosen partner. Rónmór looked at her when she looked at him and she could not read those dark eyes. But then she remembered what the Mentor had said, when she was trying not to mention Geana.

"Lord Aclaí?" she asked, "Do you know the dances of Anleacán?"

"I do, Favourite," he answered. "But I have never danced them. If you chose something simple..."

"I was thinking of The Crab, my lord," she answered.

"That is not a dance for two," he said, surprised.

"It is not, my lord." She turned back to the Mentor. "The Crab is a dance for four or more partners and it goes around: every boy dances with every girl for one verse. The steps are simple and follow the music well, so if my lord will help me to demonstrate, we can show them, and maybe some more of us can join in."

"All right," answered the Mentor.

"I think I can improve on that," said Aclaí. "I will use the Words of Many Images."

"That's clever," smiled Eala.

Aclaí took her hand and led her out.

Then he turned to the musicians and said, "Play slowly and softly and we will explain the steps."

In a clear voice, he called them out and he and Eala walked slowly through. They finished not quite before each other: if there had been other partners, they would have had new partners before them. Then he said the Words and, as the band played faster, Eala saw from the corners of her eyes that there were many of them in the hall dancing with identical steps: Geana dancing with the Lord Aclaí, beautiful, confident, the centre of attention, her blue robe swaying as she turned. She tried not to look again.

Then the last verse came and she was before Aclaí again. When she reached for his appearance, she felt his strong arms. The verse concluded and she found herself before him as the music stopped. She knew that by tradition they should kiss but she hoped he didn't. She saw in his face that it was a tradition that he would not impose upon her.

Aclaí ended the illusion of his Words as the last notes ended and turned back to the hall.

"Who will dance, then?" he asked. He looked up at Liús and Éise, calling, "Come on you two, it would be good for you to be in someone else's arms on the Night of Light."

Liús looked reluctant but Éise took him firmly and led him over. Aclaí looked elsewhere in the hall too and other boys and girls came up, not just Favourites. Then the Mentor came down, stood before Eala, and several more got up and lined up too.

The Mentor leaned close to her, and said, "If I end up a fool doing this, you will be blamed."

To her relief, she saw that he was teasing. "There are many feet to tread on now, Mentor."

"What is the matter, niece?" asked Miotal. "You have not danced all evening."

"Do I look like a peasant?" Eibheara answered.

"Be careful," answered Miotal, quietly. "The Mentor has danced more than you have."

He glanced over to where the Mentor was watching and then to where the couples were dancing.

"Aclaí has danced more than the Mentor, too," she observed.

She looked over at Aclaí with Eala in his arms, bodies pressed together, swaying gently as they stepped through the dance they had chosen.

"I see it," he said. "Aclaí knows the dances of Anleacán. You know why."

"I know what I can see," she answered. "Look at them. That stupid little girl has taken enough that is mine. If he kisses her, I will kill her."

"Now, niece, you be careful."

"Oh, don't worry, Uncle, I'll be careful. I will wait until she is no longer Favourite, I will take my time. But I swear, if he kisses her, she will die a miserable, undignified, dishonourable death, at a time and place of my choosing."

The music stopped and Aclaí brought Eala over to the Mentor. They were laughing and Eala said, "Will you dance with me now, Mentor? One last one? You see, the Willows is a simple enough dance."

"I see that. Aclaí, she told me she had never been kissed on the Night of Light before. Do you believe her?"

Aclaí looked at her a long time before answering and Eala was reminded of trying to keep secrets from her sister.

He said, "I do believe her, Mentor."

"That's not right. Do you want to kiss her?"

"She is a lovely girl," answered Aclaí carefully, "but I have always found I enjoy it best when I kiss girls who want to be kissed. I think she would prefer to be kissed by you. You should dance The Willows with her."

Eala woke up. Her mind was full of bad dreams, of being watched by something in the shadows: something like a death-head but with something dark and evil in the eyes. She was not in her own bed. The Mentor was looking down at her. She turned over.

"I'm sorry, Mentor, I fell asleep again."

"I don't mind. You know I don't mind if you sleep here."

She sat up and looked around. She had never seen the room in full daylight: she had arrived at the Autumn Feast, the traditional time for Selection, and the nights had got longer after that. Light was shining from behind the tapestry opposite the door. It must be covering a window.

The Mentor saw her looking.

"What is it, Eala?" he asked.

"I was wondering about the window behind the tapestry. I never knew it was there. I've never been here in the day. This room is right on the top of the hill: the view must be fantastic. Can I see?"

"You can try. I never open it. I don't know if the tapestry moves."

She got up, pulled her cloak around her, and lifted the tapestry. It opened easily, like curtains. There was a big window, as big as a door, all the way to the ground. The window was not shuttered: it was closed with a clear, greenish sheet of Crystal. Eala knew that like Metal, Crystal was unbreakable, but the largest pieces she'd seen, in lectures on spirit and magic, were no larger than a pea. The window must be as old as the room, as old as the City. It was clean: the servants knew it was here. Beyond it she saw a balcony, two chairs and a table, and bushes in pots. And beyond the balcony she could see the harbour, and beyond it the sea, glittering in the sun. "It's beautiful," she exclaimed and opened the frame. The south wind came in, full of scents from the Garden of the Favourites and, above it all, the clean air of the Atlantic. She turned back, took his hand and led him out. He looked around, as surprised as she was.

"I knew there was a window, but I never knew any of this was here, Eala."

She led him out on to the balcony, to the chairs. They could see over the trees in the garden and they could see the whole City.

"This is a lovely spot," he said.

He looked around, trying to see another way to get to the balcony. There was none.

"The servants have kept all this for me, when they attend to my room, and I never knew it was here. I wonder: how long they have been doing that?"

"A little while, Mentor. See how the chairs have been repainted, and how the lemon trees have grown? The plants have been at the City much longer than me, I'm sure."

"But you haven't been here long."

He turned his head, hearing something, then went back into the room, through the door. She heard him lift the bars, lower the wards, and then she heard him speaking.

"Come," he said, to someone in the room. Then he said, "Come through. I want to ask ye questions."

Two servant girls followed him on to the balcony. Eala could see they looked very scared: he must never talk to them.

"This morning I found this," he asked. "How long have ye been taking care of it?"

The darker one spoke. "I have been taking care of it for nineteen years, my lord. My grandmother showed it to me and said it was part of caring for your chambers."

"How long had she been taking care of it, I wonder?"

"I don't know, my lord." Both the servants were shaking. "Does it no longer please you, my lord?"

"I think it's lovely," said Eala. "It's a lovely place to sit in the morning."

"It is," the Mentor added. "Thank ye both," he said to the servant girls, "And pass on my thanks to the others who take care of this." He could see they were still frightened. "Ye may go. Send someone up with breakfast and send enough for two people. We will eat out here."

They went as quickly as they could and he came over and sat with Eala at the table.

"There is a lot of care gone into this place, Mentor," she said.

"I can see. You have shown me something I never knew and in my own bedroom. Thank you, Eala."

— 12 —

Venus and the Sea People

"My lords!" Féileacána stood up as they entered.

It was Aclaí that she looked at but he stood and watched as Foscúil spoke.

"You manage the watches, don't you?"

"I draw the lots, my lord. Is something wrong?"

"Well, not wrong. I need another patrol team drawn. They will not be assigned a patrol but I want to be able to call on them at any time, day or night. I expect them to be assembled in the City and ready to go out into the Forest in less than a hundred breaths."

"Very well," she replied. "What strength?"

"I want sixty. And I want each group led by an Immortal and five Veterans."

Féileacána didn't answer immediately.

Then she said, "How shall I choose? The lots are drawn from Novices."

"You will need a new lottery, of course," Foscúil replied.

She wondered if he knew how much trouble this would cause. Judging from his face, she concluded that if he did, he was amused by it.

"My lord?" she asked, hesitating. "Will there be an announcement?"

"You will have to make an announcement, of course."

"And," she wondered how to tactfully put it, "How will I choose who to put into the lots? My lord, there are no Immortals living in the City that are not Favourites."

Then Aclaí spoke.

"I have talked with some of the Retired. Foscúil, Miotal and Damhánalla will help. But you will have to include Favourites in your lottery. I will expect my name to be among them."

"Oh," she replied. "No exceptions?"

"No exceptions," agreed Foscúil.

"Well," clarified Aclaí, "Cathúa would tell you that there is one exception. The Mentor is immortal and he will not be among them. But he has

231

no Rank."

"Oh," she said again. "Well, I don't have Immortal Rank, my lord. How will I persuade Immortals to accept this?"

"You can tell them that Lord Aclaí commanded it," suggested Foscúil.

"They won't like it, lords," said Féileacána.

"You can tell them that the Mentor's life depends on it," Aclaí growled. "Or that the City will fall if they don't do their jobs right."

"Come on, sleepyhead," the Mentor told Eala. "I think I hear breakfast."

"I need a few breaths," Eala replied.

"You're always like this in the mornings now," he teased her. "What is the matter with you?"

She reached down and grasped.

"Too much of this, I think," she grinned at him.

"I see," he breathed. "Well, you aren't going to get any breakfast that way."

"I suppose not, Mentor." She sat up, and whispered her Words of Freshness. "Come on then," she said over her shoulder. "You promised me a surprise today, didn't you?"

"All in good time," he said.

Together they went out on to the balcony where the servants were ready with food. The Mentor said Words of Light: the sun had not risen.

Eala picked at the food but she was wondering. She knew that something was coming. She didn't know what, but she kept catching him thinking of saying something to her and never getting around to saying it. She wondered if today's surprise was when she would find out. As Eala ate, the Mentor put his hand on his sword.

mentor

"Aclaí," he thought, "is everything ready for this morning?"

it is

"I suppose you have a bunch of Novices to march with us?"

i have organised a patrol

"How many?"

sixty mentor came the reply.

"And who is their leader? Crannóg?"

cathúa is leading them mentor

"Favourites?"

i have made no exceptions mentor foscúil is going too

"It seems excessive, Aclaí. We're not going deep into the Forest."

the city depends on you and humanity depends on the city

"We've already had this argument."

we have came the reply. *it is because we all care about you*

"My lady?"

Eibheara turned around to see who was interrupting her walking. It was some Veteran, someone she didn't recognise. She didn't bother to keep the irritation out of her voice.

"What do you want?"

Abhainne stopped beside Eibheara, quietly waiting for their conversation to continue. She would not interrupt a Veteran.

The Veteran said, "My lady, I am the Watch-keeper. It is my duty to run the lottery of..."

"I know what the Watch-keeper does. What do you want?"

The Watch-keeper looked nervous.

"My lady, your name has been drawn for tomorrow."

Eibheara didn't answer. Abhainne spoke for her.

"Lady Féileacána, surely Lady Eibheara's name has not been in the lottery since she was a Novice – six hundred years ago."

"That is true, Novice, but Lord Aclaí commanded that a new lottery be drawn..."

"What is your name?" demanded Eibheara, her sword in her hand.

"I am Féileacána, my lady. Watch-keeper for –"

"I will call Lord Aclaí. If he denies your ridiculous tale, then you will die." A glow appeared under her hand, on the sword-hilt.

It took a while for Eibheara to converse with Aclaí. As she concentrated on the sword, a small crowd gathered around, waiting to see if Eibheara would kill Féileacána, and if she would resist. Sometimes when an Immortal killed a lower Rank, they would resist and there would be a fight. And perhaps, with a great deal of luck, a senior Veteran might defeat a younger Immortal. The gathering crowd hoped for such entertainment.

Féileacána was not defiant enough to have her sword on her hip, but perhaps she hoped her Silver Cord could bring it to her hand in time to parry the first blow. Féileacána knew that many of them would have liked to see her die. Being Watch-keeper was not a position that led to popularity, even if it could lead to favours.

The glow on the hilt of Eibheara's sword faded and she looked up.

"It appears that Lord Aclaí has chosen to spare your life. But I will remember this." She thrust the sword into the scabbard, now riding on her hip, and she released the sword-hilt. "Now get out of my sight."

Féileacána walked away, past the disappointed faces, as quickly as dignity would permit.

Abhainne walked with Eibheara, back up the Hill.

As they entered the stables she said, "What was that, my lady?"

"Aclaí wants a patrol on call, at a hundred-breaths' notice, day and night. He didn't say why."

"Perhaps, my lady, there is a good reason."

"There had better be."

Cathúa reached for the sword-hilt. The caller was Eighteenth Rank.

"Who is this?" she asked.

its eibheara came the reply. *would you like to come riding*

"Riding horses?"

not in the forest cathúa we are on the beach beyond the hill

"Why do you think I might want to ride?"

perhaps riding would be something to do while we talk

"But we could talk here and I could work on this Record at the same time."

remember cathúa how you want me to tell you when you have missed something

"Oh. And I'm missing something?" Cathúa tried to imagine what, but then she gave up. "I'll come," she said. And she released the sword-hilt.

They found her a horse and riding wasn't so demanding: her dread of it was left over from her days as a Novice. It was quite pleasant, actually, to relax and feel the horse bump and sway beneath her. Eibheara and some Novice girl were waiting on the beach. Cathúa was trying to remember if she knew the Novice girl but the Novice girl wandered off before she had a chance.

"So, Eibheara," Cathúa asked, "What did I miss this time?"

Cathúa could see the pitying look cross Eibheara's face.

"I come to the beach when I want to talk with people without being overheard."

"I see. What did you want to say?" Cathúa asked. "Is this about your old enemy?"

"It is. I know you don't believe in him, but ..."

"I'm still trying to prove it, one way or the other. It could be true but it could simply be coincidence." Cathúa made a face. "Very unlucky coincidence, perhaps, but it could be."

"It's the prophecies that convince me," Eibheara replied.

"I know, but I would prefer to understand how prophecy works before accepting that."

Eibheara laughed. "You know, everyone in the City offers your brain-interprets-noise theory for prophecy as if it is proven fact."

"Not everybody, Eibheara," Cathúa corrected. "Neither of us does."

"Oh, you," Eibheara teased. Then the anger returned to her face. "Have you investigated Eala yet?"

"Not yet," Cathúa replied.

"She is a prime suspect for it: look at the effect she's having on him. If she is one of them, I could finally get to interrogate one of my enemy's agents." Eibheara looked at Cathúa's face. "You don't believe me?"

"I don't think Eala is significant enough yet."

"What? She's got Favourites on patrol, like purple Novices. You don't think she's important?"

"I think she might be forgotten in a few months."

"That is what Aclaí says. I think they are missing the obvious."

"Aclaí has known the Mentor longer than anyone else alive."

"That doesn't mean he knows everything. Aclaí isn't so smart. Anyway, I did some tests on her myself."

"You tested her background?"

"Her genes. She has the Gift."

"And why is that a problem? Éirime had the Gift."

"And look at the trouble she caused. And look at who dumped Eala on us!"

The Governor of the Town of the Two Rivers was having an afternoon drink with his favourite architect when the guard ran in. He looked up. The man was excited and out of breath from running.

"What is it?" he asked, a little bored.

"Flyers, my lord. Coming from the West. More than a score of them."

"Big, or small?"

"They are small, my lord. But all but one of them are of the same design."

He realised that meant the City. He got up.

"You understand?" he said to the architect.

"Of course, my lord. May I go?"

"Go on."

The Flyers were landing as the Governor walked into the courtyard of his palace. His household were rushing around, getting themselves ready for this sudden visitation. He had barely had time to put on his best kilt and brush his beard. He was surrounded by a handful of servants, bearing fans, food and drink for the guests.

The Flyers were a small design that he had not seen before, their underside and front fared in Metal. Each had three eager-looking blue-robes, in full armour. Among them, surrounded by them, was a larger Flyer, as big as his royal barge and as well appointed. Four of the smaller ones landed, blue-robes came out and they walked towards him. The leader of their group had a helm that showed Immortal Rank.

The Immortal raised the visor, still looking all around him. His hair was red, his eyes blue and looking everywhere, searching the courtyard for danger.

"Governor," he began, "do you have guests?"

"It appears I do, my lord," he answered.

The Immortal placed his hand on his sword-hilt and the Governor felt a shock of fear. Was he about to die for a misplaced word? But the Immortal's voice was laughing.

"Other than us?"

"Nobody else, my lord," answered the Governor. "How many of you are there?"

"In the guard I have sixty and there is the Mentor's party: three Sea People and their servants."

"The Mentor is here?"

Fear showed on the Governor's face and he imagined the Immortal's grin grew wider, more fierce. The Immortal glanced up and the barge-Flyer began to descend, surrounded by the smaller craft, like pilot-fish around a shark. It landed in his courtyard, the other blue-robes directing the servants to clear a space. On the descending Flyer, he could see another Immortal, with a sword but no armour, standing, looking down, and directing the Flyer by moving her outstretched arms, her cloak swirling around in the wind. Behind her two more stood, arm in arm, for all like two young lovers on their honeymoon. Both had the fair hair and skin of northmen.

He took his eyes away from the Flyer to look around his courtyard. The dozen blue-robes had cleared his court, shooed out his own palace guard, and he could only see half of them. If they had come for his life, it was too late for him now: the discipline of them had overwhelmed his own men before he had a chance to notice. He glanced back at the red-haired Immortal.

"Don't be afraid," laughed the Immortal. "My men are not here to harm you. They are here to protect him."

The front of the barge swung down and the couple walked out. The Immortal spoke as they approached.

"Mentor," he said, "this is the Governor of the Town of the Two Rivers. And this, Governor, is the Mentor and his Favourite."

"Ye are welcome my lord, my lady," said the Governor, keeping his voice under control. "What brings ye to the Two Rivers?"

The Mentor turned to the girl beside him.

"Eala here was told that the gardens here are a marvel and she wanted to see."

"Governor," the girl added, "I was told that ye have tamed the rivers to make gardens that feed whole cities. Perhaps you can spare someone who could show us around?"

"I will take ye myself," he answered.

The Governor would not leave them, not until they had been all over the surrounding land in their Flyers. The tour was interesting: the people of the Two Rivers region had cut channels, and used slaves with buckets to lift the water from the rivers to wet the fields. Some variety of grass was used, not the same variety as Ólachán used for beer, and the bread it made fed more people than the City. The cropping method they used around the City was simple: maize mixed with beans mixed with squashes, left all summer to grow tall, and cut down and harvested together when the season ended. But here, hundreds of labourers worked every day and the crop they grew could feed thousands.

Cathúa guided the Flyer back over the river and they looked down at the boats unloading on the waterfront. In between the piles of merchandise, the wood and stone, the furs and grain, Eala thought she could see an inn, where the dock-workers and sailors collected. *Arrachtaíumar* worked, loading and unloading, and she was reminded of the waterfront at the City.

People looked up as the great Flyer passed low overhead and a dark-haired child looked up and waved. Eala waved back. The Mentor leaned over the rail to see the child.

"You have no dignity at all," he whispered to Eala.

"I'm sorry, Mentor."

"Don't be."

The Flyer passed over the town and descended into the courtyard of the Governor's palace. The Governor's servants were waiting for them and they were led to where a canopy had been set out, shading tables and chairs.

"Will ye dine?" asked the Governor.

Cathúa and Foscúil looked at the Mentor and the Mentor looked at Eala.

"The Sun is setting here," the Mentor explained, "But we are a third of the way around the planet. It is not yet noon on the City Hill. Do you want to eat lunch?"

Eala shook her head at the strangeness of it all.

"I'm not used to the idea of living on a ball," she told him. She eyed the darkening sky, where Venus heralded the stars. "But I will eat my midday meal with you, Mentor."

The Governor sat the Mentor beside him and wanted Eala to sit on the other side. But the Mentor would not allow it.

"Cathúa is highest Rank," he said. "She should sit on your left side."

Male servants, bare-chested and in linen kilts, wafted them with fans on poles. Serving girls with dark plaited hair and long dresses brought food in pottery bowls: lamb, fish, boiled barley, and a fine selection of salad fruits and vegetables. Thick heavy beer was served and a harpist and a drummer came out to play music as they dined.

Eala found the beer and the strangeness of night-time at mid-day going to her head. She felt the Mentor's foot on hers, his toes finding her sandaled foot below the table. Eala could see that the Governor was not comfortable surrounded by so much power.

"How much land do ye need to feed a family, exactly?" Cathúa asked.

He looked around, beyond Foscúil.

"I showed ye the land, my lords, my ladies. Ye saw how much space we use."

"But I did not measure it," she answered. "How many man-height squares are needed?"

"Man-height squares?" the Governor asked, completely baffled.

Eala rescued him.

"You imagine a square where each side is the height of a man. If your field is fifty man-heights long, and forty wide, then it has two thousand man-height squares in it." She saw his head snap around to look the other way. "If you tell us the size of a typical field ye would assign to feed a family, we can calculate the number of man-height squares."

The Governor looked a little more relieved.

He called his own servants: "Fetch the Accounter of Farmland, please." Then he looked back at Eala. "How do you count that many squares, my lady?"

"You don't. There's a trick to it. You order them in tens: there are four rows of ten and five columns of ten. And ten tens are a hundred, four fives are twenty and one hundred twenties are two thousand."

"Are they?" the Governor asked. Then, rather than counting it on his fingers, he said "Of course it is."

Eala saw Cathúa smile, trying not to laugh, and she felt the pressure of the Mentor's foot on hers.

Foscúil said, "Don't worry, Governor. Not all blue-robes think in numbers. These two are freaks."

"We each have our talents," replied Cathúa. "Some of us are better with our brains. We can't all be the muscle-bound kind of freak."

Foscúil laughed. "I think it is time we played the Flanking Game together, Cathúa."

"You two!" laughed the Mentor. "If you're going to issue that sort of challenge, there should be forfeits!" He looked around at Eala. "And this one, every time I speak to her I seem to learn a new thing about her. Did Éirime teach you mathematics, my Favourite?"

"She did, Mentor. But my mother taught me before she did. I've been figuring since I was a little girl."

"It's the Gift of Anleacán," answered the Mentor.

The Governor looked confused. "What is the Gift of Anleacán, my lords?"

Cathúa replied, "Do you know what a gene is?"

"I don't, my lady," he answered.

"A gene is a part of the design that is in our bodies, that makes us grow the way we do. You have brown eyes, because a gene paints your eyes brown. But none of us have the gene: our eyes are blue and the Mentor and Favourite have green eyes. The paint in our bodies is brown but the paint gene in Lord Foscúil's and the Favourite's bodies is different: their paint is red. It is an Art of the Sea People, now forbidden, to create new genes that make creatures that have not existed before. The Forest People are one example and similar monsters do many things for us." She looked at him, to see if he was following, and Eala wondered if she had learned to do that from their friendship. "It is possible to make a gene that contains Words of Power. The Gift of Anleacán is one such gene. If you carry two copies of it in your body, you have a gift, a talent."

The Mentor spoke up.

"Cathúa," he said, "I didn't know the Gift of Anleacán was a gene. Who found that out?"

"It is in Iolar's last journal, Mentor."

Eala felt the Mentor's hand find hers, beneath the table. He held her fingers.

"I thought it was just a phrase people used," Eala said. "I didn't know there was a material explanation."

The Mentor mused to himself. "Iolar must have found it in Éirime."

"Éirime is a special case, Mentor," explained Cathúa. "In most cases, the Gift of Anleacán comes out as something trivial, like being able to speak in rhyme or sex newly hatched chickens with just a glance. It requires other factors: high intelligence, good manual dexterity, the bone-structure for singing, things like that, to turn it into someone like Éirime."

The Mentor looked around at Eala.

"Is your family related to Éirime?"

"Almost everyone in Áthaiteorann is related to Lady Éirime, Mentor. It doesn't mean anything, except that Áthaiteorann is her home village."

Cathúa said, "So the Gift of Anleacán is in your family."

"I don't know," Eala answered, reluctantly. But the Mentor's hand encouraged her. "My father always told everyone that he married my mother because of the beer she brewed and he said she has the Gift. And his grandfather certainly had it: he could carve anyone's face in wood, just from having met them, even if it was decades before." She was embarrassed talking about these peasant tricks. "As Lady Cathúa said, it is something trivial."

"Mathematical ability isn't trivial, Mentor," Cathúa contradicted.

"But the Gift of Anleacán isn't an ordinary thing either, is it?" the Mentor asked. "Is she the best mathematician you have ever taught, Cathúa?"

"She is not," answered Cathúa. "Eibheara was as quick, at her age."

"Then it cannot really be the Gift," answered the Mentor. "The Gift makes someone the best at something, I believe. Not just good."

Eala was relieved. "But Mentor, if someone from Anleacán is good at something, people call it The Gift anyway."

"Or perhaps mathematics is tangential to her main skill," said Cathúa.

Eala looked at the baffled Governor.

"Lady Éirime is a good mathematician, but there is mathematics in music and she does have the Gift." She smiled. "But if I am best at something that needs mathematics, I haven't found out what, yet. It can't be that important if I have reached adulthood without anybody noticing."

Foscúil said, "Are you twenty summers yet, Favourite? Get some experience, get Immortal Rank, and tell us again after your first quarter millennium."

Eala didn't like the conversation: it was far too personal and felt dangerous. She remembered Éirime praising her mother's beer: Caora had been drinking beer for much more than a quarter millennium. She didn't want to have the Gift of Anleacán and, she suddenly thought, she didn't want her sister to have it either. Her peasant sister deserved not to come to the attention of the Mentor again. She glanced around and saw an official was patiently standing by, wearing a formal kilt hastily wrapped around his hips.

"Governor," she said, "is this your Accounter of Farmland?"

"It is."

The discussion went back to farmland and productivity and Eala listened to Cathúa pick out the details. But as the pattern emerged, she wondered more and more. Eventually she spoke up.

"So, Governor," she said gently, "I'm trying to understand what ye are doing here. Ye have found a way to make less land feed more people, by making them work hard and eat the same thing every day?"

"Well, that's true," he agreed.

"And the reason they come to the Town of the Two Rivers is to work hard growing food?"

"That's right."

"Why don't they stay on their own land, eat better, and not work so hard?"

When the stars had come out over the Town of Two Rivers, Cathúa steered the Flyer home along the Inland Sea and then to the Ocean. They watched the sun rise again, in the West, as they caught it up: they would still be back in time for the Evening Meal. Servants brought wine and the Mentor sat with her, watching the rising-setting sun glint off the Flyers of Manoieas.

"Did you find out what you wanted to know?" the Mentor asked Eala.

"Answers lead to more questions," she replied. "I see that organising food enables them to do more but there doesn't seem much point in it. I suppose I am still thinking like a girl from Anleacán."

"Eala, I like girls from Anleacán."

"How many of us have you known?"

"Not many. Anleacán is a small place and Aclaí doesn't often bring Candidates." Eala saw his face change and knew he was remembering. "I think he is protective of his creation."

"His creation, Mentor?"

"Aclaí devised a way to create a whole new world, a whole new universe. He needed the House of Power, at first, because he was still low-Rank, but he could make anything. He chose the rules of the world and the Words of Power he had devised filled in the details, to make his creation work."

"What does that have to do with Anleacán, Mentor?"

"I was concerned that his created worlds could be a threat to the City. I asked him to make a world where someone in it was the greatest at something. I wanted to see if he could do it and if we could handle his creations."

Eala remembered that Universe Creation was among the forbidden Arts. But she was curious about where her home came from.

"And he created Anleacán?"

"You don't think a flat slab of a world is natural, do you?"

"Of course not," Eala smiled, thinking. "So, did he make someone who

..?" and she stopped as she realised she already knew the answer. "He made Lady Éirime?"

"I guess he knew I was considering making it a forbidden Art. He did as I had asked but he I guess he tried to make his creation as non-threatening, as appealing to me as possible. Éirime was the reason Anleacán was created. The Gift of Anleacán is a side-effect, a genetic explanation for what he was trying to achieve. The Words of Creation fill in the details and, to make her the greatest at something, the Words created the Gift of Anleacán."

"The Gift is meant to make her appeal to you?" She imagined being able to design her own world, her own people. She had wondered why Anleacán culture seemed so simple compared to the rich complexity of everywhere else.

"I asked for someone who was the best ever. I didn't say at what: it was Aclaí that chose singing. He could have chosen Words of Power, or sword-craft, or anything. But he probably thought that if he chose those things or, if I didn't like his example, I'd forbid his Art. Of course he made her pretty. People trust pretty faces."

"How old was he?" she wondered out loud.

"I don't remember. Twenty summers, I think. Maybe more, maybe less. Cathúa would know."

"So Lady Éirime is some young man's dream of the ideal girl?" Suddenly Eala remembered spotting that Caora had lied about her Nativity and she realised why. It meant that she was created, not born. Eala wondered if she remembered a childhood, or if she just woke up one morning with no history, no real memories.

"I'm sure you have the Gift, you know," the Mentor told Eala.

She looked up, distracted, uncomfortable.

"As Lady Cathúa said, I am not the best mathematician –"

"I think your Gift is for making me happy, Eala," the Mentor interrupted.

They walked up from the Evening Meal, the Mentor leading, holding Eala's hand.

Aclaí turned to Cathúa, and whispered, "Thank you for your help today."

"It's nothing," she answered. "I've never seen him so happy. You've never seen him leave the City before this month, Aclaí?"

"I haven't," Aclaí answered. "I do not believe he has left the City since he raised the island from the ocean. Before I was born, certainly."

"I wonder..." she began.

"Cathúa, I have to go. I have guests here."

"Of course," she answered. She looked awkward. "I want to help," she added.

"I know," he agreed. "Thank you."

He turned aside and let the rest of them go up into the Court of the Favourites. At Foscúil's house, he was about to call to them, when he noticed that Cathúa had followed him.

"What is it?" he asked her.

"I am concerned," she explained. "I love to see him happy but I think not everyone feels the same." She frowned. "I think there is jealousy."

"I am sure there is jealousy," he agreed. "We have to do what we can to prevent it being a problem. It could make him very unhappy." He looked at her trying to understand. "Are you concerned about tomorrow's patrol?"

"I am," she admitted. "If the patrol is led by someone who is too jealous ... they might not concentrate on the right things."

"Possibly. That is why I am coming along too."

"I guessed." Then she frowned again. "Why do you think it would make him unhappy?"

"Because I think that, if someone was to arrange for Eala to have an accident, he would miss her."

He watched Cathúa look scared.

"Do you think someone will do that?"

"I thought you were our historian."

"It has happened before," she agreed, "But not to someone like Eala."

"Why not? I don't remember anybody upsetting as many people as she has."

"But she is so nice."

"Come on, Cathúa. Don't you know anyone who would rejoice if she died?"

"Oh." He watched her think a moment. "What can I do to help?" she asked.

"Be vigilant. Eala is your friend, isn't she?"

"She is," Cathúa agreed.

"Then if you hear or see people wishing her harm, watch them. You are one of the oldest on the Hill, Cathúa. You should be able to protect Eala, if you want to."

"I will. Are you going to protect her?"

"Of course," Aclaí answered. "I saw him when he lost Iolar. I wouldn't want to see him like that again."

Cathúa turned and walked back up to the gateway, to the Court of the Favourites. Aclaí watched her leave, curious, then turned back to the door.

Foscúil's servant let him in and led him into the room. Miotal got up and greeted Aclaí.

"Foscúil and Damhánalla are on their way." He pulled a face. "I think."

"Well, we shouldn't begrudge them that," Aclaí laughed. "Foscúil has been watching the Mentor in love all day. Playing with Damhánalla will get it out of his system."

"Do you need to get it out of your system, Aclaí?"

"Probably," he agreed, "But not now. I ought to try and get it out of your grand-niece's system."

"Is she jealous?"

"Cathúa thinks so."

"How serious do you think that is?"

"I think we don't just need to protect the Mentor and his Favourite from the Forest. I think we need to protect the Favourite from the City."

"Have you heard of any actual plot?"

"I haven't. But I don't think I would. Immortals are good at intrigue or they wouldn't have survived."

"Except Cathúa," Miotal sneered.

"Cathúa is good at avoiding intrigue, Miotal. It works for her."

"But what a boring life."

"She has different hobbies."

"Boring hobbies. Only last month she –"

But whatever she did was lost, as Foscúil and Damhánalla returned. Damhánalla hugged Aclaí, and Foscúil looked on, smiling.

"How did it go?" she asked his chest.

"They both survived. They both had fun."

Foscúil asked, "Do ye think this will be the end of this travelling ambition?"

"Probably not," Aclaí answered. "I would think it will carry on until he realises the danger."

"And how will you arrange that?" Miotal slyly asked.

"I think the Forest will arrange that," Aclaí replied. "The reason to have a large and strong Patrol with him is to get him out safely."

"Do you think he'd still want to wander if he didn't have her by his side?" Miotal asked.

Damhánalla turned her head, still with her arms around Aclaí.

"Are you suggesting what I think you're suggesting?" she asked.

"Oh, there are other ways to deal with it than to kill her," Miotal said. "If she was caught in bed with someone else, that would probably be sufficient."

"It would," agreed Damhánalla, "But it might be as good as killing her. You know how jealous he can be."

"It would certainly be fatal for the boy she was in bed with," Aclaí added. "Boy or girl."

"Does she like girls too?" asked Foscúil.

"Her sister does," said Damhánalla.

"Or perhaps she fakes it well enough to fool Éirime," added Miotal.

"They are identical," mused Damhánalla. "I wonder if *we* could fake something..."

"We will not involve Éirime in this," commanded Aclaí. He looked at the others and saw the assent appear in their faces. "Anyway, I don't think ye would have much luck with that kind of intrigue. She is still a country girl at heart and, even if ye set the trap, ye would not get her to take the bait."

"How do you know?" asked Damhánalla.

"He knows," Miotal offered. "Ye know how Aclaí works. If Eala could be persuaded to take that bait, he'd have caught her by now."

"Well, if that's not going to work, we need another plan," said Foscúil. "She has gained too much power to be allowed to be outside our control. And if she won't fall for Aclaí, we need something else to bring her into line."

"Maybe when she is no longer The Favourite..." suggested Damhánalla.

"I'm not sure we should wait that long," Aclaí answered. "Initiations have stopped. He hasn't called anyone else to his bed for six months and some of the favourites are angry. The Initiation itself will protect him from the worst of the jealousy but it might not protect her."

"With no Initiations, the City will die," added Foscúil. "The Novices cannot progress and, when word gets around, the Selections will be empty. When the current Veterans die or Retire, there'll be just the favourites left."

"I suspect some favourites will Retire, too," Aclaí answered. "Five years of this and the City will be in trouble. Fifty years of this and the City will be gone." He turned to Foscúil. "How long before the Forest People can keep humanity safe without the City?"

"Five centuries," suggested Foscúil. "Three if we get lucky or you are willing to take risks. I told you many times, Aclaí, they breed slowly. It will take time."

"Time is what we may not have," grumbled Aclaí.

Aclaí kissed Miotal in the darkness and turned and walked up through the gate to the Court of the Favourites. He called softly at one of the doors and then, hearing no answer, he walked around the fountain and beneath the cypress, down to the wall that overlooked the sea.

Eibheara was there, sitting in the lovers' seat, looking at the Moon reflected on the ocean. She looked up as he approached.

"Eibheara," he greeted her, softly in the darkness.

"Oh Aclaí," she answered, making room for him beside her.

He heard the emotion in her voice, but he could not see her face. He gently reached his arm around her and felt her anger and then her relaxation, as she reminded herself that she was not angry with him.

"I hate her," she whispered.

"You're not alone in that, Eibheara," Aclaí agreed.

"Do you?"

"I feel sorry for her. She's a purple Novice, put in a situation far beyond her experience. And what we know is that the Mentor's attention is like fire: either it smoulders and lasts or it burns brightly and quickly fades. When it fades she will still be a Novice. And everyone will hate her."

"Will you take her to your bed?"

"I don't think so. She will have too many enemies by then."

"I thought she was about your type."

"Perhaps she might be but that doesn't make it wise. Besides, her sister is Éirime's girl."

"I don't understand you and Éirime..."

"It's not that, Eibheara. If she is wise, when the Mentor sends her back down the Hill she will Retire and return to Áthaiteorann and her sister."

"That won't put her out of reach."

"It will put her under Éirime's protection. Do you feel ready to challenge Éirime? She may be gentle but she is Nineteenth Rank."

"She is Retired and I am not. One day my Rank will be greater than hers."

"But not in Eala's lifetime. She will be long dead before you gain Twentieth Rank."

"You're not making me feel any better, you know."

"I didn't come down here to argue about Eala, Eibheara. I came down here to find you."

"Well, she is all I can think about now. This whole summer, we've had this ridiculous game."

"It won't be long now."

"You have a plot?"

"Not really. Eibheara, I saw what he was like when he lost Iolar. I don't want to see that again. I want to see him tire of her and discard her. If she Retires after that and goes back to Éirime, then that is the best result for everyone."

"What about my revenge?"

"I cannot help you with that, Eibheara. I am thinking about what is best for the Mentor and the City."

"Don't you ever think about me?"

"Of course I think about you. That is why I am here."

"I hate you sometimes. I ought to slap you."

"If that helps you feel better, then..." and she slapped him. He looked back at her and she thought she could see him smile.

"Aren't you going to fight back?" she demanded.

"Whatever pleases you, my lady," he answered. But, however sincere he sounded, she knew it was games and she was sure he was laughing inside.

But she sighed inside. She knew it would help her forget. She set her face in the stern expression that was her part in this game and she slapped him again.

It was the night of Midsummer and again Rónmór had arranged the band to come and play them the dances of Anleacán. This time he was more confident and, when the Mentor took Eala's hand and led her out to dance, he knew he had done the right thing.

Eibheara was watching the dancers when Éise came up to her.

"My lady?" she said.

"Not dancing?" Eibheara asked in reply. "Where is that boy of yours?"

"Getting drinks, my lady. But that Novice you have been taking an interest in, she's involved in a fight outside."

"Thank you for telling me," Eibheara said, smiling as she put her drink down. "Show me where."

Éise led the way outside the Hall, into the twilight. She couldn't see where the trouble was, but she could hear them. Éise led the way and among the trees, screened from the Hall, they found the crowd, encircling some action, watching. A few noticed Eibheara approaching and they gave way.

Two boys were facing up to one another, circling carefully, armoured, and Abhainne was watching, her sword in her hand. She looked angry, and there was another girl beside her, who looked like she had been crying. Abhainne looked around.

"My lady," she greeted Eibheara.

The two boys noticed Eibheara and stood down. One raised his visor. His face was from the Great Ocean and looked angry.

"Lady Eibheara," he said. His voice was full of emotion and slightly slurred.

"What is going on here?"

"My lady," the boy explained, "Spéire says that Gallán raped her. Gallán –"

The other boy raised his visor too. "Spéire said it was all right. She wanted it."

"I didn't, you filthy dog," she screamed at him. "First thing I knew, you were –"

"All right, that's enough," ordered Eibheara. "So ye boys are going to settle this by fighting?"

Abhainne answered, "Don't you want to judge, my lady?"

Eibheara laughed. "Of course not." She turned to the combatants. "Ye boys carry on."

"My lady?" Spéire protested.

"Oh, come on, girl. Boys fighting over you? To the death? How sweet is that?"

"What if Soilbhir loses, my lady?"

"What of it? You have a sword to protect him, don't you?" Eibheara walked around the periphery of the crowd, Abhainne and Spéire following. The crowd watched her and those before her gave way. She sat on one of the lover-seats and put her drink on the arm. Abhainne sat beside her and she gave room.

"Go on then," she told the boys, "if ye're going to."

The boys looked back at one another, hesitating, then lowered their visors.

They staggered back into the room and he led her to the bed. She sat down heavily.

"Happy Midsummer," he told her.

"Uh." Eala opened her eyes. "I'm sorry, Mentor. I think I had too much wine."

"Lie still, then," he said, gently. "Close your eyes." Then, softly, he spoke Words.

Eala felt his touch and the way the bed seemed to be tipping, rotating. She wondered if she would be sick. Then she felt a strange sensation and the nausea cleared.

"What did you do?" she asked.

"It was The Purification of the Blood," he explained. "It's meant for poisons and deep infections. But alcohol is a poison. It works on drunkenness."

She opened her eyes.

"Thank you, Mentor."

"It's nothing," he told her. "I don't want you unwell. I have other plans for you."

Afterwards, he asked her, "You were born in Midsummer, weren't you?"

"Not just me, Mentor. Lord Aclaí's nativity is two days before mine."

"Do they celebrate nativities among your people, Eala?"

"Some do," she agreed. "Do others on the Hill?"

"I was thinking of taking you off the Hill for your nativity. Perhaps you would take me to your home village."

Eala tried to keep the panic off her face.

"I am not sure that would be so wise, Mentor," she explained carefully. "My home village is only a small place and, with more than sixty of us landing there, we would outnumber them."

She watched, but he wasn't convinced.

"Perhaps we could go without taking everyone with us."

"Lord Aclaí's friends live in Anleacán. They would find us straight away." She carried on watching him, trying to gauge how she was affecting him. "Lady Éirime is in my home village, Mentor," she added.

"I miss her, Eala."

"I know, Mentor. But I think if you visit her, it will drive her away more. Your best chance with her is to wait, Mentor."

The Mentor looked sad and Eala hated herself for hurting him.

"Don't you want to go home?" he asked.

She found a happier voice. "Couldn't we see your home?" she suggested.

"It's probably no bigger than your village," he explained. "It was tiny when I left but that was ... it must be over a thousand years ago. If we go, we should find a way to escape Aclaí and his guard." She saw him smile and saw his face brighten. "Would you like to spend a few days, just you and me with no blue robes?"

"Will it be safe, Mentor?"

"We won't be going into the Forest. We'll be staying in this world. Of course it will be safe."

"Then I would love to."

"All right, Eala. We will go to my village, if it is still there."

He opened his eyes. His girl was asleep by him, one arm over his neck. He lay there a moment, remembering his dreams, then carefully, he lifted her arm and folded it back on her. She stirred a little but she did not wake. It was still dark, even though it was midsummer and he knew she would sleep for hours.

But to be sure, as he climbed out of their bed, he whispered the Words of Concealment before he went to his desk. He sat down, reached to the back, and took the leather bag. As he picked it up, he knew it would come under the illusion and be Concealed with him. If she awoke, he could tidy up before breaking the Concealment: he knew that she woke up slowly. But he was sure she would not wake. His fingers shook as he undid the drawstring of the bag.

"Ceann," he whispered, "I don't want to do this anymore."

Then who will? the reply came. *The City belongs to you, they all belong to you. You have earned it and you should not let another take it from you.*

He looked over at the bed.

"I want something else..."

You have her, you know it.

"What about Geana?"

You didn't Initiate Geana.

"I Initiated Éirime. And it was a terrible mistake."

You would rather have let Aclaí have her?

"She is gone."

Only because you let her go. You could call her, she would return. She still belongs to you, she would obey you.

"I believe it. But I cannot make her want to return."

Then call her, if you want her.

"I want her to want to return. And I don't want Eala to ever want to leave."

Méar, you are a fool. She will never choose to leave, whatever you do to her. If you tell her to come back to you, she always will.

"That is not what I want."

Then what you want is a dream, not reality. Real people don't behave as you want. Have you loved anyone all your life? Méar knew he had never loved anyone the way he expected them to love him. Then he looked away from the eye-sockets of the skull, and over to Eala's form on the bed. But the words called his attention back. *No ordinary emotion can last through the centuries of immortality. Only Initiation can do that.*

"Perhaps that is true, Ceann. Perhaps love only lasts a few months. Then I will ask you again in a few months, when it is over."

You mean when she is dead? the words asked.

Angrily he pushed the skull back into the bag and pulled the strings tight.

— 13 —

Summer's End

"All summer long, the grass grows tall," Caora sang, clear up into the hazy summer sky.

"And now we cut new hay for all," the reapers responded.

"The hay is green, but soon turns gold," she led, again...

The hay was cut from a field that had been fenced off and guarded from the livestock all summer. It was divided into allotments, one for each family. Cutting hay was heavy work, with men cutting and women stacking what was cut. Flannbhúia had no men in her family so, being a widow, she had teamed up with Reo and Ordóg. Éilite had prodded Reo into helping but Duille had ordered Ordóg's wife not to stack the hay, telling her that a woman of her years carrying her first child should not work so hard. Geana was not sure what complicated arrangements balanced that debt but her mother would know.

And others in the village knew that the weather would not break until Flannbhúia's allotment was cut. That her daughter's lover had power over the elements was common knowledge. They called over, joking, to Reo and Ordóg, inviting them not to work so hard.

But it was exhausting work in the heat, with the dust and the insects. One part of Geana's mind railed against the injustice of it and she told herself not to be foolish. Her mother's animals needed feeding over the winter and so did Ordóg's and Reo's.

She still couldn't help wondering if her sister was having a better Nativity Day than her own.

"Promise me you'll hide the cloaks as soon as we get there."

The Mentor laughed indulgently.

"All right, all right. As soon as we are safely on the beach they go away."

He looked down at the coastline as they approached. He couldn't help

251

it: knowing where they were meant a lot to him.

"The coastline has changed so much. There was beach stretching out for miles here but now it's all gone. Now the sea comes right up to the cliffs but then there were dunes as far as you could see."

"In our Nature lectures they talked about how the seas are rising." Eala held his arm, looking down, happy. "I didn't think that it would be noticeable, though."

"My home village is still there: look, you can see the smoke. Flyer, go low. I'm doing better than Aclaí: the village where his parents were Stewards, where he grew up, has long gone beneath the ocean."

He put his hand on hers.

"Are you excited?" she asked.

"Flyer, follow my gaze and land," he said. "I am excited. I thought I would only be interested in something new, not something old."

"If it's old enough it might as well be new. Things change, don't they? When were you last here?"

"We raised the Isle of the Forever-Young in the one hundred and ninetieth year of the Sea People. I never returned to Tircúpla. I felt old then and thought I would never want to see my home ever again. Now I feel young. I haven't felt this since before my brother died. What have you done to me?"

"Just my duty, Mentor. The Favourites have to keep you entertained. You are entertained, aren't you?"

"I am entertained. Do you know what you have done to me, Eala? You are like someone out of one of Éirime's songs."

"I hope I am not: some of Éirime's songs tell very dark stories." She looked out at the sea, beyond the rocks. "What can we see? And what did it look like before?"

"This bit here was all dunes and marshes: you could only see the sea in the distance. The fishermen used to go out across the marshes along the path of this stream. That path, that looks like a sheep-trail, that was where we used to walk down to the sea and back up to the village."

"Can we walk to the village now?"

"We can. But if we are pretending to be peasants we should put our cloaks away."

Eala unwrapped her cloak. Beneath it she had warm clothes made of sheep's leather with the fur left on. The Mentor was wearing a jacket of bearskin, much thicker and warmer than hers. The cloaks went in the locker on the Flyer. They could have them at a moment's notice.

"Are we sure they'll be there?" Eala asked. "Aren't the tribes of the Archipelago nomadic?"

"Some are," he answered. "Most are, all through the Archipelago and along the coast to the south and east. They move with the seasons, because they need to go where the food is."

"Some day, there will be conflict between planters and gatherers," Eala suggested.

"There is conflict between planters and gatherers already," the Mentor answered. "We don't talk about it to peasants, or to Novices, but it's one of the biggest ... Wait, how do you know? I thought all of the Anleacán tribes were planters."

"Planters, herders or fishermen, Mentor. But it's obvious, isn't it? Gatherers think they own what they find, but planters think they own the fields they planted. If a gatherer gathers food that a planter has planted, then there will be conflict of ownership."

"Eala, have you ever met a gatherer tribe?"

"Only the Adepts who came from them. Isn't Lord Foscúil from a gatherer tribe?"

"From the Sea Hounds: on the West Island of the Archipelago, away to the south and west. But this is a small island and there can be no wandering here. The people of my tribe were fishermen even when I was a boy."

"There are boats and it's not far from the mainland."

"When I was a boy the mainland was covered in Forest."

"Oh," said Eala. She thought a moment, out loud. "So the tribes that we know, they have spread since the Sea People tamed the Forest?"

"That's right," answered the Mentor.

Eala made no reply to that. She tried to imagine what life had been like for him, growing up. Then she tried not to. She took his hand and he held hers.

"It's cold," the Mentor said.

"It is only cold because of the wind coming up from the sea. When we are walking in the sun, it will be hot."

Hand in hand, they walked up to see what was left of the Mentor's home.

By the time they got to the village, they were hot and hungry. Tircúpla people still lived in half-buried long houses, much as he remembered. There was an inn but they had nothing to trade. Never mind, he thought, I have the Key of Creation. It was a tiny use for one of the Great Principles, but today, in the summer afternoon, making Eala happy didn't seem so tiny. He led Eala into the inn.

Everyone looked at them. They obviously didn't see so many strangers

around here. The pots and the kitchen were over one end of the room and
he led her to it.

"I smell fish stew and cider," he said. "Will you trade for them?"

"Good day, strangers," answered the keeper, obviously surprised at the
directness of his speech. "They are both for sale if you have something to
trade. I am Tonn. Who are ye and where are ye from?"

"I am Méar and this is Eala. I am from the City, Eala is from Anleacán."

"Brother and sister?" he asked. It was not unreasonable: they both
had green eyes.

"Husband and wife," Méar replied. "We have been together only this
year."

Eala held his arm but inside she was amazed. *The Sea People do not
marry*, she reminded herself. Those peasant ideas would need to be kept
in check, she knew: but more, she knew that he was happy to say it, to
pretend it was true.

"Well, may ye have many grandchildren and many years and love one
another for all of them." It was a well-wishing Eala had heard in her own
village. "And what brings ye to Úlloileán?"

"With a name like that, I had to know if there was good cider to be
had." Méar laughed, a sound Eala had rarely heard. "My wife was born
in the country but I have spent most of my life in the City. In a few days
we will go back, but it is her nativity, the first we've been together and I
wanted to see the country with her."

"More to congratulate ye for. What do your family do, Eala? Are they
fishermen?"

"They are sheep-farmers. My father died when I was a little girl but
my mother still keeps a few sheep. There are no fishermen in my village,
at least not fishermen with boats. A few salmon are caught in season but
we are many days' walk from the sea. Before I met Méar, I had never seen
the sea."

"And you, Méar? What do your family do?"

"I have no family: my mother died three hours after I was born. My
father was a fisherman in a village very like this: he used to go out in a
little boat made of skin and twigs and catch fish with a net. He's dead
now. I work in the City, helping the Sea People research Words of Power."

Eala reflected that the last was true.

"Didn't you ever want to be Selected?" Tonn asked.

"I couldn't be an Adept. And as time has gone by, I think I've realised
that I wouldn't want to be even if I could: the Adepts have rather a sad
life."

Tonn was shocked at this open disrespect of the Sea People and, looking from Tonn to Méar, Eala could see he was surprised at the reaction.

"We don't want bad talk like that here," Tonn warned. "We all owe a great deal to the Sea People."

Eala spoke, trying to smooth things over.

"My husband is used to plain talking. Sometimes in the City people see things and say things that would seem disrespectful to my mother. It is true that life for the Sea People is dangerous: our families and our safety depends on their taking dangerous work. But not everyone at the City is unhappy. Sometimes things happen unexpectedly and a Lady of the Sea People can be as happy as any peasant girl in love."

Tonn seemed to grudgingly accept this.

"This is not the City, Mr. Méar. Find somewhere to sit and I will bring you your things."

He led her over to a table and they sat. Méar leaned over to Eala, as a young husband would.

"This house used to be mine," he said quietly. "I drew a whole fir-tree in off the ocean and they roofed this house with the timber. It used to be my laboratory. I slept in a small room back there."

He stopped talking: a girl was bringing mugs. She set them on the table before them.

"Are you really from the City?" she asked.

"I am," Méar replied.

She seemed about to say something, then shyness overcame her and she fled.

"Is your name really Méar?" asked Eala.

"It is. My brother was born first and the midwife wasn't sure what was happening, so I stuck my hand out and waved. At least that's what my father told us when I was little. So they named us for the parts of us they'd seen first: Ceann because they'd seen his head and Méar because they'd seen my fingers."

"You're a twin?" Eala asked, pleased at the coincidence, pleased to have learned it today of all days.

"I am the younger of twins. My brother died when we were twelve years old. He used to lead the two of us. When he died I thought I would have to do all the leading."

Something about the way he said it made Eala scared and alert, all at once. Something was wrong, her instinct told her. But he was still speaking.

"That is why I asked you about leading, at the Selection. We are both the following twin and we both grew under our sibling's shadow."

Eala knew the superstition about marrying people who were in the same position in the family as you: that eldests would marry eldests, second sons second daughters, and so on. She also knew enough about how emotions worked to know it was more than just superstition. But she had never expected to have a relationship with a following-twin, not really: and she certainly never thought that the Mentor might be one. She was going to answer, but a woman was coming over with bowls on a tray.

"Here it is: I hope you like it. There is salt in the bowl, please don't waste it. If there is anything else you need, call. I am right over there in the kitchen."

"There is one thing," Méar told her. "We would like to stay here a few days. It looks to me like there might be a bedroom through that door. Do you take guests?"

"That is a store-room," she said. "Nobody ever sleeps in the inn. I could ask around to see if someone would take in a guest."

Méar produced a handful of pieces of gold, each a rough cylinder about the size of his thumb.

"Would one each be enough for the food and drink?" he asked.

The woman stared at the gold.

Eala asked, "Why does nobody sleep in the inn?"

She leaned over close, not to be overheard.

"They say the building is haunted."

Eala looked at Méar. Méar looked thoughtful. She looked back at the woman.

"A haunting is normally a tale," Eala said. "What is the tale?"

The woman looked embarrassed. "We don't normally tell it to strangers."

"We won't tell anyone who will harm you," she said, and turned. "Will we, Méar?"

"We won't," he agreed.

"All right. But remember this is just a village tale and there might be nothing in it: but the story is that the Mentor was born here. Before he went over the sea to the Land of the Forever Young, this building was built for him." She looked about her, making sure nobody was listening. "They say that it was here he made dark pacts with evil Powers, that allowed the Sea People to come to being."

She looked at them, gauging their reaction. Méar took the story seriously.

"I know that the Mentor came from this island: it might be your village that was his birthplace. Perhaps your story is true. But I also know nobody in the City believes in ghosts. I was telling Tonn – your husband, is he?" she moved her head, agreeing, "– I was telling your husband that I help the Adepts with research. If there is anything bad in this house that comes out at night I can see it and tell you what to do about it. But the Land of the Young was raised from the ocean a thousand years ago. If there was any shadow here, chances are it is long gone." He looked her in the eye. "And I will pay to stay, if you will get a bed for us."

"I will ask my husband," she said.

When she was gone, Méar was smiling.

"Don't laugh at them," Eala said. "Their story is almost the same as yours and all they have is word-of-mouth, tales handed down the generations. She is scared you will tell the Mentor. Look at them arguing: he has just learned that his wife has told a City-man that the Mentor 'made dark pacts with evil Powers.' Be nice to them."

He got it under control.

"I am sorry, Eala. You really are very good at reading people, you know. Anyway, I am laughing because they are closer than you think. I made the Key of Creation in this room, over there where those two women with the dog are drinking: that is as dark a *pact* as you get. I'm sitting here, a thousand years old, with one of the most powerful of the Great Principles for a necklace and she's telling me the place is haunted." He composed his face again. "It is just so strange for me to see how they view us." Eala was smiling, too, but inside she was upset to see how different his view was to theirs. He put his hand on hers. "You show me such surprising things. Thank you, Eala."

She turned to look at him and he leaned over and kissed her mouth. As they embraced, she whispered in his ear.

"Mentor, you realise you offered enough gold to buy the inn?"

"Use my name, Eala," he replied, "they're coming over."

Eala let go of him with one arm and they turned. Tonn was coming over.

"Gaotha tells me you want to stay."

"I would like to, if you would put a bed in the room through that door."

"You told me that you help the Sea People with their research. Would you sleep in the rooms where they research Words of Power?"

"I would, once the researches are ended. Look, I wanted to know if there were any stories about the Mentor. He was born on this island, not far from here: this building might well have been his place of research, and he might well have slept in that very room. I will be safe, I can tell you if others will be safe and I will pay. In case you are worried that at midnight my entrails will be feasted on by elemental chaos, I will pay for five days in advance."

"Very well," he replied, "You say you know the risks. I will take your gold: but if you are too scared to stay, you won't get your gold back."

They brought in a bed, and they brought in a table, a washbowl, a jug

and mugs, and a pot: everything they needed. Meanwhile Méar took her
walking around the village.

"This is where my father lived," he said, indicating a door in the long
house that made the frontage of the square. "Sit with me." They sat. "We
sat on a wooden bench, just here, the day we got married."

Eala looked around at him and held his hand, all attentive.

"You got married, Méar?"

"I did. It was only a few months after the First Year of the Sea People.
I had the first Novices there and I wanted her to be one of them. She
had been my brother's girlfriend and my brother wanted ..." again, Eala's
instincts told her something was very wrong "... well, my brother would
have wanted us to be together."

"What happened?"

"I think the same thing happened as happened with Éirime. She wasn't
suited to our life and I hurt her trying to force her into it."

"Do I look like her?"

"It is hard to know. It has been over a thousand years. I think you do.
I think her hair was more red than yours and her eyes blue, not green."
A look of surprise crossed his face, momentarily. "I just remembered: her
nativity was yesterday. Or would have been." Then he looked at her face.
"Anyway, I think you are prettier than she was. But it's all right. I care
about you, not her."

That hadn't been what Eala was thinking.

"What was her name?"

"Oh, I see," he replied. "Her name was Geanúile: but Ceann called her,
well, everybody called her Geana." He looked at Eala's face, trying to see
behind the smile she always wore. "You knew, didn't you?" She saw a
moment of suspicion on his face. "How did you find out?"

"I had guessed," she replied. "It wasn't a hard guess. I am sure Lady
Éirime didn't mean to upset you, Me...Méar. Most people who bring Can-
didates know. They even check when the Candidates are brought, but
I guess nobody thought to check the Candidates brought by someone of
Nineteenth Rank and Éirime never took an interest in Selection before we
nagged her. Really, it was our fault for nagging her, I suppose."

"I've spent all this time hating Geanúile for being a peasant when she
should have been more like you. If she was at Selection today, I'd probably
walk past her without stopping."

"You'd stop if she told you her name, Méar."

"I don't know. Sitting here, with you, it all seems a bit silly and remote."
He looked at her again, with the full intensity of his gaze. "Do you want
your sister to be Selected, Eala?"

"May I ask her what she wants before answering?"

"All right. If you bring her to Selection, we'll see what happens. But I promise I won't hurt her." He watched Eala's face, wondering what she was thinking. "She doesn't have to come."

She put her arms around him and their mouths met again.

Flannbhúia's allotment in the hayfield was cleared and they had helped finish Reo's and Fléanna's before the sun had set. The hay was stacked in the fields, drying. Then Caora led them back to the Songbird and, as Geana followed her back, feeling the rubbery exhaustion in her legs, her mother fell in beside her. She felt her mother's fingers in her hand and looked around.

"Mammy," she said.

"She's not coming home, love," her mother answered.

Geana felt her eyes sting. She looked back and ahead: Caora was nearly at the inn and they were not being followed. She led her mother between the cottages, out of sight, and her mother was hugging her. She was crying.

"I miss her, Mammy. I miss her all the time. It's not fair."

"It certainly isn't," answered Flannbhúia. "But there is nothing that can be done for that. You say you cannot go back to Selection and, even if you did, Eala is Favourite. You will not best that. Your little sister is gone."

Geana laughed with the sobbing. "You remember how I used to complain about having to share my nativity, Mammy? Today I have it all to myself and it hurts worse than sharing it ever did."

"I felt the same when your father died, you know. The grief doesn't go away but life doesn't go away either. You have to live it."

"Don't you miss her too?"

"Of course. She is my daughter as well as your sister. I am so proud of her but she is gone. She will never come home to me."

"Mammy, how do you bear it?"

"What else is there to do?" she answered, holding Geana's hands in her own. "You have to decide what you want to do with your life."

"What can I do that has any meaning? Everyone compares me to her."

"They don't. The only person who does that is you. Hardly anyone noticed her when she was by your side and, now she is gone, she is more of a story than a real memory. These are still your friends, Geancacha. They are waiting for you to have time for them again."

"Lady Caora needs me, Mammy."

"I know and so do they. You are the only person in the village who knows how to talk to her, how to take care of her, and everybody knows that. Intelligent as you are, you know that makes you the most powerful person in Áthaiteorann."

"I am not as powerful a person as Lady Caora, or even as my *little sister*, Mammy."

"You know that blue-robes are not real people." Flannbhúia smiled, showing her daughter that she might be joking. "Everyone in Áthaiteorann is waiting for you." The smile became wider. "Especially the boys."

"So a few village boys are lusting after me. That's happened since we had twelve summers."

"Longer than that," Flannbhúia laughed.

"Mammy," answered Geana wearily, "You must be able to see that I cannot have another boyfriend. Eala is forbidden to be unfaithful to the Mentor. If a stranger saw me with a boy and mistook me for Eala, what then? And you know what boys are like: a boy boasting of sleeping with the identical twin of the Favourite... it would be too dangerous for us both. While she is Favourite, I must leave boys alone."

She could see Flannbhúia hadn't thought of that. For a moment it seemed to Geana that her mother was about to give some answer. Then she saw her mother's expression change, as she decided to keep a secret.

"That could be years," she answered instead.

"It could be," Geana agreed, wondering if someone had already asked her mother for her hand. Wondering who. But she said, "Eala might outlive us all. But there is no help for it."

"Then you must help yourself," Flannbhúia answered. "What do you enjoy doing?"

"I love to read," answered Geana. "I love to learn."

"You are the only person – the only *real* person – in the village who can read. I envy you that, daughter."

"I could teach you."

"I would like that very much."

"All right, I will. First you must learn a song." And she drew breath and sang the scribe's song that Caora had taught them. It surprised her that her mother learned as quickly as Eala had learned.

The next day, as they were eating breakfast, Eala asked, "How far is Gainmheach?"

"It is a short ride along the coast. Or even a short walk: we could be there by midday." Méar looked at her, suspicious and amused at once that she should ask. "How do you know about Gainmheach? I thought you'd never been to Úlloileán."

"One of the Novices used to talk about it. I wanted to see it for myself."

"Well, if that's what you want. Shall we hire horses?"

"We will not be able to go faster than a walk, Méar. I haven't done many riding lessons."

"I will show you. Riding is fun. You'll like it. Most girls do."

They hired horses and she rode with him, getting more confident. Inevitably she fell off, as there was nothing to hold on to, but he knew Words of Healing and she didn't even have bruises when they arrived.

"This is Gainmheach. The big strip of sea over there separates the two islands." He looked around. "Is it what you expected?"

She held his hand. "Thank you for bringing me. I think that is an inn over there."

"Food! Drink!" he said. "Or maybe: Drink! Food!"

"I just get giggly if you give me too much to drink. And we still have the ride home."

"The drink will relax you and it will hurt less."

"But we should wait until we are back before we try that."

"I meant falling off the horse. You are such a naughty girl, aren't you?"

"Hush," she said. They were going in. She looked around and got her bearings. The drink and food were served at one end. She went over, Méar following.

The woman who was waiting said, "I'm Cearca. How can I help you, Freckles?"

"I'm trying to take care of a thirsty husband. My name is Eala. My husband here is Méar. I'm also looking for someone. I don't know his name, but I know his son went to Selection this year. The son's name was Lách."

Cearca looked sad a moment.

"That would be Bradán. He works by the stream, in the house with the two pear trees outside." She smiled, remembering she was talking to strangers. "He makes boats. They are very good boats, people come from all over Úlloileán to buy his boats. What does your husband like to drink?"

"He's been drinking a lot of cider recently."

"Cider can do terrible things to a man," she warned. But she fetched some.

As she was fetching it, Eala turned to him.

"I have an errand, Méar. Would you like to stay and drink while I run it?"

"I would like to find out what this mysterious errand is."

"It's something I feel I need to do: a low-Rank matter. It won't be fun."

"Eala, I'm not just interested in having fun. Haven't you realised that yet? If it's important to you, I want to know what it is."

"Will you let me do it and not interfere?"

"Is that so important?" He looked at her. "I won't interfere, then. I'm now really curious."

"You will be disappointed."

"If I am, I'm sure you'll make it up to me." He held her hand. "I really want to see the rest of you. You laugh too much and you don't cry enough. I know you are hiding half of yourself from me and I want to see it."

"You really will be disappointed, Méar."

"Let's just see. Maybe it is time I learned to deal with a little disappointment. Or maybe you are so beautiful that whatever I do with you will be good. Just let's go and see."

The landlady arrived with the drink. Eala gave her gold and said, "We are going to Bradán's house. Do you mind if we take the mug? We will bring it back, we need to eat."

"All right," she said. "As long as you leave that piece of gold for when you return."

"Thank you," Eala replied.

They went out. There was a house by the stream, with a ridge-line sagged around the smoke-hole. As they approached, they could hear children. One young boy, that Eala thought looked like Lách might have looked when he was Spideog's age, ran down the path and into the house, yelling. "It's strangers! There's a man and a woman. Come quick!"

A man appeared from behind the house, a woodworking tool in his hand. He had a heavy leather apron.

Eala asked, "Are you Bradán?"

"I am," he replied suspiciously. "Who are ye?"

"I am Eala."

"Oh." He put the tool down and straightened up.

"Welcome, my lady," he said. "Come inside. Would you like to eat?"

She thought of her mother's pride and wondered what she should answer.

"A little, perhaps. Did Lord Rian speak to you?"

"He did, my lady. He said that you had asked him to."

"I am sorry for your loss," she said. "Lách was my friend. When I came to the City, he was the first person to give me a kind word."

"Come inside," he said.

He led the way into their house. His wife was there.

"This is Lady Eala," Bradán said, and they saw that his wife recognised the name. He looked at Méar.

"This is my friend Méar," said Eala.

"Is he one of the Sea People too?"

"He is."

"Welcome, my lord," Bradán said. "I did not mean to disrespect you, my lord, but I did not see a blue cloak. Lady Eala I know only through Lord Rian mentioning her name."

"It is not your fault, Bradán," said Méar. "I thought we were hiding our blue cloaks today. This visit comes as a surprise to me, too."

"Did you know Lách, my lord?"

"I only met him once, although I liked him when I saw him." Méar had learned how Eala lied: she told the truth. He knew he must have met and liked Lách at Selection, or he would have walked by. "I didn't get to know Eala for several days after the Selection. She was moved to a dormitory near me. Lách's dormitory is in a different part of the City. But I trust Eala's judgement: she says he was a good friend to her and that alone is enough recommendation for me."

"Your words are kind, my lord," said Bradán. He turned to Eala. "How did it happen?"

"They were patrolling the Forest and they encountered monsters. The monsters outnumbered them and they were defeated. A patrol, the following day, discovered what had happened to them. The man who led the patrol that found them, Lord Aclaí, tells me that they did not suffer long."

"Lord Aclaí is an important man, Lady Eala. Does he normally investigate the deaths of Novices?"

"Lord Aclaí is very good in the Forest: he can track the paths others leave behind. The three Novices that died were my friends and one of them was the younger brother of the Mentor's Chamberlain."

"I didn't know that," said Méar.

"It's true, Méar. Léaró was Rónmór's younger brother."

"Rónmór never said anything to me."

"Do you remember he went home for one evening a few days before Midwinter's Day?"

"I don't, Eala. There are a lot of things go on that I don't hear about."

Bradán's wife brought oat pancakes with honey.

"Thank you," said Eala.

"We hardly saw him, you know," she said. "For the last three years, he has been at Lord Rian's household."

"I served at the house of my Sponsor for seven months before Selection. I never forgot my mother. But I have not slept under her roof since then. It has been nearly sixteen months now. I still haven't forgotten her. I hope she is proud of me."

"I'm sure she is, Lady Eala," she replied. "Was he happy there?"

"I think Lách was the sort of person who was happy anywhere."

She smiled, remembering him. "That was my Lách."

* * *

As they walked back from Bradán's house, Méar spoke to Eala.

"Do you normally go and speak to the parents of dead Novices?"

"I don't, Méar, but Léaró, Lách and Rósa were my friends. Rónmór took the news to his family and I asked Lord Rian to take the news to Lách's family. I took the news to Rósa's family myself but they live in the City and I could walk. Anyway, that's my errand done. Would you like to go down to the sea and swim?"

"It would be cold."

"I think it would. I have never been in the sea. I have seen it from Flyers and I have seen the harbour in the City, but that is all. The water in the harbour is vile."

"Of course it is: that is where all the refuse from the City goes. Look, Eala, I remember Rónmór's brother: he was the first Novice Initiated this year. I didn't know he was dead." Méar stopped, looking at Eala, wondering something. But then he continued, "I certainly didn't know he was your friend: if I'd known, I'd have moved him away from dangerous assignments." He looked confused. "Why didn't Rónmór ask me, Eala?"

"I can't tell you. I am not Rónmór, Me ... Méar, and sometimes the reasons why Rónmór does things don't make any sense to me at all." She looked at him, checking she was not getting Rónmór into trouble, and seeing that she was not, even if Méar was agreeing with her. "But you do not encourage us to speak to you about what is really in our hearts," she continued.

"I don't just encourage it, Eala, I demand it. I want to know what you really think and feel, not the things you have been taught you should allow me to see."

"I know, Méar, but even now I am cautious about what I show you and how. I won't hide things from you but, if you don't like something about me, it would have big consequences for my life." She saw that it was not a view of himself that he recognised. "Even if you misunderstood me or thought I was thinking something bad when I wasn't, it might still have profound consequences."

"The consequences would not be that profound. I'm not that bad."

"The day you met me, Méar, you nearly killed me."

He did not reply immediately and, again, Eala wondered if she had gone too far.

Then he said, "I know. You are showing me how I look from outside and I don't always like what you show me." He looked at her, searching her face for something, and she realised he wanted her to show him that she still liked him. She smiled for him, and he continued, "I'm glad I came on the errand with you. It hasn't been *fun* but I've seen something that I hadn't seen before." He stopped her, turned her to face him, and took both her hands. "I don't like what I am seeing. But it is not your fault for showing it to me. There is something about you, some way you have of looking at the world, and some way you have of showing me what you can see. I said yesterday that the Adepts have a rather sad life but I wasn't thinking of this. Those two are really hurt by this but they are trying to understand it. Does something like this happen every time a Novice dies?"

"Something like this happens every time anyone dies. Death always touches people, because people are bound together."

"The dead don't feel anything, Eala. You know that, don't you?"

Eala looked at his face and, for a moment, she was reminded of talking to the Novices: he was repeating the official beliefs of the City but it was as if he didn't believe it. The superstitions he had been raised with still lingered in his mind, she saw.

"I know it, Méar. Nobody from Anleacán has that kind of superstition. But those who they leave behind do feel things."

"And when they die, the people they leave behind feel things, and so out, like ripples in a pond. It only stops when they're all dead. Do you know that I was over two hundred years old when Aclaí was born? That nobody is alive who was alive when I was born? They are all gone. Only a handful of people are alive who were alive when I turned five hundred. Half my life is remembered only by me: and when I am gone, that will be gone too."

"Then let's remember it now, Méar. Will you show me the sea?"

The sea was cold and the beach was lonely. But when they came out of the water, they found a sheltered spot in the dunes, which was bathed in sunlight and surrounded by rough sea grass, and they lay together. Eala found that, when he reached for her, it was different in some way. It was not that he was gentle, it was that she felt he was really trying to care for her – not concentrating on what she felt but on who she was.

The horses walked slowly along the trail. Méar watched Eala lead him and admired the slight sway in her back as she rode. Then she stopped. They heard laughter.

"Can we help?" Eala asked the men in front of her.

"Oh, I'm sure your husband can help us," he laughed. "We want his gold."

His companion looked at Eala in a way she did not like.

"And we want his wife," he added.

Eala looked directly at the one who had first spoken.

"What would your mother say if she could see you now?"

She saw it have the effect she hoped, but another voice behind them called, "My mother knows you strangers have too much gold. We all want it. Don't listen to her."

"That's right," said another voice behind them. "Be quiet, girl. If you don't be quiet I'll quieten you with a rope around your neck."

Eala looked around. There were seven of them, gathered around the horses, and armed with flint spears. They also had bows, which meant riding away was not an option. She recognised a couple of faces from Tonn's Inn. Méar had shown too much gold.

"We have friends in the City," she warned them. "If we get hurt or mistreated it will go very badly here."

"I'm not afraid of your friends," said the one whose mother knew. "If we kill ye, how will they ever know?"

"If Méar is hurt, Lord Rian will come to your village. He can use the Words of Truthful Aura and anyone who knows anything will have to tell. Aren't any of ye wise enough to be scared of blue-robes?"

"Shut up," he replied, coming over and pulling out rope. "Your husband is wise enough to be scared of us. Look at him," he added to the others. "He's about to piss himself." Eala glanced over and saw he was right: Méar was terrified.

Knowing what Méar could do, Eala knew she had only moments to save the robbers' lives. She found her naked sword on her Silver Cord, brandished it, so they could see her Rank on the hilt.

"Now run," she told them. "While ye still have time."

But they had no time. As they turned, Méar shouted Words. It seemed to Eala that the figures of the robbers collapsed in front of her. Their clothing was empty and from the clothes she saw tiny creatures run. He had turned them into mice.

She guided her horse over next to his and reached for him. He was shaking and pale and she leaned towards him, knowing the horses would stand still under his Breath.

"Don't be angry," she soothed. "They couldn't have hurt us."

"How could they dare?" he demanded, when he had calmed down.

"They didn't know," she explained. "They thought we had gold and not the strength to keep it."

"I don't care about the gold," he answered. "They wanted to rape you."

"I know. But lots of people want to rape me, Méar. A girl learns how to look after herself."

"You are a blue-robe now, Eala. You are my favourite. Nobody should want to rape you anymore."

"More want to since you have chosen me than ever did before, Mentor," she replied.

"They dare?"

"They dare to want it. Wouldn't you, if you were them?"

He was quiet a moment. Then he asked, "What about the Initiation? Don't they care about me?"

"They care about you. But it was you that Initiated them, not me. If you turned your back on me, I would have to be very careful. Favourites fall, Mentor. When you let me fall I will have to be very careful to land gracefully."

"Like a cat," he quipped. "I wonder if those mice have found out about cats yet." He laughed and looked over at Eala. "What, won't you smile? They wanted to hurt us. How did you want it to end?"

"I wish you hadn't ... I wish you hadn't had to do that," she told him. "They have families. It is hard for a family to lose their father."

"They should have thought of that." He looked back at her and, instead of arguing, she smiled forgiveness at him. "You'd better get rid of that sword," he added.

She discarded it in some thick bushes and then they made their way back to Tonn's Inn. They spoke no more about the robbers, but by next morning it was obvious that some people were missing from the village. Gaotha spoke to them over breakfast.

"When you were out riding," she asked, "did you see a group of men hunting?"

"We didn't," Méar answered.

Eala added, "Were they looking for us?"

Gaotha's ears reddened but her voice was unchanged. "They were hunting, Eala," she replied.

Méar commented, "If they weren't looking for us then we wouldn't have seen them, would we? Hunters are stealthy. But there are dangerous animals out and sometimes the hunters can find they are hunted."

"Are there dangerous animals in the City, Méar?" she risked.

"The most dangerous animals in the City are the blue-robes," Méar replied. "And they look after those they care about."

"I see," said Gaotha, and hurried away.

They stayed on the island for their five days, sleeping in Tonn's Inn, walking and riding around, meeting people, being peasants. Méar loved it and Eala loved to see him so free.

On the fifth day, in the evening, instead of going to bed they went down to the sea. The night was warm and the wind surprisingly calm, although Méar knew that it was calm because he had used the Key of Creation to affect the weather. One little heat wave in the middle of the Month of Midsummer wouldn't hurt, would it?

They lay on the shore, feeding driftwood to a fire, listening to the ocean, eating bread and fish and drinking wine, until the stars came out as midnight approached. Méar remembered how he had first heard the whisperings of his brother's voice out here and thought back to all the advice he had received since then. It was the one thing he had kept from her these last few days and he found that he didn't want to keep anything from her.

But how would he explain it? As he thought about the explanation, he realised that it didn't make any sense to him either. He heard Ceann's voice but Ceann was dead and the City had proved, beyond any doubt, that intelligence did not survive after death. Ceann's voice was no echo. It had taught him the Words of Power: it was Ceann's voice that had founded the City. Ceann's voice had told him he could marry Geanúile. Ceann's voice had taught him to use the Words of Initiation to capture the loyalty of the Adepts. Ceann's voice had told him to trap the Great Principle of Creation and wear it on a chain around his neck. Ceann's voice had told him he should raise the Land of the Young. Ceann's voice had told him he could live forever. But Ceann's voice didn't tell him what to do with Eala – or if it did, he wasn't listening.

He had realised a long time ago that Ceann's voice was something that he couldn't explain. Someone else needed to perform the experiment because he was the subject, not the observer. But that meant his trusting someone else and there had never been anyone else that he could trust. *Before now*, he suddenly realised. So he had left Ceann's voice unexplained and trusted it, because it worked. Now looking back over his life, he was not sure that Ceann's voice had worked. It might have got results, but it hadn't brought him happiness. Instead Ceann's advice had resulted in his being trapped. He had escaped from his prison a few days but tomorrow they would go back. Looking down at Eala, curled up on the blanket beside him, sleeping in the moonlight, he knew, if he didn't change something quickly, that when they returned she would go back to being the Favourite and he would go back to being the Mentor: and Méar and Eala would be lost to one another forever. He knew he couldn't bear that. He looked down at her and realised that, if they escaped their prison walls, it would be because she was strong enough to break them down. He knew he wasn't.

The Immortals need little sleep and he sat there beside her, trying to work out what he needed to tell her, until the sun rose and she looked up at him.

"Did you sleep, Méar love? You are worried, aren't you?"

He looked down at her and she looked up at him. He knew how to enlist her help to escape this prison of his and Ceann's making.

"Eala?" he asked her, "Will you marry me?"

Her eyes filled as she looked at him, although she was still trying to smile.

"The Sea People do not marry, Mentor."

"Don't call me 'Mentor', Eala. Not now. Give me my answer with my name, please."

"Méar, I don't believe you are free to marry and neither am I. If we were, there is nothing I would like more. But we both have duties to the City, to the Sea People, to humanity."

"Can't we set aside those duties?"

"For a few days we have and I have loved being with you for those few days. But the way the Sea People are now, it will be hard to change those duties to ones that leave us free to marry. For me it would be easy: the Mentor could give me permission and I could Retire. Favourites do sometimes Retire, although I would like to continue making the Mentor happy so I wouldn't want to. But for you, your duties are harder to change. The whole way the City derives loyalty would need to change, to make space for a wife for you."

"You have a wise head, Eala, when it comes to understanding people. Do you think it could be done?"

"It might, but it would be a long and difficult process. The quicker it happened, the more difficult it would be. And if anyone realised we were doing it and rumours started, it would make it many times more difficult."

"It could be a secret, Eala."

"Méar, everywhere you go people listen to you and discuss what you say. It is easy to overhear things in the Court of the Favourites. And, anyway, Lord Rónmór, or whoever is on watch, can hear what happens in your room."

"It's true," he answered. "We can't be overheard talking about this."

"There's always the swords."

"There could be ways the swords might be overheard," he answered, surprising her. Everyone had told her the swords were totally private. "We must not change how we behave."

"We've already changed the way we behave," she answered. "Probably too much."

He looked at her, agreeing. But then he seemed to doubt her resolve.

"Do you want it done?" he asked her.

"I want it, Méar, more than anything else since I've come to the City."

"If you will help me, we will do it together." They embraced again. "And when we've done it, will you marry me?"

"If we're both free, then I will."

"Then let us get free."

"It is going to take time, Méar. In the meantime we're going to spend
a lot of time fighting with our *peasant ideas*. Let me go back to being
Favourite and you..." She looked up at something climbing down the cliff.
"What's that, Méar?"

He looked around. "Where?"

"On the cliff, there. The thing climbing down, that looks like a man
with too many arms."

He squinted; she pointed.

Then he said, "It's a Forest thing of some sort, heavily tainted by chaos.
I wonder what it is doing here. It has got past the Forest People and the
patrols. We should get back to the Flyer, just in case."

They got up and gathered the blankets and things. Eala was shivering
and, knowing they were going back anyway, she twisted the Silver Cord
and her cloak was with her. Méar looked over at her and did the same,
but he got his sword too. His eyes looked up at the cliff and hers followed.
More over-legged forms were clambering down.

"I think we'd better run," he said.

They ran across the beach towards the stream. The shingle and sand
gave under their feet, slowing them down. Now there were dozens of those
things on the cliff, climbing down. Then there were hundreds, all the way
along the beach and coming down the stream. Eala reached for her sword
on her Silver Cord and for armour for her body. She wondered what good
she would do with a sword, though, standing beside the Mentor and his
thousand years of experience.

"When we get close, you will have to keep them off while I use Words
of Power," Méar told her. "They are only little things but there are so
many of them. When we get back to the Flyer, you will have to steer away,
south-west towards the City. Then we will have to get a patrol down here
to sort this out. A big patrol."

"I don't know much sword-craft, Méar," she replied, now scared.

"You've had lessons. Foscúil came down and taught you Favourites only
a ten-day ago."

"I know. But I've never killed anything. I don't know if I can do it."

"You can. It's one of the things I check at Selection. I check before I
even stop walking."

"Can't you help?"

"I have less sword-craft than you, Eala. I've never had lessons and I've
never had to fight anything with a sword. All I've used a sword for is
executions. I can't take lessons: if the Sea People knew that I had no skill,
I would be in great danger." She could see that. "If I have to use a sword
to kill things, we will be finished."

They were off the shingle, running up the path next to the Flyer. Between them and the Flyer, the things ran down the path. They were black, charcoal black and, although they had arms that could also be legs, and had taloned fingers, they had no heads or faces. Méar shouted Words of Power as they ran and suddenly they were flying over the things, across the stream and down on to the Flyer. Three of the things waited and Eala had her sword in her hand. She glanced over at him before they attacked.

"Méar," she screamed, "get your armour on!"

Then they were down among them. Eala slashed across and two of them just came apart. The third one clutched at Méar, distracting him, and Eala screamed and swung the blade down. She felt herself crouching over the blade as it cut, linking it to the motion of her hips, the way Foscúil had taught her. Fortunately Méar had his armour on now: the blade passed through the thing but skidded off the armour on his back. His sword was uselessly waving around: he really had no sword skill at all.

More were running up. Méar said Words and made a gesture towards them. They flew back, as if running into an invisible wall. Eala leaped down, waving the Flyer into action. She had never flown one before and although it seemed obvious, she wanted height not speed. It would do them no good if they crashed into the sea.

As they rose up, they saw over the cliff. The ground was crawling with monsters, like ants when the hill has been kicked over, as far as the eye could see. Thick smoke hung over the village and she could see that some of the buildings were burning. Among the little things near the cliff edge there were great creatures in cloaks, twice as tall as Eala or Méar. One turned to them and gestured with a staff. The Flyer collapsed and they fell.

Méar pointed with his sword, his other hand clutching the Flyer. Green fire leaped out, crossed the space between him and the great figure, and consumed it in a bright flash. As they plunged down, Eala regained a little control of the Flyer. But then they struck the rock on the cliff's edge. For long moments she saw sky and rock, sea and shingle, alternating as they fell, punctuated by hard impacts as they struck the rocks. The last impact was the hardest. She felt something snap low in her belly. Her body didn't feel right: somehow she felt both bent and straight. But she felt no pain as she came to rest.

Méar ran over. She could see the Flyer behind him, ruined. The smaller things were all over the beach, running towards them from every direction.

He reached his hand to her and said, "We have to get going."

There was something wrong with his voice. It was lost in the wind and the sea and her sight was narrowing, as greyness spread from the edges of her vision.

The last thing she thought was that if this was dying, then dying wasn't so bad.

Glossary

The Sea People spoke the language which was the ancestor of the Gaelic family, and I have rendered the spelling of their names using Irish: the Gaelic language that is closest to that ancestor. However, I have borrowed a gender-convention for names from the romance languages: names ending in an A or an E are feminine and names ending in other letters are masculine.

The language of the Sea People, like most Gaelic languages, has a distinction between second person singular and plural, and this has carried over into Hiberno-English. I have used these second person plural forms, ye for (all) you, yere for (all) your, to communicate this distinction.

In the pronunciation guides, any single vowel is short. They should be pronounced as p*a*t, p*e*t, p*i*t, p*o*t, p*u*tt. Long vowels are represented as vowels in combination with other letters: aw, ay, ee, oh and uu, pronounced approximately s*aw*, s*ay*, s*ee*, s*ew* and s*ue* respectively. Remember that an e at the end of a word is never silent, unlike English.

The sound represented by TCH is a blend of the T and the CH; the sound represented by KH varies from the hard sound of the German *ich* and the softer sound of the Scottish *loch*, depending on the nearest vowel: the softer sound is next to an A, an O or a U; the harder sound is next to an I or an E.

The pronunciations offered are only very approximate. Irish is a very rich language phonetically, and those of us who have grown up speaking English struggle to distinguish all the sounds. Even among the Sea People, there would have been different accents, and certainly in modern Ireland and Scotland there are several pronunciations. These are outside the scope of this appendix, but there are some excellent sources available.

273

Abhainne (*AH-wan-e*; in the old City accent, *AW-en-e*) abhainn is a river.

Aclaí (*AK-lee*), means agility.

Anleacán (*un-LEKH-awn*), means The Slab.

Arracht (*ARR-akht*) is a monster.

Arrachtumair (*ARR-akht-um-ir*) is a monster from a tank: an artificial lifeform or genetically engineered organism.

Áthaiminn (*aw-ha-MIN*) the ford over the Minn, a river to the north of the Teorainn. The atha- prefix on a place-name is equivalent to the English suffix -ford, and means a river crossing.

Áthaiteorann (*aw-ha-TCHOR-an*): ford over the Teorainn.

Beatha (*BA-ha*) means life.

Blátha (*BLAW-ha*) bláth means a flower.

Bradán (*BRAD-awn*) is a salmon.

Cabairí (*KAB-a-ree*) cabaire means talkative.

Caora (*KIR-a*) is a sheep

Cathúa (*KA-huu-a*): cathú is guilt.

Ceann (*KEE-an*) is a head.

Cearca (*KEE-ar-ka*) cearc is a hen.

Ceatha (*KYA-ha*) means a rainstorm.

Ceathrua (*kaha-ROO-a*) from ceathru, fourth.

Colm (*KOL-um*) means a dove or a pigeon.

Damhánalla (*DA-wawn-ola*; in the old City accent, *DAUWN-alah*): damhán alla is a spider.

Duille (*DIL-le*) means a leaf.

Eala (*A-la*), means a swan.

Éirime (*ay-RIM-e*) from éirim, a talent.

Eibheara (*ey-VAR-a*) from eibhear, granite.

Eile (*E-le*) means other, another.

Eilite (*AY-lit-e*): eilit is a doe.

Éise (*AYSH-e*): éis means after, or following.

Féileacána (*FAY-la-qawn-a*) féileacán is a butterfly or moth.

Flannbhuía (*FLANN-wee-a*): flannbhuí literally means a fiery yellow – orange was not a distinct colour in the language of the Sea People.

Fleánna (*FLAW-na*) fleá is a festival.

Fómhara (*fo-WAR-a*) an Fómhar is the autumn.

Foscúil (*FOS-kuul*) closed, hidden.

Fuiseoga (*FWISH-og-a*) fuiseog is a lark.

Gainmheach (*GAN-vakh*) means sandy.

Gaotha (*GWAY-ha*) gaoth is wind.

Geana (*GYAN-na*): gean means affection.

Geancacha (*GYAN-ko-kha*): geancach suggests something twisted or malformed, and although her mother looked at her nose and gave her this name as a term of endearment for a baby, now she is grown Geana doesn't let anyone else but her mother call her *Geancacha*.

Geanúile (*GYAN-uul-a*) means affectionate.

Idireatarthu (*id-IR-ath-er-hu*) means inbetween

Iorai (*UR-ree*) iora is a squirrel.

Innealta (*INN-iltch-a*) neat and tidy.

Iolar, (*UL-ar*) means an eagle.

Lách (*LAWKH*) kind, good-natured.

Léaró (*LAY-roh*) means a spark.

Leathar (*LA-har*) means leather.

Liús (*LYUUS*) means the fish called a pike.

Longeán (*LON-gawn*) means gristle.

Lorgcoiseaigéan (*lorg-KOSH-a-gaynn*) means the footprint of the ocean, and refers to a big natural harbour over the ocean, East of the City.

Luchóg (*LUKH-ohg*) means a mouse.

Méar (*MAYR*) is a finger.

Miotal (*MITTH-al*), means metal. The Sea People knew gold and copper and another metal that is not known to us, but is simply referred to in the text as Metal. It is a synonym for hardness and is the material out of which they forged their weapons and armour.

Nóiníne (*NO-neen-e*) níinín is a daisy.

Óire (*OH-ir-e*) from óir, gold.

Ólachán (*OH-lakh-awn*) ól is drink, possibly an unfortunate name for an innkeeper

Ordóg (*OHR-dohg*) means a thumb.

Reo, (*ROH*) frost.

Rian (*REE-an*) mark, trace, track.

Rónmór (*ROHN-mohr*), literally big-seal, is a sea-lion.

Rósa (*ROH-sa*) rós means a rose.

Saonta (*SAY-un-tah*) naive, gullible.

Seilidí (*SHEL-id-ee*) seilide is a snail or a slug.

Sneachta (*SHNAKHT-a*) means snow.

Spéire (*SHPAY-reh*), sky.

Stail (*sthall*) means a male horse.

Spideog (*SHPID-ogg*) means a robin.

Teorainn (*TCHOR-inn*) means border.

Tírcapall (*TCHEER-kop-al*) horse-land.

Tírcúpla, (*tcheer-KOOP-lah*), double-land, twin-land. Tírcupla is a pair of islands separated by a narrow strait.

Toirneach (*THOR-nyakh*) thunder.
Tonn (*THUN*) is a wave, as in the sea.
Úlloileán (*ool-ILL-lawn*) isle of apples.

Calendar

The Sea People calendar divides the year into two seasons: winter, and summer; each divided into six months of three ten-days each. The new year starts on the first day of the winter seasons, the Autumn Day.

The winter months start with the day of the autumn equinox (in the northern hemisphere) and the winter months are:-
- Autumn (September-October)
- Death (October-November)
- Fruits (November-December)
- Midwinter (December-January)
- Light (January-February)
- Planting (February-March)

The summer months start with the day of the spring equinox, and are:-
- Spring (March-April)
- Life (April-May)
- Flowers (May-June)
- Midsummer (June-July)
- Darkness (July-August)
- Harvest (August-September)

Feast days fall on the first day of the first and fourth months; the eleventh days of the second and fifth months and the twenty-first days of the third and fifth months. That means the feasts of Fruits and Flowers are only one ten-day behind the feasts of Midwinter and Midsummer, respectively.

The timetable of the City is based on the ten-days, and the first, second and sixth days are assigned as rest days, although the patrols still continue and the servants still work.

It will be seen that this calendar adds up to 360 days: accordingly there are two or three days at the end of each season: the Lost Days of Winter and the Lost Days of Summer. The length of these are determined by astronomical observation: when the calendar runs out, the new calendar starts after measurement of day and night length shows that the equinox has arrived.

Lightning Source UK Ltd.
Milton Keynes UK
UKOW030201030312

188260UK00001B/18/P